# PURGATION

A Novel by:

**Mark W. Stevens**

THIRD MOUNTAIN PUBLISHING

Text copyright © 2022 by Mark W. Stevens
All rights reserved.
*Library of Congress Cataloging-in-Publication Data*
ISBN 978-1-7352062-7-1
Printed in the United States of America

Cover & Interior Art Credit: Mark W. Stevens
Cover design by: Waleed Rabin
Back Cover Art by: Mark W. Stevens
Layout by: Katarina Simkova

# DEDICATION

To those who are engaged in the act of reaching across differences of ethnicity, skin tone, gender, religious beliefs, or any of the myriad of other superficial designations that have and still do serve to divide us from one another, and cause unfathomable pain and suffering.

# DISCLAIMER

Most of the characters and events found in this book are fictional. However, as depicted in this story, the forced removal of the Cherokee people and other Native American tribes from their ancestral homelands to eastern Oklahoma, sadly, and astoundingly enough, did actually happen. Therefore, where I deemed it appropriate, and to maintain continuity of the story, I did integrate the names of some of the people involved in The Trail of Tears event from accounts drawn from historical references.

# BOOKS BY MARK W. STEVENS

— ADULT FICTION —

Abducted

Purgation

Prey

The Grape Vine

— CHILDREN'S BOOKS —

The Daisy Starshine Series

Book 1. Daisy Goes to the Races

Book 2. Daisy: Lost in the Rainforest

Book 3. Daisy's Grand Canyon Adventure

# INTRODUCTION

The tragic event which resulted in the immeasurable suffering, and loss of thousands of Native American lives is known today as The Trail of Tears. It was perpetrated against otherwise innocent men, women, and children, solely because some of those with political clout saw the Indian as different from them and the early American settlers steadfastly populating the burgeoning country. As the population grew, so too did the demand for more cropland, especially cotton, and along with that, the need for someone to pick it. With the invention of the Cotton Gin, that need and demand reached a tipping point, the government proclaimed that the Indian people stood in the way of progress, and deemed them a threat to the ultimate survival of the United States.

Franklin Carlyle, like those who judged both Native and Black Americans as servants and tools at best, and ultimately as subhumans to be swept out of the way, viewed anyone he deemed different from himself with suspicion and loathing. An old saying suggests that before any person judges another, that person must first walk a mile in the other's shoes. In the case of The Trail of Tears, the distance walked turned out to be closer to twelve hundred miles, and most of those forced to walk it, did so without the luxury of shoes or moccasins. In other words, shoes were an extremely rare commodity, and Franklin's were quickly wearing out.

# CONTENTS

# CHAPTER 1

A near empty beer can slipped silently from Franklin Carlyle's hand to the carpet, following the trajectory of the four before it. Each of these had held just enough remnant of the lager that together, small rivulets from each of them gathered together forming a stream and traced their way across the top selection of a stack of history magazines. Upon reaching the edge, the beer cascaded in an amber colored waterfall down the dog-eared pages of the pile of magazines and periodicals forming a small pool on floor. Franklin's chin drooped so slowly to his chest it was nearly imperceptible to anyone who might have been looking in his direction, the motion reminiscent of a lazy water droplet hanging from a faucet, and never letting go. But just when one might think he was out for good, he snapped it upright again with a snort. The noise blasting his sensitivities gradually became coherent to him as cheering that was coming from the television broke through his stupor, and the half asleep, half drunken man shook his head to clear it so he could focus once more on the game.

A wildly exuberant, helmeted player slammed the oblong ball to the ground, which then bounced haphazardly in multiple directions as whistles blew and crowds roared.

Franklin chuckled to himself, thinking he felt a little like that ball on his last trip to the bathroom. Then casting a furtive glance toward the kitchen, as if worried it might be possible that his wife might somehow possess the ability to read his thoughts, he furrowed his brow, cleared his throat, and tugged his teeshirt back over his protruding belly. Franklin believed himself to be a self-made man, and in total control of his life, and was quick to challenge anyone who dared try to prove otherwise. The way he saw it, other than being breastfed and having his diaper changed as an infant, he had never relied on anyone for anything his entire life.

Franklin frowned and groaned as he bent forward to reach for the runaway beer can. Unfortunately, despite his efforts, it was still a good twelve inches beyond the reach of his outstretched fingers. He noticed with a frustrated grimace, the beer stained cover of one of his favorite history magazines that celebrated the military prowess of General Lee before and during the Civil War, and groaned out loud when he followed the trail of beer down the edges of his treasured stack. "Gwen! Bring me a towel!" He yelled through clenched teeth, loud enough, so as not to have to turn the volume down on the Sunday morning game, and despite the fact that his wife was in plain view a mere fifteen feet away. "And another beer!" he added. He reasoned to himself, based upon the stories he'd read of General Lee, and other such military and/or political giants, that there was a clear and important distinction between asking for something, and ordering it. He prided himself that like them, he never did the former.

Gwen was on her knees and shoulder deep in a cabinet.

*What's the hold up*, he thought with irritation? *You'd think she'd been working hard all day.*

Rather than admit he ever required assistance from anyone, Franklin maintained that he got where he was by knowing how to work the system, which for him translated to using others to his advantage. To him, to do otherwise would be pointless. Because of the considerable amount of money he had accumulated over the course of his career, Franklin Carlyle retired at relatively young age of fifty-six. By most accounts, and without looking beyond the surface, he appeared to have done well.

Gwen muttered under her breath and steadied the pans she'd bumped with her shoulder at the sound of her husband's demanding voice. She glanced over her shoulder in time to see Franklin's body slouched in his chair, and his chin just coming to rest on his chest. She shook her head while wiping her hands on her apron, and sighed.

Franklin, who had quite suddenly nodded off, neither saw nor heard his wife's approach. Instead, he found himself peering into a murky, otherworldly, darkness that seemed to have somehow replaced his living room. He willed himself to his feet, explosions of bright light and stabbing pain simultaneously flashing and throbbing in his skull. To say he felt queasy would be an understatement, and he was drenched with sweat. Attempting to straighten up, Franklin felt like he was moving in slow motion. After steadying his wobbling legs, he lurched toward an opening that was covered, of all things, by what appeared to be an animal skin. But with each faltering step, the opening matched his effort by receding further away.

*If I didn't know any better, I'd think I was having one of them flash backs like back in the day*—a reference to his brief experimentation with psychedelics as a youth—he thought to himself, then muttered, "I'd swear I've been past that Goddamn flap already!"

Franklin had indeed been past the flap several times over the last few weekends. But each time—and just before his eyes could adjust to a blinding light on the other side—he'd awake to find himself in his easy chair, in his own living room, in front of his blaring television. This time, he resolved, would be different. This time he was determined to see what was on the other side of the flap. As certain as Franklin was that he'd already been to the other side of the animal skin covering, he also knew that this phenomenon which he assumed was induced by alcohol, had at other times transported him to moments that preceded this one. But for the life of him he couldn't remember any more than the briefest of fragments of those experiences. Most vivid to him were the moments during which he was running frantic and barefoot through a forest, the branches of trees slashing across his chest and arms.

A second wave of nausea swept over Franklin, bringing him back to his current predicament. He swallowed hard, trying to keep whatever he had inside of him from coming back up, and focused on the task at hand. Once the nausea subsided, with one concentrated effort, he burst past the fur-lined skin. On the other side—in stark contrast to where he'd been—was such brightness, he reflexively squeezed his eyes shut.

After catching his breath, Franklin reached deep inside himself, and with sheer will staggered several more wobbly steps, and fell to his knees. A persistent drumming sound that had invaded his head, and seemed to fill the atmosphere with an unseen thickness the moment before he broke into the light, stopped abruptly, and Franklin leaned forward, supporting himself with his hands flattened upon a hard-packed, dirt ground. Just as he thought with relief that the queasiness was over, a third wave of nausea, more violent than the previous two overtook him building in his gut, then seemingly spreading out with increasing intensity to all the extremities of his body. Franklin started to think he might burst open from the building pressure like an exploding watermelon, but instead, he began to retch. What gushed from him as from a fire hose, was thick and hot, and felt as though it came all the way from his fingers and toes.

Dizzy and spent, he sprawled out in the dirt, and Franklin spit out as much of the foulness he could then wiped his mouth with his trembling forearm. His throat burned with each breath, so regardless of the stench Franklin thought he would experience, he focused on inhaling through his nose, and was instead, rewarded with an aroma that was fresh and sweet. After several seconds—his eyes still shut tight—he managed to push himself back up onto his knees. Though his arms hung heavy and useless at his sides, he was grateful for the cool air and wonderful fragrance wafting about him. Franklin knew he hadn't come this far before, and the silence—that only moments before was such a relief—suddenly seemed uncomfortably loud. He sensed that he wasn't alone, and for the first time in a long while, he was afraid.

As though in a film that moved slowly frame by frame, Franklin opened his eyes which revealed not far from him, the presence of perhaps a dozen blurred, humanoid shapes, unmoving and silhouetted against the bright light. Before his vision cleared enough to make out who or what the objects were, he felt himself grabbed from behind, under his arms by powerful hands, and lifted until his toes dangled just above the ground. Franklin still felt too sick and unsteady to put up a fight, but it turned out that he didn't need to. The hands that held him released their vice-like grip, and he abruptly dropped to his feet.

Though the fall was less than a couple of inches, Franklin reflexively closed his eyes, and a flutter of butterflies stirred in his gut signaling another wave of nausea. When the soles of his feet touched ground, he popped his eyes wide open expecting for reasons incomprehensible to him, to see Indians, or as he often referred to them, savages. Instead, the dreadfully worried face of his wife, Gwen, appeared. She was shaking him by the arm, but upon seeing him open his eyes, took a quick step back.

Franklin noticed she was holding a can of beer in one hand, while she wiped his magazines down with the cloth she held in the other. He shook his head in an attempt to clear it of a profound drowsiness, and straightened himself up in his easy chair from a deep slouch. Irritated that he might have appeared foolish to Gwen, he coughed and cleared his throat in a futile attempt to display a semblance of self-control.

The TV was blaring from behind Gwen, and Franklin recognized the ending of a hemorrhoid ointment commercial, that had played repeatedly throughout the game. This was followed by a referee's whistle and the sound of a cheering crowd.

Still feeling a little confused, Franklin snatched the can of beer from his wife's trembling hands and swept her to the side of the television screen. "What the hell're you doing Gwen?" He blurted as he wiped a string of drool from his chin. Then he snarled, "I'm watching the game," and took a slug of beer to put emphasis on his point.

"*Honey,*" Gwen replied, which was drawn out in a nasally, and sing-song manner, that once endearing to him, now had the same effect on Franklin as the high-pitched scream of a dentist's drill. "I couldn't hear you over the TV for all your snoring!" she continued. Then she turned and walked back into the kitchen, her husband's grumbling following her there. When she reached the sink, Gwen stood with her back to him. While wiping her hands on her apron, she offered in a tone that was as non-accusatory as she could manage, "Maybe five beers is too much this early in the morning Honey. You just fall asleep, and this time you seemed confused." As she continued, her voice shifted from pensive to that irritating whine Franklin had grown to abhor. "I'm worried about you, Honey. I really wish you would talk to your doctor about your drinking."

"I told you I'm fine," Franklin barked, "and I know right where I am!" Mumbling under his breath he added, "If someone's confused around here, it sure as hell isn't me." Raising his voice again, his eyes never leaving the TV, Franklin employed one of his usual tactics to change what had become for him an uncomfortable subject. "Anyway, where the fuck's the gardener?"

"I wish you wouldn't use that word Honey."

"Gwen!" Franklin shouted over her and lifted his beer. "It's wet!" He wrapped the can in his shirt, twisted it dry, then complained, "Aw shit! It's past ten! Now I'll have to listen to weed wackers and that polka music those beaners play while I'm trying to watch the game! Is it too much to expect for those illegals to get here on time? You'd think they'd be grateful to have the work!" He lowered his voice and continued grumbling to himself. "Hell, I'd show up early if I was in their shoes! That's what it takes if you want to be successful." He took a swig of beer then muttered one of his long-held truisms while nodding to himself, "What goes around comes around! If they get themselves deported, they've got it coming to them! Good riddance!"

"Honey, it's early! It's not even nine-thirty!" Gwen offered, her voice elevated in competition with the television. While endlessly drying her hands on her apron, she finished, "You said you didn't want them here too early, so you could sleep in, remember?!"

Franklin had gotten so worked up by this back and forth with Gwen that his face was flushed beet red, and he was momentarily, and uncharacteristically speechless. Unaware of her husband's current emotional state, Gwen continued. "Since it's going to be so hot today, I made some nice lemonade."

In Franklin's mind, Gwen's voice had now become as irritating to him as nails on a chalkboard. A loud chorus of cheering erupted from the television, and Franklin smacked the recliner with his hand and yelled something unintelligible.

"Honeeey! Would you like some fresh, cold lemonade?" Gwen called again from the kitchen. Then in a voice that vaguely reminded Franklin of his mother's, she said, "That reminds me, your eyes look a little yellow. Have you noticed? I think that thing on your cheek is getting darker too. I really think you should see the doctor."

Franklin's face had turned from beet to fire engine red. "No, I don't want any damned lemonade!" he raged, shaking his head. Snickering under his breath so that Gwen couldn't hear him, he added, "Lemonade's a black man's drink." He glanced up at a crystal decanter he kept on a mantle above the fireplace. It was half full of Jack Daniels. Shifting his gaze approvingly between the can of beer in his hand and the whiskey on the mantle, he smacked his lips thinking, *who needs lemonade*? While admiring the golden-brown hue in the decanter, the game whistle blew, redirecting his attention to the television. Nearly dropping his beer, he screamed at the set "Lame-ass! What kind of call is that?"

"I'm sorry Honey, what did I do?" Gwen asked. Her voice was muffled by the kitchen cabinet she was head and shoulders inside of. But the high-pitched whine of it pierced Franklin's skull just the same.

"I'm not talking to you," Franklin barked. "I'm talking to ... oh, never mind!" Still angry about Gwen's comment regarding the odd discoloration that had been developing on his cheek, he mumbled, "I might be getting older, but my eyes are just fine. Old people get spots on their skin! I could play connect the dots on my hands for God's sake! It's nothing!" Franklin held his beer can out dangling it from his finger tips, and raised his voice, "Don't wander off after you're through making all that racket with those pots and pans. I'm almost done with this."

Franklin hadn't seen his doctor in more than a year. Gwen went with him the last time, and as far as he was concerned, threw him under the bus by telling the doctor about the drinking. His face twisted in anger as the episode flashed fresh in his mind. "What do those quacks know anyway?" he'd fumed at her after they'd left the office. As he stormed to the car with Gwen struggling to keep up, he continued to lash out at her. Pulling an imaginary zipper across his lips, he said, "You need to learn to keep your mouth shut! What I drink, and how much, is nobody's business! They get some letters after their names, and they think they're God for Christ sake!" An eruption from the crowd brought Franklin's attention back to the game.

Although he had never laid a hand on her, Gwen believed it was best to keep her distance when Franklin was angry. After a sleight hesitation she said, "Honey, do you think it's okay if I offer some lemonade to the workers? It's already getting hot outside, and they work so hard."

"You do one nice thing for them, and they'll only expect more! Nobody ever got anywhere that way! I never took a handout from anybody, and look what I accomplished!" Under his breath he fumed, "They work so hard, my ass. They'll be taking a siesta by twelve! It amazes me how lazy these people are. They might be a shade lighter, but they're no better than the niggers."

# CHAPTER 2

The game broke for commercial, and the volume on the television increased. The distinctive crack of a cap being twisted off of a bottle of beer was followed by the light and festive fizz of carbonated bubbles, then the gurgle of a light amber lager as it was being poured into a frosty-cold glass by a woman who was young, large-breasted, and blonde. Her buttoned-down sports jersey, the three top buttons undone, was barely containing her, as she fawned over an older looking, sharply dressed gentleman. The object of her affections kept shifting his eyes from the beer to her breasts and back again, while the refreshing sound of the carbonated lager fizzing in the background grew steadily louder. The man finally settled on the overpowering allure of the beer, and took a generous gulp. Pouting, the woman turned around, and strutted away while the crowd in the bar cheered and clinked their bottles together.

Oblivious to his recent comment about never having taken a handout, Franklin shouted at his wife. "Gwen! Bring me a beer already!"

As far as Franklin was concerned, the possibilities were limitless for anyone—and by anyone, he meant men, and white men at that—who knew how to work the system, like those he'd read about. Men like Andrew

Jackson, the seventh president of the United States, and in his opinion, the man largely responsible for ridding the country of the nuisance of the Indians. In doing this, he opened up the land to the will, and to his reasoning, the rightful control of white men. In his view, there was absolutely nothing a man could not have, or do, if he played it right. To Franklin that was how the world worked. "After all, it's a dog eat dog world, is it not?" were words he'd often employ when challenging whoever he happened to be talking with should the subject be brought up.

Although he had been quite industrious in his youth, these days Franklin could be defined much more by what he had than what he actually did. In part, this was because most of what he did was accomplished from within the confines and comfort of his own home utilizing his smart phone or the internet. These tools greatly reduced the necessity of him having to go out to do anything. Although this was greatly disappointing to Gwen, it suited him just fine. He didn't like having to leave his house unless it was unavoidable, or if it was for something he really wanted to do. His resistance to going out was nothing new, however, it had become much more pronounced since he joined the ranks of the retired seven years ago.

It would be incorrect to suggest that Franklin never did anything at all since his retirement. Besides drinking and watching endless hours of news and sports, he somehow managed to fill much of his time by reading his beloved history, and accumulating possessions. Of particular interest to him was memorabilia he'd collected from World War One and Two, the Revolutionary War, and his favorite period of history, the Civil War, all of which helped to form his sense of white and male superiority. But these days, other than him puttering around tending to his property or admiring his collection of things, most of what got done around his home was taken care of by his wife, or hired help.

In addition to his money, nicely appointed home, and numerous belongings, Franklin had a beautiful wife, Gwen, who he married almost forty years ago. Gwen Carlyle was the proverbial trophy wife; on his arm at appropriate moments, and otherwise in the kitchen preparing his meals, or within earshot to run him a beer when called for. As with most trophy wives, Gwen had become more of a possession than a partner.

Franklin turned down a commercial on hemorrhoids he'd seen four times already this morning and watched as Gwen scurried over to the fridge.

"Why not? Haven't I worked hard all my life?" Or, "You know, just desserts, and all that, right?" were among his ready responses to anyone who dared to cast even a questioning glance at him after witnessing any of the numerous beer hand offs from Gwen. Then as if to settle it once and for all he'd add, "After all, I've given her everything she has."

It hadn't always been this way with them, but just as in his relationships with others, Franklin's attentions for his wife shifted over time to favor her more as an asset—perhaps tool would be more accurate—than a friend, partner, or lover. And though Franklin proclaimed a certain pride of his children, he rarely spent time with them while they were growing up. Now that they were living on their own, he rarely saw them.

As Gwen was popping the tab on his next beer, a time out was called in the game. Disappointed that the commercial that came up had to do with company promoting their premier funeral, burial, cremation, and life celebration services, followed by another on life insurance rather than beers and blondes, Franklin took his eyes off the TV and gazed around the room. A trophy possessing mentality seemed to apply to everything Franklin owned, and he owned many things, from an eclectic collection of antiques, odds and ends, and knickknacks, to objects of history and war. He was particularly fond of his guns, most of which, other than a couple of Civil War era weapons he'd managed to acquire and proudly displayed, he kept locked away. It would seem to many that Franklin had accumulated nearly every imaginable toy a man could want, even though he often used them only once, and many of them not at all.

"Here Honey," Gwen said sweetly, placing the opened beer can into Franklin's waiting hand.

Caught up in his thoughts, Franklin barely noticed, and he nearly dropped the offering. The cold wetness of the can brought him back to the moment, and he was just about to snap at her for her carelessness when cheering erupted from the game, causing him to almost drop the beer a second time. His team had scored a touch down, which was enough to distract him from Gwen, and he hooted ecstatically, took a long swig of his beer, then hit the replay button on the remote.

Franklin, at sixty-three years of age, was still a decent looking man, although he often went unshaven for days, and had developed quite a gut. So for the casual observer, it would seem that he had everything; looks, intelligence, money, power. However, to those who spent much time with Franklin, it eventually became apparent that everything seemed to be about him. While Franklin could at first appear quite generous, given enough time, one could tell that this was merely his way of satisfying his need to be viewed by others as magnanimous. Parties and gatherings were always at his house, where it was quickly understood that you listened to what he was listening to, watched what he was watching, or joined him in whatever it was he was doing. If giving of himself for the sake of others, or at the expense of his own comfort, and with no expectation of receiving anything in return were tools Franklin contained in his wheelhouse, the man appeared to be either incapable, or unwilling to use them.

The whistle blew for half time startling Franklin from a slow slide into another midmorning doze. Noticing the score was in his team's favor, he hooted again and slugged down the rest of his beer that he'd somehow managed to keep clenched in his hand. "The damned beer is warm!" he scowled in Gwen's general direction. "Gotta take a leak. Grab me another cold one, will ya?"

He watched with practiced irritation as his wife first turned off the water in the sink, then dried her hands on her apron, and finally turned toward the fridge. It seemed to him she moved with the speed of a turtle that had just gotten into one of his aggravatingly younger neighbor's backyard marijuana patches. In a voice dripping with sarcasm he said, "See if you can find a cold one this time," then limped stiffly and wobbled to the bathroom, while holding his stomach. He felt especially sore this morning, and his stomach was sour. "A cold beer will fix that right up," he mumbled. Franklin had discovered a little over a year ago—to his relief and delight—that drinking a beer worked like magic for both his muscle pain and stomach aches, and had been treating these ailments this way religiously ever since. "Doctor would just want to shove some pills down my throat," he reasoned. Laughing to himself he thought, "MD must stand for mildly delusional."

Gwen watched in silence as her husband shuffle out of the den, and thought wistfully back to when the two of them first met. Back then he was a blond, handsome, surfer-boy, fresh out of high school. He had charmed her with his good looks, wit, and bravado, and pursued her in ways that reminded her of the handsome men who courted the beautiful women she had seen in romantic movies—what Franklin now referred to dismissively as "chick flicks".

Early on, Franklin seemed responsive to her feelings, and tended quickly to her every whim. He had a job and money, and showered her with gifts. If she so much as expressed a desire for a soda, he would drop everything to get it for her. When she walked along side of him, her arm entwined in his, she felt like Cinderella, and the envy of all who saw them. On the off-chance that he would somehow disappoint her, he was quick to apologize. Gwen laughed softly, and sighed, remembering how he would virtually do cartwheels and backflips to make it up to her. But this idyllic, loving attention proved to be deceptive, and ultimately, short-lived. It wasn't long before she understood that one thing always led to another, and that other was sex.

Gwen chalked this up to their youth and believed in her heart that behind all of the lust and bravado, Franklin truly loved her. But Franklin's tendency of being opinionated, and of using others, particularly women, had already begun to develop during his high school days. As time went on she met several girls who shared their experiences of him back then. She shuddered when she was told by one after the other how Franklin had seemed preoccupied not so much with looking for a girlfriend at Friday night parties, as searching for a girl he could score with. They told her how he treated them like princesses so long as he could get them into bed. According to these girls it was all about the conquest for him, and then it wasn't long before he was off looking for the next.

From these girls as well as from some of his male companions, Gwen learned not only of his penchant for exploiting women, but his tendency to judge and mock others he deemed unworthy or unacceptable, including and most notably people of color. It wasn't long before Gwen began to experience these things for herself.

At first she spoke up when he was crude or unkind, and he always apologized. But he'd always do it again, and it wasn't long before he reacted toward her with anger, and eventually a rage so intense it frightened her.

On one occasion during which Franklin was publicly mocking a man who was blind and asking for handouts from those passing by, she decided to walk away. Franklin grabbed her by the arm, twisted it behind her back, and looked her in the eye with such penetrating intensity her blood went suddenly cold. He told her through clenched teeth, and in no uncertain terms, she was never to attempt to walk away from him again. For weeks afterwards, he treated her with disdain, followed by cold indifference. Just when she thought the relationship might be over, and she began to mentally prepare her self for the break-up, Franklin would do something sweet; bring her a gift, take her to dinner and a movie, and tell her he loved her, and that she meant the world to him. This became a pattern of behavior that repeated itself in cycles.

It was during one of Franklin's reprieves that Gwen became pregnant, and for a few short months their relationship seemed to be as wonderful as it had been in the beginning. But as her pregnancy progressed, Franklin's attitude and behaviors began to slip. The change was gradual, but it slowly shifted from bad to worse. And while she once had nerves strong enough to stand up to him, now that she was carrying a child, these weakened and eventually became nonexistent. As Gwen contemplated these things, she thought of a story Franklin once told her about how one goes about cooking a frog.

"You start by placing a live frog in a pan of cool water so that they feel safe," he'd told her. "Then you slowly turn the heat up so the frog doesn't notice the changing temperature. Before the frog knows it, the water eventually begins to boil, and by then, it's too late. The frog is doomed, and it croaks without a fuss."

Gwen remembered how he laughed while a chill ran through her at the coldness with which he told his story, and she thought sadly that this is exactly what had become of her. She'd lost her fight. In fact, she felt she no longer recognized herself at all. She looked around the room at the things she'd brought into the home, and realized for the first time that they had lost their appeal. It felt like a punch to her gut when it occurred to her that just as it now was with these mere things, her friends—people she had valued and enjoyed over the years—had become as tools that she used to help herself cope with her life with Franklin. She cried silently until she realized she was wringing her hands; something that had become a useless habit, over the years, and symbolic of her impotency, and utter lack of happiness. Unclenching her entwined fingers, Gwen turned back to the dishes in the sink.

# CHAPTER 3

Franklin gently removed the porcelain lid off the back of the toilet, being careful not to let it bump up against the tank. He then reached inside the tank and pulled out a sealed, plastic baggie inside of which was a pint of Jack Daniels. Wobbling a little, he rinsed the bottle under the faucet, twisted the cap off, and took a swig, then steadied himself once more in front of the toilet. He saluted himself in the mirror, and took another swig while relieving himself. Feeling comforted by the familiar burn sliding down his throat and into his stomach, Franklin allowed his thoughts to drift to things that had dominated the news for the past year.

He stared into the toilet at his stream of yellow tinted urine and smirked. "Don't get me started," he said to himself in the mirror. "Illegal immigration, Muslims, and now it's Black Lives Matter! This is supposed to be the home of the brave, not the piñata, hijab, and the slave!"

"And those crazy Indians," he grumbled, "always crying about their so called sacred land. They oughta get with the program!" He zipped up, wiped his hands on his pants, and continued with his rant. "They should've seen it coming a long time ago and just got the hell out of the way like we told 'em!" He took a final nip of whiskey, then after slipping the bottle back into the zip-lock bag, returned it carefully to his hiding place. Calmed from the drink Franklin's tone softened and he waxed philosophical. "If history teaches us anything, it's that life is hard on those who buck the system. And that's just what they did. If I said it once, I've said it a thousand times, what goes around, comes around. Simple as that!"

Finished with his business, Franklin looked into the mirror at his stubbled face. His eyes did indeed look yellowish, but he blamed the lighting in the bathroom for that. He tilted his head to look at the brown spot on his cheek. He leaned closer and was surprised to see that it had sprouted reddish spidery lines around its edges. Shrugging his shoulders he quipped, "Nobody said getting old was easy."

Stutter-stepping on the way back to his easy chair Franklin caught his shoulder against the corner of a wall nearly spinning himself around. Recovering his balance, he looked around himself warily, but Gwen's voice, singing in the kitchen, satisfied him that she hadn't seen his blunder. Angling himself back toward the den, he said to himself smugly, "If I could go back in time, I'd look the chief, hell, the whole lot of them Indians right in the eye and tell 'em, if you fail to prepare, you might as well prepare to fail!"

Despite his irritation with those he considered as losers in the world, he believed the country was becoming a better place. Perhaps more importantly, in Franklin's personal world it already had. Because of these two factors he felt more validated than ever, and justified for his convictions. As a result, Franklin freely and vehemently vented his opinions. Thus, apart from the few internet relationships who shared his cynical and bigoted points of view, the distance in his relationship with Gwen, and his isolation from everyone else became increasingly pronounced.

None of this seemed to trouble Franklin. His perception that he did not need anyone else remained steadfast. He believed he had achieved and acquired all he needed in his life, and that all that remained for him now was to enjoy what he had, and if necessary, defend his spoils. The closest Franklin came to anything that to some might resemble prayer—and he did this often—was when he thanked his nation's forefathers and the second amendment every day for his guns. As far as he was concerned, these two things gave him both the right and the means to do just that.

Hoping to avoid another of Franklin's tirades, Gwen wiped down the beer can a second time with her apron, then handed it to Franklin after he was seated. "It's nice and cold Honey, and dry as can be!" she said brightly.

She stood there a little too long for Franklin's liking, so he waived her off with his free hand as though swatting at a pesky fly. His mind had already begun to drift back to the dissatisfactions he had been mulling over during his bathroom break. *If it ain't the blacks, or the Indians, it's the damned Mexicans, he thought. Then, as if that's not enough, now we have to deal with the Muslims.* As this last thought rose to the surface in his mind, he envisioned his most recent trip to the corner fast-mart for a six-pack. The man behind the counter greeted him with a broad, friendly smile, but what stood out to Franklin was the brown fabric he wore wrapped around his head. *I don't know what language he was speaking, but that gibberish sure as hell ain't english!* Franklin grumbled internally. *Gotta be some kind of conspiracy!*

Women too made Franklin uncomfortable. He longed for the day when they knew their place and minded their manners like they did when he was still a kid. He often complained to Gwen, or to anyone nearby whenever the topic was raised, "A man can't look at them sideways anymore without being accused of molesting them or some such thing! If they're supposed to be so special, then why didn't God make them first instead of only as an after thought?"

Franklin's thoughts bubbled and popped within him now with an increasing pace, drowning out the noise from the TV. And Franklin spiraled down deeper into those places within his memory from which they came, believing that each of them were justifications for his anger.

He was the second of three children. His brother was five years younger than him, and as Franklin remembered it, was babied by their mother. Franklin also recalled that his sister, who was a year older than him, was the proverbial princess of the family. As Franklin often told it, his siblings formed an alliance between them, discovering early on that by working together, they could get away with almost anything, including picking on him, and Franklin would take the brunt of it. Individually, or as a team, whether they caused some kind of disturbance, start a fight, or made a mess, they would blame

Franklin for it, and he would pay the price. In an attempt to keep himself out of their sight, and out of trouble, Franklin took to reading, and became quickly enamored by tales of the brave and powerful men who fought for, founded, and shaped the United States. He was particularly drawn to the tales that were presented largely through the lens of white men, and which established his view that it was men, white men, who's rightful place was to be in charge. His favorite reading was of a series of American Heritage books, written for children and tees, which covered the history of the conquering and development of America from pre-Revolutionary War times to the present.

Franklin smiled to himself as he remembered those books, and nodded as the memory of the turning point with his siblings came to his mind. Somewhere during his fourteenth year of life, his sister threw a punch at him. He had been preparing himself for this for the two weeks after the last time she'd slugged him, bloodying his nose. This time, stirred by his reading about civil war generals, J.E.B. Stuart, and Stonewall Jackson, he caught her fist in mid air. Franklin snickered to out loud as he remembered the look on his sister's face. He held her fist tightly in his own for what seemed like several minutes, then squeezed and twisted it until he brought her to her knees, where she gave in, her eyes brimming with tears. His brother was peeking around the corner, watching the whole thing with a look of shear terror on his face. Neither of them attacked him physically again after that.

The smirk on Franklin's face while he relived the memory faded, and was replaced by one of longing as his thoughts turned to memories of his father. "I could never eat fast enough for him," he murmured. "And the second I'd speed it up, he'd yell at me to slow down! Either way, I always had hell to pay."

Aside from the chores he was given as punishment for what his father deemed transgressions, Franklin was hurt deeply by all of the things his dad never did with him. Unlike the other boys in the neighborhood he saw playing catch, or shooting hoops with their fathers, and despite the fact that his dad attended his sister's dance recitals and brother's ball games, Franklin couldn't remember ever playing with his dad. Nor could he remember his father ever showing up for a game of his.

In an attempt to escape from the pain he felt from these memories, Franklin shifted his thoughts to another area of his mind, where he stored recollections of his mother. But this led to only further disappointment. His mother was what is often referred to as a functional alcoholic, meaning for her that although she regularly drank herself into a submissive stupor, she managed to hold a job outside of the home. She often made a fuss over Franklin, but even as a young boy, her show of affection felt superficial to him. It had irritated him to no end that she would sometimes fawn over him in public, telling him for example, and for all to hear, how cute he was. Worse, she even did it when picking him up from school. Of course this wasn't lost on the other kids. They rubbed it in, and never let him forget it.

Franklin knew she loved him in her own peculiar way, and tried to chalk her behavior up to being a mom. What really aggravated him was her silence about and lack of interference with her husband's handling of him. Perhaps even more than this, Franklin resented that she put up with how his dad treated her like his personal servant. As a young boy he hated these things, and swore to himself he'd never be like that. But as sometimes happens to those who make similar resolutions, he found himself years later mimicking his father's behavior in his own marriage. *Why shouldn't she bring me what I ask? he thought to himself. Haven't I done my job supporting her all these years? Mom knew her place, so should Gwen!*

Franklin's thoughts swung back to his Dad. He was a veteran of the second world war, and although he never saw combat, he talked to no end about his hatred of "them krauts." In the sixties and seventies this changed to "the chinks," then "those gooks". Interspersed with those derogatory terms, were the ever popular "lazy niggers" or "beaners," followed by "them good-for-nothing queers."

***

The living room was Franklin's dad's domain. There he seemed permanently planted in his easy chair all weekend long, watching sports or the news, and smoking one of his smelly cigars. One might not even know he was there but for the acrid smoke wafting out from behind the newspaper that concealed his face. But Franklin came to count on him being there, dressed in only a tee shirt and his boxer shorts.

One of the rare times that Franklin could recall his dad speaking to him, was when he had worked up the nerve to ask him why he kept a rifle next to his chair.

His dad didn't bother putting the paper down to answer. Instead, a cloud of smoke billowed up from behind it, as if announcing that the master was about to speak. "In case the niggers from a couple towns over try to sneak into our neighborhood," was the matter of fact reply. He shook the paper, noisily turned a page, and while acrid smelling cigar smoke wafted over the top edge of the paper, instructed Franklin to, "Take the trash to the curb. You should know by now tomorrow's pick-up."

Franklin's hatred for his father grew, and he swore to himself that in addition to treating women properly, he'd be nothing like him when it came to people of color. While a freshman in high school, this was easy, as the town he lived in was populated by whites. That year Franklin waltzed in to the gym and made a name for himself on the basketball team, quickly becoming the star player. He then did the same thing on the track team. He got along with others and became popular with both the boys and the girls. Both teams won their respective league championships that year. But the success was lackluster for Franklin because his Dad never attended a game or a meet, nor asked about a single event.

During his sophomore year, Franklin's school participated in a meet at one of the local Indian reservation schools. The Indian team out performed every one of Franklin's teammates, and Franklin himself was soundly defeated at his specialty, the long-distance run. For the first time, outside of his own home, he felt humiliated. As a junior, Franklin's skill and aggressive style of play at basketball earned him the role of team captain. Two weeks before the first game of the season, Franklin was confident that he would redeem himself from last years defeat. That was when a new kid showed up on campus, and the news spread like a wild fire. Not that it was unusual for new kids to trickle in mid year, but this time was different. This guy was black.

Franklin viewed this as an opportunity to be a better man than his Dad, and he went out of his way to befriend the new boy. To Franklin, he looked athletic enough, and like himself, he was taller than the average high school boy, so he encouraged him to try out for the basketball team. It quickly became apparent to all that this kid's skills surpassed Franklin's, and with that realization the attention of the entire school shifted from Franklin to his new team mate. In spite of his resolve to be the better man, Franklin found himself beginning to resent the kid. A rivalry developed between the two of them that often became heated.

Later in the season, Franklin's school played an away game at an inner city school where the student population was primarily black. The schools all black team tested Franklin's to its limits, and although Franklin's team ultimately won the game, there was an altercation afterwards during which a couple of black boys began roughing Franklin up.

Franklin was mad as hell, but taking a pounding. While he was trying to get his footing, his nemesis jumped in and broke up the fight, essentially rescuing Franklin, to the cheers of the crowd.

With that, a powerful sense of failure descended upon Franklin. He knew this would make it into the local news, and in spite of the fact that his dad never came to a game, he never missed the sports section in the paper. In his mind, Franklin saw his dad billowing out huge puffs of cigar smoke as he shook his head in shame at his pathetic son.

Franklin never forgave the Indian boy for defeating him in track or the black boy for bettering him in basketball and interfering with his fight. To this day, while Franklin drank his beer in front of the television recalling these events, he seethed. His emotions worked up to a lather a whistle blew in the game he had all but forgotten, snapping him back to the present moment. He watched the replay, then roared at the screen, "Now, that's a fucking bad call!" With that, he snatched the remote from the coffee table, and oblivious to Gwen's objection to his language, surfed the channels for another game, or news, or anything that made sense to him. He finished his beer, which once more helped to sooth his raging nerves, and blissfully unaware that his narcissistic world view was on the verge of a rude awakening, his eyes drooped incrementally until they were closed. As he drifted off to sleep, he wondered with sluggish irritation where the drumming was coming from.

# CHAPTER 4

Sunlight slanted across Franklin's face like a white hot laser, and he groaned as the brightness elicited a stabbing pain behind his tightly closed eyelids. Pressing his palms against his temples in an attempt to quiet the throbbing that was going on deep in the center of his skull, and miraculously both the pounding and the searing light suddenly disappeared. To Franklin's relief, he was engulfed again in the comfort of darkness. He turned over in an attempt to sleep off the beer a bit longer, wondering vaguely how he'd made it to bed, and as a distant afterthought, why the bed felt so coarse.

Like bubbles rising to the surface of thick molasses, a new sensation slowly formed itself in his mind. *Almost like fur*, he thought, and he began to doze. But Franklin hadn't been sleeping long when the pounding in his skull returned with a vengeance. He sat up and realized that although his head still ached and felt as though it was being squeezed in a vise, the noise was coming from somewhere outside.

"Damn it Gwen! I'm trying to sleep!" he grumbled as loud as his parched throat would allow, but the words came out course and garbled. Clearing his throat noisely, he tried to stifle a feeling of nausea, and laid back down.

The drumming stopped and started, softened and intensified, and unable to tolerate the disturbance a second longer, Franklin sat up angrily and tried to open his swollen, gummy eyes. He was dripping with sweat, and his head spun so that he placed his hands on the bed on either side of himself to keep from keeling over. He stared straight ahead, waiting for his eyes to adjust to the darkness, and noticed once more the curious roughness of the bed. To reduce the discomfort of his raw, dry throat, Franklin breathed through his nose, and recoiled from a pungent odor that permeated the room so thickly, he could taste it and feel the griminess of it on his tongue. It reminded him of a mixture of dirty wet dogs, grease, and smoke, and things so primitive he had no idea what they might be.

As his eyes adjusted to the darkness, the walls slowly came into focus, and Franklin was astonished to see that they were comprised of a rough patchwork of bark covered, and interlaced branches, and the skins of animals. Objects that resembled baskets or bowls, began to take shape on a floor of dirt in the musty darkness.

"I must have put a few too many away this time," he admitted to himself through his alcohol induced fog. Franklin tried again to clear his throat, but razor blades of pain burned up and down its length. As smacking himself in the head was definitely out of the question, he sat in a bewildered agony, waiting for his aching head to clear, and for something to make sense.

Franklin involuntarily jumped, when he noticed a low, smoldering fire in the middle of the room. There was a large, smoke-blackened pot hanging over it. He followed the smoke with his eyes as it drifted up and out through an opening in the ceiling. Then tracing the fumes back to their source, he saw the silhouette of a figure, seated, facing away from him on the other side of the fire.

"This can't be real," he managed with a faint whisper, but the scene remained as it was. With his eyebrows scrunched and forehead crinkled with a profound feeling of disorientation, he called out weakly, "Gwen?"

Instead of Gwen's familiar short cropped, silver hair, the figure he hoped was his wife, wore her hair long and braided, and it was black as coal. The woman was bent forward, and was cupping her hands up from a bowl on the ground to her face. Right away, Franklin noticed that her back was bare, and despite the oddness of the moment, and the queasy feeling in his gut, he licked his parched, cracked lips and thought, *This could get interesting.*

Amazed at how realistic the primitive feel and animal smell of everything was, Franklin chuckled, "Crazy dream. Just my luck I wind up with damned Indians." He decided it wasn't worth worrying about, believing he'd wake from this annoying experience soon. Besides, his head still hurt like hell, and the pounding, which now sounded more like rhythmic drumming had started up again.

He coughed then cursed at the pain in his head, and the figure seated across the room from Franklin turned around. Although her features were partially hidden in shadow, he could see that she was naked from the waist up, and without questioning himself for a second, he greedily traced her curves. As Franklin's mind began to consider the opportunities his odd dream might be presenting him with, the thought that he might have to wake up shifted from what just a moment ago couldn't happen soon enough, to one of utter disappointment. This was followed by a surge of profound nausea.

"Svnalei Ostu," the woman said softly, then added in broken english, "good morning." She tilted her head to the side, and her dark eyes reflected the flicker and glow of the fire. Franklin's eyes had become like saucers, and with a look of understanding, and one swift movement of her arm, she covered her nakedness with a fur she grasped from beside her.

Franklin thought sourly to himself, *Can you believe this? Even in a fucking dream! That's exactly what's wrong with women. They don't understand a man's needs. A man's a man, and a woman is, well ... a man's!* He chuckled at his clever quip.

The woman rose and padded over to the fire where she stirred the contents of a bowl with a spoon that looked like it had been carved from a gourd. She then brought the spoon brimming with its steaming contents to Franklin, mimicked sipping from the gourd herself, then offered it to him.

"Usdi," she said pinching her index finger and thumb together to emphasize only a little.

Franklin reached out his hand to stroke the woman's arm, only to receive from her a surprisingly sharp slap to his fingers. He recoiled in pain licking his stinging fingertips, then shifted his focus to the gourd. *Okay, have it your way, let's focus on the food first,* he thought, and tipped his head down to take a tentative sip of the broth. The sip turned out to be more of a noisy slurp, and Franklin jerked his head back, a sour expression on his face.

The woman smiled patiently while Franklin allowed the concoction to slide down his ravaged throat. He was immediately rewarded with a sooth-ing sensation to both his throat and stomach, which prompted him to grab the gourd from the woman's hand and drink deeply. He eagerly drank in more of the broth, then closed his eyes, enjoying the feeling of warmth mak-ing its way into his stomach. For a moment he felt relaxed, and his stomach settled. Even his aching head felt the beginnings of relief. He took several more greedy drinks, draining the spoon of the rest of its contents without noticing that the woman had moved off to the far side of the room.

For a moment, Franklin thought he had never felt better, and his lasciv-ious thoughts towards the woman returned, then the nausea hit him again with a vengeance. "Shit!" he gurgled, bolting to his feet. Hi eyes bulging, and a look of desperation on his face, he didn't know which end of him would erupt first.

The woman moved quickly to the oiled flap and lifted it, revealing an opening through which blinding light immediately flooded into the enclo-sure. Franklin lurched blindly through it, ran to the first bush he saw, and dropped his pants. Relieved at that end, his discomfort now concentrated itself in his stomach. He stood and quickstepped to a new location, lost his balance, and fell to his knees with his eyes squeezed shut. Before he could catch his breath, Franklin leaned forward, his hands bracing him up from the ground, and vomited violently and profusely.

Even in his anguish Franklin knew what he was to do next. He'd come this far in the dream before, and the familiarity of all that had happened in it up to now became clear to him. So he inhaled deeply relishing the cool, fresh, pine-scented, air. Then, straightening back up, his hands still filled with dirt, he allowed his clenched fists to hang at his sides. He gradually opened his eyes against the brightness outside the enclosure, and once more saw the dozen or more amorphous figures slowly begin to solidify. Their shapes at first undulated, defying description against the bright light of day, then as Franklin's eyes adjusted, the objects began to solidify into men and women. "Jesus," Franklin uttered in awe of the phenomenon.

The woman behind him giggled.

"Goddam Indians," he moaned with disgust, then passed out while crumpling to the ground.

When Franklin came to again, he felt much better. The bed still felt hard against his back, and the place reeked of a musky animal scent. He heard movement, and hoping he was back in his own bed, rolled over expecting to see Gwen puttering around the bedroom. But instead he saw the Indian woman, back where he'd first seen her, her body fully draped in what looked like the fur of a bear.

"Shit, if I don't wake up soon..." he grumbled, but stopped short when the woman stirred.

She stood and turned around at the sound of Franklin's voice, then padded back to the large cook pot. The fire was only smoldering coals now. The woman ladled out some more broth, walked over to him, knelt on the ground, and offered him the spoon-shaped gourd. Nodding her head, she again indicated he should only take a little. As she knelt before Franklin, the bear skin parted.

Franklin thought for a moment that the woman was offering herself to him, and his pulse quickened at the prospect. But he frowned noticing that beneath the fur, she was also wearing a blouse that looked like the soft and much more supple skin of another animal, most likely a deer. Shaking off his disappointment at her modesty while looking into her fathomless, unblinking eyes, he took a sip from the gourd, and noticed there were small chunks of meat in the broth this time. The stew was gamey, but he felt it settle comfortably in his stomach. After a moment, he took some more and chewed slowly on the tender meat.

The woman stepped away, and returned with a bowl which she set on the ground in front of Franklin.

He studied it with suspicion.

The woman made a guttural noise deep in her throat, then mimicked holding the bowl to her lips and drinking.

He picked the bowl up, sniffed at its contents, then touched the surface of a clear liquid with the tip of his tongue, sipped a minuscule amount, then gulped. It was water, cool, clear water, unlike any he thought he had ever tasted, and he drank as though he hadn't had a drop in weeks.

The woman gently touched his arm, distracting him from his effort to drain the bowl dry, and once more Franklin reached for her. He quickly slipped his hand under her garment and felt the warmth and softness of her skin, then shifted his position to add to his reach so that he could grope her breast. But before he could move his hand, the woman, who had somehow managed to get her hands on a rock from around the cook fire, and brought it down hard on his skull.

Figuring he was done for, he expected the woman to cry for help, but instead, after stepping back, she offered him the gourd once again.

Franklin accepted the gourd and sipped.

"Utsati," she said, then cupped both of her hands together to her mouth and tilted her head back.

Franklin grunted his understanding, then took a long, deep, satisfying drink of the hot broth. Sitting back, he felt it going all the way down. His eyes fluttered and his vision blurred, then darkened altogether. Almost as quickly, he could see again and he caught his breath. The entire environment had changed, and he was no longer with the Indian woman. Instead, he was now at a party with his high school buddies. The perpetual drumming he had just begun to get accustomed to was replaced by ear-splitting, head-banging metal music. And as the initial shock of the drastic transition subsided, he sensed he was on the verge of scoring with a girl clad in cut-off jeans, fishnet stockings, and a man's tank top teeshirt. Her face was adorned with black lipstick and mascara matching all but one of her badly gnawed fingernails which was painted red.

Just as Franklin was settling into the new dreamscape, the scene shifted again, fast-forwarding to a few years out of high school, and another party. Although he could not remember the date, he recognized the place and the moment. This was when he met Gwen, and more importantly to him, the night he stole her virginity. They had moved to a back room, and Gwen had just excused herself to the bathroom. He was waiting for his moment.

Cute and curvy were high prerequisites on Franklin's list, and she possessed these attributes in spades. But perhaps more importantly, he deduced that Gwen was the kind of girl that needed to take care of a boy, and he played that tendency for everything it was worth.

They eventually married, had children, and grew old. In between, Franklin pursued his dreams and accumulated his things. Regardless of how much effort Gwen put into satisfying her husband's needs, the few stimulating conversations they once had were soon replaced by his penchant for televised sports while draining beer cans dry.

"Turn off the lights," Gwen teased with a trembling voice from the bathroom. Then added, "Close your eyes, okay?"

Her voice brought Franklin back to the moment of his dream state. "No problem," he crooned, rolling his eyes and flicking off the light switch beside the bed. Gamely closing his eyes to the narrowest of slits by which, undetected, he'd still be able to see her, he lied, "Okay, they're closed." It was quiet and warm in the room, but darker than he'd hoped. He could hear muffled voices outside, but was unable to understand them. Wondering what was taking Gwen so long, he opened his eyes a bit further, and saw to his profound disappointment that he was back inside the Indian dwelling.

"Shit!, just when I... oh well, maybe after whatever the hell this is, I'll get back to the party," he mumbled in an attempt to reassure himself.

He marveled again at the realness of his surroundings, and thought it odd that given his disdain for Indians, he was dreaming so much about them. Resigning himself to the place for the moment, he hoped that the sick and painful part would at least be over. He saw that he was alone, and noticed too that he was bare footed. Shrugging this off, he stretched and made his way toward the opening. He took a breath of the thick, musty atmosphere in the enclosure and pushed aside the greasy flap. Once again Franklin's lungs filled with the aroma of pines and fresh air, and squinting against the brightness, he saw them.

# CHAPTER 5

Several primitive looking men talked quietly to one another, while several more were working on some kind of wooden contraption. Two others were skinning a deer that was hanging upside down from a tree branch. Franklin also saw a woman sweeping the dirt ground with a pine bough, while another he recognized as the one who had fed him earlier, was using a rock pestle to pound something like seeds, or maybe corn inside of another rock that was shaped roughly like a bowl. Two more other women were interacting with five children, apparently playing some kind of game, while one of them was combing and braiding one of the children's hair.

They were Indians, and for the moment Franklin marveled at the sight of them. Despite his history of disregard for them, he found something majestic about the people before him. Including the children, Franklin counted eighteen of them. They all had black hair, some long and straight, others in braids. Several of the younger men looked as though their heads had been shaved, leaving only a shank of hair right down the middle that was combed and greased back. Many of the men wore one or two feathers sticking straight up from the crown of their head, while others wore them hanging down on the side, nearly to their shoulder.

Even to one such as Franklin, the scene before him appeared idyllic until the men with the shaved heads suddenly and in unison, turned to look at him. Their faces had been painted in bold and provocative colors, reminiscent of movies he'd seen with Indians painted for war. These men were also nearly naked, wearing only a leather breechcloth fastened around their waist. Their skin glistened, as if smeared with grease, and their bodies rippled with muscle marked with jagged lines, hand-prints, and geometric shapes.

The children were bundled up in furs, looking to Franklin very much like Eskimo dolls, and he suddenly realized that he was cold. Two of the men looked older, their shoulders draped with furs. Underneath them they wore the same soft leathery looking stuff the woman from the dwelling had on, except these were adorned with beads and feathers. The older looking man motioned to the others, then took a step toward him, and stopped.

"Otahitsu asgaya oudunsohnunhe asgaya?" he said to Franklin, while lightly rubbing his belly. His voice sounded like time itself, guttural and authoritative, yet worn smooth with age. "How you feel old man?" he followed in broken English.

Taken aback, Franklin sputtered, "Well, Chief, I don't feel like shit anymore."

"I am happy you feel better. You drank much whiskey last night."

At this comment, the other men laughed and shook their heads while the women held their heads down. One of the children, a boy, giggled and slapped his thigh in imitation of one of the men who sported a shaved head and red handprint across his face. The Indian brave barked something unintelligible at the boy who stopped laughing immediately and buried his head in the furs of a woman who was holding his hand.

*It's only a dream*, Franklin thought, deciding to play along. "Yeah, I must've really tied one on last night. Damn Redskins made me do it!"

The Indian who had addressed him scowled, and as the other men tensed and grumbled amongst themselves, Franklin took a quick step back.

"I am not a Chief, I am only the head of this family. But why you blame us? We did not make you drink that," the old Indian said, pointing to an empty, ceramic, quart-sized jug laying in the dirt in front of the dwelling behind Franklin. "We know what the poison can do."

Detecting the annoyance in the old Indian and the others, Franklin quickly said, "Oh, I didn't mean you guys, I was talking about the game yesterday. You know the Lions and the Redski ..." Seeing confusion on their faces and sensing their increasing agitation, Franklin changed the subject mid-sentence, "Never mind. Anyways, the soup was nice, but I could really use some solid food, you know, a burger, anything? I'm starving." Franklin had worked himself up emotionally, and no longer thinking about his safety, he lobbed an insult. "What I really want to know is, what are we doing in this God-forsaken place?"

The old Indian breathed a sigh of controlled exasperation, signaled the others to stand down, and focused once more on Franklin. "This is our land," he said solemnly. "It has been so since the earth was formed and the first two humans Kana'ti and his sister Selu inhabited this place."

"Whoa chief," Franklin interrupted. "That's a wild story there. But I don't see what that has to do with me being here."

The group of Indians, collectively, emitted a low groan. Some of them were shaking their heads and clenching their fists.

The old Indian quieted the men down again, then spoke to Franklin, his voice rising with intensity. "Once again you call me Chief. But I have told you already that I am not." He paused a moment, as if reigning himself in, then continued calmly. "I lead these few people who are my family in the best way I can. This has been made many times more difficult now that our people have been broken and forced by the white man to leave our homes. To call me Austenaco is great disrespect to the true chief of our Nation, Guwisguwi, who we now call John Ross."

Feeling both threatened and outnumbered, Franklin feigned contriteness. "Sorry," he chuckled sheepishly. "Always had a thing for good whiskey, guess it got the better of me. But I'm shaking it off." He saw the Indian appear to relax, and thought to himself, *Now, if I could just wake up, I could be done with all this nonsense.* Clearing his throat, Franklin politely asked, "What do I call you, sir?"

The old Indian took a step closer to Franklin. He tapped himself on the chest with his fist and said, "I am Degataga. My name means *standing together*, because from my birth, I have always held my family and those close to us together. It saddens me you remember so little. You have been sleeping much of the time as we nursed you back to health and protected you. But, we still do not know your name. You have not even been able to tell us where you are from, but we know what brought you here."

Franklin's eyebrows raised at this comment, but before he could say anything, the old Indian continued.

"If not for these people," he said, referring to the whole group with a sweep of his arm, "you might be dead by now, or walking in chains. Instead, you are among the Cherokee people. My sons, Chea Sequa and Kanuna," he continued, indicating two of the men with shaved skulls, "found you sick with whiskey, and lost in the forest. They carried you here. Then, my wife, Ayita, nursed you to health. Do you not remember any of this?"

Franklin was not accustomed to being lectured by anyone, let alone an Indian. "Listen Degadadavidda, or whatever you call yourself," he answered, his voice laced with derision. "I don't know what the lot of you will do after I wake up from this frickin' nightmare. But all I have to do is sleep it off, grab me a beer, and watch the game."

"You have talked of game for the second time," Degataga said with interest. "The government has shown us they do not intend to make things easier on us with the stipend they offer for food. And we know that when we leave here, the white men will mark up their price for food that is not even fit for dogs. Once we leave the world's center we have no way to know how the Great Spirit will care for us. We know only that the direction the government tells us we must go is associated with death." The old Indian looked at the deer his men had been cleaning, then back at Franklin again. "The only game for miles is hanging from that tree. Those who left the homeland before us have hunted nearly all the animals already, leaving us very little. Will you tell us where you have seen this game you speak of so we don't starve?"

Franklin was feeling frustrated enough already that his dream had put him in such circumstances. Aside from the prospect of the half-naked woman being of interest to him, everything else was harsh and uncomfortable. All this talk of starvation and death was pushing things too far, and he resolved to wake himself up if there was anything he could do about it.

"Gwen!" he called out, thinking this might break the spell of sleep.

At Franklin's sudden outburst, the Indian called Degataga staggered back several steps, and the other Indians looked nervously back and forth at one another.

"Gwen!" he called out a second time with more force, but nothing changed. Franklin cursed, called out louder still, and slapped himself in the head. When nothing happened still, he slapped his cheeks repeatedly, thinking he must look like Curly of the Three Stooges. Not caring what the Indians might have thought, he kept it up while calling Gwen's name over and over, hoping this would wake him from his nightmare.

Degataga motioned to his sons, who without hesitation walked briskly over to Franklin, grasped him firmly under his arms, and dragged him back into the dwelling. After dropping him onto his bed of furs, they positioned themselves on either side of the flap.

Franklin worried he may have crossed the line, and was about to pay for it, when the woman, Ayita, entered, brushed past the two men, and mixed something into the cooking pot. After stirring its contents briskly, she ladled some of it up with the gourd spoon, and brought it to Franklin indicating for him to drink.

Grateful for the moment to be back in the relative comfort of the dwelling, Franklin eagerly slurped the broth, then laid back on the fur covered bed, and immediately felt groggy. The woman covered him with furs, and he didn't feel like resisting. And despite the presence of the two braves, Franklin was still surprised that he didn't feel the least bit amorous. This was so uncharacteristic of him that he tried to manifest sexual interest, but was unable to feel even the slightest hint of arousal, and only became increasingly drowsy. In frustration, he decided to turn over on his side and try to get some sleep, hoping he'd wake up in his own bed. But he was startled to find he couldn't move a muscle. Able only to breath and shift his eyes from side to side, the fear that had been building inside of him was taken over by a profound relaxation, and he fell into a deep sleep.

# CHAPTER 6

Franklin awoke to the sound of muffled voices outside the dwelling, and he strained his ears to listen. Although he wasn't able to make out what was being said, the exchange sounded tense. Someone shouted, and another joined in, then he heard footsteps coming toward the dwelling entrance. His instinct driven muscles told him to bolt upright and prepare for a fight, but he found that he was still unable to move. Knowing there was only one way out, and trouble was coming his way, it was all he could do to grind his teeth with dread.

"If ya got that nigger with ya, there's gonna be real trouble chief!" growled a deep voice spoken with a country twang. "We knows a runaway was hightailin' it in this here direction, and we been paid ta bring it back ta its rightful owner. Now step back so I kin take a look fer mahself."

"My wife is sick and needs to rest. I cannot let you go inside."

Franklin recognized Degataga's voice, imploring whoever it was out there to not enter the dwelling. His plea was met by a metallic click, then another.

"That's fine by me, chief. Ah kin kill you dead, then check it out for mahself, or you kin stand aside and live ta take care of yer sick wife when we're gone."

Franklin looked around himself in the darkened enclosure. Except for Degataga's wife, Ayita, he was alone. Even while straining his eyes, he could barely see her form, hurriedly filling the drinking gourd with broth. Her hands shaking, she tipped the gourd and swallowed a good mouthful. Not taking the time to wipe her mouth, she motioned for him to get back under his furs. She then bulged her eyes theatrically and bolted out of the dwelling. The flap caught on the wall which allowed Franklin to see outside. He watched as Ayita groaned and stumbled forward, then fell to her knees vomiting in roughly the same spot he had earlier. She didn't move after that, but lay there panting heavily and moaning in pain.

Franklin saw Degataga just beyond Ayita's fallen body, standing with his arms crossed and facing two scowling strangers. Although he could see that they were not Indians, they looked every bit like what might pass as a white man's version of them. One was thick bearded, wore clothing made of leather that was heavily patched together underneath a fur cloak draped over his shoulders. The fur included the animals legs complete with four inch long claws. On the man's head, curled up as if asleep, was another animal he wore as a hat. The man beside the first, and bristling with anger, sported a handle-bar mustache, the hairs of which looked slicked together with grease. He wore a hat like the one Franklin had seen in pictures of Abraham Lincoln, and a filthy woolen coat that hung from his shoulders to his ankles.

The two strangers had quickly jumped backwards to avoid the mess when Ayita retched.

As they struggled to recover their composure, Degataga knelt down beside his wife, and put his hand on her shoulder. Rifles slung over their backs, the two pulled pistols from inside their coats and waved them back and forth warily from Degataga to the rest of the Indians to keep them honest.

Tugging nervously on his beard, the first man stuttered, "Ah don't know 'bout you, Jeb, but ah sure as hell don't wanna be gettin' none of that sickness. Word is it's real bad."

"We'll be comin' back straight away, chief!" the man with the stove-pipe hat muttered. With that, he and his partner back-peddled their way out of the camp. As soon as they had moved out of the clearing, they turned and bolted headlong into the surrounding forest.

Degataga's two sons picked their mother up off the ground and carried her inside. They laid her down on a bed of furs across the dwelling from Franklin, and gently pulled another fur over her. After tucking it under her chin, they left without so much as looking at him.

Despite the fact that he could not move, Franklin felt comfortable. Beyond that he understood that Ayita, Degataga, and the others had just protected him, but from what? He wondered what the old Indian meant when he said that he knew what brought him here, and what the hell the strangers were talking about when they mentioned a nigger, and getting it back to its rightful owner. As these and other questions cycled receptively through his mind, drowsiness overcame him. Hoping to awaken in his own home, Franklin tried once more to call out for Gwen. But before he could utter her name, he drifted off to sleep.

Franklin had no idea how long he'd been lying there, but upon waking, saw with dismay that he was still in the confounded Indian dream. He found that he was able to move, so he pinched himself hard, hoping this would wake him up in his easy chair back home. Instead, he yelp and cursed in pain. From the narrow shaft of yellow-orange light that crept past the flap, Franklin deduced that the sun was setting. Once again he heard muted voices and soft drumming coming from outside. The savory aroma of cooking meat wafted in through the flap triggering his hunger, and he decided to see if he could get himself some of whatever it was that smelled so good.

Upon exiting the dwelling, Franklin saw Degataga and his men sitting on rocks arranged around a low fire. The deer he'd seen the braves cleaning earlier was being roasted over the coals. The old Indian puffed on a pipe, stirred the bowl with a twig from the fire, then took a long drag and exhaled smoke that in the dimming light of early evening, appeared blue. The drumming stopped, and Degataga reached to his hip. From a leather sheath that hung there, he pulled out the most magnificent knife Franklin had ever seen. It looked as though its handle had been fashioned from the antler of a deer, and if he wasn't mistaken, the blade was made of black flint.

*Maybe this isn't such a good idea*, Franklin thought while taking a step backwards towards the relative safety of the dwelling.

"Galutsv," Degataga said, and motioned for Franklin to join him. With his knife, he sliced a piece of meat from the carcass of the deer, then skewered it on the end of a stick. He held it out to Franklin and motioned again for him to sit beside him.

Franklin complied while keeping one eye on the knife and the other on the braves seated just feet away from him. One of them poked listlessly at the fire with the charred end of a pointed stick, a look of despondency on his face. Franklin looked from one face to the next, and saw that they all looked upset. No one spoke. He could see their breath, and suddenly aware of how cold it was, he threw caution to the wind and scooted his rock closer to the fire.

Degataga took another puff on his pipe, then spoke up, breaking the uneasy silence. "You look much better, Unaduti. Ayita has taken good care of you."

Franklin was so enraptured with the sizzle and aroma of the cooking meat, he had no idea he was being spoken to.

Degataga laughed, then said, "Perhaps we should have called you Chuquilatague after all. You are here with us at this fire, but seem to be in another place, or in another head. Like when we found you, but somehow different."

The others looked up and smiled or chuckled softly while shaking their heads at Degataga's observation.

Franklin, startled out of his stupor by the laughter, picked up that he was the butt of a light-hearted joke. Changing the subject, he pointed to the knife Degataga had laid on a rock beside him. "Where'd you get such a beautiful knife? I collect such things, but I've never seen one like that."

Degataga picked up and fingered the handle while he lightly dragged his thumb across the stone blade. "My father made this. He gave it to me when he passed from this world. I must give it one day to my eldest son when it is time for me to go where my father is now." He took a long, slow, drag on his pipe, and held the knife before his eyes. The obsidian blade reflected the fire beautifully, but Degataga appeared to be looking far beyond it.

Uncomfortable with the silence, Franklin asked the old man, "What do those words you said mean? Chewka whata-whata?"

"Chuquilatague," Degataga corrected. "This word means double headed. We called you that because you seemed to have two ways of thinking when we found you. One was angry, and the other crazy, which we believed was because of the liquor. But two heads seems to still be true for you. With one head, you are here, and with the other, you are somewhere else."

Franklin thought that maybe the Indian was referring to his dream state. But a couple of the Indians around the fire stood and wobbled, mimicking intoxication, then sat back down laughing with the others, and he realized he was once more being teased.

"But we decided to call you Unaduti," Degataga continued, "because of your hair. Unaduti means wooly head."

Again, the others laughed good naturedly.

"I hate to spoil your fun, but my name is Franklin. And, what the hell's the matter with my hair?" he asked. Franklin reached to run his fingers through the thinning, silver-white strands that as of late barely covered his skull, but instead found that they became snagged in matted, coarse, and wiry, coils. Astounded, he gasped, "What the ...?" Then he erupted in anger, "Did you do this to me while I was out cold?" he demanded. "Is that why you had me drugged? This feels like... it feels like nigger hair!" he croaked.

"Is that not the hair of your people?" Degataga said, amusement in his voice? "Has the whiskey made you forget who you are?"

Franklin spit into the fire and jumped to his feet. His hands balled into fists, he snarled, "I told you my name is Franklin, and if there's one thing I know, it's who and what the hell I am, and am not! This is just some crazy dream I'm having because I drank a little too much. None of you are even real. As soon as I wake up, you will be nothing but a memory, one I'll be sure to forget. I'll be who I've always been, and all of you will be nothing at all."

In response to Franklin's sudden and erratic outburst, the Indians jumped up and assumed a defensive stance, except for Degataga, who remained seated and calmly motioned for the others to sit. After the braves had settled back down, he turned back and regarded Franklin for a moment then slowly and quietly spoke, "Unaduti ... Franklin, do you not know that you are gvnagei?" Holding his hands out and rubbing the backs of them lightly, he said, "You need only look at your skin."

Barely containing his indignation, at the feeling he was being mocked, Franklin looked down at his clenched fists. They did look different somehow, but then it was dark, he reasoned. "Things will look normal again when the drug Ayita fed me wears off," he thought. He stretched his arms out, turning them so to catch the light from the fire, and unclenched his fingers. Then he slowly held the backs of his hands before his eyes, and passed out cold.

***

"I think he's coming around!" an excited voice said from just inches away.

Franklin opened his eyes to a blinding light flicking from one eye to the other, as someone held each eye lid open respectively.

"Yep! He's with us!" The voice said just before Franklin closed his eyes again to a new wave of nausea.

"Oh my God! Franklin!" Gwen cried.

Her voice sounded so distant to Franklin, it might as well have been coming from another world. The nausea passed, and his eyes fluttered open again, then squinted in the glare of a bright white light that returned and resumed its relentless flicking from eye to eye. He heard a siren blaring nearby, and concentrating hard, managed to see the face beyond the light. "Where am I?" he croaked, feeling queasy again.

"Increase the drip," the face said. "He's seriously dehydrated."

"I got a better idea," Franklin groaned. "Get me a beer... that always works." He saw Gwen sitting next to a woman in a blue smock with the name Cyndi embroidered onto it surrounded by colorful stitched flowers, and below this, the words, We Care, and Believe.

"Heeey Cyyndiii," Franklin slurred. "If you expect me to believe that you care, tell that woman next to you wringing her hands to go get me a beer. And get somebody to shut off that Goddamned siren for Christ's sake!"

"I'm afraid you've had your last beer Mr. Carlyle," said the face. But you need to understand that it's going to take even more than that to get you up and walking again. I'm nearly certain you're going to need a new liver, and give the demand on them, you'd be lucky to get one."

"Then get me my JD... I keep it in the toilet," Franklin grumbled. Although disoriented, he realized he had just given up his hiding spot. He saw tears brimming in Gwen's eyes, and quickly tried to change the subject by addressing the face again. "There's no such thing as luck, you know! A man decides what to do, and that's all there is to it! Anyone who thinks otherwise is no better than, than a savage!" For a moment he thought he could smell the smoky, sweet aroma of roasting meat. It didn't seem to be coming from anywhere nearby. Something inside told him he should know where it was coming from, but he couldn't remember.

The face looked back over his shoulder at Gwen, who was sobbing and shaking her head. Turning back to Franklin, he said, "Sir, you're here because of your drinking, which although we can clearly see for ourselves, your wife tells us has been quite excessive."

"That's nobodies business!" Franklin grunted, then added, raising his voice. "What the hell do you know, whoever you are?"

"Quite a lot," the face answered. "I'm a paramedic. My name is Jim. If your wife is even close to accurate about your drinking history, I'd say you're lucky to be alive right now."

"Won't anybody turn that damned siren off?" Franklin hollered. "And what's with all these blinking lights? You'd think I was in a frickin' hospital. And Jim, or whoever you are," he said with a steely look in his eye, "number one, I told you already, luck has nothing to do with it. Secondly, how am I supposed to be able to hear the game over all that confounded noise? And third, where the hell's the TV anyway?"

"Sir,... Mr. Carlyle, do you know where you are?"

"Now that's an interesting question, Jim,... Mr. Paramedic, sir." Chuckling to himself under his breath as his memory started to return, Franklin slurred, "A second ago, I was with some Indians, and just before that, I was about to score at a party. Matter of fact, a nice looking squaw was about to give me a drink." He chuckled again, and tried to wink, but the pain in his head stopped him short, and he winced instead. "Now," he continued, his voice rising with every word, "I'm in some kind of shaking, blinking, blaring, box, with a wanna be doctor, and my hand-wringing, worry-wort, wife! Now, if I can put up with the bat-shit craziness of these blasted dreams just a little longer, I'm gonna find myself in my living room, sitting in my comfy-ass easy chair, and I'll be watching the game instead of looking at your ugly face!" With his voice at full volume, he yelled, "And I better have a cold one in my hand, Goddamn it!"

Franklin coughed ferociously, causing pain up and down every inch of his throat as if he'd swallowed a rasp. Unable to catch his breath, he clutched at the paramedic. The lights blurred, and the sounds around him began to warble out of tune like the organ music at a baseball game had just come unplugged. He felt as though he was free falling, and he heard the paramedic telling someone in a voice that echoed in his head, that he'd be lucky if he made it through this, and luckier still if a liver came available for him in time. Franklin clutched at his chest trying to catch his breath just before passing out.

\*\*\*

# CHAPTER 7

Franklin lay still in the darkness and tried to ascertain his whereabouts. As disquieting as his dream of being amongst the Indians had been, this last episode with the Paramedic and Gwen felt even more troubling. As his head slowly cleared, he realized immediately and with some relief, that he was back in the Indian dwelling. Voices and the sounds of activity filtered in from outside, and he smelled broth steaming in the pot over the cook fire. Detecting no tension in the sounds he heard, and sensing that he was alone, Franklin stretched out his hands before his face and turned them slowly back to front, then back again, studying them as best he could, but the soft glow of the cook fire did not provide enough light to reveal if there was anything to Degataga's earlier pronouncement.

"Maybe Gwen's right. Maybe drinkin's finally catching up with me," he chuckled weakly. "I wonder how long it'll take to sleep this off?"

With no answer to his question, Franklin's thoughts turned once more to his stomach. He crawled out from under the furs, and padded lightly over to the pot. There, he grasped a wooden ladle and sipped just enough to know that the broth was good, then he tipped the spoon fully and drank his fill, finishing off the concoction of tender meat, vegetables, and broth with a loud belch. Satisfied for the moment, Franklin wiped his mouth on his forearm, and wandered over to where he had seen Ayita washing herself. He squatted down, cupped his hands, and brought cool water from a large, rough hewn, wooden bowl to his face.

"Ahhh," he breathed, feeling refreshed. "Time to see what the savages are up to."

Franklin brushed the flap aside and stepped out into a cold, grey morning. He inhaled and exhaled, and upon seeing his own breath, turned promptly back around and went back inside. Groping around in the darkness, he felt the fur on his bed, removed it, and draped the heavy skin around his shoulders, then went back outside. The sight of a nicely burning fire, and children warming themselves beside it greeted him. The men and women appeared to be busy, so he stole a glance at his hands in a thin ray of sunlight that had managed to filter through the pines and the mist, and saw with a start that they were clearly a soft cocoa brown. Further, he noticed that they looked more gnarled than he remembered, as if they hadn't been strangers to hard physical labor. There was so much dirt crammed under his fingernails, they were filthy, even by his standards. As he stretched his arms out in front of him, the bear pelt slipped back revealing several jagged, swollen scars on each forearm.

"Fucking dreams," he sighed with exasperation. "They make no damn sense."

The Indians paid him little mind as he looked about himself and the camp. There were three other dwellings similar to the one he'd been sleeping in, and he saw strips of meat stretched on woven wooden racks and leaning over another fire pit that was engulfing them in smoke.

"Was that what you fed me last night?" Franklin asked, directing his question to Degataga. Franklin pointed at the deer carcass hanging from the tree, it's flank stripped of meat. "Really good, a little gamey, but good," he said sarcastically while making an unpleasant face.

Degataga was busy helping another man lash some branches together into something that resembled a crude sled. Franklin remembered seeing something like it referred to as a travois in a book he had at home about General Custer and the battle of Little Big Horn.

"No Unaduti," the old Indian answered. "We are drying the awi for the trail. Last night we ate tsisdetsi."

"My name is Kanuna, it means bull frog," one of the larger braves sporting a shaved head said with a deep booming voice, "I caught many tsisdetsi," he added with obvious pride.

Startled by the young man, Franklin replied, "Well, whatever I ate, it was tasty." Still unsettled, he rubbed his belly, and added, "Mmm, mmm," unsure if the brave understood what he said.

"The Great Spirit has been good to us," Kanuna continued, and pointed to a woven basket that was hanging from a nearby branch. "If you are still hungry, we have much more of what you ate."

Franklin reached out and tipped the basket politely to peer inside, then jerked his head back. "Rats?" he shrieked. "You fed me rats?" His stomach turned, and he doubled over fighting the urge to heave.

Several of the braves laughed and shook their heads, while the children mimicked Franklin's antics. But Degataga's wife along with the other women quieted them all with a sharp clap of their hands and casting stern looks of disapproval all around.

Franklin, his stomach curdling from the prospect of having consumed rat meat asked Kanuna in a choking voice, "So, what's everybody doing? You look like you're packing up."

"Yesterday, two men came to our camp looking for a runaway slave."

"Looked to me like they ran off in a hurry," Franklin replied.

"It is good that you were sick in bed so they did not see you. They would have found you and taken you away if my mother had not made herself sick to frighten them off. But they will come back. They were looking for you, Unaduti, so we must leave this place."

"What the hell would those men want me for?"

"If these men found you here with us, they would have taken you with them to trade back to the one who owns you. And then they would have punished us. My mother saved all of us, but we are no longer safe here. So we are going home to get our belongings for the trail ahead of us."

Not comprehending what he'd heard, Franklin asked, "Why would someone take me and trade me? Trade me to who, and for what? What have I done?"

"Unaduti, do you still not remember who you are?"

Franklin crossed his arms. "Just for fun, why don't you tell me," he retorted in a huff.

Kanuna looked at his father, and Degataga nodded his head.

"Before my brother and I found you," Kanuna said, turning back to Franklin, "you were what we call nahsa'i, one who is owned."

Franklin stared at the brave, blinking uncomprehendingly.

"Has the drink made you forget, Unaduti? You are a slave."

"Okay, okay," Franklin chuckled dryly. "I'm out." Then, with rising indignation he scowled at the group of Indians that had gathered around him. "I'm not the one with a memory problem. I told you already. I'm just in a dream, and you're all part of it," he said, pointing at them. "I'm not really here with you savages, you see? And you're not here either. And I'm sure as hell no damned slave!" Franklin shook his head and laughed again at the absurdity of the idea.

The Indians stepped back collectively from Franklin, and looked questioningly from one to the other.

"You'll see," Franklin continued, "I'll wake up any minute now, and I'll be back home in my easy chair. Then you and your family can go on your trail or whatever the hell it is you're doing."

"Degataga approached Franklin, stopping a mere foot away, and bringing his face to within inches of the fuming stranger. His eyes softened, reminding Franklin of the look he might see on the face of a deer as it chewed contentedly on the grass it had just clipped in a meadow. The old Indian spoke with a measured, yet soothing voice, "Until you leave us, Unaduti, you must come with us. You are not safe here alone. We must leave the center of the world, the place given to my people by the Great Spirit, together. There is a price on your head that many will want to take advantage of. My son, Kanuna, speaks the truth. If the white man finds you, he will take you back to your owner, who might then decide to kill you because he is angry that you ran, or because you, like me, are old, and of little use to him. We must leave this place, because we believe the white man will come back to burn it. If we don't go soon, we may find he has burned our homes as well. If you "wake up" and disappear as you say, then you will be truly safe, but for now we will do what we can to protect you. Now, we must go."

Franklin felt disturbed by what Kanuna and his father, Degataga, told him. He still felt he was merely dreaming, but he had to admit the content of the dream was peculiar. In fact, it was becoming more like a nightmare, and frighteningly real. Worse, he was seemingly unable to wake up from it. From what he read about slaves, if in this nightmare, a slave was what he was, he worried things could become extremely unpleasant for him to say the least. Besides these things, something else was bothering him. He knew from his interest in history, that even Indians kept and owned slaves. He thought to himself, *So why did these Indians care enough to rescue me as they claimed? And why did they nurse and care for me, and even now offer to protect me? Why did they give me food, and treat me so kindly despite my behavior?* He just didn't know what to make of it. He knew he'd been rude and thoughtless to them, ogling Degataga's wife and selfishly eating more than his share of their meager ration of food. *Yet they said nothing,* Franklin marveled at these thoughts.

Franklin had always felt that historically speaking, the Indians had just been in the way of progress, and should have gotten out of the way in a hurry when the Europeans arrived. He wondered why they didn't see the writing on the wall? *Why they didn't know their place?* he thought. When Degataga referred to this place as the center of the world, it struck something deep inside of him. Something he was having trouble identifying. Something about home and belonging and a right order of things that had gotten horribly mixed up in his head. He'd owned lots of things, but couldn't honestly say that he ever felt like he truly belonged anywhere.

Franklin noticed the other Indians had loaded the travois while he'd been talking with Degataga and Kanuna, and now all was packed and ready to move. Since he was still not waking up, and there seemed no where else to go, he shook off his thoughts for the moment and decided he'd better join them.

Degataga signaled the group to leave camp, and Franklin fell in half-heartedly behind them.

The pace they kept was strong and steady, and they quickly covered several miles. A couple of the women and some of the children rode horses. Franklin and most of the Indians walked, and it wasn't long before he tired.

Fortunately for him the group stopped and rested often, but Franklin was amazed at how strong even the women were.

Rounding a bend, a deer was startled and leaped away into the forest. Later in the day, they inadvertently flushed a flock of turkeys from the undergrowth, and Franklin anticipated a good dinner. But to his surprise, the Indians continued their way without trying to catch even one of them.

"If I'm not mistaken, there's no grocery store nearby," he piped up. "If game is supposed to be as scarce as you said it was, why didn't you go after the deer, or shoot those birds?"

Degataga's other son, Chea Sequa slowed down until he walked alongside of Franklin. "It is not the way of the aniyun-wiva, the real people. We only take what we can eat. If we take more, the meat will turn bad, and that is a disrespect to the animal," he explained.

"That's ridiculous!" Franklin retorted. "The dumb animals don't know you're killing them. Besides they're just there for the taking, aren't they? Maybe if you killed what God put right in front of you a little more often, we wouldn't be having rats for supper. But I don't suppose you thought of that." Chea Sequa didn't respond, and seeing a look of disappointment on the young brave's face, Franklin decided to change the subject. "I get how your brother got his name," he said, then made a deep croaking sound, "but how did you get yours?"

"My name," Chea Sequa said, laughing at Franklin's antics, "means red bird. My parents say that the red birds were always around just before I was born. They said this was a good omen." As he spoke, the young brave reached up and stroked the feathers that hung from a shock of his glossy black hair. Intertwined with what Franklin suspected were the large feathers of an eagle, was a small, bright, crimson red feather. "Good luck came to our people after my birth. Some say I too bring good luck to those close to me."

Franklin clucked his tongue dismissively. "I don't believe in luck. I believe what goes around comes around. Life is what you make of it, that's all. People just get what they deserve, if you want my opinion."

"So Unaduti," Chea Sequa responded quietly, "do you think my people deserve to be forced to leave our home that was given to them by the Great Spirit? Do you believe we did something to deserve this?"

Franklin, rarely at a loss for words, did not respond.

"And you," Chea Sequa pressed. "Do you deserve the marks on your body, and to be a slave? Like the Cherokee, you too have been forced from your homeland that was given to your people by the Great Spirit of us all. What did you do to deserve such treatment?"

Franklin was trying to process what Chea Sequa was telling him. He was also wondering if there was any difference between becoming black in a dream, and actually being born black, when the brave suddenly grabbed his arm firmly and yanked him nearly off his feet and to the side.

"Hey! What the hell?" Franklin blurted.

"Is it not lucky for you that I am walking beside you?"

Franklin scowled. "And why would that be lucky?"

"If I was not beside you, I could not have pulled you away before you stepped into that!" the young Indian said chuckling and pointing out a large pile of bear scat. Franklin just shook his head as the Indian smirked good naturedly, then left his side and caught up with the others.

As the group made their way through the mountains heading south, Franklin walked in silence, deep in thought. Although he couldn't be sure of precisely 'when' it was, he surmised the time portrayed in his dream had to have been at least a couple of hundred years earlier in history because of the talk about slaves. He also figured he was somewhere in the southeastern part of the country since these were Cherokee Indians he was walking amongst. He knew from his reading of history that the Cherokee Nation had at one time encompassed parts of Georgia, North Carolina, and Tennessee, but he had no way of knowing exactly 'where' he was at the moment.

After many more bone-tiring miles, the group came to stop in a clearing at the top of a hill. From this vantage point Franklin could see homes down below them, and about a quarter-mile beyond them, a small town. The homes were one and two story structures, like those he'd expect a white man and his family to live in. But unlike white men's homes, these were arranged in a large circle facing one another. Each structure had what looked like an established, fenced in garden beside it. The houses were separated by a patch of forest from the banks of a river that flowed toward the town.

From the group's viewpoint everything seemed in order. They looked down at the homes and across to the town for several minutes until Degataga indicated it was time to move in for a closer look. With Degataga in the lead, the Indians formed a single-file line, and threaded their way down the forested flank of the hill toward the homes.

# CHAPTER 8

Though exhausted, Franklin worked his way up beside Degataga, and asked him to stop. Doubled over and gasping for air, he asked, "Why are we going down there?" He wondered to himself if the Indians were planning to raid the small circle of houses.

"These are our homes," he replied, a touch of sadness in his voice. "The white man told us we could get along better if we became more like them, so we came here, built these homes, and took white man jobs. This is as close as they would let us live to them." Then he pointed beyond the circle of homes to the town. "Some of the men had jobs in the mill. I," he said with obvious pride, "ran a newspaper for twelve years." Degataga directed Franklin's view toward a single story building that resembled a school house he'd seen in photographs of the past. "The children went to school there," Degataga said, "but over the last few years the people in town began to turn on our people. The children became afraid to go to school, and fights often broke out for those who worked in the mill. Often I would find windows busted out in my office. In these ways and others we saw that we were not welcome."

Degataga began walking again, and struggled to keep up. After moving several yards in silence, the old Indian continued. "The government made many promises to our people but broke them all. We made many sacrifices, and learned to live much like them, but their chief, the one they call President Jackson, decided this was not enough. He told us we must leave our land, the land of our ancestors, and go far to the west, which for us is the direction of death. He said we no longer have a choice, that our own people have signed agreements for all of us to leave. Even before the soldiers came, white men began to move onto our lands promised to us in treaties."

Franklin felt reasonably certain now about the answer to his question about what time in history his dream was taking place in. It had to be somewhere around the early 1800s, at about the time of the Trail of Tears. He knew this was when the government of the United States under President Andrew Jackson finally ordered all of the Indians living in the southeastern part of the country to leave, and resettle in what eventually became the state of Oklahoma. However, he didn't know the exact date, and he realized this could be important. Franklin remembered from history that many of the Indians, including the Cherokees left for the west voluntarily, or at least under reasonably peaceful circumstances. But things got rough around the late 1830s. He'd read that at that time, the Indians tried to take their homes back from squatters who had come in and chased them off. Then in 1838 the remainder of the Cherokee people were forcibly removed from the land they claimed was theirs, and forced to walk the infamous Trail of Tears', during which many Cherokees suffered and died.

Worried that this might be the actual 'when' of his dream and that he might be going along for the ride, his attitude soured again.

"Well chief, er, I mean Degataga, if your own people signed agreements, how can you argue with that?" Franklin challenged. "Besides, couldn't you people see the way things were going? You should have been smart enough to get out of the way ... you know, read the writing on the wall!"

"You do not understand, Unaduti." With a wistful look in his eyes, Degataga continued. "Our people have lived in the center of the world since the Great Spirit brought it into being. Generation after generation have lived here in peace and with respect for the land and it's creatures. When the white man came, we welcomed them. And when they asked us to be like them, we made many changes so they would not feel threatened by us. We became so alike in many ways that even the white man called us one of the 'civilized tribes'."

Degataga's eyes narrowed. "In spite of this," he said barely able to control his anger, "they told many lies. Even though we gave and shared much with the white man, they always demanded more. And when we resisted, they just came and took it. The men they say signed the agreements, did not have the authority of our Chief, John Ross, and the Cherokee Nation to do so. This was just another lie. But since then the white man has come in ever increasing numbers and has taken more of that which rightly belongs to us. There has been fighting, and even killing, and we have heard of other Cherokee who have had their homes, and other property taken by force by white men. We thought that if we moved out into the woods, the evil might be satisfied, but we now know that the white man will never be satisfied until we leave."

Lowering his voice, Degataga said, "We came to get our things now hoping we would be able to leave in peace, and not be driven away by townspeople, squatters, or soldiers. You have told us that you are here in a dream. That you are not a black man as you appear to be, and that where you are from, you have family and property, and rights. I ask the Great Spirit that if this is true, you are allowed to return there. But while you are still with us, we will continue to protect you, because even though you do not understand, if the white man decides it, he will take you from us, and you will know our misery, and perhaps even greater suffering." Degataga drew a long breath, shook his head slowly as he exhaled, then said, "But I don't imagine that you could ever know our sorrow."

As they drew within a hundred yards from the homes, Franklin began to see signs that all was not as well as the view from the hilltop had suggested. Upon entering the property he saw clothing, lamps, furniture and cooking implements littered about everywhere. Much of it was broken, and everything appeared to have been tossed in the mud. Several busted up picture frames were among the litter, and many of the photographs were torn and mutilated. Franklin was surprised to see among these some which depicted in black and white, various members of the group including Degataga, his wife, and sons. He was impressed at how clear the photos were, and surprised that in several of them the family was dressed as any white man or woman of the period. Entering one of the houses, he picked up a broken frame containing a color lithograph image of a man he did not recognize. Although the picture had been torn and appeared to have been ground beneath the heal of a muddy boot, Franklin could see the image of a man wearing a formal looking coat and bow tie. He looked official.

"Who's this chief, uh,... Degataga?"

"He,... is the Principle Chief of our nation. His name is Koowisguwi, who we know as John Ross. He has done everything he could to persuade the white political powers to allow us to stay on our lands, but his efforts were undermined by others of our people who were bought with a price. I no longer wish to speak their names. I believe they are not long for this world."

This last comment caught Franklin's attention. As he was about to ask Degataga what he meant by it, one of the women rushed into the house.

"I am sorry to disturb you," she blurted, "but Kanuna spotted soldiers coming from the town on horseback. He said there are eight of them."

"Gather the women and the children into this room," Degataga replied. Then turning to Chea Sequa, who was picking through some of the debris near by, he said, "call the men together, and tell them to remove their markings."

Franklin wanted to follow Degataga outside, but the old Indian grasped his arm with a firmness that stopped Franklin in his tracks.

"Stay here for now, it is not safe for you. I will talk to the soldiers to let them know you are with us and part of our family." Degataga spoke again to his son, "Chea Sequa, cover his head with my feather cap," he said nodding at Franklin. "And put my coat on him. I will tell the soldiers he is our brother from the northern tribe of our people." To Franklin he said, "Try to stay behind others and do not show your face." He then put a finger to his lips and added, "And do not speak."

Even though Franklin still believed he'd wake from his dream, the urgency in Degataga's voice, and the swiftness with which the others moved alarmed him enough to comply.

Ayita and another woman, who had taken several of the children to the river, had not returned, but just as the soldiers pulled up on their horses,

Ayita appeared rushing out from the woods, followed by a soldier on horse-back. Upon rejoining the Indians, she ran in tears into the house and to Degataga's side.

Kanuna stepped back from Franklin, and disappeared into a back room.

"He would not let me call for Tsula!" Ayita cried.

"We don't have time ta round all you people up!" the man who had been driving her forward bellowed loudly with a southern drawl. Still sitting on his horse just outside the door, he spit in the mud and continued, "You all had your opportunity to leave in peace, but that time has past! You're all leaving now! Your failure to plan was as good as planing ta fail! Simple as that!"

The last two sentences spoken by the soldier struck deep in Franklin as he did his best to stay out of sight.

"Hawley! That's enough!" commanded a man who appeared to be in charge. Upon entering the house, he addressed himself to Degataga. "I am Second Lieutenant Rayford, and I have been given charge by Captain Wain-scott to see that you get to the holding camp immediately!"

"We know we must go. We have only come here to get our things," Degataga said. "But can we not wait here until the woman and children return from the river?"

Before the horseman had made it to the house with Ayita, Franklin saw Kanuna slip out the backdoor, and thread his way unseen by the soldiers amongst the trees toward the river. He suspected the brave was going for Tsula and the children.

"What I see," growled the soldier in charge, "is a belligerent savage, and as you've no doubt already discovered, there's nothing much left here for you to take. Besides, this property no longer belongs to you, so you can come along peacefully, or I can put you in chains. Either way we're moving out,... now!"

Degataga reached out and pulled Ayita to his side then called to the women and children in the house, and they gathered behind him. They held in their arms several furs and skins and a few trinkets, pictures, and other keepsakes. Degataga, moving slowly, arranged the men and women so that several braves were in front of and several behind the women and children who he placed in the middle with Franklin and himself. He then had a brave gather up the belongings the women had scavenged from their damaged properties, and load them onto horses.

Franklin kept his head down in an attempt to remain inconspicuous as he had been instructed.

"We are ready, Lieutenant," Degataga said, "but I ask you once again, to allow us a little more time for our children to return from the river. They will come back soon."

Ignoring Degataga's plea, the Lieutenant pulled back on his reigns and briskly turned the sweat drenched horse around. He waved his arm above his head and gave the order, "Move out!"

The collective groan of the muscle and hide of horses straining against harness and saddle leather, the clomp of soldier's boots, and the shuffling feet of Indians on hard ground, filled the air. Miraculously, over this cacophony of sound, a commotion was heard coming from the direction of the river. Franklin wiped the sudden whirlwind of dust from his eyes, and turned his head to see Kanuna with two children, one cradled in each arm, and Tsula beside him with another child, hand in hand. They were sprinting out from a towering stand of Cottonwoods and brush, herding two more children ahead of them.

"Halt!" Lieutenant Rayford called out and signaled his men and the ragged line of Indians with a gloved hand.

The group came to a lurching stop, and two soldiers swung their mounts around, put their rifles to their shoulders, and tracked the oncoming Indians awaiting further instructions.

Kanuna and Tsula stopped dead in their tracks, held the children behind them, and looked imploringly at Degataga.

"There is no need to kill them, Lieutenant," Degataga pleaded. "They will not give you trouble."

"My men know how to deal with trouble, chief," the Lieutenant replied dryly. He signaled his men to lower their weapons, then to Tsula, Kanuna, and the children, he snarled, "Get in line. Georgia has had enough of you, alive, or dead." He then swung his horse around and signaled the group forward again.

Franklin noticed the soldier the lieutenant addressed as Hawley, eyeing Tsula up and down. He wore an insidious grin on his face and a look in his eye that he recognized all too well. Ragged, fresh looking scabs that ran from just above the soldier's right eye, diagonally down the bridge of his nose, and over the left side of his mouth caused Franklin to wonder who had clawed him. The why of it seemed obvious. Degataga's warning was momentarily lost on him, and he was about to call the man out, but the Lieutenant beat him to it.

"Hawley, you're riding beside me. Best keep your eyes on the trail lest their wandering gets you into more trouble than they already have."

Hawley dropped his gaze, spit a line of brown colored juice into the mud, then pulled his mount back around, lining himself up beside the lieutenant.

The group began moving with two soldiers riding before them, and two more along either side of them. The lieutenant and Hawley took up the rear.

Halfway up the hill they had come down from earlier, one of the children called out. "Wagons!"

Franklin turned with the rest of the group and saw several wagons bumping along a road from the town. They were just approaching the Indian's homes. The soldiers and their captives watched transfixed as the men guiding the wagons reigned in the horses, bringing them to a stop near the center of the circle of dwellings. Franklin saw a couple of the men take kegs from the back of the wagons, then carry them in and out of the homes from one to another. The other men disappeared into the dwellings, then reappeared with their arms loaded with the Indian's remaining belonging. They then dropped the items on the ground, making a single pile. The men with the casks shook their contents over the mound of belongings, then stepped back. Several of the men were smoking cigars, and they proceeded to puff vigorously on them while the other men backed further away forming a widening circle. In unison, the men with the cigars tossed them onto the pile which all but exploded into flames.

After the initial inferno had subsided, the men took pieces of burning material from the fire and tossed them into the homes. Roaring fire quickly consumed the structures and belongings, and huge volumes of black smoke rose into the air. The soldiers cheered and guffawed at the sight, drowning out the crackling and popping fire while Degataga and his men wailed in anguish, and pounded their fists against their chests and their skulls. The children cried and buried their faces in the skirts of their mothers, and as the women consoled their children, they watched as great plumes of acrid smelling smoke billowed out from the windows and doors of what they once called home, and drifted ominously in the dreaded westerly direction.

# CHAPTER 9

"Move out!" Lieutenant Rayford's shout broke through the din of grieving Indians and hooting soldiers.

The Indians hesitated, unable to take their eyes off the destruction, until a pistol shot rang out. Franklin, ears ringing, jerked his head in the direction of the sound, and saw the lieutenant, and smoke still trailing from the revolver he held high in the air. In response, and without a word, the Indians began trudging away from the scene, and Franklin was swept up in the movement.

He doubled over to try to catch his breath after what he figured amounted to a mere quarter of a mile, but the crack of a whip and a searing sting just below his shoulder blade got his attention, and stood him upright again before buckling his knees. Grimacing with pain, he saw Hawley curling the serpentine weapon back along side of his horse preparing to lash him again.

Before Franklin knew it, Kanuna and Chea Sequa moved quickly to either side of him, each of them grabbing him by an elbow. They lifted and carried him along, his feet skidding along the ground out of range of Hawley's whip.

"Young or old, woman or man, doesn't matter!" hollered Lieutenant Rayford. "I'm already behind getting you people to the pens, and I'm not letting any of you hand my ass over to Captain Wainscott for failing to do so! Carry him, or leave him behind. Makes no difference to me."

Jerking himself free from the two braves, Franklin caught a glimpse of Degataga's and the other's tear-streaked and broken faces, and the words the old man had spoken earlier resurfaced in his mind. *'You will never know our sorrow.'* He bowed his head and hoped he never would know a sorrow so profound.

Franklin surmised from the lieutenant's earlier comment that they were probably moving through the hills and low mountains of northwestern Georgia. He thought they might be making their way toward the southern tip of the Appalachian Mountains, an area he knew as the Smokies, toward Tennessee. As they gained in altitude the temperature became cool, dry, and crisp again, a relief from the humidity Franklin felt at the Indian's valley home site.

After walking several miles, and despite the soldiers continually goading them on, the children were tiring, causing the group to move at a pace that was too slow for the lieutenant's liking. The soldiers, who had been prodding the Indians with the butts of their rifles, occasionally causing one or the other of them to trip and fall, had apparently grown tired of this form of entertainment, and were grumbling amongst themselves. Two of the soldiers turned their attention to the women. Using the tips of their bayonets they hooted and hollered salaciously as they lifted the leather skirts and blouses of the women.

Kanuna made sure he was always beside Tsula in an attempt to spare her from this humiliation. The lieutenant, preoccupied with a map, didn't seem to notice what was going on, but Hawley slapped his thigh and whistled with delight at the show.

Franklin realized that ordinarily, he'd be enjoying such behavior if not engaging in it himself. But despite this fact, his body tensed with anger. He wanted to do something, but before he could move or even utter a sound in the women's defense he felt the firm grip of Degataga's hand squeezing his arm.

"No," the Indian whispered sharply. "You might think this is only a dream, but still you felt the sting of the soldier's whip, you could be shot dead."

Franklin reached a hand to his injured shoulder blade and remembered hearing somewhere that if a person dies in a dream, they might never wake up. Dream or no dream, this shit feels real, he thought, and held his tongue.

"Lieutenant!" Degataga said, raising his voice for the first time. "Is this necessary? My people are going with you. We are not resisting. They do not deserve to be treated this way."

"Why Lieutenant," Hawley drawled, "this here savage is gettin' all worked up. Want me ta cool him down some?" he asked while he was staring at Tsula with a predatory gleam in his eye.

"That's enough, Hawley!" Rayford barked, his eyes focused on Degataga. "Listen to me, chief. If we don't keep moving, it'll take us weeks to get to Fort Cass. And we don't have enough to eat for that long!" Then to his men he ordered, "Leave the women alone!"

"Shit," Hawley grumbled. Then challenging the lieutenant, he said, "Thought they was government property."

The other soldiers nodded emphatically in agreement with Hawley.

"My orders!" snapped the Lieutenant. "Any man goes against them will answer to me here and now!" Turning back to Degataga, he continued, "My first priority is my men. So if you insist on moving slowly, you are the ones who will go without food, not them. You should also know that the longer we take to get to Fort Cass, the more out of hand these men will undoubtably get. I can't account for their every move, you understand? Plus, winter's coming on, and you're a long ways from your new home. I don't have to tell you how cold things can get."

As if in response to the Lieutenant's words, a cold wind rustled the branches of a stand of pines nearby. The sky suddenly darkened, and a thin rain pelted the group, dropping the temperature sharply within seconds.

Franklin winced at the rain that stabbed his face like thousands of tiny needles, and pulled Degataga's coat up around his ears. Leaning forward into the wind, he shoved his hands into the folds of thick fur and longed for the comfort of his easy chair and the warmth of a shot of whiskey. The only good thing about the change in weather was that it made the soldiers just as miserable. Everyone, including them, moved on in silence, and with no further disruption, the group arrived back at the Indian's mountain dwelling by that evening.

Lieutenant Rayford ordered his men to make camp for the night, and after erecting their tents, the soldiers gathered at one of the fire pits and began passing a bottle around between them. The Indians readied the fire pit Franklin had sat at with them the night before, while Kanuna took some of the dried deer meat from the travois and handed it to Ayita. She in turn sliced the meat into chunks, then placed it along with some roots and vegetables into a large pot that had been suspended over the fire.

The aroma of the food was intoxicating to him, and after such the extraordinarily difficult day, Franklin couldn't wait to eat. He shivered along with the dropping temperature and clutched under his furs at his belly, anxious to fill it. He planned to climb under some additional furs immediately after eating, hoping he'd wake up in his own bed next to Gwen. Drunken laughter coming from the soldiers interrupted his thoughts. Seeing them hard at their drinking—something he was only too familiar with—Franklin hoped the aroma of the cooking meat would escape their attention. But no sooner had he had the thought, Hawley stood up, wiped his mouth on his sleeve, and leered in the Indian's direction.

The drunken soldier cleared his throat and pointed at the pot of stew. "By order of Second Lieutenant Rayford," he slurred, "that food is no longer yers to do with as ya please. You, and everything you have, is now the property of the U. S. Government." He directed one of the other soldiers to come for the pot, and ordered the food doled out to himself and the rest of the men. After the pot had made the rounds amongst Hawley and his men, the soldier who'd taken it away, returned and sat the nearly empty pot down unceremoniously at Degataga's feet. Hawley, a sneer on his face, burped loudly, then said, "Y'all understand now why we have ta move along chief?"

"Share what is left," Degataga said to his people, ignoring Hawley. "We must stay strong and sleep well." He lowered his voice and continued, "We must remember who we are. The white man may be able to remove us from this land, and separate us from one another, but he cannot separate us from the spirit that forever binds us together. In that same spirit we must continue to care for each other. In this way we will survive whatever comes."

After this encouragement, the Indians shared what food was left to them, then wandered off each to their own dwelling, and Franklin wondered miserably how he was going to stay warm. He knew he didn't belong here, that he wasn't one of them. He was also quite aware of how calloused and rudely he had treated them, so he was uncomfortable asking them for help. But he knew he couldn't go to the soldiers either. As long as he was in this dream, he felt he was safer with the Indians.

Franklin pulled his coat of fur tightly around himself. He worried again about the fact that he was not waking up, and wondered if he was going to freeze overnight, and if that would kill him, and he would never wake up again. "Unaduti," the calm but tired voice of Degataga called out, interrupting Franklin's thoughts. He turned and saw the old Indian peering out from the dwelling behind him.

"Come, sleep. As long as you remain among us, you are safe. We will protect you."

Franklin sheepishly entered the dwelling, and Degataga directed him back to the bed he had used earlier, then retired with Ayita in their bed on the other side of the cooking pit. Franklin lay awake, incredulous at how Degataga seemed to read his thoughts. Even more remarkable to him, was how Degataga and the others continued to care for him, even after all of his insults and condescending remarks. It struck Franklin that Degataga's treatment of him would understandably be quite different if Ayita had told him of his salacious behavior toward her, and he wondered if it suggested any willingness on her part to entertain his advances at some point. Overcome with weariness, he felt himself drifting off. But before he succumbed to sleep, Franklin recalled Degataga's explanation for his name, and he thought it fitting. It seemed to him that everything Degataga said or did was geared toward encouraging his people. But he shook the thought off just as quickly as it had entered his mind, deciding that the old Indian's philosophy was not a strength, but a weakness, proven by the very predicament Degataga and his people were currently in. Franklin decided to take this up with Degataga the next opportunity he got. That is if he wasn't at home in his own bed when he awoke again. Just before he dozed off, he wondered vaguely whether he'd have another opportunity to try his luck with Ayita.

The following morning Franklin woke up to the now familiar primitiveness of the darkened, and musky smelling dwelling. He heard the voices of the soldiers outside, and knew they were gearing up for the trail ahead. He thought it strange that although he was apparently a black man in his dream, he felt no different than he always had. He was distracted from straining his eyes against the darkness in a futile attempt to look at the color of his forearm by whispers coming from the other side of the dwelling.

Ayita was crying quietly, and Degataga was soothing her. The soft glow of the cooking fire cast enough light that Franklin could just make out the shapes of them slipping out from under their furs. Though he couldn't understand a word being said, he was struck with the tenderness with which Degataga spoke to his wife. The gentleness with which he stroked her cheek caused him to wince with guilt at the memory of the callousness and disregard he routinely showed Gwen. Unaccustomed to entertaining disparaging thoughts about himself, he immediately shook them off, and feeling more himself again, he peered wantonly into the darkness to see if he could make out a little more detail of Ayita's body as she arose from the furs. But, once more, as if he was privy to Franklin's thoughts, Degataga, with one swift movement, stood from a reclining posture and held up a fur as a shield of modesty for his wife's unclothed body while she dressed.

Just then, the door flap was lifted, and the face of a bearded soldier thrust itself into the dwelling accompanied by a shaft of light which fell upon the two Indians. "Outside, now! Let's move!" drawled the demanding soldier. Then he abruptly withdrew his face, and let the flap fall back in place. Franklin heard the man stomping away, and the repeat of his rudeness at each of the other dwellings.

"Unaduti, remember to act as one of us," Degataga said. "You have seen their unkindness. For them to discover that you are a runaway slave could cost you and us our lives."

"I got it," replied Franklin. "I have no intention of getting myself killed before I wake up. I heard that can happen in dreams." Franklin got up from his bed, and emerged stiff kneed from the dwelling to a light dusting of snow on the ground. The trees too were coated with a thin, white, powdery layer that caused their otherwise buoyant branches to droop. The air was not brisk, it was frigid. Franklin knew intellectually that late spring and early summer snows can occur in mountainous regions, but seeing it made it real. The soldiers were driving the Indians northwest which, if his geography was correct, would take them to the even higher altitudes of the southern end of the Appalachian Mountains.

Some of the Indians, wrapped in their furs, were already busy loading up their belongings from the camp on the travois.

"Put it back!" Lieutenant Rayford ordered. "Put it all back! We have nearly a hundred more miles to go, and the mountains won't be getting any easier. That junk will just slow us down."

A couple of the soldiers rushed over, and pushed the Indians away from the travois with the butt of their rifles.

"Now line up," the lieutenant growled. "If you want to keep warm, walk closer together."

"Lieutenant, we have not eaten," Degataga said. "You must let us give the children something to eat."

The lieutenant had already turned to tend to other business, and Hawley seized the opportunity to cut in. "Ya'll are gonna have ta make do with trail rations," he said flatly. He reached down and picked up a branch from the fire pit. It was still glowing and he blew on it producing a flame. "Maybe now ya understand why ya gotta get up early, chief," he said turning back to Degataga while cupping the flame until it strengthened. Apparently satisfied with the small torch, he walked from dwelling to dwelling, and as the Indians looked on with knowing sadness, he set fire to each doorway. Once these were aflame, Hawley tossed the burning branch onto the still laden travois. As crackling flames rocketed upward into the forest canopy, the lieutenant gave the command to move out.

The Indians trudged through the snow for miles, receiving meager rations only after Degataga again reminded the lieutenant that the children had not yet eaten. After a meal of dried meat and brick-hard biscuits, the soldiers prodded the Indians for most of the day on a trail that wound ever upward.

Franklin was eager to talk with Degataga. He wanted to ask why the Indians didn't put up more of a fight when the white settlers began encroaching on their land, but he put the question off for now. He figured it was all any of them could do to just maintain their focus, try to stay warm, and keep moving. He had draped himself with additional furs from his bed before he stepped out of the dwelling that morning and was grateful he managed to keep them, but the cold was biting nonetheless.

*Must be my Californian blood*, he reasoned to himself, after noticing that the others seemed to be holding up better than him. Up to now, his ego had kept him silent about his discomfort, but unable to keep it to himself any longer, he wheezed through his chattering teeth, "Degataga! I'm freezing my ass off!"

It was Kanuna who responded by taking one of his own furs which looked to be that of a thick, luxuriant black bear, and without a word, draped it over Franklin's shoulders.

Franklin basked in the warmth of the fur. If he took any notice of Kanuna who was left wearing an obviously lighter garment, he didn't show it. No longer tasked with fighting the bitter cold, he had already begun worrying about how he was going to sleep that night now that they were without dwellings.

"Back in line!" a soldier yelled at Kanuna, who was still walking beside Franklin and just outside the line of the procession of Indians.

Franklin looked up and saw Hawley reaching for his whip. He nudged Kanuna in the ribs, and the young brave stepped back alongside Tsula.

Hawley spit in the snow accumulating on the trail, and left the whip in place. The rest of the day passed without incident.

Bone-tired, Franklin was relieved when the lieutenant called for a halt. Thanks to the bear fur Kanuna had gifted him, he felt as though he could climb inside a hollow log near the camp, and sleep through the night no matter how cold it got. But first there was a gnawing hunger he hoped to attend to, and he took his place amongst the Indians in their dinner circle. He didn't like that they were forced to wait for the rations to be doled out by the soldiers, but his aching, famished body overruled his mind, and he tolerated this humiliation with the others.

Just as he had feared, the rations were the same as the night before. He choked down dry deer meat and tried not to chip a tooth on a flat, rock-hard biscuit. While doing this, he couldn't help but notice the soldiers seated around their own fire, who between slugs of liquor, or mugs of steaming coffee, were digging into a hot stew. He seethed with anger. It was all he could do to sit there and stay quiet, but he hated to think what would happen if he spoke up.

As Indians finished their meager scraps, the soldiers helped themselves to seconds. Then, adding insult to injury, they tossed the food left on their plates into their fire. The steaming aroma wafted over to the hungry Indians who remained silent.

Franklin saw Hawley, the scars on his face glowing in the light of the fire, and he wasn't sure if he was more angry at the audacity of the soldiers, or for the fact that he knew the Indians never wasted anything out of their respect for nature and the earth. He could only imagine how the Indians must have been feeling as they observed the blatant waste and disregard for the animal they had killed according to their understanding of the right order of things.

After supper, the soldiers set up tents for themselves, and the Indians dispersed and went about gathering boughs from the pine trees. Franklin watched in disbelief as Kanuna collected the furs they wore. He turned away from the scene and shook his head as his body anticipated the coming cold, and he pulled his furs more tightly around his body hoping the brave would let him be.

Franklin turned around at the sound of footsteps crunching through the snow and looked into the young face of Degataga's eldest son. He had several furs draped over his shoulder, and held a couple more cradled in his arms.

"Unaduti, I am gathering the furs to make our beds."

"Are you crazy? It's freezing out here. I'll die! You people might be used to this stuff but I'm from California where we laugh at people stuck in weather like this."

Kanuna didn't argue. Instead he nodded his head then turned back to his work with the others. They were busy laying out a large circular shaped platform of pine boughs and grass that was already several inches thick. On top of this they placed a layer of furs. Ayita called the children and instructed them to lay in the center of the platform. The women were next, and they arranged themselves in a circle around the children. The women were followed by the men, who began to lay arranging themselves around the women.

"Come sleep, Unaduti," Degataga called to him. Other than Franklin, he and his two sons were all that remained standing.

"You're not getting me into that dog pile."

"You can do as you wish Unaduti, but I am afraid you will only suffer unless you join us. Here there is warmth from the furs and our bodies." The Indian pointed to an open space in the group which featured the backside of one of the women.

After reassessing the arrangement, Franklin's predatory instinct kicked in. "You might have something there chie... uh, Degataga," Franklin replied with a mischievous chuckle, and he crawled into position.

Degataga and his sons placed four shorter branches, one each at the respective corners of the sleeping platform, then pulled several large furs over them all, so that they overlapped each other and a taller branch that had been placed in the center. Once all was ready, they too climbed in.

At first Franklin was certain he would suffocate. But he soon noticed there were small openings in the overlapping of the furs, enough to allow for air circulation. Before long, he was amazed at the warmth in this otherwise cramped configuration. Comfortable at last, his thoughts turned back to the woman he was curled up against. He had gotten used to the musky smell of the natives, and noticed appreciatively how soft the leather was that she wore, such that he could feel her breathing and the shape of her against him. But as fate would have it, his immense exhaustion overwhelmed his base tendency, and instead of copping a feel, he passed right out.

# CHAPTER 10

Long, paper-dry leaves, clinging to the stalks of corn, and deceptively silky in appearance, tore mercilessly at Franklin's face, and arms. Interspersed between the thudding of his own feet and those of unseen others somewhere behind him on the hard ground, and the relentless slashing of corn leaves against him, Franklin heard the shouts of men and the baying of dogs somewhere far behind him. A shot rang out as he plunged headlong through a furrowed field.

His breath came in short, ragged bursts as he blundered forward. Something hot grazed his right arm, and he wondered in sheer terror if he'd been hit by a bullet. Still on his feet, Franklin realized that his dream had shifted once again. He wound his hand in the end of a rope that was fastened around his waist, the other end of which was tied off through a finger loop on the side of a glazed jug. Franklin slowed to a trot and sniffed at a cork that plugged the neck of the container and smiled knowingly, until an ear of corn just above his shoulder was shattered by another bullet. Back at full speed, he pulled the bottle against his body to keep it from slamming against him as he ran.

A stand of trees came into focus up ahead and on his left. Between the tree trunks Franklin saw the unmistakable glint of sunlight on water. He veered toward them and quickly merged into their undergrowth and shadow. After another twenty-five feet, Franklin reached the river. Eyeing the other side, he stopped running long enough to kick off his shoes, then noticed he wasn't wearing any. He stepped into cold water and sank immediately to his shins in mud.

The voices of those chasing him drew near, and Franklin laid himself prone in the water, only his nose and eyes above its surface. A loud splash several yards to his left followed by a second startled him. Peering along the marshy bank, Franklin saw two gaunt men, their skin a mahogany brown, and clothes so frayed he wondered how they stayed on their bodies. Like him, the men submerged themselves in the water. One of them whistled softly, and immediately, a third splash caused Franklin to jump. The whistler, reached out and pulled a yellow, fur covered, bag of bones resembling a dog to himself.

"That damn mutt of yers gonna get us caught!" the other man hissed. He clambered to his feet and bent at the waist, sloshed through the muck further along the riverbank.

The percussion of a rifle was followed by bullets tearing through the air, and ripping through the leaves of the trees nearby. The man who had gotten up and was distancing himself from the other, thudded to the ground some forty feet away. He thrashed around on his back while grasping at his thigh. Seconds later, two howling dogs emerged from the corn, followed by two white men carrying rifles. The front dog grasped the fallen man's ankle, and while growling, viciously shook his head. The other animal snapped at the screaming man's arms. A swift, and solid crack to his chin silenced all but the yapping dogs until their owners called them off.

"Shit," Franklin heard the man with the yellow dog curse under his breath.

The heads of the men with the guns bolted up from their quarry.

"Go get em, fella!" one of them encouraged the hound who was still snapping at the fallen man's leg.

Franklin feared he'd been seen, and was wondering whether he should give himself up, when the man laying with the dog pushed himself off from the bank and into deeper water. Pulling the mud caked hound with him by a short rope leash, the two of them were quickly drawn into the rivers silent, but powerful current. Franklin watched amazed as the two of them were swept downstream.

The oncoming hound bounded into the water, only to become stuck in the mud. While one man waded in after the dog, the other knelt on the murky bank, took a bead on the flailing escapee and his dog, and fired. The shot fell harmlessly short, and the hound, now free from mud, took off along the bank baying wildly.

"Damn it, Chester! We can't let em get away!" growled one of the men.

As the two of them crashed through the brush after their dog, Franklin breathed a sigh of relief. Then, after enough time had passed, and he could no longer hear the wailing dog, he felt safe enough to pull himself from the fowl smelling river bank. Franklin sat with his back against the trunk of a tree, and feeling safe, felt for the jug. Somehow, it had survived the last few minutes. He pulled out the cork and tilted the bottle to his lips. Anticipating a long and tasty pull, the brassy sound of a lone horn startled him, and he woke to find himself nuzzled up once more against the backside of an Indian woman.

***

Franklin and the Indians were jarred from their communal bed by the racket of soldiers who were busy breaking camp. Before he had the chance to wipe the crust of sleep from his eyes, other soldiers were hollering for him and his companions to line up for the next leg of their journey. The day ahead held the promise of clear skies and sun, but despite the possibility that there would be no additional snow, Franklin felt as though he was wandering through a vast and natural open-air freezer. As the day wore on, the existing snow developed a brittle crust, and despite the care with which the Indians navigated its surface, they often broke through up to their thighs, slowing their movement to a crawl. This in turn evoked the wrath of the soldiers, who in addition to delivering brutal kicks and lashings to their captives, made up for the loss of time by doling out the rations to them while on the move.

Franklin was relieved to see that they had begun descending into a valley far below. Although his knees and thighs burned, and his legs became like jelly from the downward movement, the warmth he expected to find there gave him the hope he needed to continue. He found himself along side of Degataga, and was about to ask him why the Cherokee Nation didn't put up a fight over the treatment they'd received from the United States Government when Hawley rode up to them.

Degataga looked up at him. "The children are not doing well. They are hungry and have used up most of their energy trying to keep warm."

"Actually, chief, ya might wanna talk ta yer people about that. In my opinion, they ain't been careful enough with the rations we been givin' ya. We still have a week or so left 'fore reachin' Fort Cass." Hawley paused with a smirk on his face as if to let that information sink in. "It'll be no different from here on out, so we'll only be givin' you and yer people half rations the rest of the way. That is unless we get lucky and scare up some game."

"But you give us so little now. The deer meat that we smoked, you give to your men who only throw away what they can no longer eat."

"Ya see chief? This is 'xactly why we can't live together in peace. You and yer people are always cryin' about what you claim is yers. What you claim yer great spirit gave ya. Well, yer great spirit's not in charge here. We are. You'll eat what we give ya and go where we tell ya. I rode up here to give ya some kindly advice, and for that all I get is yer complaints." At that, Hawley spit at Degataga's feet.

No longer able to contain himself, Franklin blurted out, "Can't you at least give a little more to the children?"

"Well,... what have we here? I don't recall addressing you, savage," Hawley said coldly. "What's yer name?"

"Frank..."

"Unaduti," Degataga interrupted. He put his hand firmly on Franklin's shoulder and turned him half way around in an attempt to keep his identity concealed. "His name is Unaduti. Please forgive him. He has forgotten his place."

"Ya'll are right about that, chief. I 'spect ya ta get better control of yer people! He should have better manners, but then, once a savage, always a savage. For his outburst he'll get even less rations. I'll beat him the next time he speaks up, and ya'll as well! Ya got that?"

"I understand. It will not happen again," Degataga said as he casually maneuvered himself between Franklin and the soldier.

Hawley clucked his tongue, reigned his horse roughly around, and positioned himself at the back of the group again, along side of the lieutenant.

Franklin, still in the surprisingly firm grip of Degataga, bristled at the two men. He saw the gleam of malice in Hawley's eyes, and while squeezing his hands into fists, thought to himself that if he didn't wake up soon, the two of them would surely exchange more than heated words.

Shaken both by anger and the threat of being beaten, Franklin held his tongue. He and Degataga trudged along side by side in silence for several miles. The path became easier as they descended into areas the snow had not reached, and the weather warmed.

When the noon break came, the lieutenant, true to Hawley's word, rationed Franklin barely enough of a slice of meat to chew on. That, and a broken off piece of biscuit. As he chewed on the stringy sliver of venison, he felt a body brush against his side and heard the unmistakably jovial voice of Chea Sequa, Degataga's youngest son.

"Unaduti, are you certain you do not believe in luck?"

Franklin looked into the Indian's eyes which virtually seemed to dance with exuberance. Perturbed by the young man's perpetually bright demeanor, Franklin snapped. "I don't say anything that I don't mean. Besides I don't see anything lucky in all of this!"

Without hesitation, the young man replied, "I think it is lucky for you Unaduti, that I did not eat all of my ration."

Franklin turned and scowled, "And why is the fact that you're too stupid to eat, lucky for me? And by the way, how the hell is being on this God forsaken trail good luck for you? " Forgetful of the hardness of the biscuit in his hand, Franklin bit down with force, and he winced when his teeth made a sound as though he'd bit into a piece of ceramic tile. Reflexively, Franklin jerked his hand back to fling the remainder of the biscuit into the brush, but thought better of it. He stuck the hard tack in his mouth and sucked on it instead, resenting the soulful eyes of Chea Sequa still fixed upon him.

"Because I am on this trail, and because I chose not to eat," the young man spoke quietly and slowly, carefully enunciating each word, "I have food to give to you." His eyes twinkling with a mirth Franklin could not fathom, the young brave opened his fist revealing a slice of venison. As I told you before, the luck I received at my birth, although not always for me, is meant for others. This he secreted into Franklin's hand before slipping away.

Franklin spit the biscuit into the fire pit and replaced it with the meat. *Luck be damned, but stupid is one thing I'm not,* he thought closing his eyes to savor both the meats malleability and flavor.

With Franklin still chewing, the soldiers rounded up the group and drove them out along the trail into the afternoon. The morning sun at their backs, they wound their way down the mountain switchbacks toward the valleys below without incident. The soldiers, perhaps because of the promise of warmth and food to come, were in a relaxed mood, and Franklin wondered if this was as good a time as any to approach Degataga with his question. He felt he was justified to question the Indians. *After all,* he thought, *if they really were such a noble people, why the hell wouldn't they fight?* The fact that they did not, didn't sit right with his sensibilities.

Whenever conversation regarding injustices perpetrated upon the Indians, blacks, migrants, and most recently refugees came up in social situations back at home, Franklin always cried foul. When it came to people from other countries wanting to come to America, he'd argue they should stay put wherever it was they were from, no matter the conditions there. On one hand, whenever a dispute arose over land that had been given by treaty to the Indians, he'd argue vehemently that the Indians should just get out of the way of progress. On the other hand, he swore to high heaven that he would fight anyone who dared tried to get him off his property to build a highway, or clear land for industry. He neither understood nor acknowledged the contradiction.

For a brief moment, Franklin wondered why he was so adamant about confronting Degataga. Already, during the short amount of time he'd been in the company of the Indians, he was becoming increasingly impressed not only with their compassion, but their seeming integrity. *Maybe I've been wrong,* he thought, but shook the notion off just as quickly as it arose. He remembered how he'd tell people that he knew what was what, because he was there when it all happened. No one ever questioned him over such an audacious statement, knowing if they did, they would suffer his wrath.

Franklin chuckled at the irony that now—at least when it came to the Indians—he could tell people he *actually had* been there. He reminded himself that this was only a dream, albeit, a damned long one, fueled by too much liquor, and picked up his pace to catch up with Degataga who was walking amongst the women and children. Before he got close enough, one of the soldiers at the front of the procession lifted his hand, stopping the group's movement. Next, he signaled for them to be quiet. A soldier from the rear rode up along side of the man, and after conferring briefly with him turned to Lieutenant Rayford and mimed firing a rifle at a moving target, then raised both of his hands up above his ears with the fingers extended.

The Second Lieutenant signaled back, then ordered the rest of the group to stay put while the two men dismounted and moved off into the trees on foot. The first soldier took to his left up ahead, and the other swung back and to the right.

After several moments of waiting in silence a shot was heard followed by a second, and several deer charged out the trees toward the Indians and remaining soldiers. Franklin counted three young deer and four adults. As they came crashing through the brush, eyes bulging, they split from one another and ran in all directions, springing and leaping frantically for safety.

Hawley and the other soldiers still on their horses and positioned around the Indians raised their rifles and fired.

Franklin recognized the gun fired by Hawley. It was a British Enfield Pattern 1853 rifle, identical to the one he had in his collection back at home. The only thing missing from the soldier's weapon was the fixed bayonet. Franklin knew that this rifle was the improvement from the muskets that proceeded it, boasting a much improved range and accuracy that could take down a moving target twelve hundred and fifty yards away, and that it was used by both the north and south during the Civil War.

One of the adult deer buckled and skidded on its knees. Its shoulder virtually exploded, the creature flopped on its side panting in the darkening crimson colored snow. Another deer was knocked backwards after taking a direct hit to its chest, and fell with a thud to the ground. Until that moment, Franklin had never heard a deer cry, a sound he now knew he would never forget. A third adult and one of the youngsters fell under a fresh volley of shots, summersaulting grotesquely in the brush where they lay dead or dying.

The soldiers hooted elatedly at their kills while the remaining adult deer, a large buck, bounded off to the side, crossed the trail ahead of the group, and headed for the forest on the other side. The two young deer ran, bumping into one another out of sheer terror back to the brush they came from. Franklin thought they might actually make it to safety until the two soldiers who had flushed them initially broke from the trees and stood, rifles in hand, directly in their path. One of the men dropped to one knee while the other remained standing. Simultaneously, both raised their rifles and fired, dropping the two youngsters in a deep drift of snow. The buck seemingly lost and in a panic, bolted nervously first back toward the path, then sprung back again toward the cover of the surrounding forest.

In the midst of this shooting frenzy, Franklin noticed that two Indian braves had managed to free themselves from the group. The ropes that bound them together at the ankles were still in place, so they scrambled across a thigh high thicket looking as though they were running in a three-legged race. They were a couple hundred yards away from the cover of the forest, and making slow progress, when they were spotted by Hawley and another soldier.

Hawley had already drawn his pistol and was taking a bead on the frantic buck, supporting his gun hand with the other. "Save one for me!" he asserted, then fired a single round, and the deer summersaulted, a section of antler breaking off in the process, and skidded to a stop. Hawley dismounted, and seemingly without looking, fired side-armed at one of the escaping braves at the same time that the other soldier pulled his trigger, sending them skidding to the ground on their chins.

While Degataga and the rest of his group gasped collectively, and without pausing, Hawley fixed a bayonet to the end of his rifle, and strutted over to the panting deer. He stomped his boot on the animal's neck and held it to the ground, although this was clearly unnecessary. The only sign of life Franklin could see was the mist that hung in the cold air from the still living buck's gasps for breath. Without ceremony, Hawley plunged the bayonet into the creature's heart, releasing a crimson geyser that spurted blood into the killer's face.

Aside from the macabre scene of blood-drenched snow and carcasses, Hawley's reaction was comical. He flopped backwards in a fruitless effort to dodge the dark red stream jetting from the big buck, and fell flat on his back, coughing and spitting profusely, blood dripping from his face and staining his overcoat. The soldiers whooped it up, elated at their perceived good fortune in taking out an entire herd of deer. In all, seven of them lay dead in the field. "I got me another buck back in the trees yonder!" shouted one of the soldiers ecstatically. "A big un'! Had 'em a nice rack too! Gonna carve them sons-a-bitches off for a trophy!" Hawley, apparently satisfied that the men's celebration wasn't at his expense, joined in their fun.

In dramatic juxtaposition to the soldier's antics, the Indians stood in stunned silence as they took in the carnage, both of the dead and dying animals, and two of their own, who lay motionless in their own blood. Even Franklin was taken aback by the sheer brutality of the soldiers as they mowed the animals and the two young men down with such unabashed glee. Somehow, he understood that the two braves had courted their own deaths. And although he had never hunted, he had vocally advocated for the rights of men to bare arms and take the life of any animal as their God-given right. He had scoffed at people who complained about trophy hunting displayed on the news or the internet. But he'd never witnessed a slaughter of such ferocious heartlessness. To him, it seemed as though the soldiers had lost their minds. But he shook this off as he had so many other things and decided to focus on the positive side of things. At least there would be plenty of meat to go around for the rest of the journey.

"Alright!" hollered Lieutenant Rayford. "Let's get some order here, men! You boys," he said to a couple of the soldiers, "clean out the fattest of the three runts and do it quick. That meat should be nice and tender. Then we'll move out. It's getting late. Matt, Hawley!" he yelled at the soldiers who had each killed a buck, "You boys have time to take those antlers if you want 'em, but be in formation when we're ready to head out. Chief!" he hollered emotionlessly at Degataga, "you and your people have the time it takes my men to get their jobs done to bury your dead, no more, no less!"

"Yes sir!" Shouted Matt. He let out a celebratory, "Whoop!", and took off into the woods.

Hawley was already hacking away at the skull of his kill, seeking a trophy of his own.

The other men groaned realizing they weren't going to get the pleasure of carving out their kills.

"Knock off your grumbling boys! We don't have time for that nonsense, and we can't take it all with us. The meat'll never last the trip, and it'll just slow us down." He turned and looked directly at Degataga, who appeared to be looking up at the sky, his mouth moving but not making a sound. "Besides," the lieutenant continued, "unlike savages, we know there's plenty of food waiting for us when we get back to the fort. Leave the rest of this mess for the buzzards."

Except for Degataga, and the four Indians dispatched to bury the dead braves, the rest of his group stood with their heads down, not speaking as the designated animals were butchered. Hawley and Matt returned with their prized antlers, and the lieutenant gave the orders to move out.

They had been on the trail for about an hour, and Franklin could not contain himself any more. He drew up beside Degataga, matching his pace, then after checking to be sure he wasn't overheard by the soldiers, leaned in closer. "So, tell me Degataga. I don't get it. Why did your people not fight these bastards when you had the chance? Why did you just roll over and let them take your world?"

Degataga did not answer for what felt like a couple of minutes, and Franklin was about to walk away and try his question another time, figuring the old Indian wasn't up to conversation so soon after the incident with the deer. But he felt a soft grip on his wrist, and looking down he saw a dry, wrinkled hand. He looked up and saw Degataga's eyes glistening with tears.

# CHAPTER 11

The deepening snow muffled the steady clopping of the horses hooves. It even softened the sound of the soldier's prolific, coarse banter, and made it seem as though it was coming from far away. Light from the sun angled in through the pines refracting prisms of color that glowed softly like stain glass windows, reminding Franklin of long ago, childhood days when he'd gone to church.

Degataga, lightly grasped Franklin's arm, and finally spoke to him. "By your words, you show that you do not understand," the old Indian said softly. "But you have asked, and I believe with my heart that you truly want to know, so I will try to answer your question." He stooped over as they walked, and with surprising agility slid a hand through the snow, scooping up some dirt from underneath. He shook the soil in his two cupped, weathered hands, then rubbed his palms together, letting the dirt filter through his fingers back to the ground. "Everything is of the earth, everything," he began. He lifted his eyes and cast them from the left side of the road to the right as if he was looking past the forests on either side, far away to where the land ended and the seas began. "These trees and bushes, the animals, fishes, birds, and the humans, are all of the earth. The seeds of the plants can be moved by the wind or the animals from one place to another, and if the soil is suitable, the plants can grow again there. Animals too, can roam far away, and have babies who then grow to bare their own young in that new place." Degataga took a deep breath and exhaled for a long time. He looked weary beyond words, but he had enough left in him to say one more thing. "The dead, give themselves back to the earth. And from them, she makes new life."

Franklin grimaced as Degataga told him these things. He wasn't used to listening to anyone for very long, especially if they were trying to tell him the shape of things for which he had already formed an opinion. Irritated with the way the conversation was going, he blurted out a bit too loudly, "What the hell does that have to do with my question?"

"You there!" yelled Hawley. The soldier kicked his horse forward, and drew up alongside Franklin, then reached down and grabbed him by the collar of his furs. "I thought I told ya, I don't wanna hear you runnin' yer mouth no more!"

The smell of blood was still thick on the soldier's clothing, turning Franklin's stomach, and he fought back the urge to vomit.

Ignoring Hawley, Degataga looked back and called out loudly to Lieutenant Rayford. "Call your man off, and I will deal with mine, Lieutenant!"

The Second Lieutenant waved Hawley off.

Hawley spit in disgust, then wiped his mouth with the dirty, bloodstained sleeve of his military regulation overcoat. "See that ya do that chief,... next time he's mine." He kicked his horse again and drew it back around to the rear of the formation.

"You must try listen with your heart, Unaduti," Degataga resumed with composure, "to understand what I tell you. Then you will begin to see with your heart what the eyes do not, and the mind cannot comprehend."

Franklin rolled his eyes wearily, and shrugged his shoulders. To himself he thought, *There's where you're wrong, chief. All I gotta do is wake up.*

"As it is with the plants and the animals," Degataga continued patiently, "so it is with men. So when the white man came to the earth's center, we welcomed and accepted him as we would any of earth's creatures."

Franklin raised his eyebrows. *Creature? That's a laugh,* he thought.

"At that time the Cherokee were many, as were the Choctaw, Seminole, Creek, and Chickasaw. If we had joined together to fight the white man we would have easily overwhelmed them, but we did not see the need to fight. We believed the white man's words when he told us he wanted to live peacefully among us. But the white man brought the invisible enemy of disease with him, and many people of this land died because of this. Our numbers became less, but still we trusted the white man's good will. We did not believe the diseases were his intention." Degataga seemed to look off into the distance, as if he was carefully weighing what he wanted to say next. When he finally did continue, his voice had a tone to it that indicated that a reservoir of anger was just barely below the surface and he was struggling to contain it.

"More and more white men came to our world. They were hungry for land, and we made room for them. Then, they began to move in to our sacred places. All this time they also hunted the animals without discrimination or respect for the lives they took. They killed for food, but also to satisfy their lust for blood in the same way we all witnessed today. They hunted so much, it became difficult for the animals to replenish themselves, and the Cherokee began to suffer this loss. All of this led to fighting, which brought death to both white man and Indian."

"The white man's numbers continued to grow, and our advantage became less. Still they made their treaties. They promised if we became more like them in the way we farm, dress, and speak, that we could work and live among them in peace. They encouraged us often to believe in their god, while showing no respect for our beliefs. "

"We began to see that the time of living in the world's center on our own was ending, and we saw that we would need to learn the white man's ways for us to continue to survive. The Cherokee have always been a trusting people, and people ready to learn new ways. Although we already had a system of growing our food, we learned the white man's ways. We adapted our own way of doing many things to that of the white man. We had our own way of buying, trading and sharing information, but we developed banks and newspapers like the white man. We built and lived in dwellings like theirs, and learned to dress like them as you saw in the photographs left behind in our homes. We even developed our own constitution."

Franklin stumbled with surprise at Degataga's last comment, then regaining his stride, wondered again how such a strong group of people could have become, in his estimation, so beaten down.

"We believed at first that these things were good," Degataga said. "That the white man meant to keep their word that we would live together in harmony, but as more and more of them poured into this world, their needs outweighed their promises. They broke treaty after treaty, and each time the land upon which we walked free was made smaller, and game less plentiful."

"Although we worked with them and adapted to their way of doing things, they never worked with ours. Instead, they used those of us who are weak to their advantage. That is often how treaties were signed. Not by our true chief, not by what the tribe wanted, but by Indians they bought with money, and always with empty promises. The very system they encouraged us to become a part of was never for our good as they said, but was a trap designed to make us dependent upon them, and to weaken our resolve, and then our society. By the time we realized this, it was too late. We no longer had the numbers, and our leadership had become divided. We did not fight the white man because we trusted. Many of our people left this land still believing that the white man's government will take care of them. But others like ourselves refused to go because we stopped believing them. Now we are being forced to leave because of three things. The white man has discovered that there is a yellow rock they call gold in the ground near the place we were living, our sacred ground that they now call Georgia. Also, a white man invented a machine that can be used to help with a plant they call cotton, which is very important to their people. This machine has made it possible for them to grow cotton on much larger areas of land, and they decided that both in the name of gold, and the money they make from cotton, to remove us from that which they now want for themselves. But most of all, I believe we are being removed from our land because the white man never wanted us here in the first place. To them, we are savages, and we have always been in their way."

"So fight them!" Franklin uttered through clenched teeth, his exasperation distorting his face.

"As I have told you," Degataga continued with patience. "It is too late for us to fight a direct battle. The kind you seem to suggest. Our fight now is to survive, to see our children grow, and our numbers increase again. Our fight is to preserve our heritage so that future generations will know from where they came, have an understanding of their place in the world of things, and eventually be able to have input into the human journey through which the Cherokee may one day return to health and right order."

"Back where I'm from we call that losing the battle to win the war," said Franklin, nodding with understanding. "When, or if, you ever regain the numbers of your people, I hope you'll kick these bastard's asses!" He shook his head as he made his last comment in disbelief he'd even say such a thing.

"I do not mean disrespect, Unaduti, but if you are from where you say," Degataga said slowly as if he was measuring his words, "and white men still think anything like you, a man who knows terrible suffering, it is obvious this has not happened," Degataga finished with unfathomable sadness deepening the lines of his weathered face.

Franklin looked down at his hands and winced for the umpteenth time. Closing his eyes, he shook his head again, hoping that when he reopened them he'd see the white, manicured hands of a successful, and retired white man. Instead, he saw what Degataga was undoubtedly referring to. As he stretched out his arms, the fur cloak he wore fell away and revealed only the gnarled, scared, coco-brown hands and forearms of a runaway slave, his fingernails still caked with dirt.

The group plodded along, and the setting sun elongated their forms in shadows that reminded Franklin of marionette puppets until the lieutenant ordered them to stop and make camp. The rations the Indians received while gathered around their fire were the same as they had been, meager and dry. Franklin's portion was even smaller this time as a result of his outburst during the conversation he had with Degataga after the slaughtering of the deer and the braves. He was certain that if he didn't wake up soon, he would starve to death. But, as he sat amongst the Indians he had openly mocked, they, one by one, got up, and dropped a sliver of their own pathetic rations in his lap as they passed by.

The night was not as cold as the previous one which was fortunate because there wasn't enough room in this location for the Indians to build a platform as before. Instead, they gathered boughs and piled them up high enough to provide insulation from the cold ground. Most could be used individually, and some of them looked large enough for two. Along with the use of furs Franklin found an available pile of branches which proved sufficient to keep warm enough through the night.

In his slumber, Franklin dreamed he was awake in his own bed, and he thought with great relief that his troubles were over. He felt a nudge to his backside and when he rolled over, he saw Gwen laying beside him. She was curled up as usual, her back to him, and he breathed a long sigh of relief, believing that he had at last awoken in his own bed. Franklin's hand trembled, something he could not remember ever happening before, as he stretched out to touch her side. But with a cruel twist of his perception, the distance between them widened as if the bed itself was stretching, creating a gulf between them. No matter how hard he tried, he couldn't reach her.

"Gwen," he croaked helplessly, and she moved in response, stretching her arms in catlike fashion, such that the covers slipped off her shoulders and down her back. Franklin recoiled and gasped in shock when he saw that Gwen's back was crisscrossed with deep, oozing slashes and thick, ugly scars. It looked to Franklin as though his wife had leaned her back against a hot waffle maker that had been designed with an erratically laid out grid.

Intuitively, he knew that these scars were caused not physically, but emotionally, by him. And though he believed them to be mere manifestations of his imagination, he wanted with every fiber of his being to heal them. Stretching with tremendous effort, he finally managed to grasp his wife's shoulder. Despite her wounds, he thrilled at the prospect of being able to speak to her again. Franklin couldn't remember the last time they'd really talked, and there were things he wanted to say to her. He relished the opportunity to make things right.

"Don't touch me!" she screamed, and she jerked her body around to face him.

Franklin recoiled in horror. What he saw was not the soft, acceptant face he expected. Gwen's countenance was twisted; contorted with a look of intense hatred. He tried to speak, but words would not come.

Gwen sat upright in the bed. "What makes you think you can do this now, after *all* of these years? I've waited for you,... I waited *on* you!" She seethed with anger, every two or three words broken by a haggard and labored breath. "You cut me again and again with your hurtful words, and even more deeply with your silence."

Gwen climbed out of the bed and turned her back to him again. "You only needed me to show that you had someone, just like all your other,... *things*," She moaned, and one of the scars opened up and began to bleed. "You *needed* me to cater to your needs." At these words another scar bled. "You *needed* me to distract yourself from your own fears, and you treated me with the same hatred you had for everything you didn't understand!" With each accusation blood so dark it appeared black, oozed from other scars until her back was covered with a thick flow that dripped to the floor, staining the bottom of her gown before puddling at her feet.

Franklin was bewildered and terrified. His distress pounded in his skull, and ached throughout his being. He searched for something to say, words that could make things better, make things what they *should* be. But the words, if they were there at all, seemed to be lodged in a place deep with him, a place he'd long forgotten even existed and like his wife, he seemed unable to reach.

Gwen was not only physically distant, it looked to Franklin as though she was actually being drawn away from him in space and time, while ghost-like, her visage was fading slowly from sight. Sobbing, he frantically reached out his hands once more in vain. Just before she disappeared completely, words from deep with him broke free, and at last escaped his lips, "I'm sorry I hurt you so,... I do love you, I do,... but,... I treated you... like... a slave."

Nothing was left of Gwen but the faintest aura that shimmered, fragmented into dust-like flecks, which disappeared altogether, and Franklin recoiled from a bright light stabbing first into his right eye, then his left. It seemed there was nothing he could do to evade it. Which ever way he turned his head, the blinding light followed and stabbed again. He clenched both eyes tightly shut, and the light mercifully snapped away as quickly as it had come. He slowly opened his eyes to slits and peered around himself. Lying on his back, he noticed he had an IV in his arm. He felt a solid bump and his body was roughly jostled. Then he heard the scream of a siren that reminded him of an ambulance. A woman in a blue uniform was adjusting the IV bag.

"He's with us," a man's voice said quietly. "His heart rate is normalizing."

"Honey!"

Franklin recognized Gwen's nerve racked voice. At first he was afraid to look at her, but then opened his eyes wide. Seeing she was herself again, he grumbled, "What the hell am I doing in an ambulance?" Then accusingly, he snapped, "Gwen, what did you do?"

"Calm down sir," the male attendant soothed. "You're going to be all right."

"Of course I'm all right! I don't belong here!" Franklin blurted out. "I should be at home, not in a fucking ambulance!" He shook off the remnants of the dream and accompanying feelings he'd just had, pointed a shaking finger at his wife and snarled, "Don't you people know a lunatic when you see one?" Slowly and cautiously, he opened his eyes wider than slits. When he saw that the light was tolerable, he opened them fully. He saw that he was lying on his back, and had an IV in his arm. And based on the amount of jostling he felt, and the scream of a siren he heard, he decided that he must be in an ambulance. A woman in a blue uniform was adjusting the IV bag.

"He's back," a man's voice said quietly. "Mr. Carlyle, you must calm down," the male attendant insisted.

"Franklin, Honey, you wouldn't wake up! I tried and tried, but you looked... dead!" Gwen shook her head, burst into tears, and buried her face in her hands.

"Sir, we're taking you to the hospital. We'll be there soon," the attendant's voice cut in.

"Damned if we are!" Franklin hollered, his eyes bulged in anger. He began to cough, and his head suddenly hurt like hell. Then if felt as though something heavy had just sat on his chest. He grasped his head with one hand and his chest with the other and groaned. Struggling to catch his breath he choked out, "I... didn't... ask for this." But he didn't finish his complaint because the attendant, Gwen, and everything else began to tunnel out and away from him, and the crushing sensation relaxed.

"He's passing out again," Franklin heard the attendant say as he drifted into a calm, warm, gradually darkening void. "He'll be okay. He'll rest now."

In the background Franklin could hear his wife blubbering from somewhere far away, something about knowing this was going to happen someday. He wanted to be angry, but consciousness evaded him.

# CHAPTER 12

When Franklin opened his eyes again it was morning. If the slant of dim sunlight that filtered in to him through the forest canopy didn't tell him he was back with the Indians, the fur he was wrapped in certainly did. For the moment, even as his ears were being assaulted by the coarse and obnoxious grunting, farting, and cussing of the soldiers as they ate their meals, and went about breaking camp, he felt relieved to be there instead of the nightmare ambulance scene he'd just left.

Puffs of breath, momentarily crystalized in the crisp, cold of morning, drifted in the air around camp while the Indians gathered together the children, then quietly waited for their food. Franklin gazed dismally at the halved ration that was dropped on the ground at his feet. He was about to complain, but before he could say anything, Degataga slipped him a slice of his own meat as before.

"Are we going to make it on the food we've got?" Franklin asked him while considering if the stone-hard biscuit he held in his other hand was worth risking a chipped tooth for.

"No, not on this alone," the old Indian answered, matter of factly. "We will gather roots and any berries we find. They will help. Perhaps we will come upon more game, although I did not expect to see the deer."

Franklin finished the meat, then managed to chip off an edge of his biscuit, shifted it inside his cheek, and sucked on the stone-like crumb while contemplating Degataga's words.

Once underway, Franklin was amazed at how much food was available along the trail when one knows what to look for. The blackberries and huckleberries were obvious, but the Indians also found mulberries. Also gathered by Degataga's people was chicory, which they brewed into a drink Franklin thought tasted something like coffee. Surprisingly, the Indians gathered an abundance of pine needles, which they later soaked and brewed into a steaming hot tea. Wild onions were everywhere, as were wild grapes, and a bewildering variety of mushrooms, and roots Franklin didn't recognize. Awed by the Indian's knowledge for gathering food, Franklin was stumped when he saw them collecting thistle.

Incredulous, he snapped at Degataga, "Isn't it more important for us to search for food, than for weeds? I know you people like to wear feathers and paint yourselves, but thistles? Really?"

Ignoring his outburst, the Indians went on with their gathering.

Franklin put his head down and muttered to himself as he plodded along. "You're all crazy."

The weather gradually improved as the group made their way down from the mountains into a valley, lightening the dispositions of the soldiers who, other than the hunting incident, and periodically poking at the women as a distraction, had been mostly on the sullen side.

From time to time Indians and soldiers alike needed to relieve themselves, and would step off the trail to take care of business. The soldiers displayed no humility. They simply hopped off their mount and urinated, or dropped their pants and a steaming pile of waste, seemingly unconcerned that anyone could see them. The Indian's, in contrast, used discretion, stepping into the bushes, and the women always took along another woman as extra cover when their time came. While this took place, the lieutenant kept the rest of the group moving forward, with the promise that a guard would be dispatched to round up, "And not in a kindly manner!" he'd bark, "anyone foolish enough to fail to catch up," in a reasonable amount of time.

Tsula, whether by luck or determination, seemed to limit these occasions to the times they stopped to eat or camp, but a moment eventually came when she was visibly struggling to hold on, and there was no indication the group was going to stop any time soon. She asked the lieutenant for permission, and stepped out of line with another woman. Together they walked into the deep brush apart from the soldiers and the protection of their men, and waited for the group to move ahead.

Franklin turned and saw the lieutenant lean over to Hawley and overheard him say he needed to discuss some things with one of the men up front, then watched as he kicked his horse forward, then send another soldier back to accompany Hawley at the rear.

"Take my reins for me will ya Davis?" Hawley said leaning over to the man now riding beside him. "Must be contagious," he laughed, "cause *now* I gotta *go* like nobody's business." Davis mutely took the reins, and Hawley slid down from his mount and stomped into the brush.

Franklin craned his neck to look back and saw that Hawley was not in his usual place. Beyond that, he saw the woman who had accompanied Tsula standing guard for her friend at the edge of a tall stand of brush. A movement in the woods behind the two women drew his attention. At first he thought it might be an animal, but then realized that it was Hawley. The obnoxious soldier was squatting by some trees, and appeared to be looking directly in the women's direction. Franklin understood immediately that Hawley had circled around undetected, and gotten behind the women, affording himself a birds-eye view of Tsula.

Franklin fumed out loud, "Son of a bitch!" and grabbed Degataga's arm, spinning the startled man around in the direction of the women. At that moment, having apparently lost his balance, Hawley flailed his arms and fell backwards, which was followed immediately by the screams of the two women, both of whom burst out from the brush at a run as if they'd seen a bear.

Besides Degataga, the rest of the Indians were startled, as were the soldiers, drawing their attention to the women's plight. Kanuna strained to break free from the group but Degataga and Chea Sequa managed to hold him back.

Hawley cried out, his voice a higher pitch than usual, "Caught them squaws trying to make off into the woods! He scrambled over and cut the women off from rejoining their families, and added, "I circled round 'n flushed 'em back!" He drew his pistol and pointed it at the two women with one hand, holding them in place, while he seemed to be struggling with his pants that were noticeably sagging, with the other.

Lieutenant Rayford made his way through the brush toward Hawley, and signaled to the man to stay put.

Kanuna strained to break free, but his father and brother held on to him to prevent him from being shot.

Hawley wheeled around and pointed his gun at Franklin. "That's right chief! Hold that injun right there!" Hawley screamed. "If he takes one step this way, I'll split him, and both them women in two!" Keeping his gun on Franklin, he pointed at the soldiers with the other. "Just in case I miss, there's four more guns'll stop that boy right in his tracks." But as soon as Hawley released his pants to point toward the soldiers, they slid down around his ankles, revealing a pair of thread bare, army issue long johns, promptly eliciting a chorus of hoots, and guffaws from his comrades.

"Put down your gun, Hawley!" commanded the lieutenant. "I don't want to lose anyone if I don't have to. And for God sakes, pull your britches up! You look like a damned fool!" Turning to the women Rayford said, "Now, I don't know what happened here ladies, but just to be safe I'm gonna take precautions." Speaking to another soldier, he ordered, "Bind their hands behind their backs, and use another rope to connect the two to them at the waist, then put them up in front so we can all keep an eye on them."

Degataga and the rest of the Indians glared in disbelief at the lieutenant and Hawley.

Rayford stared back at Degataga, and apparently satisfied the old man had his son under control, turned his attention once more to Hawley. In a voice tinged with thinly veiled disgust he said, "I suspect you were up to something, and now is not the time I'm choosing to deal with it. But if you so much as leer at that woman again, I'll have you tied and walking behind my horse the rest of the way to Fort Cass. Is that understood?"

Hawley spit and said with a grin that was twisted in the shape of a backwards letter z by the scars on his face, "Yes sir. I s'pose I can save my appetite a might longer."

"You do that. The rest of you men," Lieutenant Rayford said sternly, "stop messing with the women and focus on moving along now. You've had your fun. It's time we got these savages to the pens." Then in a rare show of what Franklin thought might qualify as compassion he added. "They have a long journey ahead of them after that with plenty more problems coming their way. They don't need anymore grief from the likes of any of you. Now let's move! I want to make another few miles before dark."

The rest of the day and that evening passed without additional disruption, and the group wound their way through a series of connected valleys which allowed them to remain at low altitudes thus avoid the cold of the higher climes. Finally, just at dusk, the Lieutenant ordered camp. The Indians went about setting up their sleeping arrangements, then settled down to await the evening dinner rations.

"We're plum outta biscuits," said a soldier as he passed out the expected scraps to Degataga and the others. "Yer lucky we're only a day 'r two out from the fort. They got food there."

Franklin gnawed on a dry, paper-thin slice of deer meat as he waited for some broth being prepared by Ayita. He scowled in the direction of the soldiers who were noisily slurping their overflowing bowls of fresh venison stew and wondered what the fruit, roots, mushrooms, and thistles the Indians collected that day would taste like. Suddenly, a shout from the bushes drew everyone's attention

"Look-here Lieutenant!" a soldier called out. His belt was undone, and his pants were loose around his waist as he waddled back from the trees, legs splayed awkwardly trying to keep them up. He had a colored man by the collar with one hand and a pistol pointed at the man's head with the other.

"I was jes' takin' a leak," the soldier continued, "and I nearly tripped over this here darkie! Didn't want 'im running off, so I had to leave my drawers undone ta grab 'im right quick! Strong son-of-a-bitch! Tried to pull loose, but I got a good grip on 'im. Think he smelled the food and hoped he'd get ta swipe some scraps after we was sleepin'."

Franklin stared, transfixed at the man being held in the soldier's grip. He couldn't imagine how, but he was sure he'd seen him before. As he racked his brain, a shiver went up his spine. *He's the man in my dream. The one who got away,* he thought confused. Franklin squeezed his eyes shut and tried to think of another explanation. *This doesn't make sense. I'm only dreaming,* he reasoned, *and a person can't dream inside of a dream, can he?*

"Yer not planning ta whip 'im with that are ya boy?" said another soldier, interrupting Franklin's thoughts. He pointed at the man whose pants, as Hawley's had before, slipped down to his ankles, while the rest of the men roared with laughter at the scene before them, and the memory of the scene they'd witnessed earlier that day.

"Pull your drawers up soldier!" Lieutenant Rayford yelled over his men. "Bring him to me."

The soldier knocked his captive in the side of his head with the barrel of his pistol, who slumped to the ground, then pulled his pants back up and cinched his belt. Once he was properly situated, he yanked the frightened man back to his feet and pushed him stumbling to the lieutenant. The other soldiers gawked as though they'd never seen a black man before.

"What are you doing out here boy?" questioned the lieutenant.

"I wasn't doin' nothin' suh. Jus' minin my own biznes."

"Yeah, Lieutenant, he was just wanderin' about the woods at night enjoyin' the moonlight," offered Hawley, which brought a chorus of snickers and jeers from the others.

"Loss, thas all. I don't know where I is. I smelt some food'n I reckon I oughta check on it. I's real hungry, suh."

"I bet you are boy," Rayford continued. "Who you running from? Tell the truth now." "Don't make us have ta beat it out of you boy," Hawley threatened.

"Well, yessuh. I's runnin' away cuz,... my massah, he be real cruel. He done whip me for no reason but to enertain hisself. I said to mysef, ain't nobody put on this earth ta be somebody's enertainment. If y'all don' min', I think I be off 'n these-here woods now, an' leave y'all ta yer biznes."

Just then, the sound of something crashing through the brush drew everyone's attention back to the dark forest. While the soldiers fumbled at their guns, a large, yellow dog, its coat so caked in dried mud it looked like plastic, bounded into the clearing.

Franklin gasped realizing that these were in fact the man and dog from his earlier dream. The foul smelling mutt raced up to the colored man who was standing in front of the lieutenant, and proceeded to circle around the man's legs whimpering with its tail whipping back and forth showering everyone with dried mud.

"Y'all don' gots to shoot," the colored man pleaded. "This here's just ol' Lazarus. I named 'em Lazarus cuz he got hisself swiped good by a bear he was protectin' me from," he rambled, chuckling intermittently, looking from the lieutenant to Hawley, and back again. "Lord knows that bear woulda ate me." He pointed to three prominent scars along the right side of the dog's head and shoulder. "This ol' boy n' me both be lucky we still livin'."

"Looks like yer luck done run out," Hawley drawled, then he pointed his pistol straight into the forehead of the dog and pulled back the hammer with an audible click.

Franklin's blood had been at a low boil over Hawley's antics since the incident at the Indian's town homestead. And like a pot of heating water intensifying from a simmer, to lukewarm, to a full boil, his anger had been building with each new ugly action or word from the man. In a blur of sudden movement Franklin launched himself, aching knees and all, from the rock he was sitting on. He burst through the fire before anyone could react, and barreled shoulder first into Hawley's side, slamming him to the ground. Hawley's gun fired and dropped, and the dog yelped. Franklin scrabbled in the dirt for the weapon, but the lieutenant kicked it out of his reach while the dog wailed in pain and the black man knelt cooing quietly to it, stroking its fur.

Hawley was a good head taller, twenty pounds of muscle heavier, and fifteen years younger than Franklin. Recovering quickly, he easily flung Franklin, groaning in pain, off of him onto his back. "Y... you're!" Hawley stammered gawking at him incredulous. "You're a nigger! I'm gonna kill you, you black son-of-a-bitch!" Blood was running down Hawley's face from a scab that got scraped off when he hit the ground, and he spit blood from a busted lip.

Franklin attempted to push himself up from the dirt, but Hawley kicked him solidly in the ribs, sending him flying back to the ground. Gasping for breath, Franklin reached for his assailant's pistol.

"Leave it!" The Second Lieutenant hollered. Rayford had his own gun trained on Franklin. "Now, leave it and back away Hawley. I'll take care of this." His eyes nearly protruded their sockets, and as were everyone else's, were fixed upon the nappy-haired head of Franklin who, dazed, was sprawled out on the ground.

"The jig is up," was the only thing Franklin thought between his rasping breaths, and he laughed weakly to himself at his pun.

# CHAPTER 13

The faces of the soldiers standing around him, and the Indians behind them, gradually solidified from blurs. All of them were all staring at Franklin. Several of the soldiers removed their hats and ran their fingers through their hair while talking animatedly with one another. Franklin attempted to pull his fur cloak up and over his salt and pepper colored, frizzy, head of hair, though he realized it was probably too late.

Hawley sucked at his teeth, then said with a smirk, "I ain't never seen no injun with hair like that. Looks like we got us not one, but two niggers!"

"Take these two and tie them up together at that tree!" Lieutenant Rayford ordered. "And someone take this mutt and put it out of its misery. We don't need no dog hanging around with the little food we have left."

As one of the soldiers reached down to grab the whimpering animal by its rope collar, Franklin stuck out his foot causing the man to trip. The dog, not waiting for a better opportunity, took its cue and bolted in a blur of yellow fur, and lanky, scrabbling legs into the forest.

"Let it go!" hollered the Lieutenant, as the soldier scrambled back to his feet and launched into several stumbling steps after it. "It won't last out there on its own for long. And after what just happened here, it won't come back! If it does, you can shoot it then." Addressing the man they had just caught, he said, "Turn around boy and lift up your coat. Let's see what we have here."

The man turned and slowly did as he was told, exposing a back criss-crossed with thick, old scars and scabs from more recent punishment to the lieutenant.

"Who do you belong to boy? What's your name?"

"Oh, there's no need to worry 'bout me. No, suh. My massa be done worry'n 'bout me. He like ta kill me, thas all. Thas why I run. Please don't be taken me back to him. He jus' try killin' me again."

"Your name boy, what's your name?" The lieutenant repeated.

"Yessuh, sorry suh. My name is Nathaniel, Nathaniel Bowden, suh."

Franklin, as everybody else was doing, stared, transfixed on the terri-fied man, and didn't see Hawley approach. Suddenly, he was yanked to his feet by the man who then flipped Franklin's fur up and over his head, then ripped his thread-bare cloth shirt up the middle of his back.

"Well, I'll be. By the look of all these scars, this boy's a slave same as that nigger over there! And both of 'em is runaways ta boot!"

The new man scooted on his butt to a tree and sat with his back against it. He drew his knees up to his chest, wrapped his arms around them, and rocked back and forth in a fetal-like position.

Degataga hurriedly stepped forward and gestured toward Franklin. "He is ours, Lieutenant. We found him lost in the forest, and took him with us to prevent him from dying. Much time passed and no one came to claim him, so we made him as one with us. This is our way."

Franklin, for once was utterly speechless, and still in Hawley's grasp, he fixed his eyes on the ground. As disrespectful as he had been to Degataga and his people, mocking them, ogling the women, and eating more than his fair share of their food, he couldn't understand why the old Indian was once more willing to put himself in danger to protect the likes of him.

"Take them both, and tie them up for the night," Lieutenant Rayford ordered pointing at Franklin and Nathaniel. To Degataga, he said, "We'll sort this out at Fort Cass." Then turning back to the others he continued, "Get some sleep. Tomorrow we have a long haul. If we're lucky we'll have one more day on the trail after that, and make the fort by nightfall." Finished, Rayford turned sharply on his heel and walked briskly away.

Hawley watched the lieutenant until he disappeared into his tent, then turned to Degataga. "Say, isn't Fort Cass where you Indians used ta have yer so called capitol?" he taunted.

"Our capital is in the east," replied Degataga somberly, and in the volume of a whisper.

Hawley spit in the dirt, displaying utter disgust, his eyes flashing with hatred. "This ain't no more yer land, than it ever was fer this nigger friend of yers."

Hawley and another soldier grasped Franklin roughly, one by each arm, then dragged him away and slammed him down on the ground with his back to a tree about three feet away from Nathaniel. They tied him securely to the tree, then secured Nathaniel in the same manner to another tree, three feet away and facing him.

Franklin never got the chance to finish his meager ration, but knew better than to ask for food. Nathaniel seemed to understand this as well and the two of them remained silent, each of them slouched chin to chest.

The soldiers hadn't finished eating, and went back to it, noisily as ever, talking about the excitement that just went down. They ignored the two colored men except that every so often one of them would sling a piece of gristle or some other barely edible scrap at them. This devolved into a game of seeing who could toss the scrap the closest to the two men, yet keep it just out of their reach. Franklin's stomach growled relentlessly, but he worried that other than his hunger, the food might attract the rodents he heard scurrying about in the brush nearby.

The Indians weren't allowed near the prisoners, and eventually everyone was ordered to bed down for the night. Although they had been out of the snow for a couple of days, it was still quite cold, and the two prisoners were left wearing only their torn shirts, pants, and worn out shoes. Franklin sat miserable, his feet stretched out in front of him. His head and ribs ached beyond anything he'd felt before. And he was weak, the ropes the only thing keeping him from slumping over in a heap.

As the camp fires burnt lower, the night set in around the two men. And as the fire gradually dwindled to mere ashes, the sounds of the forest became incrementally more obvious. Franklin strained his eyes into the darkness hoping he wouldn't see a shadow lurking about, or a pair of eyes reflecting the fading light of the embers. But it wasn't more than an hour after the erratic snores and farts of the sleeping soldiers had settled into a rhythm of their own that he heard something stirring in the woods behind him. A subtle snapping of twigs and rustling of brush increased his trepidation. Whatever beast was out there seemed to be circling around the two men until it stopped directly in front of Franklin.

Franklin's heart pounded wildly in his chest, and he called out to the other man, despite the fact that his throat had gone dry. "Are you awake?" he managed to whisper. "Nathaniel, do you hear it?"

"I hears it alright, but I don't believe thas big enough ta be a bear."

"That's a relief," replied Franklin sarcastically.

"Could be one o' them big ol' cats."

"Cats?" Franklin asked, breathing a sigh of relief. "I wouldn't think a cat could survive out here."

"Oh, I don't mean no kitty cat. I'm talking bout them big ol' mountain cats."

His voice suddenly a full octave higher than a second ago, Franklin asked, "You mean *mountain lion?*"

"Thas what I mean."

Franklin's heart rate surged like a kid flooring the gas pedal in a street race when the light turns green. In the midst of an adrenalin spike, he realized that even if he wasn't tied up, he was too frightened to move. He was frantically trying to figure out how he could possibly defend himself from an attack by a mountain lion, when he thought he heard Nathaniel giggle. No, he was sure of it. The sheer absurdity of the man's behavior broke Franklin's temporary paralysis, and he blurted out, "What the hell's wrong with you? We could be ripped apart and eaten alive!"

Nathaniel stifled his laughter and shushed Franklin who was staring bug-eyed into the darkness, and breathing rapidly.

Accompanying the occasional rustling noise coming from the bushes, was a sound like something sniffing around, and Franklin looked in horror in the direction of the scraps of food he knew were laying near him. He tried to kick dirt in the direction he had seen them in the hope he could cover the food up and conceal the scent. For a moment the sounds seemed to be moving away, and Franklin thought maybe his effort paid off, but suddenly something large rustled the bushes just behind Nathaniel's right shoulder.

The thought occurred to Franklin that maybe the lion would be satisfied with Nathaniel, skin and bone that he was, and leave him alone. With the next thought he wondered if they prowled around in pairs. Then he saw it. The creature was crouched with its hind quarters raised and twitching, its tail flicking from side to side. Franklin tried to scream, but no sound escaped his lips, and the animal lunged from the bushes directly at Nathaniel. Terrified, Franklin reflexively squeezed his eyes tightly shut.

"Lazarus, you ol' hound! You okay, boy?" Nathaniel whispered and chuckled with joy.

Franklin opened one eye and then the other in spite of his intense fear, expecting to see a lion gnawing on Nathaniel's head, and instead saw the man's dog. He was a large, lanky golden lab, and he was leaping back and forth excitedly between Nathaniel and the cast off food laying around, alternately licking the man's face and gulping down the scraps. The dog's tail wagged so hard it was a wonder he could stay on his feet. Closing his eyes and cursing under his breath, Franklin breathed a heavy sigh of relief, then felt a big wet tongue on his face. In its excitement, the hound had pounced over to say hello, and proceeded with slathering him from ear to ear. Franklin lay helpless under the weight of the dog, unsure whether he was about to laugh or cry.

"Laz. Come boy," Nathaniel giggled, and the dog, with one last lick from Franklin's chin to his forehead, padded happily back to Nathaniel and sprawled in the dirt, panting at his side. Nathaniel lovingly scratched the hound's belly, who responded by rolling shamelessly onto his back, his legs splayed comically in the air, one of the hind ones reflexively scratching the air whenever Nathaniel found a good spot.

Franklin's nerves gradually settled down as he watched the interaction. He tossed a small stone at Nathaniel to get his attention. "If I wasn't tied to the tree, "Franklin snarled at the still smiling man, then his voice softened. "Nathaniel, are you really a run away slave? Is that how you got those scars?"

"Thas what I is now," Nathaniel replied sadly as he fed Lazarus from some scraps he'd hidden away in his clothes, "but I used ta be a free man. Nathaniel Green. Thas my whole name."

"What are you talking about? You're either a slave or you're not!" Franklin shot back irritably.

"No suh, thas not always true. Not for a whole lot of us. I has a wife and children back in Pennsylvania, ... or had 'em. I was a free man there. My whole family was free. Had me a sweet little angel girl, looks just like her momma," he smiled at the memory of them. "The two of 'em was nearly glued at the hip," Nathaniel beamed proudly. "After a spell we had us a boy and we named him Nathan, after his daddy. That be me."

Despite the darkness, Franklin could still see a sparkle in Nathaniel's eyes. "Me and Nathan was as close as a father and his son kin get. We did everythin' together, and I taught that boy everythin' I knows. We was so close, everybody took to calling him Nearest, 'cause everybody could see he was the nearest thing ta me, and that name stuck. Nearest Green," Nathaniel said wistfully, then he continued. "I had me a job workin' in a lumber mill, and the wife and I had us our own home. Wasn't much, but we could raise our little ones all right in it."

"How'd you end up a slave then?"

"Well, suh, thas a little story all by itself. The man who run the mill started havin' money troubles. I knows he be messing 'round with the women too. Seems those things go together a lot of the times, don't they?" Nathaniel asked Franklin, but not waiting for an answer, he went on. "Anyways, I always been good at makin' shine. But, seems me and shine always led ta trouble. So after startin' a family I figured I'd try ta straighten my ways."

Franklin felt he detected a knowing glance on Nathaniel's face, and met the look with one of his own. He asked, "How'd that work out for you?"

"Well suh, since my boss be havin' money troubles, he couldn't pay me no more. I couldn't let my family starve, so I took some of the money I had stuffed inside my mattress and bought me the supplies ta put up a small still." Nathaniel's eyes lit up a little more. "Turned out, everybody loved my corn liquor," he gushed." Then he narrowed his eyes conspiratorially. "Course I couldn't tell no one Nearest was the real reason my still made such fine whiskey. Must've run in the genes, cause even as a youngun, Nearest just had him a real knack for makin' the shine. I'd have hell ta pay if his momma ever found out. Truth is, I think she knew all along," he said chuckling, and his eyes twinkling more brightly yet.

Nathaniel's voice grew somber. "My mistake was the owner of the mill also be makin' shine. And he be thinkin' him and his shine is God almighty hisself's gift ta the world. But when he went ta town he saw people's drinkin' my hooch, not his. I knew his pride couldn't take this, and sure-nuff one night he bust into my home with some other men, and he take my children and wife, and he sell them. Then he takes ta beatin' me. Oh, he beat me before, but now he beatin' the daylights outta me. Barely leavin' any skin on these here skinny, old bones," he said holding his scrawny arms out as evidence. "Well, suh, first chance I gets, I skeedattle inta the woods."

"But you were a free man. How could he get away with all that?" Franklin asked incredulous.

Nathaniel rubbed his thumb back and forth across his first two finger tips and shook his head. "Money be the real massah of this world. It decides every thing. That man caught me and beat the tar outta me. Then he tells me he wants me ta sell a batch of his hootch and tell everybody it's mine. An' if I do this, he promised ta get my wife and children back. Course I aimed ta sell off the whole lot of it. I gotta if I wants ta see my family again. But now I'm really gettin' scared. It's a small world, an' everybody talks. I know they knows the difference from my whiskey and his. I knows they be mad bout my misleadin' 'em. Either way, I'm gonna have hell ta pay, but I figure I has no choice so I do it." Nathaniel stopped and shook his head, his hands out and palms up in a gesture of helplessness.

Franklin's eyes had adjusted to the darkness, and he saw that the twinkle in Nathaniel's eyes was no longer there.

"I knock on the door of this place I was told ta go to," Nathaniel finally continues. "They's music playin' inside. They let me in all friendly and pay me for the liquor. Then just as I was goin' ta leave, I get hit over the head with a chair or somethin'. When I fall to the floor, somebody puts a tore up sheet in my mouth and a sack over my head, and they throw me in the back of a wagon. Next thing I knows, I'm loaded inta a boat with a lotta other colored men and women, and we's sailing out ta sea. Things start ta rockin' and everybody is gettin' sick. They's a loud crunchin' sound, and water starts ta leakin' inta the boat. We sinkin' fast, but I so skinny I get my wrists outta the cuffs they put me inta. I try with all my might but I cain't help anybody else," Nathaniel said, his voice choking and tears forming in his eyes. "They's no time. So I climb up the steps an' push open a small door. I sticks my head out an' drink a gallon of salty water. The boat is sinkin', and men is jumpin' in the sea. I was wonderin' why the sea was red, then I sees these big grey fishes, each of 'em bigger'n two or three men, an' I hears some men cryin' and other men screamin', an' the big fish flashin' their tails an' chompin' on the men, an' draggin' them under."

Nathaniel's eyes had grown so wide during the telling of his story, it appeared to Franklin as though the man was not only seeing these terrible things all over again, he was experiencing them as an individual suffering from post traumatic stress syndrome might.

"I was thinkin' this might be my time ta meet the Almighty hisself when I sees some barrels tied together. Thas when I get me this idea," Nathaniel continued. "If I can scooch up on 'em maybe I can float back ta land. And thas jes what I did. I never beat on anything in my whole life, but I beat the daylights outta a couple them big ol' fishes when they came around tryin' to take a chunk outta my ankles!" Nathaniel chuckles at this, then cleared his throat and went on with his story. "Anyways, I start feelin' like I'm gonna make it, then I see somethin' yella coming at me and I think this a big ol' yella fish so I start to beat on it like I did the others. Well, it lets out a yip and I sees it's a dog. I figure it must've jumped off the boat hisself. Thas how I found ol' Lazarus and why I name him that, both of us coming back from the dead and all. Being he was soppin' wet he sure was heavy. But between him clawin' and me pullin', I got him up on the barrels with me and I paddled us to land. From there we headed back north. I aimed ta find my family, but they was too many people on the roads so I decided I better go west for a while first and keep ta the woods."

Franklin thought to himself while Nathaniel rattled on with his story, *That boy of his, Nearest, didn't I see that name in an article only a couple of weeks ago? What was it? Oh, yeah, something about a black man by the*

*name of Nearest Green and how he was the one who came up with the rec-
ipe for Jack Daniels?* "Ridiculous!" Franklin scoffed out loud with disgust.

"Thas jes a part of the story," Nathaniel laughed, noting, but not understanding Franklin's outburst, then he went on. "Me an' Lazarus got ourselves lost. We wandered around in the woods a long time and I thought it
was my lucky day when nearly starved to death, …"

Nathaniel droned on and on with his tale. Franklin, thoroughly exhausted and unable to help himself drifted in and out of a restless sleep,
only catching an occasional word or sentence each time his head nodded
forward enough that his chin hit his chest and woke him as it did this time
when he heard Nathaniel sobbing.

"All us men, women, an' children got put up on that platform so's men
could come have a good look at us." Nathaniel wiped his eyes on his sleeve
and his countenance hardened. "Mostly they look at us ta see if we was
strong, if we can do the work they want us for. They even look at our *teeth*."
In a voice more hushed that it had been he said, "Sometimes they make us
take off our clothes in front of everybody, and they check all over our bodies. I sees some of the men has scars. Then I sees some of the *women and
children has 'em too*. If someone like somethin' they see, they pay money
and shakes hands, and that one get sold to a massah. *Thas* the day when I
become a slave."

Nathaniel yawned and rubbed his eyes. "If it's all the same with ya, I is
gonna get some sleep now an' I recommends ya do the same. Tomorrows
gonna be a mighty ruff day. I been ta that fort before, and they ain't too kind
ta negroes. I'm just hopin' ta survive long enough so I can get myself back
north ta find my family."

Franklin didn't respond. He pondered Nathaniel's story and that of the
Cherokees' Degataga had told him earlier, and wondered how mankind had
ever become so cruel. He hoped he'd wake up from this nightmare before
he had to find out how much more cruel they could possibly be, particularly
when it came to him. Gwen's image came to mind and he thought about the
dream he had the night before, and what Gwen said as she faded away from
him. He heard her voice again, echoing in his mind, saying accusingly, *'You
made me a slave!'* Franklin shook off the chills that ran up and down his

spine and looked around himself in the darkness. Seeing that Lazarus was still laying beside Nathaniel, he felt safe enough for the moment to close his eyes. As he began to doze he wondered what the next day would be like if he woke up still tied to a tree.

# CHAPTER 14

Franklin awoke to the steady drone of tires on pavement and a blaring siren. Opening his eyes he saw the blurred image of someone bending over him, and behind that, a backdrop of blinking lights. He realized that he was no longer with the Indians, tied to a tree, but was back in the ambulance. Absurd as it seemed even to him, he couldn't decide which was the worse place to be. But before he could decide which it was, he felt the sensation of weightlessness. Then, suddenly, his body rose up toward the ceiling of the vehicle. Just before he smacked face-first into it, Franklin managed to turned over. Hovering there, he looked down upon his wife, Gwen. She was wringing her hands, and seated next to a female attendant who was trying to comfort her. He also saw the back of the paramedic's head, who was bending over his body, still strapped to a gurney.

Despite all the noise inside the ambulance, Franklin heard the steady beating of his own heart. The sound weakened until it stopped altogether, replaced by a flatline signal from the heart monitor.

"We lost him," the paramedic muttered, and Gwen gasped, then burst into a frenzy of tears.

Franklin watched disconnectedly as the paramedic placed two paddles with wires connected to them against his body's chest. Then came a horrific jolt as a powerful surge of electricity burst within him. It felt like he was being kicked in the chest by an angry mule. From his vantage point against the ceiling of the vehicle, Franklin watched his body lurch upwards at the chest and shoulders. Then he felt as though the mule had decided to sit on his chest, and the face of the Franklin he was looking at began to turn grey-blue.

"Breath, Goddamn you!" Franklin urged from above his own body, and in the next instant the flatline signal reverted to a faltering beep that quickly steadied, and suddenly, he was looking up again into the paramedic's face.

"Got him!" the paramedic exclaimed, and a moment later, the ambulance screeched to a stop. The rear doors opened, and Franklin saw a flurry of medical attendants outside. Beyond them loomed the emergency entrance to a hospital.

"He's been slipping in and out of a comma, and we lost him for a second, but he's back and otherwise seems stable," the paramedic informed the attendants, while Gwen sniffed loudly and wiped at her eyes.

Franklin, still on the gurney and hooked to an IV, was rolled out the back end of the ambulance into the waiting hands of the medical attendants. He overheard one of them consoling Gwen. "We've got him, Mrs. Carlyle. Everything is going to be okay. We're going to get your husband help."

Franklin wanted to talk. He wanted to assure Gwen himself, but he was unable to speak, let alone move. Although he couldn't see her for all of the medical personnel swarming around his gurney, he imagined her twisting her hands up into the apron she was still wearing from the house.

"He always says I make too much of his drinking," Gwen murmured.

"Ma'am, you didn't make too much of it," the attendant assured her. "You did the right thing. When he comes out of this he'll have you to thank."

*Oh, that's a good one.* Franklin laughed to himself. *Like hell I'm gonna thank her!*

An attendant continued trying to reassure Gwen as he helped wheel Franklin through the Emergency Room doors. "Ma'am, I've been doing this for six years, so believe me when I say I've seen worse."

*Finally, someone with some Goddamned sense! Franklin thought. I'll buy him a beer when they let me outta here*, he resolved, then closed his eyes.

The attendant wheeled Franklin through another set of doors into a small room. Another attendant joined the first in transferring Franklin from the gurney onto a bed, then a nurse connected him to an assortment of tubes and wires, that were themselves attached to beeping machinery. After they'd left the room, Gwen alternated between sitting near his shoulder and repeatedly pacing the length of the bed and back.

"He doesn't know you like I do," Franklin heard Gwen mumble. "All he'd have to do is take one look at our refrigerator, and he'd know. There's so much beer stacked in there, there's no room for salad dressing!" she fumed.

*The envy of any real man*, Franklin smirked to himself.

"You didn't even try to hide the empty cans you left all over the garage!" Gwen continued. "The place reeked like a bar! I can't even think of you without a can of beer in your hand. And I'll bet you think I don't know about the liquor you keep in the toilet."

Internally, Franklin cringed and then scowled. He thought he'd been especially clever about the whiskey. *And what the fuck's come over her?* he fumed. *She'd never give me lip like this to my face!* In his mind, Franklin could see Gwen's face. Her countenance was especially sour, and he soon found out why as she continued her outburst.

"I doubt that paramedic has seen anything like Franklin before," she mused.

"Mrs. Carlyle? Mrs. Carlyle?" A new voice said. "We're moving your husband to another room where we're going to take a closer look at him. The doctor would like to see you in the mean time. Follow me, please."

Franklin tried to call out to Gwen, but he could not speak. He could, however, hear. And what he heard along with the beeping of hospital monitors was the sound of a nurse's shoes squeaking on the waxed, tiled, floor, and Gwen, whose tirade had devolved into a whimper. Both sounds became fainter as they moved beyond Franklin's room and down a hospital corridor.

\*\*\*

Gwen followed the nurse around a bank of curtains providing privacy for hospital beds occupied by patients, beeping monitors, and people in hospital garb. Although she tried not to look, the various cries and moans emitted from the spaces beyond the curtains compelled her to glimpse the assortment of humanity suffering in these sterile cubicles. Gwen felt curiously comforted seeing that she was not the only person wringing her hands.

The nurse knocked lightly on a closed glass door, and then opened it for Gwen to step through. A man in a white coat whom Gwen thought looked young enough to be graduating High School soon, sat behind a desk, studying a computer screen.

"Please, sit down Mrs. Carlyle," the doctor greeted her. "Can I get you some water?"

"No,... no thank you Doctor." Unconsciously clenching then unclenching her fingers, she asked, "Is he going to be all right?"

"We're doing everything we can to see to that Mrs. Carlyle," The doctor responded while he turned the computer monitor around slightly so that she could see the screen. "I want to show you something," he said, tapping the screen with his pen. "This is your husband's liver." He sat back and taped his chin with the pen as if to allow this information to sink in.

Gwen looked at the screen and saw a display of shapes and shadows she could not identify.

Detecting her bewilderment, the doctor inhaled sharply and clicked a button on the computer which divided the screen in half. He then elaborated for Gwen the difference between the normal, and "healthy" human liver displayed on the left of the screen and the liver on the right he said belonged to her husband, then sat back and clasped his fingers together in his lap.

"I,... I don't understand," Gwen moaned. "That side looks so bright, and Franklin's looks dull,... and fat."

The doctor explained that Franklin had cirrhosis of the liver which was undoubtably due to his excessive drinking.

Even after all of the years she endured his poor treatment of her, Gwen instinctually came to her husband's defense. "Aren't there other reasons his liver could be having problems?"

"Yes, ma'am, there are. But, let me show you something else." The doctor clicked a few keys on his computer and as the first screen faded out, another screen appeared. Looking back at Gwen, the doctor said gravely.

"Franklin didn't simply smell of alcohol when he was brought in. His blood-alcohol content was over forty percent."

"Yes, I know he drank a little too much today," Gwen said, trying to minimize her husband's situation.

The doctor leaned forward placing his elbows on his desk, and said gently, but with authority, "The amount of alcohol your husband had in his system put him into a coma. I'm told his heart stopped just before the ambulance arrived. He'll be a lucky man to walk away from this, let alone survive."

Tears welled up in Gwen' eyes, but before they spilled over, the Dr. handed Gwen a tissue, then said in an upbeat tone, "The good news is that even people who have been heavy drinkers can recover with a transplant if enough of their liver is still healthy. My preliminary assessment suggests he might just have enough healthy tissue."

Gwen sat forward. "Today? Can you operate today?"

The physician explained the process of finding a suitable donor, time complications, having to wait for Franklin to awaken from the coma, and the fact that he would have to be alcohol free for at least six months to even be considered a candidate for a liver transplant.

Much of what he said was lost on Gwen. It was all hitting her so hard. Seeing this, the doctor gave her a cup of water, then instructed his nurse take her to see her husband. As Gwen, her mind spinning, followed the nurse back to Franklin's room she heard the Dr. calling after her.

"Your presence can make the difference for your husband," he encouraged. "Even in his state, he is aware when you're with him."

Gwen clasped the styrofoam cup in her hands like it was a communion wafer. She wasn't watching where she was going as much as she was following the rhythmic squeak of the nurse's crocs in front of her. She wasn't sure what was worse, worrying that Franklin might die, or what she'd have to put up with as he waited for a transplant should he come out of his coma and survive, not to mention the torment she'd receive from him once he was back at home. She was certain of two things; he wouldn't quit drinking without a fight, and even if he did, he would continue making her life miserable.

The squeaking finally stopped and Gwen waited, her head still down, while the nurse pushed the door to Franklin's room open. "I'll leave you two alone," she said, then turned and squeaked away down the corridor.

***

Franklin, as the Doctor told Gwen, was indeed aware of his wife's presence. Though his eyes were closed, he could see her beside his bed. He wondered to himself, *Does she know I'm in here? That I'm not a frickin vegetable?* He saw a look on Gwen's face like she thought the nurse might have made a mistake. "Hey! I'm here!" he called to her from inside his head. "I'm... right ... here!"

"I've never seen you look so,... so serene," Gwen began with a whisper.

*I must be losin' it,* Franklin thought. *That whisper of hers reminds me of an old locomotive venting just a hint of steam before it leaves the station.*

Gwen reached over and brushed the back of her hand down the side of Franklin's face, along his mustache and his stubbled cheeks. She took a slow, deep breath, as if to steady herself, then she touched his arm, and his flesh caved in as if she were pressing into bread dough. When she removed her hand, the indentation remained. Her eyes full of sorrow, she reached out again with her finger tips, and brushed lightly at the wrinkled flesh at the corners of her husband's eyes, across his forehead and cheeks, and hanging in a deflated sack under his chin. "How long has it been since I've looked closely at you, or you at me?" she said softly. Gwen looked at her own hands and forearms, the skin thin, almost translucent, and beginning to wrinkle. "Maybe this is why you've drawn away from me."

"I haven't gone anywhere. I've always been here," Franklin cried out on the inside, knowing his effort was futile, that Gwen could not hear him.

"Do you remember when we first met?" Gwen continued regaining some of her composure. "Just a couple of youngsters fresh out of High School, weren't we?"

"Of course I remember! I was there, wasn't I?" he groaned within.

"Even then I knew it was all ego and hormones. I wonder if you've ever known me. It's all a blur now." The sad look in her eyes, like that of a fawn, morphed into something more akin to those of a wolf defending her den.

Her head shaking side to side, and her voice beginning to tremble with anger she said, "I tried to do everything I could to satisfy you, and all you ever did was criticize me and expect me to take care of your every need! And then it was the beer, always the beer!" Gwen stopped for a moment and closed her eyes as if she was thinking, then opened them and bent a little closer to her husband's face. "Can you hear me in there? I know I complained about your drinking, but when I asked you for a glass of wine, what did you do? Do you remember *that*?"

It didn't take long for it to come back to him. "You want wine?" he remembered taunting Gwen. "Well, if you're gonna drink that crap, you might as well get yourself to the store and buy it, cuz I'm not wasting my time or money on fruit juice!"

"What was I thinking?" Gwen said, shaking her head, her lips taught and white with anger.

Franklin thought back to the image he had of the train Gwen reminded him of as it sat idling at the station. *Guess I better buckle up*, he thought. *This train looks like she's picking up a head of steam.*

Both disrupting and confirming Franklin's thoughts, Gwen's voice intensified. "You never even said please, or thank you, to me. And nothing I did was ever good enough for you, or fast enough!" Gwen slammed a hand down hard on a tray beside the bed and shouted, as a plastic pitcher of water sitting on it tumbled to the floor, "Or just fucking enough!" Gwen's eyes suddenly opened wide, and she immediately clamped both of her hands over her mouth, her face betraying a look of complete shock and embarrassment at her outburst.

Franklin, his face sunken and jaundiced, didn't budge. In addition to being in a coma, he was now in shock. He'd never heard Gwen use such language, and she had certainly never even raised her voice at him. The analogy he'd had of her as a train that was picking up steam held true, and Gwen's anger was gaining momentum, revealing deep seated bitterness and resentment.

"I guess I always knew you were more about yourself than anyone else," Gwen said, now virtually roaring down the tracks. "I never liked the way you talked everyone down. And you never respected women." With each word,

Gwen's voice began to rise and intensify. Sparks flew from the friction caused by the iron wheels grinding against the tracks. "You mocked anyone who had a different opinion than yours. And you never allowed me to have one," she shouted. "I doubt you ever wondered why I don't talk so much anymore, but, well, now you know." Taking a step back from Franklin, she said, "I know you'd say that if I was unhappy, I should just leave, right? Oh, don't think it didn't cross my mind countless times. But I'll tell you why I didn't."

Gwen approached her husband again and laid her hand on his, and for a moment Franklin thought she was finally coming out of her emotional tail spin. It was as though the raging locomotive had slowed and pulled into a station, where the engine cooled down. He knew she'd eventually talk her-self out, or as he'd put it, "zip it," when she realized he wasn't listening, and decided this must be what was happening now.

Proving her husband's perception of her incorrect, Gwen bristled, ele-vated her voice, and continued.

To Franklin, it was as if the train suddenly blew its whistle and belched its acrid, black smoke.

"When we first met, you did things to make me feel special,... like you cared," she said, then screamed, "I fell for it! I wanted to believe I meant something to someone,... to you!"

"Here we go," Franklin groaned inwardly. "And I gotta lay here and tolerate this? I must be in hell. Hey, God, the coma was one thing, but what did I ever do to deserve this?" he asked with a grumble.

Gwen turned on her heel and began to pace back and forth between the bed and the window. "I wanted to believe it was true," Gwen continued as she walked away. "So when you knew you had me and stopped your act, I pretended I didn't notice." She turned back around, her face contorted with a combination of sadness and anger. Intensity fueled by years of neglect was injected into every word, the veins bulged in her neck, and her face had turned bright red. "By the time we had our first child, I had given up so much of who I had been before we met that I forgot who I used to be. I guess I was just hoping that somehow you'd change. But you didn't! And now, here we are!" she screamed again. Then except for her breathing, she went silent.

Other than the incessant beeping of hospital equipment, Gwen stood, less than an arms length away from her husband. After a moment, Gwen stirred and leaned in close to him again. "I'm probably out of my mind, but, this is your last chance," she seethed through clenched teeth. "If you're lucky enough to survive this,... you better stop drinking."

Gwen was beyond trembling, she was now shuddering, and as she took a breath to steady her nerves, Franklin thought to himself, *I knew this would happen one of these days, but not like this, the train has finally gone off the rails!*

Gwen leaned down and exploded right into Franklin's ear. "I don't care if you have to see a therapist or go to AA! I'm going home and throwing away all your precious beer! I'm cleaning out the garage, and your whiskey stash in the toilet! Then I'm going to wait this out! I will visit you every day to encourage you. Even if it takes a year! You,... *you* will fight for *your* life! I can't do that for you! If you do all of that, and never have another drink, and if you begin to treat me with compassion and respect, I might consider staying with you." Gwen sat back, took a deep breath, and straightened back up. "Do you have any idea how lucky you are that I would still do that?" she asked.

Franklin winced at Gwen's last comment. She'd hit him where it counted.

"Oh, I know you never believed in luck, but just maybe this has given you some idea now just how lucky you are that I'm still with you! Starting right now, at this moment, the me I've been all these years with you is gone! You've lost her! I haven't been your lover, or your sweetheart, and more likely not your trophy for a very long time, but I am no longer your ser-vant either! I *am* your wife, and if you survive and still cannot treat me as a husband should treat his wife, I *will* leave you!" Gwen looked hard at her husband, and with her final comments, it was as though the freight train had finally come to a stop. "You may not understand, but this is going to be the hardest thing I've ever done," she whispered. She patted his hand and leaned over to kiss his forehead, then got up and walked away. Half way to the door, she stopped, turned around, and once more looked hard at her husband. With the faintest hint of a smirk on her face, she said, "It felt good somehow to finally tell you how I feel, but now I'm exhausted." Her fingers of her hands had begun to entwine themselves together, but she shook them loose and instead brushed the creases from her dress. With that, her hands relaxed at her sides, she turned and left the room.

As Franklin watched her walk out of the room, he felt an odd sensation. He was confused. A large part of him was angry at his wife for the things he heard her say. But there was another part, somewhere within in a place he was unable to identify, that thought she could be right. About all of it. He felt pain in his chest near his heart, and a great weariness came over him. As he found himself hoping that the train would come back, the light in the room began to fade, and everything went black.

# CHAPTER 15

Franklin slept with a furrowed brow and his chin slumped against his chest. He snapped his head back sharply at the sound of someone yelling nearby, knocking it into the tree he was tied to. Groaning with pain Franklin opened his eyes to see Hawley directly in front of him on his haunches, an arms length away. The man was picking his yellowed teeth with a knife blade.

"Looks like this here's a lucky day for you boys," Hawley drawled. "Extra rations for y'all." He spit a stream of foul colored saliva into the dirt, and sat bowls of stew in front of them with a thick slice of bread each, then unfastened their hands so they could eat while still tied securely to their trees. Looking directly at Franklin, Hawley said, "Soon enough y'all be gettin' what the both of ya deserve. What goes 'round, comes 'round's what I always say."

Franklin nearly choked at Hawley's words. He'd used them so many times himself when rebuffing his friends. But he quickly shook it off to instead join Nathaniel in gulping down a stew of meat, potatoes, and carrots without even chewing. As he sopped up the gravy with his hunk of bread that was substantial enough it could be used as a weapon, he looked up long enough to see the Indians siting with one another some ten yards away eating their pathetic rations. Then, without so much as a second thought, he put his head back down to lick his bowl clean of every drop, and held out the empty to his captor for more.

"Easy, boy" Hawley said flatly. "Ya'll be gettin' more after we been movin' along some." With a chipper lilt to his voice he added, "Gotta fatten y'all up for the market!" Then he took their bowls and skipped away doing a jig. Over his shoulder he drawled, "Course, that is if y'all'r lucky enough ta make it that far."

Sated for the moment, Franklin was surprised when the faces of Degataga and the others bore expressions of sadness toward him, rather than those of anger for the way he gluttonously ravished his food, while they ate so poorly. He decided this must have had something to do with the statement Hawley made about fattening him up for the market. He shrugged his shoulders which unleashed a loud burp, then, he noticed Lazarus wasn't laying by Nathaniel.

"Where's the mutt?"

"Oh, he always be gone afore the mornin' light. But he's okay, he's a smart hound. He be out there not too far off, and he gonna follow us ta see where's we be goin'. He know not ta let them soldiers see him, but if ya look when I tell ya to you can catch a flash of him ever now an' again. Ol' Lazarus don't forget what ya did for him. He be near to ya for as long as he can be." Then Nathaniel appeared reflective. "Don't know what he do if they split us up cuz he loves us both now."

Suddenly, Nathaniel's eyes widened, and when Franklin followed their direction he saw Hawley coming their way again. Franklin's mouth watered at the thought of more savory food until he noticed Hawley was not carrying bowls with him this time. Instead he had two lengths of rope, each with a noose at one end.

"What the hell's that for?" Franklin asked brusquely with a show of bravado to cover up the fear that ignited inside him.

"Y'all sure don't talk like no colored boy, but that skin ya got coverin' yer bones, and that kinky hair is a dead give away," Hawley said. "Course, we could be lynchin' yer sorry asses, but this here rope's gonna make sure you two don't get no idea ta run fer it on 'tween here and the fort. But don't worry," he smirked. "We'll save the lynching fer another day."

Hawley slipped one noose over Nathaniel's head and the other over Franklin's, then slung their other ends over his shoulder. Next, he released them from the trees and jerked both men to their feet, then walked away pulling them behind him over to a couple of soldiers seated on horses. "Synch these up tight around yer saddle horns," he instructed his comrades, "then one of ya ride on the right side of the Indians, and the other on the left. Keep these niggers away from each other, and on a short leash." That said, he mounted his own horse, and brought it up along side Second Lieutenant Rayford as before.

Rayford gave the signal to move out, and the group began another day on the trail which alternated from valleys to mountains and back to valleys as they moved into the southern region of the Appalachian Mountains in southeastern Tennessee. The weather fluctuated with the elevation, providing the group warmth in the valleys and a brisk chill air in the mountains, and the afternoon passed without trouble.

The rope around Franklin's neck limited his mobility, and was jerked firmly any time he tried to talk with the Indians. He also had to work harder than before at keeping pace with the group or the horse he was secured to would get ahead of him. Whenever this happened, the soldier in charge of him apparently thought nothing of wrenching his neck, and Franklin felt the skin beneath his rope bleed from the almost constant friction.

When Franklin or Nathaniel needed to relieve themselves, their only option was doing so right where they were and while continuing to walk because the group did not stop for them. Franklin learned this the hard way when he tried to walk sideways to avoid getting wet. His feet quickly became entangled, and he stumbled awkwardly, fighting to stay upright only to fall. He was dragged several yards as he scrambled to get back on his feet, losing his hat in the process.

In spite of these hardships, he enjoyed the noontime meal. He and Nathaniel were fed copious amounts of food, and he felt the difference in his strength and energy quickly. Every once in a while he noticed an unmistakable flash of yellow in the trees alongside of the trail, and knew that Lazarus was indeed following along as Nathaniel had said he would. Somehow, just knowing Lazarus was there gave Franklin a feeling of comfort, and he made sure to leave some bits of food behind when the group got moving again.

Not long after resuming the trail, Lieutenant Rayford called for a halt. He ordered all of the Indians secured with rope one to the other in a straight line, and assigned three soldiers to split them off from the detachment of soldiers and take them on a side path that led up a steep grade to the right. Rayford kept Franklin and Nathaniel with him and the other soldiers, and continued moving forward.

After about a half a mile the trail widened to a deeply rutted dirt road. On either side of the road a scattering of dilapidated looking one or two story wooden structures came into view that looked as though a strong wind could blow them over. Beyond these there appeared a small shantytown, and above it, an assortment of rustic looking cabins.

At first, besides a couple of mangy-looking dogs lapping at a mud puddle, the place appeared abandoned. Then Franklin heard a "whump - whump" sound. Looking up and to his right, he saw a woman with a wooden paddle beating on a piece of laundry hanging from a tree branch. Beside the woman, a line heavy with drying clothing was strung between two other trees. As Franklin watched, the woman stopped long enough to wipe her brow with her forearm, shade her eyes, and look back at him and the rest of the spectacle trudging by.

Franklin's eyes wandered to the woman's left to what he could only surmise must be a dwelling of sorts. On the porch of the dilapidated structure sat a man with a scraggily beard who was leaning back against the wall of the cabin in a rickety looking chair, smoking a pipe. The glint of metal caught Franklin's eye when the man reached over and grabbed a rifle leaning against a wall just beside him. The man bumped the butt of the rifle sharply against the porch floorboards, and immediately the woman took a piece of laundry, got down on her knees, and began to scrub it in a large basin next to the clothes line. The man sat the gun back, spat off the porch into the dirt, then picked up a tin cup and took a drink.

"Looks like things haven't changed much," Franklin muttered to himself feeling as though he was looking at a version of himself and Gwen.

"Sumpthin the matter?" Nathaniel asked.

Franklin just shook his head. People had come out from an assortment of hovels, and worn out looking buildings along the road. They were gaunt, their skin drawn and grey-white, and their eyes deep in their sockets. They gawked in silence at the procession moving by. The soldiers, Franklin, and Nathaniel, trudged to the other end of town past a livery stable, ironsmith shed, dry goods store, and something that probably served as a tavern, each place emitting its own unique sounds and smells. The citizens of the place never spoke or raised a hand in welcome, dashing any hope Franklin may have entertained about resting here or escaping his captors.

After they had walked for about a mile to the other side of the town, the group met up with the Indians who had been led down a path from the surrounding woods that intersected with the road again. This procedure was repeated several miles later when the trail passed through a town nearly identical in appearance and habitation to the last.

Franklin wondered if Rayford sent the Indians around to prevent them being seen by sympathizers. If his memory served him right, he knew from history that although it seemed the whole country was adamant about getting rid of the Indians, this was not true of everyone. There had been sympathizers. Most notable among those he could remember from his reading who spoke out against the forced removal of the Indians were Henry Clay, John Quincy Adams, Davy Crockett, and Ralph Waldo Emerson. These names surprised him as he had thought all of them with the possible exception of Emerson were patriots. Franklin had no appreciation for poets or their words.

As they trudged through the center of town, a man stepped out onto the rutted road from what Franklin took to be the town saloon, and hailed the lieutenant who reigned his horse over to the side. Rayford signaled for the group to stop then dismounted. The two men spoke as the stranger peered over the lieutenant's shoulder at Franklin and Nathaniel. He wrote something down in a small notebook he produced from inside his knee-length coat, then shook the lieutenant's hand, and disappeared back into the murky looking drinking establishment. The lieutenant rejoined the group and signaled them to continue.

After another few steeply inclining miles, the lieutenant ordered the men to make camp. Darkness came early in these mountains, and the group scrambled to arrange their sleeping areas before settling in for a meal.

Franklin and Nathaniel were led to a couple of trees on the northern edge of the camp and secured there as they had been before.

As he settled back against his tree to wait for his meager rations, Franklin gazed into the gathering darkness of the valley below, and was startled to see what appeared to be hundreds of fires stretched out for what he estimated must have been at least a mile.

"What the hell is that?" he asked Nathaniel.

"Tha's Fort Cass."

"I've never seen a fort like that," Franklin retorted.

"Oh," Nathaniel replied. "Them fires you lookin' at is the holdin' pens. The fort is over ta the side there. And them lights yonder," he said pointing just to the north of the fires, "is Charleston, Tennessee. When we gets down there," he said pointing back in the direction of the fort, "your Indian friends be put inta one of them pens, and you and me be put inta jail for sure. I knows it cause I was there before I was caught in them mountains by the soldiers."

Franklin looked at Nathaniel with a puzzled expression on his face.

"I never finished my story," Nathaniel said.

Franklin closed his eyes.

"I was bought at a slave auction by a man who lived in Virginia," Nathaniel began. "He was taken me back with some other coloreds when some Indians attacked his wagons. We scattered in all directions, and I found a hollow to crawl into. I waited till everythin' was quiet again and started back North. Thas when soldiers found me and took me to Fort Cass. I was put on a work detail while they was tryin' to find my massah. The guards that was watchin' us were drinkin' of course. They *always* be drinkin'. They loosed us from our chains so we could work better," Nathaniel said chuckling. "I guess they just forgot how to count 'cause when it was time to go back to the pen, I had already strayed a bit from the rest, and they left me behind."

"Well, ol' Lazarus was out there watchin' like he does. So we scooted away into the woods together and ended up where y'all was when that ol' Hawley found me. Guess that makes me a three time loser," Nathaniel added shaking his head.

Franklin thought for perhaps the first time how strange it was that Nathaniel, and the Indians, because of the color of their skin, were considered some variant of ignorant, sub-human, or savage. He shuddered knowing that he'd held these same beliefs, and wondered at the irony that at least for the time being, he was counted among them. The image of the woman he saw in the first small town they passed through, pounding away at the laundry while her husband relaxed on the porch came to his mind, and he shook his head. It reminded him painfully how he'd treated Gwen. From what he had experienced over that past several days, he thought that if anyone here was to be considered civilized, it was the Cherokee people. They seemed to be the only ones who treated people, animals, and the earth itself, with respect.

That night, after the soldiers had turned in to their tents for sleep, after their raucous celebration for being within sight of Fort Cass, Franklin heard a rustle in the nearby scrub, and out from the dark bounded Lazarus. This time the hound enjoyed treats from both men, and Franklin enjoyed stroking the dogs muzzle and oversized floppy ears. He noticed Lazarus' ear wound didn't look as bad as he thought it would be, but the bullet had managed to put a rip in that right ear that would be there from now on.

Suddenly, the fur on Lazarus's neck rose and he emitted a low growl. Franklin peered anxiously around himself, and froze when he saw a stooped figure coming towards him from the direction of the Indian's beds. Another figure, bent down as the first, appeared out of the darkness, followed by one more. He couldn't make out who they were in the darkness, and he feared in the pit of his stomach that the Indians had finally had enough of his rude and selfish behavior, and decided to do away with him.

*Serves me right if they do*, he thought to himself miserably.

"Unaduti," the figure closest to Franklin whispered. "I fear our paths are soon to part. My sons and I wish to tell you that we have been honored to have had you among us. You have been sent to us for a reason that we cannot understand. We are sorry we cannot prevent what is now to come, but we have something to give you. We hope these will help you." The old Indian held out three eagle feathers. They were trimmed so that the black portion of the feathers were rounded and came to a point at the white tip. Each was threaded on a single string of deer sinew, and one of them had the crimson red feather of a cardinal attached to it with an additional bit of leather string.

"To us," Chea Sequa said, "the awa'hili is our great sacred bird. I know that you do not believe in luck, but this, Unaduti, is not only luck. It is medicine which gives much strength and bravery for the fight. My father, my brother, and I have each removed one of our feathers to give to you for your medicine. Wear them around your neck, and keep them safe so that in your time of need they will carry you through."

Franklin sat, stunned. He couldn't make sense of what was happening. Finally, he stuttered in a voice filled with shame, "I... don't deserve your kindness. I have disrespected you all of this time, and for years before you ever knew of me."

"It is not a matter of deserving," Kanuna responded in his deep baritone voice. "It is a matter of needing. Kindness is a sacrifice we make, and a gift we give for the good of the world. We do this as much for your need as for those who you may show kindness to tomorrow, in this time, or in your own."

Degataga reached out and draped the necklace over Franklin's bowed head. "My son's and I pray the Great Spirit looks upon you with mercy as your journey unfolds."

Then as silently and without ceremony as they had materialized out of the darkness, they slipped back to their people, and their words filtered deep into Franklin's aching, and gradually softening heart where he pondered them through the night.

# CHAPTER 16

The whinny of a horse woke Franklin from an unsettled sleep. He opened his eyes, and through the soft light of the moon saw the tail end of Lazarus disappearing into the forest. A glow could be seen through the wall of one of the tents, and the lieutenant came out holding a lantern. Hawley, his own lantern in hand, exited another tent. The sound of a horse clopping on damp ground was followed by the dark figure of horse and rider entering camp. Dismounting the beast, its rider approached the two soldiers with a shuffling gate. After some time together, talking quietly, all three men walked over to Franklin and Nathaniel.

The lieutenant held his lantern up to Nathaniel's face. "Found this one a couple of days ago, Mr. Calhoun." Then he shifted the lantern close to Franklin. "This one here was with these Indians when we started moving them out of Georgia."

"Ooo-wee, Lieutenant, these *coloreds*! They move like molasses when you want some work out of 'em, but they sure can skedaddle once they slip away from the farm!" Mr. Calhoun chuckled.

"You wanna watch this one here *real* close," Hawley offered, kicking Franklin just below the knee. "Jumped me by surprise and 'bout took my head off a couple days ago."

"Oh, don't you worry sir. I may look soft around the middle," Calhoun said laughing and patting his bulging belly, "but I know how to take the spit out of the rough ones, yes sir I do." Calhoun eyed Hawley, then said in a tone dripping with sarcasm, "I wouldn't have taken you for one to let a colored get the drop on you."

Hawley shifted on his feet, squaring himself to face Calhoun. Even from where Franklin sat he could see there was no love lost between these two.

"Just caught him off his guard, that's all," the lieutenant said, coming to Hawley's defense. "Let's just stick to business, shall we?" He cleared his throat and continued. "This one talks almost as good as a white man," he said, kicking Franklin's foot with his boot. "Could be he might bring a better price."

"We'll see once I get 'em to Fort Cass. If these two are runaways like you say, you'll get the rest of the payment when you get in tomorrow. If not, I'll deal with 'em as I can and you can consider yourself paid in full. In the meantime, I'll be taking them off your hands. Chuckling, he added, "So Hawley there can focus on the trail instead of watching his back."

Rayford grabbed Hawley before he could lunge at the slave trader, and walked him back to his tent.

Mr. Calhoun shuffled over to Franklin and Nathaniel, and placed an iron collar around each of their necks with a length of chain that connected one collar to the other, then untied them from their trees. "Get up boys, I'm taking you for an early morning stroll. If you give me no trouble, you can walk with your hands and feet free. But start any kind of ruckus, and I can chain 'em for you real quick." Mr. Calhoun indicated that they walk out ahead of him with Nathaniel up front, followed by Franklin. "With only the two of you, we should make real good time." With a grunt, Calhoun hoisted his bulging form into his saddle, prompting a side step from his mount as the animal adjusted to the man's bulk.

It took a little over an hour for the three of them to make it down from the mountain and to a road that wound its way into a valley connecting with another road that ran east and west. The men hadn't spoken since leaving camp until Mr. Calhoun, guiding them as if they were cattle, ordered Franklin and Nathaniel to take the new road heading west. The moon was still visible ahead of them as the sun began to rise over the mountains they's left behind.

"What is that?" Franklin asked having spotted a cloud of dust rising up off the road in the distance.

"Prob'ly just some coloreds bein' moved along ta market," Nathaniel answered.

"That's a good-sized coffle," added Mr. Calhoun, holding a pocket-sized, brass telescope to his eye. "They come through here from as far away as Virginia. Could be some of them are friends of yours, maybe even family." Calhoun unfurled a long leather whip, flicked it out and over Franklin and Nathaniel's heads with a crack. "Now, keep your mouths shut when we get closer and pass 'em. Understand?" Then he rolled the whip back up and hung it on his saddle horn.

It wasn't long before Franklin saw for himself that the dust was being kicked up by a large group of people. The three men caught up with the mass of humanity, and Mr. Calhoun moved the two men off the road and proceeded to pass forty or more bedraggled, colored men, women, and children.

Franklin noticed that the men were in the front, chained together at the ankles, followed by the women. A few of the women closer to the front, and who appeared younger and healthier than the others, were connected together with ropes. The older ones, and those who appeared to have injuries walked free behind them. Children were either carried by the women, or walked along side them. Behind the group were four wagons, pulled by a team of horses. Filled with supplies, the wheels, rusty shocks, and sun-dried wooden frames groaned under the load they carried. A white man drove each of the wagons, each of them bearing a whip, and with a rifle across their knee, or laying close at hand on the spring-fitted, plank seat beside them. A couple of colored women and several more children were sitting in the back of the second wagon in line, and an older colored man sat in the third. The old man's skin looked so dry and wrinkled, it appeared he might be as old as the earth itself.

The large group shuffled along, amidst a swarm of flies that nearly matched the thickness of the dust they stirred. None of them other than a child or two cast a glance in the three men's direction. Franklin was surprised at how quiet they were until it dawned on him that like he and Nathaniel, they probably weren't allowed to talk to another group of slaves. He estimated that if they came from Richmond, Virginia, they'd have travelled about 500 miles. Their tattered, and thread-bare clothes bore witness to their struggle. Many of them had no shoes, and those that did were as worn as the man, or woman wearing them. Figuring that he'd walked around a hundred miles since the soldiers moved him and the Indians out of Georgia, Franklin wondered how they could have come all this way and still be on their feet. Just looking at them brought on a fresh wave of weariness. The faces of the men and women in the coffle were sullen, downcast, and as dirty as their feet, but surprisingly, they didn't appear to be starving. In his head Franklin heard Hawley telling him, "Gotta fatten ya up for the market!"

An hour or so after passing the mass of slaves, the three men crested a rise in the road which afforded them a view of the valley beyond. Not far to their right was a river, and ahead, what appeared to be a mile or two away, was a large structure that Franklin took to be the fort. His gaze shifted to the left, where just South of the fort, separated by a space of maybe one or two-hundred yards, a fence stretched for a mile or more out and away from the structure, and then turned west disappearing into the distance. Enclosed within this fenced space, there appeared to be hundreds of smoking fires, and thousands of dots moving around amongst them like a hoard of ants. Upon closing the distance, Franklin could see that there were soldiers posted at a gate to the enclosure and at increments of approximately twenty-five yards along the outside of the fence. Drawing closer, the moving dots became Indians. In comparison to the coffle of slaves, they looked like walking skeletons, and Franklin felt a combination of guilt and concern for Degataga and his family.

Unable to contain his awe at the sight before him, Franklin exclaimed, "My God! What is this place?"

Mr. Calhoun coughed, then hawked a wad of phlegm that hit the road to the right of Franklin's worn boot, sending up a small puff of dust. "That, boy, is Fort Cass, and that over there is a holding pen. But you coloreds don't have to be worrying about that. There's a special place in there for *you*. If you're *lucky*, you won't be here for long anyways. On the other hand, there's really no telling."

"What's that supposed to mean?" Franklin grumbled, the mere mention of luck aggravating him to his core.

"Well, the good news is like I said. You won't have to stay in this God-forsaken place too long. But that good luck's probably going to turn bad because the both of you will be going back to your rightful owner, and as glad as he'll likely be to get you back, I don't expect he'll be too kind to you for running. Paid good money for you old man," Calhoun explained. "And he lost money during your absence. Spent more of his money to locate you. Now he'll have to spend more to get you back again." Calhoun spit, and wiped his chin. "In case you're missing my meaning, I think he'll be fit to whoop your ass good for all the trouble you caused him. Tell you the truth, at your age, I don't know what anybody would want with you anyways. You'll be lucky if he takes you back."

"What if he doesn't?" asked Franklin, although he thought he knew the answer.

Calhoun drew a deep breath, "If he doesn't take you back, I doubt there's too many others'd want you either. An old colored man out on his own with no master to care for him... well, suh, he ain't worth much of anything to anyone. And if you've got no value,... well, you aren't long for this world."

"Couldn't I just go North?"

"Oh, I suspect you could. But first you're going to have to find a way out of this fort. Then, second, supposing you did that, you're going to have to make it there, and there is a long ways from here. Then there's your partner there. He came from the North, and yet, here he is with a chain around his neck just like you. No, suh, you best be hoping your master wants to take you back. Long as you survive the beating, you oughta do just fine."

They were stopped at the gates to Fort Cass by a soldier who asked Mr. Calhoun for documents, then abruptly left the three of them waiting as he disappeared through the open gate. After a few minutes, the soldier returned and led the three men into the interior grounds. He instructed Mr. Calhoun to tether Franklin and Nathaniel to a post, then led the slave handler into an office.

Nathaniel seemed to be taking it in stride, but Franklin felt unsettled. The two men stood tied to the post as though invisible. No one paid the least bit of attention to them, only walked by as if they weren't there. He felt like a piece of meat that would rot if left out in the sun for too long. Franklin watched as soldiers milled about, tethered horses, or led them from one place to another, as he had been led over the course of the past several days. He saw that there were a number of small structures along the right and the left walls of the fort. Each had a post anchored in the ground in front of it. An iron gate stood along each of the two side walls, blocking an opening to a dark room on the other side. A guard was posted in front of each of them.

A large grouping of tents were assembled toward the back of the grounds, that looked as though they probably housed soldiers. To the right of the office was another much larger tent, and through the open flap, a raised platform was visible. Flies buzzed around Franklin's head. The place smelled like horses, urine, dust, and the sweat of men. He was suddenly struck by a profound irony. He realized that he hadn't felt threatened while being cared for by the Indians. But now, surrounded by his own kind, he did.

"Like the man said, I been here afore," Nathaniel offered, disrupting Franklin's thoughts. "They's no doubt exchangin' money inside, and gonna put us inta the holdin' pen for coloreds till our massah come for us, or ask for us ta be took to him. Either way ain't good."

"I don't plan to be here much longer," Franklin grumbled. "But as long as they're feeding us good, it's better than starving. I don't know about you, but I'm bone tired from all that walking."

"Oh, they gonna feed us alright, till we be sold. But they is nothing else good 'bout bein' here. And believe me, they got some work for us ta do while we waitin' that'll make ya wish we was still walkin' up and down them mountains. Sides, just where ya planning ta be going?"

"You wouldn't believe me if I told you. Let's just say I'm planning on waking up from this nightmare."

Nathaniel gave Franklin a look, then shrugged his shoulders.

Mr. Calhoun reappeared from the office tucking an envelope into an inner breast pocket of his coat. He walked back out the entry gate without a word, or so much as a look at the two men. A moment after that, a soldier came out from the same office and untied the tether. He pointed toward the south wall of the fort and instructed the men to head in that direction.

"I been in this nightmare my whole life," Nathaniel said. "I'm near fifty now and I ain't woke up yet. So if ya figure a way ta do that, let me know."

"Hush up niggers!" the soldier ordered. "Y'all're now the guests of Brigadier General Winfield Scott! You'd be wise to save your gabbing for the pen."

The name rang a bell in Franklin's head. Sifting through his memory of historical data he recalled that General Scott had been one of the more important military figures of early 19th century America. He was credited to a large degree for transforming the army from poorly trained citizens to a force of professional level fighters.

Franklin first came across General Scott in his readings regarding one of his true heroes, Robert E. Lee, who while at the rank of captain served under him. Franklin used to muse over how great it would have been if Scott had decided to serve the confederates during the civil war rather than taking the side of the North. His battle strategies helped to facilitate the ultimate success of the union. Together, Franklin thought during his reading, the two men could have influenced the outcome in the South's favor. In his current circumstances, Franklin suddenly found himself uncharacteristically questioning himself on his own line of thinking.

Franklin and Nathaniel were taken to the large iron gate in the South wall of the fort. A guard stood at attention about ten paces out in front of it. Upon the order of the soldier who'd led the two captives there, the guard stepped to the great rusted gate, unlocked it, and swung it open with a rusty creak. The sound made Franklin think of the noise an ocean tanker might make should it run up against another ship at sea. He and Nathaniel were led to the opening where they were met by an overwhelming, nauseating reek coming from the darkened space beyond the gate. Franklin now understood why the guard had positioned himself so far away. The thick, rancid, stink of human waste and whatever else was inside wafted over him, provoking a gag reflex in Franklin and causing his eyes to water.

The guard removed the iron collars and lead ropes from around the prisoner's necks, and they were unceremoniously shoved from behind past the gate. Their boots were demanded of them, and upon receipt, the rusty gate was slammed closed with a loud clang and secured with an equally corroded padlock. Resuming his post, he left Franklin and Nathaniel in the dank, dark void.

Franklin tried to blink the blindness of the fort's bright inner yard from his eyes, and the residual images of horses and soldiers that had become imprinted on his retinas changed colors from red to orange, to green, then blue, before fading altogether. Then slowly his eyes adjusted to the darkness engulfing him. To his left was a rough hewn, log wall. To the right, the area opened up for about forty feet, and ended against another. Directly in front of him, at a distance of approximately twenty feet, was a third wall that had narrow slits cut into it every four or five feet. The small openings allowed narrow shafts of light, as well as a hint of fresh air from the South side of the fort—the side the immense Indian enclosure was located on—to enter the cell. Nathaniel crept away to a far corner, and Franklin heard him talking quietly and with familiarity to some men yet unseen.

Franklin was quickly drawn like a moth to a flame following a shaft of light to the slit in the wall before him. Blinking against the brightness he could see the Indian enclosure about one hundred and fifty yards away. He reached into his shirt for his eagle feather necklace and wondered if he would be able to spot Degataga and the others when they arrived, and what other God-forsaken things he'd have to endure until he finally woke up from his miserable dream.

Absently, Franklin stroked the feathers with an index finger. In spite of his disregard of such things, he found himself hoping there was something to the medicine the Indians claimed the talisman held, that it would help him, if not out of, at least through his predicament.

# CHAPTER 17

"Get 'em inside! Drag 'em by the hair if ya have ta!"

Franklin's thoughts were disrupted by the loud, coarse voice of a guard over that of a commotion coming from the direction of the Indian compound. He pushed his face up against the narrow slit opening of his cell to see if he could get a glimpse of what was happening. For a moment, his heart leapt within him when he saw that Degataga and his group had arrived. But it sunk just as quickly as he watched soldiers, rifles at the ready, grab at the tired and bedraggled Indians and push, shove, and kick them past the gate and into the holding area. They seemed to make no distinction between age or gender with the handling of their prisoners. The voice of a woman screamed, and Franklin saw Ayita, grabbed by a soldier, who shoved her with enough force she tripped and fell to the ground.

"The fuck's wrong with you people?" Franklin hollered through the slit. He pounded his fists in futility against the rough hewn wall, and yelled his voice hoarse, "Those people are human beings for Christ's sake!"

The guards and Indians at the gate turned and looked in his direction, and one of the guards levered a rifle to his shoulder and fired. A fraction of a second later, the round screamed through the air and embedded itself with a "thunk" into the wall.

"Shit!" Franklin shrieked. He dropped to the ground as a second round zipped through the opening he had been peering through, and the super heated lead buried itself in a ceiling timber. His hands covering the back of his head, Franklin trembled with both fear and indignation. So far as he could see, the Indians were getting worse treatment than even he as a supposed runaway slave had received.

As he was considering this, he realized that not much had changed in how the Indians are treated by the government. A new scuffle drew Franklin's attention back outside to the plight of the Indians being pushed into the holding pen. He slowly rose back up and stole another peek through the slit. His eye was drawn to one of the soldiers who seemed to be looking straight at him. Despite the distance, he realized it was Hawley, and at that moment, Hawley stretched out his arm, held his hand in the shape of a pistol, and mimed pulling the trigger.

Franklin turned his back to the opening, and slid back to the ground scraping his back against the rough logs. He wished he could do something for the Indians that had treated him as their friend, or at least thank Degataga and the others for being so kind to him, and for protecting him in spite of the disrespect he had shown them. He wanted to apologize for how wrongly they had been treated by the race of people he was a member of in his waking world. A dull ache of shame was beginning to form in his heart for being related to his ancestors, and for the uninformed, ignorant thoughts and comments he himself had made regarding the Indians over the course of his life.

"They's bringin' out the girl again!"

Franklin's thoughts were suddenly interrupted by an exclamation from one of the slaves who had been staring through the wrought iron gate into the forts inner grounds. The man was clenching the iron grill in his fists and shaking so hard the massive piece of iron rattled.

The rest of the men in the cell clamored around one another trying to see for themselves, but there were so many of them, that several men had to wait on the others for word of what was happening.

"How many they bringin' out?" asked a man in the back.

"Letty be the only one!" another voice answered.

"I remember her," said Nathaniel. "That be the woman who spoke her mind ta the soldier what was trying ta feel her up before I run from this place! That Letty been fightin' that one off for a while now. I knew she'd be gettin' it one of these days."

Franklin recognized Nathaniel's voice and said over the commotion. "What are you talking about, Nathaniel?"

Nathaniel left the gate allowing another man to take his spot, and sidled over to Franklin. "These soldiers be mean as the devil ta us negro men, but they sho do like the women from time ta time. Shoot, black, brown, white, red, they like 'em no matter what color they is. That woman still a child, but she be real pretty. All these soldiers been eying her since the first day she in this place. The soldier who been wanting her the most, the one she spoke her mind ta, be the same one shot my dog back on the trail. The same man almost broke your ribs. Thas Hawley. He the boss of the yard here and he gets what he wants."

Franklin cringed at the mention of Hawley's name.

"When I run from my massah," Nathaniel continued, "I get caught and brung ta this here fort. While I be in here I sees that boss soldier, Hawley, pushing that little girl, up agin a wall and feelin' things he had no right ta touch."

A chorus of disapproval arose from the other men.

"Well," Nathaniel said, "she hauled off and slapped him a hard one right in his face! Drew blood. He was so surprised, he fell over on his backside and she run off back inta the hole in the wall you see on the other side from us."

The other men erupted in laughter at the memory.

"Probably what put those scabs on his face. I knew then he meant ta get her back."

"Oh yes!" said another man, the shadows in the cell so dark Franklin couldn't see the man's face. "She just askin' for a whoopin!" the man continued. "Even after ya done run, Nathaniel, she bin callin' him names and spittin' at him every time he even get close ta her. Word is, he done her once already and hurt her somethin' bad. Can't say as I can blame her for hatin' him. He got hisself sent away by the captain couple weeks ago ta cool him down some, but it don't look like it done any good."

"There they go! They's tyin' Letty up agin that post ta whip her!" one of the men at the gate called over his shoulder. "She just a girl!" he hollered and violently rattled the gate.

The guard stomped right over and jabbed at the man's hands with the butt of his rifle. "Get back in there and shut up or your next boy!" he shouted, and the man fell away howling in pain, clutching at his bleeding knuckles.

Franklin squeezed past him into the man's previous position at the gate. From there he saw two soldiers who were pulling a young woman by her arms across the grounds of the fort. She was twisting her body and kicking out with her feet, fighting them with every fiber of her being, but loosing the battle. They dragged her screaming profanities at them to a post about ten yards out from the woman's enclosure, and tied her to it with her face up against the rough, splintered wood. One of the soldiers grabbed her flimsy, dirty garment at the neck with both of his hands and ripped it down her back, her skinny arms tied to the post the only things keeping the dress from falling to the ground and completely exposing her naked body for all to see.

Franklin couldn't believe the barbarism playing out before his own eyes. The girl, Letty, wasn't a woman at all. Not that age should matter, but she couldn't have been more that thirteen or fourteen years old. The men in the cell with Franklin, and the women being held in the enclosure across the yard shouted their objections. The girl tugged, pulled and wrenched at that pole with a desperation Franklin had never seen before.

Hawley stepped out from a doorway near the front gate of the fort, and walked slowly toward the girl. He held a rolled up whip in his left hand, which he unfurled, allowing the tail to drag menacing along behind him, making a snake-like side to side imprint in the dirt. He held a bottle in his other hand. Halfway across the yard, Hawley stopped, tilted the bottle to his lips and took a long swig draining it of its contents. He wiped his mouth with his shirt sleeve, and tossed the bottle to the ground before moving to a point about six feet behind the straining girl.

Howls of indignation from the men in Franklin's cell were matched by the wailing of the women across the yard, but all of them fell silent as Hawley recoiled his whip.

Unable to contain himself any longer, Franklin broke the silence. "Don't do it!" he yelled, and violently rattled the gate.

His outburst did nothing but curl Hawley's lip into a cruel smile, and the angry protests of the men in his cell and the mournful wailing of the women in theirs erupted anew.

Hawley looked over toward Franklin through eyes darkened by alcohol, hatred, and lust, then drew back his arm. One of the cuts on his face had left a scar that glistened with the sun reflecting off a slick coating of sweat. The tail of the whip flew up over Hawley's shoulder in a graceful arc with one smooth motion, then seemed to hang in mid air, and the collective breath drawn and held by everyone watching the spectacle was all Franklin heard. After what seemed an impossibly long amount of time, Hawley flicked his wrist and the first lash cracked the air, and laid a bright red line down the girl's back, from her right shoulder to the slight curve just above her left hip.

Letty's body fluttered like a leaf in a hard wind not yet free of its branch, quivering as it dangled from the post by her wrists, the tips of her toes just making contact with the ground.

Before anyone could take another breath, the second lash fell, then a third, each making its own ugly red slash, and each causing a reflexive jerk of pain from the girl. No one spoke, nor cried out anymore from either side of the field. A forth and fifth crack of the whip split the air, and the girl hung lifeless, blood flowing freely from the slashes in her back, down her legs, and muddying the dirt at her feet.

"I declare by the scars ya left on my face, and these I just sliced inta your skinny carcass, that you're mine," Hawley growled. "Lucky for you the captain sent me off for awhile ta calm down, or I'd of already killed ya dead, instead of the whoopin' ya just got."

A soldier stepped forward, saluted Hawley, then turned smartly away and unfastened Letty from the whipping post. Her body crumpled to the hard-packed ground so rapt with pain she didn't even curl into a fetal position. The soldier grabbed one of her arms, and with the help of another soldier, they began to drag her away toward the women's holding pen, her heels carving two blood stained squiggly lines in the dirt. A third soldier sprinted forward and attempted to drape Letty's torn garment over her exposed body, but the blood was flowing so that the fabric failed to stick.

"Leave it!" snapped Hawley. He leaned over, picked up his discarded bottle and attempted to take a swig, but seeing it was empty, cast it back to the ground, then casually walked away and disappeared back through the doorway he'd come from.

Franklin and the other men in his cell retreated in defeat to the dark recesses of their enclosure, and sat in sullen silence for the remainder of the day.

As evening approached, a new activity in the yard drew Franklin's attention away from his stupor. Soldiers were carrying branches and chunks of wood to the center of the yard. When the pile reached a height of about six feet, one of the soldiers poured fuel on it, and another lit it. Soon, bottles of liquor were produced.

The guard in front of Franklin's cell released several of the men, then along with a few of the women from the cell across the way, charged some of them with serving food and drink to the soldiers. Other men were handed musical instruments, and told to sing and play. Before long, soldiers grabbed the women and forced them to dance with them. Several men disappeared with their prize into the shadows.

Later that evening Franklin saw Hawley go to the women's enclosure, and leave with Letty, leading her now docile form by the arm. He led her through the door he'd come out from earlier, and closed it behind them. A half hour later the door opened and Letty came out and wobbled back alone to the women's cell.

The men in Franklin's enclosure had bedded down for the night on thin, straw matts. Occasionally, one of them got up and relieved himself, using one of two large wooden containers located in the two farthest corners from the cell door. Franklin would discover the following day that these containers were emptied only every other day. This was done via a two foot square door that was cut about three feet high into the exterior wall of the slave enclosure. The door was unlocked from the outside by a soldier who then signaled the men to dump their containers outside. Human waste flowed down a chute onto an ever growing mound, piling up on itself and sloughing over with the sheer weight and volume of the mess, and stinking to high heaven. Flies gathered in mass over the pile and drifted in and out of the slave pen with a nearly constant and maddening buzzing.

Unable to sleep, Franklin returned to the slit in the wall and peered toward the Indian's pen. A movement to the right of the entrance gate caught his eye. It was fairly late in the evening but a full moon illuminated the night and cast long shadows across the expanse of land between the Indians and Franklin. For a moment all was quiet and still, and Franklin thought he'd just imagined it. Then, there it was again, a subtle movement, this time followed by a shadow stretching out from a patch of weeds. A silhouetted form moved stealthily, close to the ground along the fence and towards the gate. Franklin strained his eyes to try to make out who or what the shadow belonged to, but distance and the weak light were not in his favor. Finally, the creature broke from the shadows into the moonlight, and Franklin laughed out loud, until his eyes ran, and the laugh turned into a hoarse cough.

"Hush up now!" a groggy voice called from somewhere in the cell.

"People be tryin' ta sleep in here!" agreed another, which was followed by a series of coughs, farts, and a few well chosen words.

"Lazarus! Here boy!" Franklin whispered, wiping his eyes on his sleeve, then he whistled softly.

The dog stopped and turned its head in the direction of Franklin's voice, raising its head and sniffing the air for a long moment. The animal was exceedingly lean. It's ribs appeared ready to protrude through its skin. It continued until it was several yards away from the gate to the Indian enclosure, where it dipped its head and wolfed down some scraps left over from the food delivered to the Indians earlier in the evening. Finished with this, it turned and sauntered back in the direction it had come from.

Franklin thought that would be it for the night, but just as the dog drew directly in front of the opening Franklin was peering out from, it veered off its path and headed straight towards it. Lazarus, his tongue lolling out the side of his mouth, stood on his hind legs and placed his front paws against the building, bringing his face almost level with the slit.

"Hey, boy. You have no idea how good it is to see you," Franklin said soothingly. His eyes began to water once again. Letting the tears flow, he stuck his hand out of the opening. Lazarus pushed his head against Franklin's palm and held it there, and Franklin relished its softness and warmth. Then the dog pulled his head back, licked Franklin's hand, dropped back on all fours, and sauntered back into the shadows. Franklin watched him go, then exhausted, collapsed on his thread bare mat. Despite the horrors of the day, his elation over the brief encounter with Lazarus allowed him to drift off to sleep.

# CHAPTER 18

Franklin opened his eyes, startled by the sound of someone singing. The putrid aroma of the slave cell was gone, replaced by the earthiness of Degataga's dwelling back in the mountains of northern Georgia. He peered out from under several soft furs, and saw on the other side of the cooking pot, the silhouetted figure of a woman whose back was toward him. His instincts told him the woman was not Ayita, but his wife, Gwen.

"Gwen," he said, but not responding to him, the woman only continued her singing. He crawled out from under the furs and inched closer, perplexed by the strange sounding tone and dialect of Gwen's song. It sounded like an old negro spiritual.

"I got a robe, you got a robe - all God's chillun got a robe," she sang while casually running a comb through her hair. "When I get to heaven I'm goin' ta put on my robe ..." she continued, then hummed the rest of the verse, before singing again, "I got wings, you got wings - all God's chillun got wings." Her singing began to dissolve into sobs. "When I get ta heaven, I'm goin' ta put on my wings." She began to hum again, then finished the verse while softly crying.

Franklin was able to reach his wife just as she was beginning a third verse. He carefully put his hand on her back, then stopped short. His touch caused Gwen's garment to slip from her shoulders, and he fell backwards to the ground stunned by what he saw. Thick scars, and deep lacerations criss-crossed her back, swollen and oozing, deep red blood. The woman turned and gazed at Franklin through eyes black and glossy as obsidian.

His mouth frozen open in a terrified gasp, Franklin realized this woman wasn't Gwen, but Letty, the little girl from the previous afternoon. She bent down and grasped her thread-bare and blood-stained garment, then stood back upright, the fabric partially covering her nakedness, then turned and shuffled barefooted toward the door flap. Opening this, then while holding onto her clothing with one hand, she pointed to a panoramic scene that un-folded with the sweep of her free arm. Franklin saw Degataga and his family with perhaps thousands of other Indians. Dotted here and there amongst them were a number of black men and women. Together, all of them were being driven forward by soldiers on horseback cracking their whips in a line that stretched from the mountains in the south to the northern horizon. The young girl turned to Franklin imploringly as if to ask if he was taking all of this in.

"See them tears on all of those faces? See how just like me so many don't even got shoes?" she asked in a voice tender with compassion. When she spoke again, her tone was stern, "In Heaven, all God's children goin' ta have shoes, but now they goin' ta walk this trail of tears without none. You can do what you want with me and you can do what you want with them... but it don't matter... cause all God's children got wings too. When I'm gone from this place, I'm going ta Heaven, and so are they." She let the flap fall closed, turned towards him, and let her arms drop to her sides. "Where you going ta be Franklin?"

Franklin tried to speak, but unable to form a word, only croaked in ag-ony. Sobbing and shaking his head trying to clear his mind from the images he was seeing, he finally managed to talk. "How long will I have to stay here in this nightmare?" But his words seemed to echo out to nothing. Mist, or dust swirled inside the dwelling, and when it settled, the frail and torn little girl was gone. He felt the hard ground against his back through his straw mat, and realized he had woken up. Wiping tears from his eyes, Franklin looked around the cell, relieved that nobody seemed to notice he had been crying in his sleep. A bit of sunlight crept up over the eastern wall of the fort and seeped in through the locked iron gate, and Franklin shook off the horror of his dream as best he could, while he attempted to still himself for the day to come.

As uncomfortable and unpleasant as things were, one thing Franklin couldn't complain about was hunger. Since he arrived at the fort, he noticed that he and the others were fed regularly, and although the quality of the food was nothing to write home about, there was plenty of it, especially bacon, biscuits, and butter. So much, he couldn't finish what was given to him, and neither could most of the other men. He remembered the wastefulness of the soldiers on the trail and by comparison, how the Indians made use of everything in respect for what the Great Spirit provided them. And he remembered how Degataga and his people shared with him from their lack. Out of a sense of guilt, he tried to eat more.

The men were led into the yard each day for exercise which involved running, lifting, jumping jacks, and sit-ups, all under the watchful eye and ready whip of several soldiers. The women were often seen in the yard carrying items from one area to another, or washing the soldier's uniforms until the men were through with their workout, and sent back to their cell. Then, the women, in similar fashion to their male counterparts, performed calisthenics for as long as an hour. Franklin hated to imagine what for, but it was clear to him that the slaves were meant to be appear to be fit.

A soldier arrived at the gate with a large bushel basket and ordered Franklin and the others to scrape the remains of their meals into it. When it was Franklin's turn he glanced out to the yard and spotted Hawley. He quickly deposited his leftovers, then slipped quickly back into the darkness to avoid the man's notice. As the remainder of the plates were being scraped, Hawley strode over and peered in through the iron gate. He wiped his eyes and blinked. "I'll be damned if them tar babies ain't camouflaged in there," he drawled chuckling.

He turned, and Franklin thought he might be leaving, but instead Hawley turned to the guard. "Bring out them two new boys from yesterday."

Two other soldiers appeared with their rifles at ready. The guard unlocked the gate, then summoned Franklin and Nathaniel.

The two men stepped out into the blinding morning light, wiping and blinking their eyes. Hard, cold iron rings were fastened to their ankles. Franklin looked up to the blue sky and breathed in the air. Compared to the enclosure, it was almost intoxicating.

"Stop the gawkin' boy!" Hawley hollered. "And pick up that basket!"

One of the other soldiers slammed him in the back with the butt of his rifle, driving him to his knees.

The wind knocked out of him, Franklin staggered back to his feet, and gasped for breath.

"Where you goin' boy? Look at me!"

Franklin slowly turned and saw two images of the man until they slowly morphed into the one standing right in front of him.

"If yer thinkin' I forgot about you and that boy's mutt," Hawley said, gesturing toward Nathaniel, "best be thinkin' again." Hawley leaned in with his face mere inches away from Franklin's. "Take a good look at these scars," he said pointing to his face, "and remember what I did to that nigger girl who gave 'em ta me. Maybe now you understand that what goes around comes around!" Bulging veins pulsed, and scars blanched white in Hawley's otherwise tanned and grizzled face.

As Hawley's last phrase reverberated in his head, Franklin was struck with the irony that he often had said the very same thing.

"Now, pick up that basket of slop. Y'all got some work ta do."

Franklin bent down and strained to lift the weight, then pushed by Hawley and guarded by two additional soldiers, he and Nathaniel were led to the center of the yard where three more bushel baskets full of food sat.

Along with the horses, the fort had several pens for chickens, cows, goats, and pigs. Franklin assumed he and Nathaniel would be taking the scraps to feed the animals. Instead, Hawley directed them through the gated entrance of the fort, and toward the Indian compound, and the armed soldiers posted outside the gate who had been seated on bales of hay playing cards, scrambled to attention.

Franklin counted eight Indians waiting behind the enclosure fence. He hoped to see Degataga, Kanuna, or Chea Sequa, but was disappointed they weren't among them. He gazed past the men at the countless Indians, gaunt and sickly looking, their clothes, hanging from their skeletal frames, milling about in a mass of indistinguishable humanity. They reminded him of the photos he'd seen of holocaust victims. Franklin wondered if he'd be able to recognize Degataga or the others if he did see them.

As though he'd read Franklin's mind, Hawley drawled, "Put them baskets down. Ain't nothin' here for y'all ta see."

Immediately upon setting their loads down, Franklin and Nathaniel were jerked roughly by their chains and shoved back in the direction of the fort. Relieved of the weight of the food, Franklin was overwhelmed by another burden. He felt the heaviness of guilt for his selfishness and hoarding of food when he was with Degataga. He also thought about how he ogled the man's wife, Ayita, and the other women, thinking only of his own need for pleasure. It occurred to Franklin for the first time that this was how he had handled his life for as long as he could remember. Everything was always about him. Even if it should seem that he was thinking about someone else, it was a sure bet there was something self-serving about it. Franklin suddenly realized incredulously that he never found what he was looking for, regardless of how many people he burned through, or possessions he accumulated. Even Gwen, his wife of over thirty years, didn't possess whatever this thing was that he needed.

"Or did she?" he murmured as he shuffled along through the dust. "It's more likely I just didn't recognize it." He heard the whip before he felt its sting. Hawley had flicked it only once the moment Franklin spoke, and the force and pain of leather tearing into his flesh sent him face first to the ground.

"What ya say, boy? Yer itchy?" drawled Hawley from behind him. "Y'all can count on gettin' a lot more itchy. I promise ya that. But the good news is yer gonna be gettin' cleaned up for the market soon. I reckon yer gonna feel better after that. With any luck y'all will get bought and cared for. If not," Hawley laughed, "well, it's back ta the pit stinkin' and itchin' ta high heaven."

Shaking, Franklin pushed himself up from the ground. His knees almost gave out, and he felt like he was going to retch from the searing pain he felt. But he didn't intend to give Hawley that pleasure, and managed to hold it back. He also kept his mouth shut the rest of the way back to the slave pen. Once inside he grasped Nathaniel's arm. Although he feared he knew the answer, he asked anyway. "Hawley said something about a market and getting cleaned up. What's he talking about?"

Nathaniel ripped off a piece of his already frayed shirt and spit on it, then rubbed his saliva into the fabric. "Turn around. This gonna hurt some." He dabbed the shirt against Franklin's torn flesh, soaking up the blood as Franklin held his breath. "Usually once or twice a week, the traders and the buyers come by and we get cleaned up, and they has us put on some nice, clean clothes. Then the soldiers parade us over ta that platform we seen in the big tent near the front end of the yard, and we get showed ta the traders. We 'bout due for another showin' any time now."

Franklin's mind reeled at the thought of going through the humiliation of being displayed like a piece of meat for people to inspect, not to mention the possibility of being bought by a slave trader. He'd read about it, and had seen it depicted on television. Imagining someone prying open his mouth to check his teeth disgusted him. He'd suffered pain, hunger, and seen horrors perpetrated on the Indians and the little colored girl. But the idea of someone having him remove his shirt to access his musculature, and poking at his body with their fat fingers felt more degrading and embarrassing than he could imagine, especially as he hadn't taken care of himself physically for decades. The thought of having to undergo any of these things was a major affront to his ego.

"I'd rather experience everything I've been through up to now in this nightmare all over again then go through that."

"I don't know as you and I is gonna have to on account of we already belongs ta somebody. They might be usin' us to play the music, or pass out the 'freshmints. As long as our massah still be wantin' us we be alright. That is, if they shows up."

"Fresh mints?" asked Franklin. "The way we all stink, they really care that much about our breath?"

"Vittles is what I is talkin' 'bout," Nathaniel laughed. "We gets ta pass out crackers, and meat, and cheese,... and liquor too. If we lucky we can take a bite of somethin', and maybe even a swig'r two when nobody's lookin'. The way I sees it, anythin's better than bein' holed up in this stinkin' cell all day."

Franklin sighed as he considered this last piece of information.

The rest of that day passed without incident. The only other activity was when several men, including Franklin were assigned to clean up the interior yard of the fort. They used brooms to sweep, and a shovel and wheelbarrow to collect animal waste. They took that outside and around to an area not far behind the men's enclosure and dumped it into a pit. It didn't escape Franklin's notice that the soldiers showed more concern for animal waste than for the human waste piling up outside the slave enclosure.

From where he stood, Franklin could see the Indians. But he was unable to identify any of them as they were too far away. The work was as disgusting as it was backbreaking, but he figured Nathaniel was right. Anything seemed better than sitting in the stench and darkness of the slave pen. Afterwards, while sweeping the yard, Franklin drew near to the enclosure that held the women slaves and peered through the iron gate to see if he could spot the young girl that had been whipped. He saw several women sitting near the opening. Although they appeared to be looking straight at him, Franklin had the distinct impression they took no notice of him. Their eyes seemed cold and vacant, and he moved away quickly.

Like the first night, both this one and the one after brought one of the few pleasures Franklin enjoyed during his captivity. After scouring the ground for fallen scraps at the gate to the Indian's enclosure, Lazarus, like clockwork, came to the slit in the evenings. Each time he did he stretched up on his hind legs and licked Franklin's fingers, and then enjoyed the snacks Franklin scavenged from his own meals, and the scratch on the top of his head and ears Franklin gave him before he sauntered back into the brush.

As much as Franklin knew Lazarus enjoyed the momentary attention, he felt the visits were more of a kindness the dog was showing to him. A kindness he hadn't felt since being separated from Degataga and the others nearly a week ago. A kindness he now believed had been available to him in his natural life, but that he had never appreciated or acknowledged. Each time the dog's warm, wet tongue licked his fingers, it brought tears to Franklin's eyes. Somehow this small connection gave him hope. Hope that his captivity would not last, and that things would not get any worse. Hope that if and when he ever woke up from this nightmare, he'd be given the chance to show such kindness to Gwen. He wondered once more how long he'd be stuck in his nightmare. And he wondered how much longer Lazarus would be around. The dog was looking skinnier each time he visited.

# CHAPTER 19

Another couple of days passed, and each morning Franklin woke expecting to find himself safe at home in his own bed. But instead of a soft, warm mattress, he rose up from hard, cold, ground in a place more wretched than anywhere else he could remember ever having been before. The only possible exception being the food. Saturday, while gorging himself on a breakfast of corn beef hash with biscuits and gravy, word reached the cell that the slave market was being set up for that morning. No sooner had Franklin choked on the news, two soldiers with rifles came to the men's cell and selected from the mass of stinking humanity seven of the prisoners, including Franklin and Nathaniel.

The guards shackled five of the men together, then led them out to the yard for exercise. Another guard used the butt of his rifle to prod Franklin and Nathaniel over to a large barrel full of water.

"Wash up, boys," the guard ordered, and he tossed Franklin a large slab of rough soap.

Nathaniel, wasting no time, nearly dove into the barrel, submerging himself headfirst to his shoulders. He pulled his head out and shook it like a dog would after a leap into a lake, and splattering Franklin.

"Afraid ta get a little wet, are ya?" he laughed. Then he slapped Franklin good naturedly on the shoulder. "Give me that soap if ya ain't usin' it."

Franklin dipped his hand tentatively into the barrel, and pulled it quickly right back out. The water felt like ice, but he scooped it up anyway, and splashed it onto his face, gasping from the cold.

"Gotta wash all over, boy, so strip off them rags yer wearin'."

Franklin wiped the water from his eyes and saw Hawley standing nearby with his arms crossed. He looked nervously around himself and saw that Nathaniel had already removed his shirt. He also saw two colored women about twelve feet away working on something that involved another barrel and a small fire. They looked over at him and laughed as they scraped pieces of gristle and shards of bone off a slab of wood into a large iron pot suspended over the fire.

"What are they doing over there?" Franklin asked Nathaniel. One of the women was now pouring some putrid smelling grease with chopped up bits of animal entrails into the pot, while the other stirred the mixture with a wooden paddle. Franklin could hear the concoction boiling.

"Ain't you ever seen nobody makin' soap before?"

"I'm washing with the guts of animals?"

"Ol' man," growled Hawley, "from the smell of ya, I'd say it's a good thing yer washing with anythin' at all. Take all them clothes off, and get ta scrubbin'."

Franklin, slowly and self-consciously began stripping his ragged pants down his legs. But he lost his balance and fell hard on his butt to the obvious amusement of the women. "God damn it!" he grumbled, and yanked the pants off. He wanted to position himself at the barrel so that it stood between him and the women, but Nathaniel was already there, scooping water and lathering himself with the brick of soap, his black body glistening and reflecting sunlight. Besides that, he saw that there were plenty of other women slaves about as they exercised or did various tasks, so no matter where he stood, he would be in plain view of someone. "God damn it all to hell!" he cursed again as Nathaniel snickered at his discomfort.

After vigorously scrubbing the accumulation of weeks worth of grime from their bodies, Nathaniel and Franklin dried themselves with large strips of rough burlap that was folded up on small table nearby. Franklin was gingerly patting his back where Hawley's lash had sliced him when the five other men were brought over to the wash barrel. Franklin breathed a sigh of relief, because of the relative covering of the burlap and the fact that the presence of the other men would take some of the attention off of him. But his relief lasted less than a minute.

"Y'all scrub these boys down real good," Hawley ordered, and tossed a long-handled scrub brush end over end to Franklin. "Y'all be servin' food and drinks, but these boys'll be on the sellin' block, so they gotta shine."

The humiliation Franklin felt at the prospect of having to scrub other men was mind boggling. While trying to process what he was about to do, the iron gate to the slave women's enclosure was opened and several black women were led in by a pair of soldiers over to another tub less than ten yards away. The young girl, Letty, was with them, and Hawley quickly and with obvious pleasure showing on his face, took command of the situation.

With no privacy afforded them, both men and women disrobed and proceeded with the scrubbing and drying. Hooting and hollering could be heard from the soldiers all around while they enjoyed the spectacle of the men as a comical side show to their real interest.

Afterwards all of the bathers were herded inside the large tent to a separate room and behind a platform where two tables awaited, piled with clean, pressed, and folded clothing—blue slacks and white shirts for the men, and pink or white ankle-length dresses for the women.

Franklin, for the first time he could recall in his life, felt immense shame at seeing the women frantically doing their best to cover their privates with their arms and hands, while attempting to position themselves behind one another. Letty simply turned her back to the men, and Franklin caught a glimpse of the raw lacerations her frail body suffered. Wincing, he averted his eyes and remembered how just about two weeks before, he had so eagerly ogled Degataga's wife. And this while the two of them were caring for and protecting him. He wondered at the depth of depravity that had consumed him for so many years, and whether there was any way out for him. Aside from his thoughts, Franklin tried to keep his body out of the line of sight of anyone interested by cupping his hands over his manhood and turning from side to side. He couldn't wait for permission to get dressed, but before this, Hawley shattered his sensibilities with yet another humiliation.

"Rub yerselves down before puttin' on them clothes," he commanded. Pointing to a large bowl beside the clothing on each of the tables, he added, his eyes glazed with lust at the spectacle before him, "And don't forget ta put on plenty of the sweet oil."

Moments later the men and women stood in their separate areas, their skin glistening and vibrant. Hawley hooted his approval then licked his lips. Half-heartedly, he told them to dress, had them shackled again, then more sternly said, "Stay put till yer called out front." Then turning to Nathaniel, he continued, "Y'all served the food and drink before, so I'm holdin' ya responsible ta show yer friend there how it's done."

"Yes Suh. You don't have ta worry none, Suh, 'cause we won't be making no mistakes. You can count on ol' Nathaniel, Suh."

The two men were taken to the kitchen, and Nathaniel demonstrated for Franklin how he was to bring snacks and drinks for the guests. He took a tray loaded with drinks and held it out in front of himself, his elbow bent at his waist, then draped a towel over his other arm, also bent at the elbow. To Franklin, aside from the surroundings, Nathaniel looked like a mannequin one would see in a department store. Thus postured, the man walked stiffly about, stopping occasionally, and bowing his head slightly as if offering a drink to a guest, his shackles clanking like those of Ebenezer Scrooge's ghost of Christmas past as he moved. He returned and stopped just in front of Franklin, executed a perfect pirouette, then held out the tray, indicating it was his turn.

"But try a tray with nothin' on it first," he advised.

Despite grumbling at Nathaniel's lack of faith in his abilities, Franklin selected an empty tray and assumed a rough facsimile of his demonstrated posture. He cleared his throat then took a swift step forward forgetting about his shackles. His leg was stopped short less than half way through its forward motion, but the upper half of Franklin's body kept going, and he fell headlong to the floor while his tray clattered out in front of him.

"Get up, boy!" Hawley roared. He had entered the room in time to see Franklin sprawled out on the ground. The soldier reached down and grabbed the chain connecting Franklin's feet together, and dragged him backwards on his stomach lifting his feet off the ground about knee high. With his free hand, he pulled a key from his breast pocket and unfastened the lock allowing the shackles and Franklin's feet to fall back to the ground. Hawley then stomped over to Nathaniel, pushed him down onto a bench, then roughly lifted the man's feet up to his thigh and unlocked his shackles as well. "Don't either one of y'all even think of runnin' if ya know what's good for ya," he growled, then turned smartly on his heel and stomped out of the tent leaving Franklin and Nathaniel alone.

Other than when he was locked in the slave enclosure, Franklin had not been unshackled for weeks. He rubbed the raw skin around his ankles, and realized he had nearly forgotten how it felt to be able to move about freely. But any notion he might have had of taking advantage of his current shackle-free state passed quickly as armed soldiers entered the tent. They herded Franklin and Nathaniel from the staging area, through an opening in the canvas divider that separated the back from the showroom and an elevated platform. Nathaniel handed Franklin a tray of drinks and snacks, while he hoisted another.

Inside the main room, in addition to more soldiers, Franklin saw a small group of men and women slaves seated on a long wooden bench. Curiously, the men were still in their rags, and were holding musical instruments. The women, in contrast, wore the skimpy, gaudy types of outfits one might expect to see adorning a prostitute in a brothel. He noticed Lieutenant Rayford standing near the platform, busy welcoming groups of men, smoking cigars or pipes, who looked as though they had come to do business. While patrons helped themselves to the drinks on his tray, Franklin recognized Mr. Calhoun, the trader who had brought him and Nathaniel to the fort among them.

Calhoun, in turn, spotted Franklin. He summoned him over and quickly emptied the two remaining drinks, then grabbed and gobbled down a small meat pie. "Be a good boy, and fetch some more," he drawled with a chuckle. Then he drew on his cigar and blew a cloud of rancid smelling blue smoke directly into Franklin's face. "Go on now!"

Franklin excused himself stiffly while trying not to cough, and with tears spilling down his cheeks, quick-stepped his way back to the relatively smoke free air of the refreshment room.

Upon returning to the main room, replenished tray in hand, Franklin saw a man wearing a stovepipe hat and a loud black and white pinstriped suit making his way up the steps to the platform. When the gentleman had turned to face the room, Franklin nearly laughed out loud at the sight of him. His attire was complimented by wide lapels and an oversized bowtie. He wore spats over a pair of gleaming polished boots, carried a shiny black, ivory handled walking stick, and sported a thin black mustache that curled up at each end, making him look in appearance every bit like a villainous cartoon character Franklin had watched as a kid by the name of Snidely Whiplash.

"Gentlemen! Gentlemen!" The man chuckled merely and tapped his walking stick on the stage. The crowd quieted, and he continued. "May I draw your attention to the viewing platform?" he drawled with a cadence reminiscent of an old west, side show carny. "My name is Phineas J. Guthrie, and it is my pleasure to assist you today. And a lucky day for you it is indeed! Captain Wainscott, and the good men of Fort Cass have afforded me the privilege of displaying before you only the finest of working, and breeding stock you've yet to lay eyes upon. Now, am I mistaken in thinking I saw that some among you looked a little downcast just now?"

A smattering of grumbling was emitted by several of the men in the crowd, while the majority of them laughed heartily and slapped one another on the back.

"Perhaps it's because you've been on the road much too long in getting here."

Several men somberly nodded agreement.

"For the trouble of your journey," Phineas said, pointing his walking stick at them, while holding his free hand to his heart, "I am truly sorry. Or maybe you are disappointed that I've only mentioned the working and breeding potentialities of the stock on hand today. Which I add happens to be particularly extraordinary." The garish proprietor paused briefly to allow for some excited clamoring amongst the men, then continued in a booming voice. "So let me lift your spirits!" He spun his stick nimbly between his fingers, he said with a gleam in his eye, "I declare that this day will be well worth your journey. I do believe that amongst the fine assortment of prime, number one, and yes, fancy Negros and Mulattos you are about to behold, the discerning eye will note a woman, or indeed, if so inclined, a man who will suit your pleasure, if you understand my meaning."

The men's grumbling changed to knowing nods and a smattering of laughter.

"Should any of you be new to the market, the trade descriptors I mentioned a moment ago of prime, fancy, or number one, are reserved for only the highest - quality - stock." As Phineas spoke those last three words, he tapped the cane to emphasize each of them. "Now gentlemen," he continued, "you will also be pleased to know that unlike the markets one would see further south, even in the venerable city of New Orleans, where product is often displayed one at a time, I," he said with his hand on his heart, "will be displaying our entire stock all at once, so as not to waste any more of your precious time. Furthermore, I, Phineas J. Guthrie, will have them brought up to the platform together, both men and women, for your thorough inspection. And this, long before they undergo further and inevitable wear and tear on their way to markets down south. In short, you have the privilege and exceedingly good fortune of beholding this fine stock I am about to show you in only the very freshest condition possible."

Rumblings of discontent, sounding much like the rolling thunder of an approaching storm arose from the crowd, to which Phineas immediately responded raising his hands. His walking stick dangled from the thumb and forefinger of one hand, while the rest of the fingers on that hand, and those of his other were held splayed wide apart in supplication. "Do not despair gentlemen! For those of you who would like a more, shall we say, *in depth examination*, we are able to afford a private room for that very purpose. I ask only that you please be courteous to your fellows and limit your time thus occupied to no more than ten minutes." Phineas cleared his throat. "We merely require a nominal fee for such an examination, paid of course, up front."

Sounds of anticipatory excitement at the barker's revelation, quickly fell into another unanimous groan from the impatient, prospective buyers.

Phineas loudly thumped his walking stick to no avail. So he cleared his throat and elevated his voice several decibels louder than the crowd, bringing it to a high-pitched, nasally, whine. "Should any of you require longer than the requested ten minutes, you may speak to Lieutenant Rayford, who I understand may be willing to negotiate an extended time... for an additional fee!"

Dead silence and tension thick enough to gag a less seasoned showman permeated the room.

But that was precisely when Phineas, eyes sparkling like bursting fireworks, reached the peak of his pitch. "I assure you, every penny will be a penny well spent, every dime, ten times that, in a top-grade piece of property that will provide hours, nay, years of ease around the household, and pleasure to its proud owner... on demand!" Perceiving that the crowd was still anxious he bowed at the waist, and with a hand over his heart said, "Without further delay, let us begin."

Hawley signaled the seated male slaves, who abruptly stood and began to play their instruments and sing. He then called for the group of slaves still sequestered in the room behind the stage to be led into the main area and up onto the rear edge of the viewing platform. The men, manacled to one another at the ankles, were lined up from the shortest to the tallest, and instructed to flex their muscles in a display of strength. The women, who were unshackled, assumed more delicate positions that accentuated their femininity. They were occasionally instructed to bow, pirouette, and stretch their arms out in a variety of sensual poses. The men in the crowd quickly lost interest in snacks and drinks, and clamored up close to the edge of the platform. As they jockeyed for position, Franklin and Nathaniel were left alone to observe the spectacle.

Prospective buyers were invited up onto the platform for closer inspection which included having a slave remove his or her shirt or blouse and sometimes even pants or dress while the buyer pushed and prodded at the slave's body. Each of the slaves were commanded at some point to open their mouths for a close inspection of their teeth and gums.

Franklin noticed that the male slaves were mostly sullen during the physical inspection and looked neither right not left, but straight ahead like soldiers standing at attention. And he was stunned when to the contrary, more than a few of the women seemed to encourage the buyers by inching their own skirts up and asking them outright if they'd like a closer look.

Letty, Franklin noticed, although standing amongst the other women, had a look on her face that suggested she was mentally in a place and time somewhere other than on the platform. When a man would run the rough palm of his hand over the lacerations on her back, she stood perfectly still, never uttered a word, and maintained a far away gaze.

Franklin could see that Mr. Calhoun was very interested in Letty. He came back to her over and over again after brief forays with the other women, eyeing her up and down with a lascivious grin on his grizzled face.

"This husky male here," Phineas sang out. He singled out a slave from the line-up and walked him forward before the throng of spectators and prospective buyers, "This is a fine specimen of primal strength." He pointed with his walking stick at the mans rippling musculature. "Why," he gasped, "this one is as strong as he looks, and can pull a cart load of cotton, or lumber, all day by himself."

Some of the prospective buyers tugged at their beards, their eyes rolled upwards in their sockets as they considered such a purchase. Others called on Phineas to move on with the show.

Redirecting his cane toward another man, the slave hawker continued, "I have it on good authority that this ol' boy is especially talented at fixing all things mechanical, and can shoe a horse before you can whistle Dixie." Phineas left the first man for closer inspection by a few of the men in the crowd, and summoned the next slave forward. "As you can see by the cuts and scars on his knuckles, he is no stranger to fighting, so as a bonus you can use him to win some hard cash in your local fisticuffs matches."

While some of the crowd frantically rechecked their wallets for available funds, Phineas turned his attention back to the women on stage. "That woman with skin the color of shining coal, can make biscuits and gravy, and churn butter all day." Directing the men's attention to another woman, he crooned, "This one over here not only bears the distinction of being a number one, she has the particular talent for providing a drink even before she is asked for one, and never spills a drop. After all, a gentleman should never have to fret over the discomfort of a wet hand."

Franklin cringed as a brief visualization ran through his mind of Gwen dutifully bringing him a beer, only to be coldly rejected by him for not being quick enough about it, or the can dry enough for his liking. A southern drawl coming from the stage interrupted his thoughts.

"Gentlemen, I, Phineas J. Guthrie, give you my *personal* guarantee that any of these fine specimens on display today will not only serve you to your complete satisfaction, they will mind their manners. And if all of this is not enough, I've saved the best of the lot for last. This pretty little lady," the slave seller said as he smiled broadly and swept his arm in a grand arc, his palm open, and fingers extended, toward Letty, "as you can see, has many years of service left in her. Some of you have heard she recently received a beating. I pray that does not dissuade any of you from recognizing the value of such a package. First, because I can assure you, she is receiving the finest of treatment here at Fort Cass, and should heal nicely. But secondly, should a slight scar remain, mind you, only on her backside, so to spare the exquisitely beautiful features of that young face of hers," he chuckled, "it should be a relief to you to know that at such a tender age, she has already learned the importance of respect and obedience. Perhaps even more importantly to some among you, I have it on impeccable authority," he said while winking knowingly at Hawley, "that she is easily trainable in the art of pleasing a man."

While the buyers laughed, hooted, and clapped each other on the back, Mr. Calhoun licked his lips and tossed another drink down his throat. The room had filled with clouds of blue pipe and cigar smoke, thick enough to cause Franklin's eyes to tear. He wiped them with his sleeve, then noticed a dark scowl on Hawley's face, who while fingering a revolver he wore on his hip, seemed to be staring directly at Phineas.

"My friends," Phineas continued. "Each and every one of these fine specimens can be used for labor and breeding, as well as providing for your more personal comforts. Have another drink and take as close a look as you like. As I said earlier, you may try the merchandise at an extremely generous and nominal fee. But you must seize this opportunity quickly as regrettably, I must soon take your leave for the New Orleans market. Get them now, because they will be snatched right up once they reach that great gulf city. I open the floor for your bids."

# CHAPTER 20

A torrent of offers, haggling, laughing, and bawdy language followed the trader's words. The rag-tag group of slave musicians struck up the music with a twang of banjo, fiddle, and mouth harp, the rhythmic slap and scrape of a corrugated metal wash board, and deep thump of an over-turned wooden barrel.

Franklin and Nathaniel circulated with more refreshments amongst the boisterous crowd. Every so often one of the buyers approached Lieutenant Rayford with cash in hand, then left the tent with a slave woman in tow, then returned at the specified ten minute time allotted them. With the man disheveled and sweating profusely, and the woman primping her hair as she returned to the line-up, there was no mystery to what they'd been up to.

When a prospective buyer failed to return on time, Phineas J. Guthrie, watching his merchandise like a hawk, simply signaled a couple of soldiers with his walking stick. They, in turn would storm past the partition and drag the unlucky brute, pants down around his knees, to the front entrance of the display tent, to the loud guffaws of their comrades. There, they would kick the offender soundly in his naked behind, sending him to the dusty ground outside.

Franklin was surprised the rough treatment didn't stop the men from try-ing to get more than what they paid for. Instead they cheered and dared one an-other on. It seemed the men enjoyed the show even more so for the distraction. "Animals," he murmured to himself, then felt an immediate twang of guilt as the memory of a time he spent in Mexico many years ago surfaced in his mind.

A couple of years into their marriage, Franklin had told Gwen he was going on a fishing trip with his best friend and would be gone for the weekend. Truth was he and his buddy skipped across the border for a little fun at a Mexican Brothel he'd heard rumors about. "What happens in Mexico, stays in Mexico," Franklin had said with a laugh to his friend on their way back home. Until now he hadn't thought much of it. *What Gwen didn't know couldn't hurt her, he convinced himself. Nothing wrong with a man having a little harmless fun.* Franklin shook his head with disgust at himself and made an oath that if given the chance, he'd do what he could to make things right with Gwen.

"That is entirely unacceptable!" A loud, voice broke through the frenet-ic activity in the tent as well as Franklin's thoughts, bringing his awareness back to the present. The music and raucous activity in the tent came to an immediate stop, replaced by a tension that was nearing a full boil.

Hawley glared back and forth from Lieutenant Rayford to Mr. Calhoun. Letty, wide-eyed and trembling, stood behind Calhoun, grasping his coat tails. And Calhoun, puffing furiously on a fat cigar, held cash in an out-stretched, sweaty fist.

Breaking the tension, Mr. Calhoun cleared his throat and spit in the dirt at his feet. "Now, Hawley," he slurred, "y'all heard the man as good as me. Thish here's a fair exchange for a mere ten minutes. And, if it'll make ya feel any better, I promish I won't take her away from ya againsht her will."

Hawley, his eyes now fixed on Mr. Calhoun, didn't blink.

Unperturbed by Hawley's stare, Mr. Calhoun continued, "Now if on the other hand she taaksh a liking to me..."

"Now you've gone too far, Calhoun!" Hawley roared. "She's not going nowhere with the likes of you!"

By this time the other men in the tent, including the soldiers, lost inter-est in the slaves and formed a circle around the two men. Their excitement at the possibility of a fight was palpable.

"Gentlemen, Gentlemen!" cried Phineas, rapping his stick loudly on the stage. "We are businessmen here, are we not? Perhaps you boys," he said to Calhoun and Hawley, "could settle your differences after the show?"

Calhoun hiccuped then belched. "Perhapsh" he slurred, wobbling slightly while turning to face the slave seller, "you'd like ta be the main attracshion! Why don't you come down off that platform, and you and me can settle things firsht?"

Lieutenant Rayford appeared perturbed with Hawley, but even more so with Mr. Calhoun. The man had been loud, sweaty, obnoxious, and self-righteous from the moment he entered the tent, and he often elbowed other men out of his way as he reached for a drink, or to grasp clumsily at one of the women. It was evident to Franklin that Mr. Calhoun was generally disliked by everyone there, including the Lieutenant who stepped back from the spittle that was spraying from the man's drunken mouth.

"Give me another one, boy!" Calhoun demanded Franklin. He tipped the glass he already had to his lips, spilling half the contents onto his coat and shirt, and seemed he either did not notice, or care. The drunk swung his head back toward Hawley, and said with a lilt, "Perhapsh you would like to take care of thish outshide?"

"Yer not fit for fisticuffs," Hawley replied angrily, "specially not with the likes of me. And yer not fit ta have anything ta do with that woman neither!"

"She's no woman," snickered Calhoun. "She's a child with a lot of good years still in her." He rubbed his chin as if deep in thought, then laughed, "You got that wrong about me and her, *Hogly*, and I can promish you this, I can sure as hell hit a snake with a bullet anytime I sees one." He slugged down the rest of the drink he'd snatched from Franklin's tray, then tossed the glass, shattering it on the hard packed ground next to the last one he'd let fall.

Hawley hooted, raised his eyebrows at Calhoun's comment, and fingered his revolver.

"Thash right. I'm not talking fisticuffs," Calhoun's words tumbled out thickly. "I'm talking firearms!"

"Y'all heard 'im. He's the one askin' for a fight, pure and simple!" growled Hawley. He took a step back, spread his arms out wide, then turned slowly in a circle, displaying the gun he wore on his hip to the excited spectators.

"I might be a bit rotund. You probably think I'm out of shape," Calhoun said, playing to the crowd, while slapping his belly with both hands. Then he wheeled around, nearly falling over in the process to face Hawley again. After steadying himself, his words tumbled out thickly. "But you ain't nothing but a runt in a uniform ta me! I see through those fancy blues and shiny boots ya got on. Nothing but a puny boy underneath all that." Calhoun pulled the front of his coat over revealing that he too carried a gun. "Why don't we jush step outshide and get us some fresh air? You're stinkin' this place up."

"You're drunk! It wouldn't be a fair fight," said Hawley, who for all of his bravado, began to look a little skittish to Franklin.

"I might see two of ya, but I can sure as hell shoot two of you as easy as one," Calhoun countered. "Or maybe you're jush cowering out on me." Calhoun flared his coat out with one hand, and not to be outdone by Hawley, spun in a clumsy pirouette to the amusement of the crowd.

The men roared with delight, and appeared to be near frothing at the mouth for blood.

Hawley raised his hands open fingered in the air, turned, and stomped out of the tent. To Phineas' chagrin, only a couple of buyers scuttled quickly over to settle their deals with him. The rest of the prospective buyers and soldiers alike followed Hawley out of the tent. They formed a large oval around him in the yard and began to cheer him on.

Franklin, Nathaniel, and the other slaves watched from behind the tent flap, lined up in such a way as to look over one another's shoulder. Calhoun wobbled across the sun hardened yard and elbowed his way through the circled crowd, stopping after he'd reached the traditional twenty paces away from his rival.

Rayford was among the spectators, and spoke out with authority to the prospective duelers, "If you're going through with this, turn your backs to each other."

The two men obeyed the Second Lieutenant's directive, Calhoun executing another drunken pirouette, while Hawley turned slowly, the look on his face suggesting he'd really rather not be where he was at the moment.

"Now," said Rayford, "listen carefully. I'm going to count down from seven to one. You'll have that time to reconsider. If you remain after the count with your backs to one another and pistols raised, the next thing you'll hear me say will be the word turn! On that word, and that word only, you each may turn and fire a single shot. Should both of you still be alive after firing, you will shake hands, part as gentlemen, and go your way. Anyone, and that includes all of you watching this, who attempts fisticuffs, or any other kind of altercation afterwards, will be locked up. Agreed?"

"Let's get thish over with," slurred Calhoun.

Franklin thought Hawley looked like a boy who got caught with his hand in the cookie jar, and now wanted nothing more than a way out of his predicament. But he suspected the man's ego wouldn't allow for that. After a long moment of hesitation, the soldier took a deep breath, then grumbled, "Agreed."

The Lieutenant approached each man and ordered them to empty the chamber of their weapon of all but one bullet into his gloved hand. During this procedure, the onlookers scooted away from being directly behind either of the two men to avoid being in the line of fire should a bullet go astray, and began wagering amongst themselves on the outcome.

"On my count then," Rayford continued. "Seven... six..."

The crowd hushed, clenching cigars in their teeth, and clutching money in their hands, while Franklin, Nathaniel and the other slaves, watched from the tent. Any thought he or the others may have had of trying to escape was quashed by the presence of armed guards at each exit point. Franklin noticed that the women slaves had already beat a path back to the safety of their cell.

"Five... four..."

Hawley stood ramrod straight, the pupils of his eyes narrowed to pinpoints. His hand, finger twitching, was hovering just inches from the gun on his hip. Calhoun swayed drunkenly in all directions.

"Three... two... one..."

Calhoun burped, then hiccuped.

"Turn!" Lieutenant Rayford uttered the final word.

With blurring speed, Hawley spun on his heel. His pistol was drawn and he fired at Calhoun. At the same time, in a slow motion swoon similar to what Franklin thought one might see in one of those nickel, side-show melodramas, Calhoun wobbled, hiccuped again and fell sideways, cork-screwing his legs on the way down. He hit the ground face first with an audible "umpf!" having never fired his pistol.

For a brief moment, everyone stood in hushed silence, and as smoke trailed from the barrel of Hawley's pistol, it appeared the soldier had found his mark. Hawley holstered his gun, and as if this was the signal the crowd was waiting for, hands began to exchange money. Some men grumbled, while others whooped in jubilation. The surviving gunman, his face void of emotion, turned to walk away, when a loud belch erupted from his victim's direction stopping him in his tracks.

Calhoun moaned, then with great effort, rolled over on his back, the only blood visible being a tiny dribble from his nose, presumably the result of him smacking it on the ground. Calhoun hiccuped again, pushed him-self up to a sitting position, and spat a mixture of phlegm and blood in the dirt that stirred up a tiny wisp of dust. Dull-eyed and blinking, he looked around himself, then began patting incredulously all over his chest and ro-tund stomach. "Well, I for damn sure ain't dead!" Then he chuckled, "If I'm not mishtaken, I ain't even took a bullet. How 'bout you Hawley? You shtill among the livin'?"

"How could I miss?" Hawley's exclaimed, his face an expression of frus-tration and bewilderment. "How the hell are ya still talkin' ta me? I had me a bead on your heart, ya bastard!"

Still sitting in the dirt, Calhoun only burped. As far as Franklin could sur-mise, the drunk was still too dizzy and rubber legged to stand. It seemed that Hawley's shot must have sailed harmlessly past Calhoun's slumping form.

The crowd of men were already arguing with one another over their bets and the fairness of shooting it out with a drunk, when a chorus of screams from the direction of the women's cell cut through the heated clamor.

"Somebody help!" someone hollered from the women's cell.

"She bleedin' to death!" another female voice cried.

Women stood at the bars of the cell, rattling it wildly.

Lieutenant Rayford signaled to the guard that stood posted outside the enclosure to check things out. Then he pointed to another soldier, directing him to join the first. The guard took the key ring from his belt and rattled a key into the rusty lock, then pulled the gate wide open with a loud squeak. While the two soldiers entered the darkness, several women burst out past them bawling and moaning, their hands on their heads or crossed over their hearts.

Within seconds both men re-emerged from the cell, one of them holding in his arms the limp body of a woman. Her arms and legs swung lifelessly as she was carried toward the Lieutenant. It was Letty.

The girl's dirty white, thread bare garment was turning crimson with her blood. Other than a low groan from Hawley, the only sound was the sobbing of the slave women, the occasional braying of an unseen mule, and the scrape and hollow thud of the guard's boots as he trudged closer to the group of men, and stopped in front of Lieutenant Rayford.

The Lieutenant bent close to the lifeless body, and sighed deeply while straightening up. "Well, gentlemen, as bad as it looks, it would appear you two might not have anything left to fight over."

"She ain't no good ta me in this condition," Calhoun said, staring at the ground and shaking his head. Then he looked up at the Lieutenant, seeming to brighten. "That is unless you would conshider lowering the price for damaged goods. Perhaps you can cut me a little deal on thish-un."

"Son of a bitch!" Hawley hollered. Unable to contain his rage, he lunged at Calhoun.

Several soldiers upon the lieutenant's orders, promptly stepped forward, and held the crazed man back. As he tried in vain to fight his way free, they dragged him away cursing and making oaths of retribution.

"Keep him away until he cools down," Lieutenant Rayford ordered. "Lock him up if you have to." Then he turned toward a soldier standing nearby and pointed at Calhoun without so much as looking at the man, "Get rid of this one here. If he can't sit on his horse, put him in a wagon, and dump him in town." Rayford then addressed a second soldier, while nodding toward the bleeding girl. "Take her to doc! Maybe he can fix this one. I've seen him take care of worse."

"What about the rest of us?" questioned a bystander. "Some of us still got bids up fer one of them coloreds." Murmurs coming from the crowd rose to a low rumble.

"Your bids are logged!" Rayford snapped. "None of the slaves are going anywhere. Any of you with bids in play can show up to the tent tomorrow to settle your deals. If you don't, your bid will be forfeited, and Captain Wainscott will thank you for your kind contribution to the upkeep of Fort Cass. Now everybody clear out... show's over!"

As the grumbling crowd dispersed, Franklin snatched some meat and cheese off the tray Nathaniel had set to the side during the failed duel. He went back to the changing room and hurriedly traded the serving clothes for his rags, then rolled the morsels inside his oversized shirt. He stuffed the lump into his pants just before one of the soldiers ordered the slaves back to their cells. As soon as the guard slammed the gate closed and stationed himself at his post, Franklin tore the bottom of his shirt off, and wrapped the food in it. Then by scraping and clawing with his nails in the dirt under his mat, he dug a shallow hole, stashed the food into it, and covered it back up, then laid back exhausted from the day.

# CHAPTER 21

The next few weeks passed relatively quietly. It seemed that the accidental shooting of the girl had put a damper on the entire workings of the fort. The otherwise rambunctious soldiers went about their business in an uncharacteristically subdued manner. Slaves continued to be brought into the yard daily for exercise and various cleaning duties, but without the usual excessive harassment. Even Hawley kept to himself much of the time or stayed out of sight all together.

Then, one afternoon, Franklin saw Letty being escorted to the women's slave cell. She walked stiffly, her countenance appearing dark and withdrawn. Franklin was surprised that she could walk at all, let alone be alive. He was relieved for this period of relative peace. Especially for the reprieve from Hawley's taunting. However, he was troubled by the news he'd heard of the Indians. Apparently, they weren't faring well.

Word was that the sicknesses which had been spreading through the Indian encampment had exploded into epidemic proportions. Franklin heard rumors of whooping cough, dysentery, cholera, measles, and smallpox. All of these would be problematic in his own time, but here, in this time, these diseases were deadly on a mass scale. The Indians were contained in extremely tight quarters, and because their immune systems were incapable of fighting these illnesses, they spread like wildfire. The doctors who had been brought in were of little help, and as days turned into weeks, multiple deaths were reported on a daily basis.

The weeks quickly turned into a month, then two. The last days of summer passed, and the already cool temperatures dropped rapidly. Franklin was wondering one morning how his Indian friends were managing, or if they were even still alive, when Hawley showed up unexpectedly at the cell gate, and ordered him and Nathaniel into the yard for what he called "shit duty".

The two men were handed shovels and assigned a wooden cart, then directed by Hawley with the butt of his rifle and the crack of his whip to push and pull the heavy cart out of the fort. Any question Franklin had about where they were going, or what Hawley meant by shit duty was answered soon enough when the soldier ordered the two men to stop at a large mound of human waste that was piled up outside of the women's cell.

Hawley rolled and lit a cigarette, then walked away a good twenty paces. Over his shoulder he called back to Franklin and Nathaniel, "Shovel that shit into the wagon, and be quick about it. You got the men's pile after this."

The sight and smell of the excrement nauseated Franklin. Thick clots of flies blackened the surrounding area forming a dark, frenzied, buzzing curtain. Franklin's eyes watered as he drew close swatting aimlessly at the flies. The sound of Nathaniel gaging told him his friend was faring no better.

Hawley cursed at the two men, and spit in the dirt. He looked mad as hell, or maybe crazed. Franklin assumed the man was still brooding over his failed duel with Calhoun, and accidental shooting of Letty. Hawley assailed Franklin and Nathaniel with insults while rolling and smoking a succession of cigarettes, at times moving in closer to crack his whip on each of their backs as they bent to their work. The lashing shredded their clothing and tore their flesh, sending them repeatedly to their knees. No sooner did blood begin to flow, when the wounds were immediately blackened by hoards of flies. Hawley was clearly favoring Franklin as the main target of his rage, whipping him twice for every lash that fell upon Nathaniel.

"Y'all think 'cause a little time has passed," railed Hawley, "that it's over 'tween you and me, boy? Well, think again. Ya made one big mistake gettin' in my business with that mutt back on the trail." Hawley punctuated these words by snapping his whip, ripping Franklin's shirt right down the middle of his back, opening a fresh blood-oozing gash, and dropping his target to his knees once more where he nearly passed out from the pain.

Franklin's head spun in dizzying circles. He wondered how much more his body could take. Nathaniel offered him his hand, and Franklin grasped it, then let his new friend pull him back to his feet with a grunt. He and Nathaniel bent forward at the waist, and together they pulled the cart, wheels creaking. A hoard of flies followed them like a black cloud, around to the other side of the fort where the two of them stopped just outside of the men's holding cell. There, a pile of excrement toppled over from the sheer weight of it, sending the flies wheeling in a black tornado.

The buzz of unseen Cicadas rose and fell in competition with the incessant droning of the flies surrounding the men's heads. The two men shoveled, and the cart quickly overflowed with human waste, and after Franklin and Nathaniel finished slopping the mess from the men's pile into it, the bottom of the cart bowed under the strain. Hawley ordered them to take the cart over to what Franklin had thought was a pond where they were to dump it. The men grunted and spit with exertion, but were unable to budge the cart in spite of Hawley's threatened and intermittent lashings.

"Ah kin smell them boys all the way over here!" laughed a guard seated with his back against a tree. He was picking his teeth with a long blade of dry grass, his rifle across his knees, and clearly enjoying the show.

Hawley flicked the whip in the man's direction, snapping a small branch hanging low over the soldier's head, causing a shower of brown and yellow leaves to rain down on him. Veins bulging in his neck, Hawley screamed. "Get off your ass, and bring Horace over here!"

"Sir!" the startled soldier stammered. He jumped to his feet and tried to salute at the same time, causing his rifle to drop with a clatter to the ground. Eyes wide, the soldier lunged for the weapon, then stood at attention trembling.

"Don't just stand there, numbskull! Get going before I change my mind and have you help them niggers pull that cart!" As the soldier took off at a run back to the fort, Hawley turned back toward Franklin and Nathaniel. "Y'all boys are lucky this time, but once Horace gets here the three of ya are gonna hurt plenty just moving that thing," he said, pointing at the cart sagging with its load.

Moments later, the huge, burley, ox of a man, Franklin had only seen in the darkness of the slave enclosure, came running from the fort with the soldier Hawley sent to get him on his heels.

"Y'all two pull," he told Franklin and Nathaniel. "That-a-ways I can tell if yer workin' or not." Franklin and Nathaniel, the two of them combined not half the size of the new man, grasped the front end of the cart, dug their heels into the ground, and strained backwards, while Horace bent forward and leaned into the load from behind.

The cart didn't budge, and Franklin thought he'd throw his back out for sure. But after another couple of tries, the cart's wheels creaked and began to roll forward. The three men maneuvered the rickety container along the rutted dirt road that ran alongside the Indian enclosure. Several hundred yards later, drenched in sweat and swarmed by the maddening flies, Hawley ordered them to stop alongside the same pit Franklin and Nathaniel had taken the animal waste to before. The pit, which was in actuality a medium sized pond, was about eighty feet in circumference and full of foul smelling, inky-black water. Dozens of buzzards stood around the edge of it and many more sat in overhanging tree branches, all of them eyeing the humans and their load. Several of them squawked and flew off, landing again only a few yards away. The harsh buzz of the Cicadas was replaced by the soft, sporadic chirping and croaking of frogs, but the mass of flies hadn't diminished, rather, it increased exponentially, joined by countless more flies buzzing about the buzzards and the dark bog. A ghastly reek emanated from the pit that was a sour, rank mingling of waste and something else even more foul Franklin couldn't identify.

"Stop yer gawkin and whinin', and dump that load-o-shit so we can get out of here!" Hawley demanded. "Ya act like y'all ain't seen buzzards before!" Hawley, a kerchief wrapped around his nose and mouth, cracked his whip to move things along. It appeared to Franklin, Hawley didn't like being at this place anymore than he did. In fact, he seemed unusually uncomfortable.

"Crack!" The whip found its target on Horace's back sending a spray crimson blood arcing into the air. Horace bent over trying to catch his breath, and another vicious lash loosed a chunk of the man's flesh. The sting drove the big man to his knees. "Move that shit boy!" hollered Hawley. "Get it done!"

For a brief moment, the frogs stopped croaking, and Horace grunted as he slowly righted himself, a pained expression on his face. Nathaniel looked the other way and Franklin vomited. Horace leaned over and grasped the back end of the cart, nodded to Franklin and Nathaniel, and began to push it forwards. Through some back and forth maneuvering, he managed to direct the cart toward the pit, while Franklin and Nathaniel strained with all they had to help him.

The sagging wood of the cart groaned and the wheels creaked as it slowly inched a dozen or so feet toward the the reeking pit, then gained momentum. As he struggled to keep pace, Franklin's foot caught against a root causing him to stumble backwards. Nathaniel quickly jumped out of the way of the careening cart which sent him reeling out of control, while Franklin flailed his arms wildly in the air, in an effort to regain his balance.

Hawley snorted and laughed out loud as the cart quickly accelerated, bearing down on Franklin.

Horace let go of his end, and with surprising speed ran around to the front of the cart. The big man lunged and barreled into Franklin, knocking him out of the carts path to the ground with Nathaniel. The two men lay stunned in a tumbled mass and helplessly watched as the cart crashed with a sickening thud into Horace's outstretched body. The impact catapulted him into the air like a rag doll, and he landed on his back with a loud plop in the fly encrusted pit. Horace immediately began to struggle to pull himself up from the sucking action of the muck. But the momentum of the cart had carried it off the embankment, and after a brief flight, it smashed directly into Horace's chest, submerging him with all of its weight beneath the surface of the pit below. Hordes of flies erupted from their rotten feast and swarmed aimlessly all around before settling back on the putrid sludge that had engulfed both the cart and the giant man.

Hawley roared with laughter, periodically choking while wiping his eyes with his sleeve.

Franklin and Nathaniel both called out to Horace but to no avail as he was literally buried by the heavy cart in the pit of waste. Franklin scrambled to his feet, and frantically searched the murky sludge for any sign of the man. He stepped towards the pit and tentatively lowered a foot down into the muck, when a hand suddenly grabbed his arm and yanked him back to solid ground.

"Oh my," Nathaniel whimpered, his free hand over his mouth. "Look at that." He pointed to what could only be human remains partially submerged in the muck. Franklin stared transfixed at the macabre sight, and a feeling of horror arose within him as more slime stained bone fragments broke the surface near the imprint left in the pit by the cart.

"Crack!" Hawley's whip lashed out once again, startling Franklin from his stupor. "Well, damn! Loss of a worker is bad enough, but loss of a cart is unforgivable! Y'all two better believe yer gonna pay for this with yer own black hides! Pick yer sorry asses up and get back ta the cell! I'll deal with ya proper after I report to the Lieutenant how y'all stepped aside and let yer own kind die!"

Hawley freely flicked his whip, allowing it to rip and tear across the men's backs, alternating from one to the other as they stumbled and fell along the path back to the fort. The whip sliced another strip of flesh off Franklin's back, and he fell face first in the dirt. Rolling over on his side, his face contorted with pain, he found himself looking directly at the Indian enclosure. A black circle appeared and began to thicken around the periphery of his vision and the earth he had fallen to began to tilt. Despite this and the screaming pain that engulfed him Franklin saw a cloud of dust rising up near the enclosure. He shook his head for clarity and followed the cloud to the ground. Although he heard nothing, he saw hundreds of pairs of feet lurching and dragging and staggering in the dirt. The feet were connected to bodies that appeared at first as blurs of brown colored flesh and torn furs. Without seeing them clearly, Franklin knew who these bodies belonged to. The Indians, his friends among them, were being herded out of the enclosure and along the outside fence toward the forest.

Franklin calmed his breathing and unclenched his fists. One Indian in particular caught his eye. Degataga. Then beside him, Ayita. Kanuna came into focus walking behind them, and Chea Sequa, holding Tsula's hand, was in front of them. Franklin's initial excitement quickly faded as he saw how

decrepit they each looked. Their physiques and vitality seemed to have de-
teriorated along with the condition of their clothing. Instead of the strong,
proud individuals they were when he first encountered them, they were
gaunt, their faces drawn. They dragged their feet, their shoulders stooped.

Even as he wondered about what was happening to the Indians who
had cared for and befriended him, another crack of the whip brought Franklin back to his own predicament. Scrambling to his feet, Franklin silently
wished them well.

"Crack!" Hawley let the whip flay across Franklin's shoulders, renewing
his victim's awareness of the searing pain racking his body. "Stay on yer
feet nigger! And stop worrying about them Indians. Probly die on the trail,
... and good riddance to 'em. You, on the other hand, got troubles enough
of yer own!" Hawley snapped the whip again. This time, although he connected with the ground, the tip flicked the dirt up hard enough that shards
of earth spattered into Franklin's face and eyes. "Y'all may be done with yer
work for the day, but my business with yer sorry ass ain't done that's for
damn sure."

Franklin had not given up the notion that he could wake up and escape
this nightmare. But as he and Nathaniel faltered on their way back to the
relative safety of their cell, he realized more fully now than ever how bad
things could get until then. He also understood that then could be a very
long ways off. In the meantime, even if this was only a bad dream, the horror and the pain of it felt alarmingly and painfully real.

Night fell quickly, and like a dark and soothing ointment, brought
some much needed relief from the days earlier horror. Franklin, stooped
with pain, walked stiffly to the slit and waited on Lazarus. Sure enough, like
every other night, the hound came loping out from the shadows and up to
the slit for some time with his friend. Franklin offered the treats he'd con-
fiscated from the slave market, and Lazarus chomped and swallowed them
ravenously, then offered his muzzle up for Franklin's touch.

Suddenly the quiet of the moment was broken by the loud creak of the
forts front gate, and Lazarus dropped and crouched. He emitted a deep but
barely audible growl. The silhouette of a single cart emerged from the darkness of the forts interior, followed by two men pushing it and several armed

men following behind. The cart handle had a lantern hanging off the front end illuminating the way ahead. Franklin was able to make out Hawley's face in the glow of the lamp. He appeared to be directing the men with the cart. Lazarus' growl began to rise, but Franklin soothed him quiet, and the two watched the group exit the fort, then move down the path to the gate of the Indian enclosure. Franklin had noticed on several other evenings a large fire that would suddenly erupt in the enclosure and was curious about its significance. He wondered if this procession of men had anything to do with it.

The guards at the gate of the enclosure swung it open, and the group of men entered, then fanned out with their rifles at the ready into the encampment. After several minutes they disappeared from view except for the glow of the lantern that followed the procession deeper into the interior, casting their ghoulish shadows about. Finally, the movement stopped.

A new light appeared, and quickly grew into a huge bonfire. Every few seconds it popped and erupted in a fountain of swirling sparks. The smoke from the flames wafted in the direction of the fort, and Franklin detected the unmistakable scent of meat being grilled. But the odor was peculiar, and Franklin reasoned that the soldiers were ridding the Indian's camp of rancid meat. After nearly two hours, the fire began to die, and finally disappeared altogether. On the other occasions when Franklin had observed this activity, he hadn't waited to see what would happen next, but this night he felt compelled.

Shortly, the lantern, the cart, and the men reappeared back at the front gate of the enclosure. Upon exiting, they turned down the path toward the pit Franklin worked at earlier that day, and where Horace met his end. He noticed that there appeared to be a mound covered by a tarp in the cart, and there was smoke or steam rising from it. Franklin and Lazarus watched in silence as the cart trundled into the shadows.

After the small and odd procession disappeared from view, Lazarus whined softly, and jumped up for another ear scratching, which Franklin obliged before the dog dropped back to all fours, then took several tentative steps in the direction the cart had headed.

"Be careful out there," Franklin whispered. Lazarus's tongue lolled out of his mouth, then he loped away and veered into the thick woods behind the fort. Franklin settled uncomfortably onto his flattened straw mat. He thought about Horace, and the death the man met while saving him and Nathaniel. Finally, exhausted from the work, the pain, and a feeling of immense sorrow, he succumbed to a fitful sleep. What Franklin hoped would be a brief refuge of quiet solitude, instead took a terrifying turn.

# CHAPTER 22

No sooner had Franklin dropped off to sleep, he found himself standing in his kitchen back at home where he took in with a tremendous sigh of relief, the sight of his wife Gwen. Her back to him, Gwen was tending to something in the sink. Franklin instinctively knew this couldn't be real. His place at home was typically seated in his easy chair in front of the big screen, beer in hand. Based on his recent side-dreams, he worried that like them, the initial euphoria of finding himself at home again, and so close to his wife, would soon change to some kind of disappointment, if not downright terror.

Without turning around, Gwen reached her hand behind her back. In it, she held a dripping wet can of beer. Franklin's habitually engrained reaction was anger that the can was not dry. He never could understand how she could be so careless. But he quickly caught himself and dismissed the resentment. Without his anger, Franklin wasn't sure what to do. This for him was new territory. He didn't want the beer, but Gwen seemed to want him to take it. Finally, grateful just to be near her again, Franklin meekly reached his hand out for the can. But like Lucy, who at the last minute pulls the football away from Charlie Brown's kicking foot, instead of letting Franklin take the can, Gwen opened her hand at the last moment and let it drop to the floor. The can hit with a bang rupturing the tab, and spewed white foam and amber liquid all over the floor, the cupboards, and Gwen.

Franklin jumped back, but, rivulets of beer dripping from her hair, Gwen had already produced another can of beer and held it behind her back as before—only this one she shook. Before Franklin could react, she dropped it too. The suds erupted from the can covering both of them. Franklin tried to say something, but he couldn't form words or make any sounds. Gwen continued dropping cans of beer, now using both of her hands, freakishly and frenetically, alternating one after the other, and allowing them to explode and splatter their contents in all directions.

Franklin's discomfort mounted as he watched his wife's spastic motions. As the cans hit the floor, some of them bounced and became like projectiles knocking into cupboards, breaking glasses that sat on the counter, and punching holes in the surrounding walls. One of the cans bounced hard into the refrigerator door which flew open, exposing Franklin's stash of beer inside. The cans teetered, then fell, first one, then another, then several at a time. Beer with a thick head of foam began to fill the room. Soon, it was sloshing around both Franklin's and Gwen's ankles, and steadily rising.

Suddenly, Franklin noticed a rust color forming in the golden suds swirling around Gwen's knees. He wondered if Gwen had gotten cut by a shard of metal, or some broken glass, and was bleeding, and at that moment Gwen finally stopped dropping cans and slowly turned around to face him.

The beer began draining away from the room, becoming shallower, and exposing the floor. At first relieved, Franklin groaned with a mixture of disappointment, shock, and confusion when he saw that the woman wasn't Gwen after all, but the young colored girl, Letty. Beer dripped from her chin, and soaked her hair that hung in a tangled mass over her shoulders, and there was a dark redness gurgling from the right side of her chest where the errant bullet had entered during the duel. It flowed down, spreading out and discoloring her dirty white gown all the way to the floor, where it pooled at her feet, then spread out over the beer slick floor.

At first glance the girl seemed to implore him with her deep brown eyes. But her eyes widened, and any trace of brown in them dissolved into two fathomless black holes. She opened her mouth as if to speak, but instead of words, blood bubbled from her lips. Letty reached out to Franklin with both hands, and once more opened her mouth to speak. But the voice Franklin heard was Gwen's.

"I always thought drinking would lead to your death, Franklin. But instead, it led to mine."

Franklin, still speechless, could only listen. And as he did, the girl's features blurred, distorted, and reconfigured themselves until she'd finally morphed into Gwen.

"And though you don't know it yet, it also led to the death of that little girl," she said with a moan.

He knew she meant Letty.

"Oh, it wasn't just the alcohol," Gwen continued. "And it wasn't really the bullet that killed us. It was because of you and the legion of men like you who are heartless. Men like Hawley and Calhoun. Men like those in the Mexican whore house you thought I'd never know about. Men, who like you cheer drunkenly at television sets, at news of little consequence, and games of even less, while their wives wander around their houses wringing their hands with loneliness, and die inside a little more each day, trying to think of a way to connect with their husbands again." She stopped talking for a moment, but her eyes continued to penetrate to his very soul.

Franklin winced at being likened to a monster like Hawley, or any of the others. He hoped she would stop. He wished that this apparition of his wife—as he knew this was—would just go away. The pain was too much for him. But he somehow knew she wasn't done talking yet, and he prepared himself for what she was yet to say.

"Men like you, hate," Gwen continued. "Men like you, judge. Men like you, think only of what satisfies them, and will do whatever it takes to have it. The hatred, like it is with an infection, is toxic. It's contagious, and it spreads from person to person, and from generation to generation. It was this hatred that killed that little girl. And it's what's killing your Indian friends. Even if it hasn't succeeded in taking all of their lives, it has surely killed their spirits. And it has been destroying mine. This hatred is alive and well today, doing what it has always done; destroying lives, hopes, dreams, possibilities, entire cultures, intimate relationships, personal friendships.

It pollutes the very air we breath and the planet we live on, destroying any hope of the future. It is all connected." She stopped again as if to allow all that she had said to sink deeply into Franklin. "Oh, I'm still breathing," she finally continued. "But like your Indian friends, my spirit is all but dead."

Franklin tried to speak, but still couldn't. He reached out for Gwen, but the hands she had reached out to him, she turned so the palms now faced him. The look from her eyes burned right through his heart. She stared at him for what seemed an eternity. He found it hard to breath.

"You've lost me," she finally said. And suddenly, from behind her, it was as if countless cases of beer exploded all at once. The foam quickly rose up and swelled all around, engulfing Gwen and everything else. Franklin choked on the foam as it refilled the room and began to swallow him. He shook his head and flailed with his arms to clear some space to draw a breath.

The sound of the exploding beer cans began to morph into a series of muffled thuds and Franklin woke up to find himself back on the hard-packed ground of the slave cell. He was soaking wet with sweat, and his face was pressed into the frayed fibers of his mat. Someone had stepped on the side of his face with a boot and was holding him there. Who ever it was grabbed his arms, then tied them behind his back. Before he could call out, a gag was stuffed into his mouth. He had no idea how long he had been sleeping, but it was still dark.

"Get up boy! It's reckonin' day!"

Franklin was yanked to his feet, and thrust out the gate along with Nathaniel who was bound as he was. The duty guard was laying contorted on the ground, his face frozen in a death stare, his eyes bulged and tongue lolling from his mouth. He had obviously been strangled to death. Franklin looked about frantically, but saw no one else in the yard.

Hawley shoved the guard's corpse out of the way, then pushed Franklin and Nathaniel past him. "How y'all two managed ta do that and get outside this fort is a mystery, but as fate would have it, I heard some commotion," Hawley drawled with a look of pure evil in his eyes. "Too late for me ta save him, or the guard at the women's cell, or the poor boy on duty at the front gate. But I was just in time ta stop y'all from sneakin' off very far with that little Letty girl ta do God knows what."

Hawley shoved his prisoners from behind with the barrel of his rifle. "Didn't have time ta call for reinforcements. Had ta take matters inta my own hands," Hawley continued, lowering his voice.

It sounded to Franklin like Hawley was rehearsing an explanation to the Second Lieutenant. As if Hawley had read his mind, he looked at Franklin and sneered, "Probably get an accommodation for heroism for my actions tonight."

Franklin was confused over what Hawley meant about Letty, and wondered if she had anything to do with the fresh bloody scratches he'd just seen on the man's face. His emotions shifting into a feeling of panic, Franklin glanced at Nathaniel for some reassurance, but instead saw that his friend's eyes betrayed that he too was overcome with fear. They were directed outside of the fort by a small side door beside the main gate, not making a sound. On the other side of the wall, he saw the boy Hawley had just referred to. He was laying crumpled in a heap like the first guard. Franklin prayed again to wake up, but to no avail.

"Just so ya know how much trouble y'all are in, I set a couple of my boys loose going in the other direction earlier. That's the way I told 'em I seen y'all runnin'. Nobody is gonna be lookin' for yer miserable asses this way."

Muffled by the cloth stuffed in his mouth, Nathaniel implored, "What we do wrong boss?" and immediately received a sharp crack to the head from the butt of Hawley's rifle in reply.

"Shut up or I'll be obliged ta shoot yer asses right here," Hawley hissed through clenched teeth. He hawked up some phlegm and spit, then prodded both men in the direction of the pit.

Before long Franklin could smell the putrid aroma of human waste, and the image of Horace being buried alive in the sludge flashed in his mind. Hawley pushed the two men further, past the spot where the cart had crashed into Horace's body, to a point where the fort was no longer visible. Hawley paused to light a lantern that was sitting on a rock. A soft yellow, flickering glow illuminated the men, the edge of the pit, and the trunks of trees that lined the surrounding forest. It also revealed what at first appeared to be a large burlap bag leaning against a tree. As his eyes adjusted, Franklin saw that what he thought might be a bag of supplies, was Letty.

She didn't move as they approached. Instead, she sagged against the tree trunk in an unnatural way. Franklin soon saw why. He had learned that the stray bullet from the duel had not resulted in a mortal injury, and that she had been recovering fairly well. But she had obviously been shot again, this time through her heart. She was dead.

Hawley spit. "That bastard Calhoun was wrong. He said she was no good for anythin' anymore. But there *was one last thing* she could do for me." Snickering, he got down on his haunches and lifted her chin with his dirt caked finger. The blood had drained away from her face, leaving it pallid and ghostly in appearance. "Way I see it, her being here makes it look like y'all tried ta escape, and took her along for the ride so's y'all could take advantage of her. Pity. Looks like she put up one hell of a fight."

Franklin saw that the young girl's filthy and bloodied garment had been cinched up around her waist.

"Everybody knows she was a fighter. Gotta give her that. Gave me a hard time right up ta the end. Gave me a new set of scratches and all." Hawley laughed, held the lantern up to his face, and glared at them through crazed eyes, the yellow glow accentuating the fresh, oozing scratches Letty made trying to fight him off.

"Animal," Franklin uttered with disgust. "She was just a little girl."

"Oh, but ya see? That's not how it went. Y'all are the animals! Ta take a little injured girl like that and try ta rape her... tsk, tsk, tsk,.... It's a good thing I heard that commotion and followed yer trail. Just too bad I couldn't save her. Course I would've, 'cept I tripped on a root when I fired my first shot at y'all, and tragically, I hit her instead. I pulled my knife to fight the two of ya, but like cowards, y'all just run off."

"You killed her," Franklin whispered hoarsely. He believed he knew exactly what Hawley had in mind.

Hawley set his rifle on the ground and pulled his pistol then his knife. He took a step toward them brandishing the weapons. "Nathaniel there was holding her from behind like the coward he is, and y'all had just scooted up her dress when she kicked ya a good one where it counts. Ya rolled off her tearing up like a baby. But I'd already fired. Poor girl didn't know what hit her." Laughing he added, "just like the first bullet I guess. Well, y'all tried ta high-tail it inta them woods and I fired two more times." He laughed again. "Even I was surprised at my shootin'. Specially with it bein' so dark and all. But I got both of ya in the back."

Hawley's pistol was pointed at the ground, his knife pointed at them. He cocked the pistol, and smiled with a look of pure unadulterated evil. "Tell ya what. I can make a story that'll hold up whether I slit yer throats, shoot y'all like I just said, or could be that one or both y'all somehow manage ta dodge my bullets and escape inta them woods. I like a challenge, so I'm gonna give y'all a chance. I'm gonna count ta three, and the two of y'all can start runnin'. Then I'm gonna count ta three again before I start firin'.'"

Franklin's mind was a storm of thoughts colliding one into the other. He wondered if a person can really die in their sleep if they die while dreaming. He agonized at the possibility that he might never see Gwen again; ever be able to apologize for how badly he treated her, how difficult he made her life, that he'd never be able to hold her again.

"One."

A part of him grieved for the young girl who was leaned up against the tree in her bloody rags, and he wanted to pull the garment down to cover her skinny little legs; to cover her innocence, to provide her some dignity. Another part of him felt that now at least for her, there was no pain, no fear, no more suffering.

"Get ready ta run," Nathaniel warned getting to his feet.

"Two."

Franklin, still on his knees, ached for the suffering inflicted on his Indian friends, as well as the cruelty and hatred with which the white man treated the black man, and how he himself had so callously spewed such hatred, demeaning women, people of color, or anyone he perceived as different from himself. He shook his head at the thought that his hate and disregard for others had no limits. That, like the apparition of Gwen had accused, he had caused this.

"Get up now!" Nathaniel cried. He tugged at Franklin's sleeve. "We gotta go!"

"Three ... !"

# CHAPTER 23

Franklin's and Nathaniel's muscles twitched to bolt into the forest, when a yellowish blur suddenly lunged out from the surrounding scrub. It flew through the air like a missile past the two men. But rather than the scream of a lead bullet, they heard a deep throated, blood curdling growl, and all of Lazarus's eighty pound body slammed chest high into their tormentor.

Hawley, staggered backwards from the blow and dropped his knife. Still fighting to regain his footing, he began firing his gun in rapid succession. After the first wild shot, Lazarus yelped, then sunk his teeth into the base of Hawley's neck. Hawley continued firing, but his backwards momentum sent him sprawling over the edge of the pit, and he landed on his back half a dozen feet from the rim. Lazarus stayed on top of him maintaining a death hold on his enemy's throat. Hawley continued pulling the trigger on his revolver, but the gun's bullets were already spent.

Between the soft-white light cast by the moon, and the yellow-glow of the lantern, Franklin could see that the back half of Hawley was sunk in the thick slime. He could also see bright red blood spurting out and over Lazarus's shoulder, and he knew Lazarus had punctured the man's artery.

All around Hawley, bones protruded at various angles from the putrid muck, and as Hawley flailed about under the yellow dog, he grasped at them for leverage. He managed to grasp what looked like an adult femur, and as the large bone shifted toward him, a full torso complete with ribs, collar bone, and skull, dripping slimy, black ooze, rose up vertically as if it was attempting to resume its life. The empty eye gaped, and the mouth, holding few teeth, hung open in a frozen scream. As Franklin took in the macabre carnage, he wondered if the bones belonged to the Indians, and if these were fresh from tonights fire.

The weight of Lazarus' body slowly pushed Hawley below the surface of the stinking, burbling muck. And just when Franklin thought the dog would go down too, Lazarus whimpered and leapt from the sinking body, just barely making it to solid land where he collapsed in a heap.

Franklin and Nathaniel ran to the fallen dog and were elated when they saw that the bullet had only grazed his flank. He had literally dodged another attempt on his life. Twice he should have been dead, yet twice he remained alive. Franklin thought he had not known an animal more aptly named.

A gurgling sound drew Franklin's attention back to the pit. Hawley's torso was submerged, but his head, arms, and legs were still above the surface of the muck. His mouth opened and closed, fish-like, without making a sound. Blood bubbled from his lips. He flailed intermittently now in ever weakening efforts to free himself from the sucking action on his body. The blood still pulsed from his neck, but the force and arc of it had decreased. The two men watched silently as Hawley's eyes finally rolled back in his head, and he took his last blood-gurgling breath, then disappeared from sight altogether, leaving nothing but a shallow impression in the muck that slowly coagulated back together returning to its pre-disturbed surface.

Shaking himself from the grisly scene, Franklin checked the rifle and found it was empty. Nathaniel had already tried fishing Hawley's pistol from the pit, but his efforts only served to push the gun deeper into the mess, and he finally gave up.

"We can use this for fish or squirrels," Nathaniel said picking up Hawley's knife. He looked at Letty's body. "What we gonna do 'bout her?"

"Those shots had to have been heard," Franklin replied. "We'll take her with us, and bury her when we've gotten far enough away from here, and we're sure we're not being followed. If we don't get lost, we'll catch up with Degataga, and try to blend in with the family like we did before. They can't be more than a couple hours ahead of us."

Franklin lifted Letty's body and cradled her in his arms. Nathaniel, with a groan, carried Lazarus. Shortly, they came to the Hiwassee river that flowed behind the fort. They stopped along its bank and cleaned the dog's wound with fresh water, then dressed it with a mud pack Nathaniel secured to its body with a strip from Franklin's oversized shirt. Then they continued their way, trading their loads back and forth as needed. Franklin was shocked at how light the girl was. She had been reduced to skin and bone. Lazarus, on the other hand weighed a ton, and the men found it was easier when carrying him to straddle the injured animal across their shoulders.

Franklin's concerns about getting lost were put to rest quickly. While at first he regretted not having the lantern, he soon saw that the light from the moon made the trail left by the Indians sufficiently clear. The ground was trampled by hundreds if not thousands of feet both large and small, and ran parallel to the soft bank of the river heading north, northwest. Franklin figured the Indians had at least several hours on them, and given his and Nathaniel's burden of having to carry two bodies, it could take days to catch up. Even if they did, he knew that fitting in with the group undetected by the soldiers would be tricky, and probably mean the difference between life and death.

The men trudged on for several miles before stopping to rest, each laying his load carefully down on the ground beside the river. It was still dark, and so far they'd had no indication they were being pursued. Franklin decided this was as good a time and place as any to bury the girl.

The men used a couple of branches to dig into the soft ground along the embankment. After digging a couple of feet down and making sure that water was not seeping into the hole, Franklin lifted Letty and gently placed her in the shallow grave, then stepped back. Tears trailed unchecked down his cheeks. Emotionally drained, he looked at Nathaniel. "Can you please finish this?"

Nathaniel covered Letty's eyes with a couple of smooth stones from the river. Next, he cut some pine boughs, and laid them over the girl's frail body. "This'll keep the dirt off her." Gently, he then pushed dirt into the hole until she was completely covered, tamped the dirt down firmly with his feet, and piled heavy rocks on top of the grave. "Now, the animals won't be likely ta get at her." His work done, Nathaniel sat beside Franklin, the dog between them seemingly resting comfortably. "After we sit here a spell, we kin say a prayer over her."

"What's the point?"

"Where'd ya say you was from?" Nathaniel asked.

"California."

"They don't pray for the dead in Caly-fornia?"

"I don't know how to pray. Never did it."

"Well now, prayin' ain't hard. See, we is all Gawd's children. And Gawd's children pray for one another so's we git ta heaven directly after our life is done on this earth."

Franklin stared blankly ahead. He had never felt so depleted. And prayer had never seemed so pointless.

"Look-it here," said Nathaniel, rising stiffly to his feet. "When I says the prayer, alls ya gotta do is say the amens. Come on up 'side me now. When I look at ya, just say amen! Just like that."

Franklin got slowly to his feet, and keeping his eyes downcast, sidled closer to Nathaniel.

"Thas right. Now we's gonna pray proper ta Gawd for dis girl."

Franklin had never been sure if he believed in God. He knew he didn't believe in heaven. But he had to admit, he was starting to think that he might be in hell. During his life he'd heard many versions of God. The one that seemed the most pervasive was a harsh God; judgmental and vindictive. The only time Franklin turned to this God was when he wished someone harm, or when he cursed someone who had upset him. Franklin had learned to associate this God to a heavy darkness, and this moment in time was the darkest and heaviest he could remember.

It dawned on him just then that Degataga and the other Indians often spoke of and prayed to their version of God, the Great Spirit. But, their words seemed full of light and a feeling of gratitude; quite opposite the burden and guilt infused prayers Franklin had been exposed to in his life. He had decided long ago that if God really existed, he didn't ever want to meet him. But the Indians made God seem appealing, and approachable, kind, and benevolent. He wondered how Nathaniel's prayer might portray the Almighty; this *Gawd* of his.

Nathaniel, his head down and his hands at his sides, seemed to be gathering his thoughts. His eyes were squeezed shut, and Franklin felt an energy emanating from him. Even Lazarus was looking at him curiously with one ear cocked. Without opening his eyes, Nathaniel, began to sing softly, "Steal away ... steal away ... steal away ta Jesus. Steal away ... steal away ... ." Finally, he lifted his head, opened his eyes skyward, and shouted, causing both Franklin and Lazarus to jump. "Ho-o-o-o! I ain't got long ta stay here."

Franklin stood sheepishly next to Nathaniel, and after a moment of awkward silence, he felt Nathaniel looking at him. Remembering his part, he stammered, "Amen."

Nathaniel nodded encouragement, then continued in a quiet tone that rose in intensity with each word to a crescendo, "My lord call me, he call me by the thunder!"

Startled again by Nathaniel's outburst, Franklin looked at the man with stunned amazement. Nathaniel looked back at him expectantly.

"Amen," Franklin whispered.

Nathaniel smiled faintly, then began to sing again. "The trumpets sound within a mile so-o-o, I ain't got long ta stay here. Green tree a bendin', post sitter stand a tremblin', the trumpets sound within a mile, so-o-o, we ain't got long ta stay here."

Franklin caught the emphasis on the word we, and wondered if maybe Nathaniel had changed the words to include him. Still in thought, he felt Nathaniel's eyes once more upon him, and again Franklin uttered his part.

Nathaniel shook his head, and a few of the tears streaming from his eyes wet Franklin's face. Without drying his eyes, he spoke quietly, looking at the mound of rocks. "Miss Letty, I knows we sing this song cause we wants ta be free on this earth. But it seem like the only way we gonna be free is when we leave it. When it's my time ta go, I gonna see ya again, and join ya in freedom."

Without needing to be prompted, Franklin said, "Amen", then swallowed hard and wiped tears from his own eyes. Nathaniel's prayer was so simple. It was grounded in nature, and acceptant of fate and the bigger plans of God. He thought to himself, *The Indians seemed to get this ... the slaves too. How did we miss it?* He shook his head, looked at Nathaniel and said once more, his voice choked with emotion, "Amen". Then he turned and walked over to a pile of boughs he had cut to sleep on. Spent, and eyes blurred by tears, he slumped down upon them with a heavy sigh, and saw Nathaniel walking off toward the river, gathering branches as he went.

"Aren't you tired?"

"Real tired, but we gonna be hungry in the morning. Gotta set some traps," Nathaniel answered, not looking back. Franklin watched him go, certain the man was wiping tears from his own eyes. After a while Nathaniel returned and lay close by, the hound between them.

"How far do we have to go?" Franklin asked, his voice low. He'd been staring at the countless, bright stars above him. They were so numerous, and they appeared to be so close, he thought he wouldn't have been surprised if he reached his hand up, and swished it, that they might swirl all around like the sparkling flakes in a snow globe.

"Think we got 'bout twenny ... maybe thirty miles ta the ferry where we cross the river. Then close ta another two hundred miles ta Nashville after that."

Franklin looked at Nathaniel who was laying on his back, looking up at the same stars he was. "How do you know this?"

"Been this way before. Back when I was bein' took ta market. Me and about thirty others; men, women, and children was took along this trail all the way from Virginny ta New Orleans. Just like that bunch of people we saw when we was bein' brung ta the fort. Men in front, walkin' in chains, women behind with the kids. Most of 'em with no shoes, and wearin' nothin' but rags. We walked hundreds of miles that way. Some died from freezin' in the cold, some by fryin' in the heat. Some got beat ta death by the bosses. Some just give up they spirit cause they got nothin' left inside."

"No disrespect," Franklin interrupted, "but New Orleans is far south of here. Why would they take you this way?"

"Cause they could pack us inta a boat like *fishes* and ship us down the Mississippi River," Nathaniel replied, his voice rising an octave. "I guess they figured less of us would die that way. Oh, that boat did stink!" He laughed a little at this. "We was packed in one against the other, back ta back, front ta front, in the very bottom of the boat. Lots of us got sick. If we had to puke, piss, or shit, we had ta do it right there. Can you imagine? Only good thing 'bout bein' on that boat, was I heard from some of those folks that my wife and kids never did get took south."

Franklin had no words. He couldn't fathom the circumstances of Nathaniel's life, and felt too inadequate to even make an attempt at consoling him. So he was relieved when he heard the man snoring, and he decided to give his emotions a rest, and try to follow his friend into a much needed and hopefully dreamless sleep.

He woke to find Lazarus still asleep beside him, but Nathaniel gone. Franklin sat up and shivered as he stretched his aching body. It seemed the season of summer had begun its gradual transition to fall, and cooler temperatures. He hoped he would catch up with the Indians soon. Among other things, he knew they'd have a way of managing the cold. But his concern at the moment, was the whereabouts of Nathaniel.

A rustle in the bushes behind him solved the mystery. Franklin craned his neck and saw his companion returning with several silvery fish cradled in his arms. One of them flopped its tail and arched its body, working itself free in a last ditch effort to escape. Nathaniel deftly snatched it in mid air with one hand, then knocked its head against a stone rendering it unconscious. He tossed the treat to Lazarus, who surprised the men by jumping up onto all fours. Furiously wagging his tail to the point of nearly falling over, the grateful dog chomped the fish down in three bites.

Laughing, Nathaniel got a fire going, then gutted the other two fish with Hawley's knife. As a steady blaze developed, he stuck a stick into the mouth of each of them, then handed one skewered fish to Franklin, and held his own over the fire, turning it slowly.

"How did you do this?" Franklin asked incredulously.

"Last night, I cut me some branches and wove 'em together ta make a funnel the fish could get into, but not back out of. Then I moved some big ol' rocks ta make a little pond for 'em ta swim in, and put the trap in there. These three beauties were waitin' for me this morning. I'll shows ya how ta do later, but we got ta make up some time. We still got plenty miles ta go before we cross the Tennessee River."

After finishing their breakfast, they eliminated any evidence they had ever been there, then resumed the trail. Lazarus hobbled a little but could walk, enabling them to make better progress than they had hoped.

# CHAPTER 24

Smoke curling up above the forest canopy into the evening sky, was the first indication Franklin had that he and Nathaniel might be drawing near to the Indians. Before long, he spotted the dancing glow of firelight that managed to find its way between the tree trunks and thick underbrush. The two of them moved in as close as they dared to assess the situation, and found to their relief that they had indeed caught up to their friends.

Inching closer, Franklin saw that there were Indians moving about the perimeter of the camp like guards. *They must have been threatened or bought off, to get them to corral their own people like this,* Franklin thought with disdain.

Just then a metallic click interrupted their reconnaissance, and the men turned to see a soldier on horseback, the barrel of his rifle pointed at them. The breaking of some twigs alerted them all to the presence of another, and an Indian guard made his presence known in the nearby bushes, his face shadows. Lazarus flattened his ears and emitted a low growl.

"Well, lookie here? Y'all slaves wouldn't be tryin' ta make off outta here, would ya?" Drawled the soldier on horseback. "I could shoot ya dead right here for tryin', so ya better control that mutt right now if y'all know what's good for ya."

"I will take care of them, sir," the man still in the shadows offered. "These men are not slaves. They have been with my family since we found them as infants. We have raised them as our own."

Franklin breathed a sigh of relief. Although he could still not make out his features in the dark, Franklin immediately recognized the voice of Degataga.

"Probly slaughtered their parents, and took 'em, is more likely." The soldier spat with disgust. "Y'all savages is all alike."

"Unaduti and Chuquilatague," the Indian continued, "were only chasing after the dog who must have gone after something into the forest. I believe they were only desperate for some food. But it seems the dog is hurt." Turning to Franklin, he continued, "Is he okay?"

Franklin was caught completely off guard. The look he saw on the soldier's face appeared incredulous, and he was afraid to say anything, thinking he could make a mistake and reveal Degataga's story as a lie. Nathaniel, sensing Franklin's discomfort answered. "He be just fine. But no matter how hard he try, that ol' hound still be too slow to catch a varmint," he chuckled light-heartedly, playing along with Degataga's ruse.

"Enough!" the soldier scolded. "Y'all git your sorry asses back ta camp, and take the mutt with ya! Keep him on a rope if ya know what's good for 'im. Next time any of y'all git caught away from camp, there ain't gonna be no questions. Understand?"

The two men and the dog followed Degataga into the encampment and wove their way amongst hundreds of Indian men, women and children who were gathered close together around fires. Although it was dark, the fires revealed the poor condition most of them were in. Franklin saw their gaunt faces, and that many of them wore little clothing.

When they came upon Degataga's family, they were warmly received. Franklin was hugged by Kanuna first, who even in his emaciated condition, engulfed him like a bear. Chea Sequa was next to greet him, then Ayita came up and touched his cheek lightly with the tips of her fingers. The touch was soothing, yet it stirred within him the shame he still felt for the earlier thoughts he'd entertained about her. She offered the two men some dried meat, and both of them broke a piece and gave it to Lazarus.

As they sat to eat, Degataga informed them that there were close to a thousand Cherokee in the camp and only several soldiers in control. He and some others had been chosen to act as guards to help maintain order amongst the Indians to make up for the lack of soldiers involved with their removal. This of course had been accompanied by an unveiled threat to harm their families if they didn't comply.

"If I had not been out there this evening," Degataga continued, "you both would most likely have been shot. But Ayita told me of a dream given to her by the Great Spirit, that you would be joining us again soon. She said I should go out to make sure you made it here alive."

"You don't look well, none of you do," Franklin said, his hand on his heart in gratitude.

"It is true, we are weak and tired and have not eaten well. But it was much worse for us in the fort camp. Here, we once more have the comfort of the forest, and the freshness of the air."

The excitement Degataga showed upon finding Franklin shifted into a deep sadness. He looked around the camp before continuing as if taking some kind of a measure. "Still, there has been much sickness among us, Unaduti. The sadness we felt at being taken from our homes, and led in the direction which means death has now been made worse. The soldiers at the fort would not even permit us to bury our dead and say our prayers for them. They took the bodies of our friends and burned them, then carried the remains away into the forest. We are told that if we die on this trail, our bodies will be left to rot. They have taken our home and our spirit. Now, they even take away our way of dying and returning to the earth. But, we are lucky to have survived, … many others have already been lost."

Franklin hung his head and silently chewed dried, leathery, meat. He thought he had never seen a man so dejected, and he didn't have the heart to tell Degataga about the pit. He also thought better of telling him of any of the hardships he had endured as he felt these things paled in comparison.

Chea Sequa patted Ayita and Degataga on their backs breaking the solemnity of the moment. "It was good my mother saw you in a dream and encouraged my father to go into the woods tonight." Flashing his perpetual smile, he said in a joking manner, "Do you believe in luck now, Unaduti?"

Franklin noticed the strain in the young brave's smile. He thought for a moment, then replied, "I believe in your mother and your father. And I believe in you and your brother." In his heart, Franklin still abhorred the very notion of luck. And he questioned the belief in a Great Spirit that would allow such pain and sadness to fall upon the people he or she had created. But, he also could not understand how he was still alive given all he had gone through. That night they huddled together to insulate themselves from the ever increasing chill, and fell into an exhausted sleep.

***

Franklin woke to the blare of a trumpet. He sat up and saw Degataga walking towards him and the family with a small bundle in his arms—the morning rations. Soon he was gnawing on scraps, grateful to be among friends.

As the family quietly ate, a loud wail arose from another group of Indians across the encampment. A couple of soldiers immediately headed in the direction of the crying, and the sounds of orders joined the outburst. The wailing persisted until a single shot rang out, and silence prevailed once more.

"What was that about?" whispered Franklin.

"Someone has died," Chea Sequa said gravely. He put his arm around Tsula and drew her nearer to him.

Suddenly a new commotion erupted, followed immediately by another rifle shot, then quiet again.

"Listen up!" a voice cried out. "We have already told you. We do not have the time for burial. We have a long ways ta go, rations are low, and the weather ain't gettin' any warmer. You are gonna have ta leave your dead behind, the same as you left your homes. You can pray for 'em, but only as we move along. Now let's go, line up!"

Franklin saw two soldiers carrying someone between them by the hands and feet toward the forest that encircled the encampment. Without ceremony, they swung the body out, back, and then out again, and flung the person, limbs all askew, into the bushes. A new round of wailing erupted, and another gun shot silenced the outcry.

Degataga took up a position on the flank of the Indians. Franklin looked up and down the long and wide line of bedraggled people he now knew were once proud and strong. Once rooted in their belief in the Great Spirit who brought them to their homeland of abundant and replenishing life, they now looked like a wasted mass of broken humanity, driven by a society who's God seemed based upon greed. Rather that flourishing in the peace and tranquility of their homeland, the group slowly moved out in the direction which to them, meant death.

Deep in thought, Franklin felt overwhelmed over how cruelly the Indians and slaves were being treated. More so, he was ashamed at how he had unquestioningly accepted the suppressive practices that had been utilized to control them both. Franklin had always prided himself at being a student of history, but he now realized his education had been pitifully selective. He knew that President Andrew Jackson was the primary force behind the movement to remove the Indians—and not just the Cherokee—from land he wanted for the use of the still fledgling United States. He understood that the Cherokee were just one of four other major Indian nations at the time who were inhabiting what Jackson perceived to be prime territory for America. What he conveniently, or selectively disregarded, was the fact that in 1830, the five tribes were living independent of, and for the most part peacefully with one another, and were considered "civilized" by the American settlers.

The material Franklin read, but failed to comprehend at the time indicated that this was because for among other reasons, the Cherokee, in particular, readily adopted and practiced the Christianity of the white man, and developed centralized governments along with their own constitutions. In doing so, the Indians became literate according to the standards and expectations of Anglo-European society. They engaged in the free market which included establishing and owning businesses. In some instances, they even took slaves to work their own plantations. Intermarriage between Indians and white Americans was becoming increasingly common. As Franklin trudged along, everything he'd ever read about this period in American history came flooding into his mind with startling clarity. In spite of these perceived successes in their movement toward acculturation, the Jackson administration was dissatisfied by how much of their Indian culture the various tribes still retained.

Franklin hadn't cared about any of this. Instead, he vehemently agreed with President Jackson's decision that there was no room in American society for the Indians, and that the solution was to relocate them far from where they could pose a problem to the still fledgling nation. The first to go where the Choctaw. Then after two wars, the Seminoles were forced out. The Creek Indian nation was next to be removed, then the Chickasaw. The Cherokee were the hold outs.

Franklin had read that the Cherokee were a strong people, spread out for hundreds of miles across the Southeast part of the country. When combined with the other tribes that inhabited early America, Jackson understood that if he tried to fight them, it would be a long, bloody battle, the outcome of which could very likely end unfavorably for the country. He decided instead to work toward their assimilation into American culture.

Franklin now recalled reading that the Cherokee, in comparison to the other Indian nations, were the group considered by many as most like the whites in that they already utilized a system of farming. And as he read more deeply into this piece of American history, he had discovered there was a more insidious plan at the heart of the so-called Americanization of the Cherokee. It seemed that Jackson believed if he impressed the importance of education on the Cherokee, and could get them used to methods of sustenance and economics already utilized by white culture, the Indians would grow increasingly dependent on American ways, and become less reliant on methods they had used for hundreds of years. In this way, Jackson hoped to weaken them.

By this time the country had become dependent upon the growth and development of cotton, and as fate would have it, the area inhabited by the Cherokee was considered prime cotton growing land. The nation was overwhelmed by the amount of cotton already being grown and could not transform it into product quickly enough as it was, so for the time being, the Cherokee were safe. Then an invention called the cotton gin came along and changed everything. With this new technology, Jackson considered the land occupied by the Cherokee absolutely necessary to the growth and development of the country. He went so far as to ignore a Supreme Court mandate barring the state of Georgia from intruding on Cherokee land. As it turned out, Georgia became even more interested in inhabiting Cherokee lands when in 1829 gold was discovered in Lumpkin County, Georgia, and throughout the mountains in the north region of the state.

Finally, due to the ever increasing demand for cotton production and the onslaught of white Americans who needed land, the earlier and contentiously received Treaty of New Echota negotiated by Jackson in 1835, rose to new heights of popularity. It included land on the western bank of the Mississippi River—today known as Oklahoma—where the Indians could relocate, and five million dollars for the move. But very few Cherokee accepted this offer. The majority refused.

Countering the Indian's resistance, President Martin Van Buren, ordered state militia under the command of General Winfield Scott to forcibly remove the Cherokee, and the African freedmen and slaves who lived among them. By 1837, roughly forty-six thousand Indians had been removed from their ancestral homelands.

Franklin remembered how surprised he was back then to read that the Cherokee had not gone easy. They did not—as he was fond of saying—see the writing on the wall. They put up resistance. There were skirmishes, and people on both sides died. The government infiltrated the Cherokee and bought off some so-called leaders—unrecognized as such by the Cherokee Nation—with promises they either could not or had no intention to keep. These self-proclaimed leaders signed the Treaty of New Echota. The treaty, however, was never accepted by the elected tribal leadership or by the majority of Cherokee people, and thousands of them, to no avail, signed a petition against the treaty.

What surprised Franklin more than the Indian's resistance—even disturbed him—was that such notables as Davy Crockett, who up until then Franklin had revered, and Ralph Waldo Emerson, who Franklin swore if he were to ever read poetry, he'd skip, were outspoken against the Government's treatment of the Indians.

Three of the four unrecognized leaders who signed the deal were eventually chased down and assassinated by the Cherokee for their treasonous act against their nation. An act which would invariably result in the deaths of up to six-thousand men, women and children, as they walked what the Cherokee began calling nu na hi du na to hi lu i, which, translated to English, means the trail where they cried. Historically would later refer to this as the Trail of Tears.

***

After a day and a half of trudging along—many of the men in chains— the group came to Blythe Ferry where they were to cross the Tennessee River. By the time they arrived, a group of approximately ten thousand Indians had already gathered along the riverbank. Most of them were Cherokee, but there were also a few hundred Creek Indians. All of them were jammed into enclosures, and Franklin's group was squeezed in with them.

Chea Sequa, ever the optimist, sidled up to Franklin and his father. "It looks bad, but maybe it is lucky for us to be here now that it is getting cold."

"All of them, like us, have only the clothes on their backs," groaned Franklin. "And look," he said to Degataga, "there is only enough shelter for maybe one of every four of us. We'll freeze!" Turning back to Chea Sequa, he said in a voice laced with sarcasm, "Those who have died already may have been the lucky ones." He gestured, sweeping his arm about the decrepit looking mass of humanity. "You've impressed me with your other ideas of luck, Chea Sequa, but to me, this looks more like doom."

"If we stay here for long, many will die. If we leave, many will still die. But if we are to die, I would rather we die walking the earth among the trees and rivers, not rotting in this prison," agreed Degataga, shaking his head.

# CHAPTER 25

It was becoming increasingly clear to Franklin that what had been sold to the American public for nearly two hundred years as merely a legal exchange with the Indians, was in actuality a horrific mass violation of human rights. As he was considering this, Degataga hailed someone Franklin did not recognize. The man, gaunt and limping badly, came over.

"Osiyo, Degataga!" he called out and beamed.

"Waya! Oginalii, my friend." Degataga embraced him while gesturing for the man to follow him as he made his way over to two large rocks. "Galutsv... come." The two sat side by side.

"I have no food to offer you as we have just arrived," Degataga said matter of factly.

"We too have little. I bring only myself to you," Waya responded with a sad smile. "I see your two sons, and Ayita, still with you. I am glad. My family is also alive and in this place with me," he pointed across the compound to a motley looking group of Indians, "but others lost loved ones... died on the way here. We were not allowed to bury them. Our only happiness is they died in the world given to them by the Great Spirit, and not in this dark place."

Ayita got up and turned to go to Waya's wife.

"No, you must not," Waya lamented. "She has the sickness."

"I have not allowed the soldiers or this trail to stop me caring, and I will not let the sickness stop me," she said firmly.

"Many people die from this one," Waya countered.

Ayita knelt and kissed Waya's trembling hand, then rose and walked across the compound waving to Waya's family.

Degataga nodded and patted his friend's shoulder. "We hope to leave soon so that we will not die here." His head swiveled around to gaze at the filthy, overcrowded enclosure. "This place is very bad."

Waya joined his friend's sad gaze. "Un, un, this place uyoi udohiyo,... very bad."

Franklin still could not believe what he saw in this camp; the many fires and pitifully few tents, all torn, or in various conditions of disarray, and far too few for the hundreds of Indians cooped up and milling aimlessly about. The Indians, some of whom he knew personally, were gaunt, filthy, wearing rags, and many were barefoot. The soldiers in sharp contrast were housed and dressed comfortably, and they always seemed to be eating, smoking, or drinking, often all at the same time.

"I fear we will be here for a while," Waya continued. "The river is too shallow for boat to carry us across, but also too deep for us to cross on foot. This is why so many of our people are still here, not on path. This is why so many sick."

Degataga patted his old friend's knee, and the two of them stood and clasped the other's forearm. "Stiyu."

"Stiyu," Waya replied, then headed slowly back across the encampment to his family.

Franklin wondered at such a friendship he'd just witnessed between these two men. He had noticed the tears in each of their eyes as they talked, and knew he had nothing like that in his life. Watching Waya weave his way through the mass of wasted bodies squeezed together in the compound, he saw many who were coughing with sickness. Some of them looked like they wouldn't last much longer, and he wondered how long it would be before the sickness would find him as well.

"It must be hard for you to say goodbye," Franklin said to his friend.

"We do not say goodbye. That for Cherokee means we would not see each other again. We say be strong, in the hope that we will meet again," Degataga explained, then got up and greeted Ayita who had just returned. As Degataga held and consoled her, Franklin could see that she had been crying.

"They may lose Ahyoka soon," Ayita moaned. "She is very sick, and both she and Waya try to believe this is not true, but I can see it in her eyes that she is dying."

As Degataga held his wife, he motioned to Kanuna to bring food for their supper.

They ate in silence in a cold, drizzling rain, that to Franklin matched the mood in the camp. After the meager meal, Kanuna sought out the highest ground as there were no boughs to build a sleeping platform. Franklin called to Nathaniel, and the two of them huddled together with the Indians in a circle as Franklin had before, and covered themselves with what skins they had amongst them for warmth.

Franklin woke the following morning and peered through a sliver of an opening in the protective hide that covered him. Around him, he heard the soft moans and snoring of those who were still asleep and he hoped perhaps dreaming of a better place than this. Voices caught his attention and he maneuvered the slit so he could see whom they were coming from. He spotted Degataga and both of his sons talking with two soldiers near the family's horses.

"We need our horses to carry our belongings," Degataga said to the soldiers. His sons stood quiet, their faces set, and they held tightly to the horses lead ropes.

"Look here. I understand what yer saying," said one of the soldiers, "but do ya understand that rations are so low ya ain't gonna need these horses much longer, cause they, or you, will starve ta death? 'Sides, we're only talkin' bout one of 'em. That'll make sure yer family will eat for another week, or maybe two if yer careful 'bout it. Maybe even three if ya stop feedin' them niggers of yers so much. Unless, of course," the soldier elbowed another soldier beside him, "yer planning on trading 'em yerself somewheres down the line." The two soldiers laughed as they eyed Degataga and his sons.

"We understood that the American government promised money and food enough for this journey," Degataga argued flatly.

"The government didn't account for the weather, and y'all bein' stuck here fer so long. Now, we can get the food fer ya, but the people sellin' it are jackin' the price up so high we got no choice," the soldier insisted, then smirked. "It's up ta y'all. Maybe y'all would rather eat them horses. I hear ya'll eat yer dogs." The two soldiers laughed again, slapped each other on the back, and shook their heads.

Degataga sighed and nodded to Chea Sequa, who then released one of the horses into the hands of the soldiers, then told Kanuna to go and get the morning rations.

Franklin carefully extracted himself from the huddle of sleeping bodies, then made his way through the deepening, rank smelling mud that sucked at his every step to join Degataga and Chea Sequa.

"The days are getting shorter, and it's getting colder too," Franklin observed wrapping his arms around himself for warmth after they greeted each another. "I hope this rain stops soon, before we all get stuck in this mud for good." He picked his feet up one at a time and scraped them off on a rock, only to plop them back into the mud again.

"This rain is cold and harsh, but it is also lucky for us for it to keep coming down," Chia Sequa offered.

Franklin looked at the young man, anticipating an explanation, and unsuccessfully tried to suppress his habitual scowl.

Smiling patiently, Chea Sequa went on. "Even you must understand that the rains will also cause the river to rise and make it possible for the ferries to carry us across."

"Yeah, I guess that could happen," Franklin conceded. But not willing to give in completely to the young brave's aggravating positivity, he countered with a note of pessimism. "As long as it doesn't drown us first."

Chea Sequa took a drink from a gourd he'd filled up earlier at a station that had been set up to distribute water to the Indians. He spit it out coughing with disgust. "Or kill us," he groaned. "We must boil the water," he said looking at his father.

The three of them looked up at the sound of someone approaching and saw Kanuna sloshing his way to them carrying a sack. "Cheer up" he smiled, hoisting the sack in the air. "Food."

"What is it Kanuna?" Degataga asked. But before his son could reply, he answered himself in the form of another question. "More old salted pork and dried out corn?"

"Edoda, father," Kanuna replied with a grunt as he placed the sack on a rock. "Do you think the soldiers will let us hunt for game?"

Degataga walked around his sons and Franklin in a wide circle, all the while gazing into the sky. "Even if they do, when have you seen anything more than the smallest tsiskwa? The birds are all around, but do you see how they are only as big as your thumb? And the awi have already been hunted by those who have come this way before us. The last one I saw was slaughtered for sport, and all that was missing was the antlers and hooves. The soldiers took no meat. Even as they tell us there is little food, they waste their kill." Degataga calmed himself, stopped circling, and looked back at his son. "I will ask them if we can hunt. It will give us something good to do. Perhaps we may find a sikwa and eat fresh pork, or get lucky and catch a gvna," which he pronounced slowly as, "guh nuh," for Franklin's benefit.

Chea Sequa could see that Franklin didn't understand so he strutted around craning his neck and made a "gobble, gobble, gobble" sound.

Franklin only nodded at his effervescent friend and chuckled in spite of himself.

# CHAPTER 26

Franklin was surprised at first when the soldiers gave the Indians permission to hunt. However, their efforts proved fruitless. The fact that the area had been hunted out by the thousands of Indians that had been moved in the same direction before them became more apparent each day. The unavoidable squish and sucking sounds the hunters made while walking through the mud did not help their efforts. And the fact that they had to be accompanied by two even noisier soldiers on horseback further challenged their ability to successfully surprise even the random turkey, and they returned day after day without fresh meat.

As one dreary day was replaced by the next, the sounds of lamenting the loss of a loved one from disease or starvation became all too familiar. Perhaps even more troubling, there had been rumors that some deaths were the result of Indians straying too far from the encampment and being killed by unscrupulous locals who maintained that the errant Indians were lurking about their properties.

It was said that some of the Indian women, in a desperate attempt to procure food for their starving families, allowed local men to sleep with them in exchange. One woman's battered body was found a few days later weighted down with heavy rocks below the surface of a nearby creek. Upon inspection, the consensus was that she had been beaten and raped, then her throat, slit. Sadly, this was not an isolated case. The only relief afforded the Cherokee while living like rats in a cage, and unlike while they were on the move, was that they were granted the freedom to grieve and to bury their dead.

Lazarus nuzzled his nose softly into Franklin's side asking to be pet, and Franklin did so listlessly brushing his hand along the dog's now pronounced ribs. The rain during the night had been so steady and hard that it was impossible for the Indians to build a fire. They huddled close to one another draped with their sleeping skins for warmth. Franklin felt grateful for this sentient being that had become a fixture in his life, and wondered if Nathaniel minded.

"We can share him. Lazarus can be both our dog," Nathaniel said as if he'd read Franklin's mind. He sat down and joined Franklin, stroking Lazarus' silky, soft, floppy ears.

Franklin turned to Nathaniel with an urgency in his eyes. "If Lazarus only knew the man I was all my life,... the pain I've caused others."

"He don' judge ya. It was you who saved him, thas what he knows."

"The animals have a wisdom and understanding beyond men," Chea Sequa, who was sitting nearby added. "Lazarus can feel your heart, Unaduti. He knows that under the anger, you have a deep hurt. He knows that is why you have done any of your wrongs." He chuckled and looked at Franklin with a twinkle in his eyes. "He also knows that he is lucky you have come into his life. Nathaniel told me the story of how you saved Lazarus from Hawley, and how you carried him for many miles after he was wounded, instead of leaving him to die. It is because of you he is alive."

Raindrops tapped insistently on Franklin's head, and plopped rhythmically into puddles at his feet, and he winced, not because of them, but because of Chea Sequa's words. He was about to argue against the two men's encouragement when a loud wail, joined by a chorus of them disrupted the men's conversation.

Ayita had been sitting against Degataga, his arms wrapped around her, and when the cry pierced the air, she sat upright with a start. "Ahyoka," she shrieked. She rose abruptly and pulled her husband to his feet. "We must go to them."

Franklin and the others stayed put as Degataga and Ayita sloshed away through the mud. Soon their wails could be heard merging with those of their friends, and a collective wave of mourning spread in all directions. Cries of lament drowned out all other sound. But Ayita's voice could be heard above it all, singing out her dear friend, Ahyoka's name over and over.

The ear-splitting crack of a rifle shot silenced the melee, except for the constant downpour of rain. Franklin turned with the others in the direction of the shot and saw several soldiers in the center of the camp, the one who shot the rifle was standing on a wooden box, smoking gun in his hand.

"Bury your dead, and be quick about it! Then gather your things and prepare to depart tomorrow!" the soldier hollered. "We will begin loadin' onta the ferry after the mornin' meal ta take advantage of the risin' water!" The soldier, finished with his proclamation by firing a final shot for emphasis. Then he hopped down from the barrel to join his comrades who were already scampering off to the warmth of their tents, hot stew, and liquor. Immediately after the soldiers disappeared into their tents, the wailing resumed. And while Franklin and the others huddled miserably together in stunned silence, Degataga returned.

"Kanuna, Chea Sequa, go quickly and dig a grave. All of you, we must go with our brother Waya to help him bury his adalii. Tsula, bring lavender oil from Ayita's pouch."

Franklin stood off to the side with Nathaniel, unsure what he should do.

Kanuna addressed them. "We *all* must support Waya. You too must come."

The heaviness of Waya's heart and those of his friends was mirrored in the steady, cold, rain, which had slowed to a grey drizzle. The forest was shrouded in a mist so thick that even the evergreens lost their color. The only blessings brought by the rain were those of softening the ground for digging, and serving as a liquid curtain surrounding the mourning Indians, and muting from their view the soldiers standing guard amongst the trees a couple dozen yards behind them.

Waya, was consumed with grief and unable to speak. The frail, elderly man knelt by the body of his wife, who, wrapped in skins had been laid upon a bed of furs. The grief stricken man repeatedly anointed her fore-head, hands, and feet with lavender oil, as the rains only washed it away.

The sight of this old, wasted, Indian, so lovingly and patiently tending to his deceased wife mystified Franklin. To him, the body before him was nothing more than a corpse, an empty, emaciated shell, something abhor-rent. The rain drops splashing off of her form, might just as well have been falling upon lifeless rock. But he remembered that to the Indian, the entire world was imbued with life. Even something as seemingly basic as a rock. That they showed reverence for a rock, the display of love and care going on before him now should not have been a surprise. From somewhere deep within him rose the bittersweet realization that this man loved his wife be-yond himself. Bittersweet, because although his time among the Cherokee was showing him that this kind of selfless love was possible, he knew he had failed to do so himself.

Degataga reached over and gently took the oil from Waya's hand, then anointed the old man's forehead. After doing the same for each of Waya's family members, he returned the stone vial to his friend. Standing beside the body, Degataga raised his hands and tilted his face upwards. With closed eyes, and after a prolonged silence, he spoke. "We, the children of the Great Spirit, live our lives in harmony with all created things as surely as the sun rises at daybreak and the moon and stars shine at night. The cruelty of those who force us from our lands can do nothing to remove us from the truth of our creator's heart where we belong, anymore than this rain can prevent the sun from rising again. Although we cannot now see it, we know that it is there, waiting for just the right moment to move out from behind the clouds. And although we suffer, we will not complain, for this death is a friend that comes to free our sister from her pain and suffering. It takes her beyond this shroud of torment that has engulfed us, to the land where our Great Spirit awaits the arrival of us all. There, he always rejoices in his children, and the good way we have lived our lives, in harmony amongst all of his creation."

Degataga took a feather from his hair and placed it in the crook of Ahy-oka's arm while Franklin and the others looked on in silence. Then he nod-ded at Waya, who in turn motioned to his son Mohe. With help from Chea

Sequa and Kanuna, Mohe lifted his mother's body, and gently placed her into the shallow grave that he had dug.

The silence gave way something that reminded Franklin of static electricity. The very air felt charged with energy, making the hair on his head and arms rise, and the nearby trees brightened as if lit from the inside. Finally, Ayita called out with her shrill voice. She chanted Ahyoka's name, and Waya's family and friends resumed their wailing while placing stones onto the deceased's body, gradually filling the hole completely. When finished, Waya sat still, and his tears mingled with the rain which flowed between the stones and into the grave of his beloved wife.

Franklin was so engrossed in the proceedings, he failed to notice the approach of several soldiers. The whickering of a horse drew his fixation. Looking up, he saw five of them with riders suddenly materialize from out of the fog like characters in a sci-fi movie. The manes of the horses were drenched, as was the clothing of the men that sat upon them, making them look other worldly. But Franklin knew this was no movie, and regardless of how many times he reminded himself that he was only dreaming, it had all felt too painfully real.

"Enough!" shouted one of the soldiers. "Enough of yer confounded wailin'! The dead is dead! They can't hear none of y'all! Now, get yerself up outta that mud, and skeedadle back to camp!"

No one moved.

All five soldiers cocked their rifles and leveled them at the group. The leader spit. "I ain't gonna say it again. Move now, or join yer sister, or mother, or who ever the hell she was," he said pointing to the mound of stones.

One by one, the Indians slowly turned away from Ahyoka's grave, and began moving back toward the camp. Only Waya remained, seated beside her.

"I said enough old man!" the soldier growled. And when Waya didn't move, he dismounted and began sloshing through the ankle deep mud toward him. "Last time chief," he warned, and raised his rifle at the back of Waya's head.

Degataga walked slowly back holding his hands in the air. He knelt and whispered into Waya's ear, then stood and extended his hands to his friend. Waya looked up squinting against the rain, clasped his friend's hands, and allowed Degataga to pull him to his feet. Without looking back, the two old friends joined the rest of the mourners.

In a bracingly cold, grey drizzle, Degataga, Franklin, and the others joined the rest of the Indians who had already lined up to board one of the four ferry's available for crossing the Tennessee River. Their wait in line lasted for three days, due to the sheer magnitude of the undertaking. Each and every person, animal, wagon, and supply item was checked in and accounted for, and they were forced to eat and sleep in line so not to slow the process of loading the boats any longer. There were close to two thousand people, over eighty wagons, and close to one thousand horses and oxen, in addition to all of the supplies needed to support a group of that size, and only four boats to transport all across the swollen, storm-churned river.

Finally, Degataga's group began the long, slow, miserable process of boarding. A calendar tacked to the inside wall of the cabin on the ferry Franklin was loaded onto revealed that it was Monday, November 12th, of the year 1838. The food, provisions, and even the livestock had been ferried across before them. At this point, the group of Indians Franklin was amongst had been detained for a month at Blythe Ferry. They were the last group to cross.

The ferry lurched, bobbed, slid, and shuddered its way across dark and angry waters, causing panic, nausea and vomiting in many of its passengers. And any thought that things might get better from here were dispelled immediately upon their arrival to the opposite shore of the river. Bone tired and famished, Franklin discovered that the horses and wagons of supplies had been transported to a place further along the path. With few exceptions, they would be forced to walk—many of them in chains—until they too arrived at that location. To make matters worse, the roads had become all but impassable having been reduced to thick, pasty, muck, that reeked with the waste of horses and oxen.

Franklin read a sign, stuck into the sludge and leaning heavily toward the ground. The painted lettering had long ago faded. But gouged into the weathered wood for anyone who could read were the distances between this spot and the next few towns: McMinnville – 73 miles, Murfreesboro – 118 miles, Nashville – 157 miles. The bedraggled group of Indians were surrounded by miles of wilderness, rugged terrain, and roads Franklin knew would claim the lives of many of them. *Perhaps*, he thought, *even my own.*

# CHAPTER 27

He stood transfixed before the sign, while Lazarus nosed his hand. And while Franklin absent-mindedly scratched the dog's ears, Nathaniel sloshed through the muck to join them.

"How long is it going to take for us to reach those towns?" Franklin asked. He shook his head to clear his eyes of the rivulets of rain streaming into them, only to have them immediately flood again.

"Five ta six days ta McMinnville," Nathaniel said. "An' two ta three weeks ta Nashville if we's luck..." He stopped in mid-sentence, then re-phrased his response, "I mean if the weather don't get any worse."

As if prompted by Nathaniel's reply, the rain became mixed with snow flurries. Then just when Franklin thought things couldn't possibly get any worse, the soldiers started lining everyone up and connecting them to one another with chains. Only the very oldest and weakest of men and women were spared the restraints. They, and some of the youngest children whom their mothers were too weakened to carry were allowed to walk freely or ride in the wagons. It reminded Franklin grimly of the slave coffle he had seen on their way to Fort Cass.

The chains were heavy, and it seemed everything was becoming bitter cold. With each step, their feet sank deep into cold, wet mud, followed by the pull of the muck sucking at them as they tried to free themselves from its grasp only to take another laborious step. This process was repeated for miles on end. Many who still had boots or moccasins up to this point, lost them to the unforgiving mud.

"I think Lazarus could use another lift," Franklin observed as he watched the dog struggle through the muck that reached just below his belly. The dog's yellow fur had become stiff and stained brown with the stuff.

"I don't know how long I can carry him," Nathaniel grunted as he bent over and extracted a grateful, and slippery Lazarus from the mud. The dog's coat steamed from exertion.

"That's okay, we'll share the load like before."

"Say, Franklin, what ya gonna do when ya gets ta the Indian territory where they's taken ya?"

"I haven't thought about it. I didn't think I'd be here this long to begin with. I keep telling you that all of this, including you and Lazarus are part of a very long and strange dream I'm having. I thought I'd wake up in my easy chair with nothing better to do than watch the game on TV, and drink beer," Franklin mused. "If you can believe it, my biggest concerns were the noise the Mexicans working in my yard were making, how much of the game I'd miss because of it, and if Gwen would finally bring me a cold beer that wasn't dripping wet."

"Y'all... had slaves?" Nathaniel questioned, his eyes wide with wonder.

"No, I didn't have slaves. I paid them," Franklin answered uneasily.

"Tell me 'bout these... Mexicans," Nathaniel prompted. "I think I seen me one o' them before. Aren't *they* brown people too? How come they's workin' for y'all?"

"I suppose they were having trouble in their own country, so they came to America hoping to do better. I hate to admit it, but they do the jobs most white people don't want to do."

Nathaniel chuckled. "Hmm, sounds like slaves ta me. How much ya pay them?"

Franklin, was feeling uncomfortable with the direction the conversation was going, and responded a little under his breath, "I paid them fair enough."

"Fair enough for this work y'all didn't want ta do? So's y'all could do somethin' else with your time?" Nathaniel retorted. "How ya treat them folks? Ya give 'em somethin' ta drink in the hot sun? Somethin' ta cool the sweat off their brow?" he probed.

"I never asked them to cross the border!" Franklin snapped.

"Yet y'all have 'em come ta yer house and do work y'all don't wants ta do anyways." Nathaniel scratched his chin thoughtfully. "Say," he asked, "why couldn't ya get that beer for yerself? I has got to say, Franklin, this sounds like..."

"That's her job, damn it! That's what women are supposed to do!" Franklin clenched his fists and quickened his step, trying to distance himself from the questions, and causing the mud to squish and pop loudly with each movement forward.

Nathaniel trudged behind in silence for a while.

Franklin tried to pretend Nathaniel wasn't there, but the man's breathing was becoming labored. "Give me that dog," Franklin grumbled, and took Lazarus from Nathaniel's arms, then huffed along beside him for several minutes, the two of them not speaking.

"I don't mean ta upset ya," Nathaniel began. "And I don't know nuthin' 'bout no Mexicans. But the way y'all was talkin' 'bout 'em, and the way y'all was talkin' 'bout yer missus; well, it just don't sound like the man I been walkin' aside of all this ways. Not like the man I been knowin' for a while now. Y'all is like two different people."

Chea Sequa had drawn up along side of the men and had quietly listened to the conversation. "Chuquilatague," he said, nodding his head in agreement with Nathaniel. "Two heads. You tell us of this bad man who we don't know, and of this place he comes from. But all we know is this good man we walk with. All men have two heads Unaduti. We all were given only one, but then that one head became divided into two. The first head was good. It was connected to its heart. The second head came because of something that caused pain to the first. This caused it to separate from the heart and forget right from wrong, good from bad. This is not your fault," the Indian continued. "It is not anyone's fault. But things happen in life that offer the opportunity for the second head to reconnect with the heart where the spirit of every man lives. Which head takes over depends on which of them you feed. Perhaps your time here is for you to decide which head you will feed. Perhaps if you wake up in the place you say you are from, you will wake up with your eyes open because you have become reconnected with your heart, and see things as they really are. This place and all that is happening, as bad as it is, may be lucky for you. Maybe you must wake up to your heart before you can wake up in your home again." Chea Sequa patted Franklin's shoulder. "But I think this is something that only you can choose."

"I gotta pee," Franklin muttered. He was overwhelmed by the young brave's comment. "Take the mutt," he said, and he placed Lazarus back into Nathaniel's arms. "I gotta pee!" he announced again, and he raised his arm to get the attention of a soldier riding nearby.

"Nobody stoppin' ya boy," drawled the man, his cheek bulging with a wad of chewing tobacco.

"I can't move to the side of the road. These chains are too short," Franklin said, trying to reason with the man.

"Then that's where yer gonna pee, just like the rest of y'all. We ain't stoppin' fer y'all to piss, or anythin' else. Y'all stink ta high heaven as it is. More piss ain't gonna change that," the soldier said, then he spit a stream of yellow-brown juice into the mud.

"What about the women, the children?" Franklin's voice raised angrily.

Chea Sequa and Nathaniel moved in closer beside Franklin and shushed him.

"That's right. Yer injun and yer nigger friend is right. Y'all best shut yer mouth and walk, piss, or whatever ya gotta do. Women, children, Injuns, niggers,... makes no difference."

Franklin looked straight ahead, his blood boiling. He trudged on with the support of his two friends. He held back the urge to pee as long as he could but finally had to let it go. The immediate relief was followed by a welcome but momentary warmth, quickly replaced by biting cold. The snow flurries had become continuous as the rain, and gradually replaced it altogether.

"Nathaniel, what do you plan to do when we get to..." Franklin caught himself just before he said Indian territory. Instead, he finished with, "the place they're taking us?"

Nathaniel looked around and saw that the soldier had moved up in the line. "Well, I been meanin' to tell y'all 'bout it soon enough, but I spose now's as good a time as any. I ain't plannin' on goin' there."

"Are you planning on waking up too?" Chea Sequa laughed good naturally, then dropped behind to walk with Tsula.

"I wish we could *all* wake up from this terrible place," Nathaniel said. The ground they were walking on was firm, and he leaned over and put Lazarus back on the ground. "But I ain't countin' on it. No, suh, I's planning on cuttin' back east when we comes ta the Ohia River."

"What are you talking about?" asked Franklin. "You'll die out there on your own. Once we get to Oklahoma, you'll be fine. You'll be able to start over... have a new life."

"I don't know 'bout this Okla-homie thing y'all is talkin' 'bout. 'Sides, I thought y'all was gonna wake up before then," he laughed. His eyes took on a far away look. "I lost my life already when I lost my family. So's I'm gonna go east through Kintucky and Ohio, and on inta Pennsyvania. Gonna go lookin' fer my wife and kids. Git my life back. Just like y'all is, Franklin. When I finds my family, I finds my life."

Franklin was fairly certain that getting his life couldn't be equated with what his friend was talking about, but he knew he wanted it to be, and that was something new for him. He wondered if Chea Sequa was right about his two heads, and this experience having something to do with reconnecting his bad one to his heart. He vowed to himself, he was going to pay attention to which one he fed from now on.

# CHAPTER 28

The rain lightened as they traveled north, changed gradually to snow flurries, then stopped altogether. Although the temperature remained quite cold, the group was relieved that the mud was beginning to harden into firmer footing. Despite these improvements, the sounds of moaning and coughing took the place of the previously incessant pattering of the rain.

A day did not go by that a mournful wail wasn't heard arising from somewhere along the long line of disheveled Indians. Some days were interrupted by several of these outbursts, each of which signaled the death of a loved one. As no time was allowed for burial, Franklin began to see corpses left lying along the side of the road. And as the snow drifted into deeper banks, he sometimes passed an extended arm or leg sticking up from the drifts reminiscent of morbid images he had seen of captives being led to concentration camps.

Just after the group crested a hill, Franklin rubbed his eyes. This time it wasn't to clear them of snowflakes. He thought he could see the lights of a town up ahead. Not a simple mountain village as the others had been, this looked more like an actual town. Elbowing Nathaniel, he said hoarsely, "Is that what I think it is?"

"I see it! I sure could use me some grits," Nathaniel chuckled and managed a weak smile through his chattering teeth.

"A place this size... maybe we can get some real food," Franklin responded feeling his spirits lift. "I could go for a hot bowl of soup or chili."

"Alls we gotta do is go over that hill yonder and before long we be sittin' right in the middle of town," said Nathaniel, the excitement rising in his voice.

"Then why's the line moving to the right?"

"They's probly takin' us in the back way. I don't mind. Guess I'm kinda use ta that."

Arriving at the crest of the hill, Franklin's question was answered. Several soldiers were seated on horseback right in the middle of the road with their rifles at the ready. Behind them, Franklin saw a sign post that read McMinnville. He heard the men hollering orders as they waved the Indians onto a side road. Mixed in with the soldiers were a handful of rough looking strangers. Because they were not wearing uniforms, Franklin figured they must have come from the town itself. As he followed the line and turned right in front of the soldiers and townsmen, he overheard one of them talking animatedly to one of the soldiers.

"No suh!" said a scruffy old codger in muddy boots and bib-overalls. "Don't aim ta let a single one of them savages set a foot inta this town." The man adjusted the brim of his hat down to just above his eyes, then he and another townsman next to him spit in unison out if front of themselves. "It wouldn't matter none even if they *wasn't* sick. They's vermin ta us, and they ain't comin' through!"

The soldier the townsman had addressed tipped his hat and reigned his horse back around to face the ragged line of Indians. He pointed to his left, directing the line down a trail that headed east and back into the forest.

Another townsman shouted after them, "Ain't no self respectin' town from here ta where y'all are goin' that'll let you savages step foot inside *them* neither!"

The side road skirted the town by a couple of miles, and was less maintained than the one they had been on. The ruts were deep, muddy, and crusted over thinly with ice. The Indians stumbled along in their chains, and more often than not, tripped in the ruts. Several men and women sustained twisted or broken ankles, and had to be supported by others to be able to continue. Finally, after coming to a spot Franklin decided must be the town's refuse dump, the soldiers ordered them to stop for the night.

The camp arrangement was the same as it had been on the trail up to now. The Indians were ordered to assemble themselves in a tight group. This was then encircled by the tents of the soldiers who patrolled the perimeter around them, this time with the assistance McMinnville's citizen-militia. Franklin doubted the security was necessary because of the weakened state of the Indians. Never the less, several fires were started immediately, and more sprung up by the minute. The Indians huddled as close to these and to eac other as they could while they waited for food.

Franklin remembered reading once that a person could survive for three weeks without food, three days without water, and if it was snowing, three hours without shelter. But these averages had been based upon otherwise healthy individuals. Most of the Indians on the trail had been held under concentration camp conditions from one to two months; the rations, pitifully small, the water contaminated, and neither fit for animals. Thus, many of them suffered from parasites, which in turn led to cholera, dysentery, nausea, and dehydration.

The bedraggled group of Indians had walked for miles in non-stop rain mixed with occasional snow flurries for more days than not since leaving Fort Cass. For much of this time they had been trudging through knee deep mud and dropping temperatures. Most of their clothing had been reduced to rags, and many of them were without footwear of any kind. Now they were camped alongside the town's waste dump. Franklin thought he had become immune to stench due to his own and that of the Indians all around him. The current situation proved him wrong.

Most would agree that it was a stretch for Franklin to find the positive in most things. But although the dump attracted a contagion of assorted vermin, including rats, he and his friends ate fresh meat for the first time in weeks. He settled for that.

Due to the miserable conditions in the camp, the group was only too happy to be on the move again the following morning. The military picked up a few volunteer militia men from McMinnville to assist them with watching the Indians along the trail, and the Indians soon learned that if they thought the soldiers were tough and lacked compassion, the militia men were demons by comparison. They taunted and berated the Indians ceaselessly, and in spite of the sicknesses and extreme raggedness of the Indian women, they never ceased looking for opportunities to have their way with them; a new low, even by Franklin's standards.

He had learned that to speak up would do more harm than good, so Franklin kept his mouth shut and plodded along, Lazarus at his heel. Nathaniel walked on one side of him, and Degataga, Waya, and Kanuna on the other. Chea Sequa walked behind them next to his friend, Mohe. The two young braves, their heads hanging down, lamented that they couldn't walk alongside the women they loved. All of the women now walked unshackled behind the men who were in chains. Franklin only shook his head with sadness when he overheard Chea Sequa tell his friend that he believed Tsula was pregnant. Mohe seemed happy about this, and said he believed that Ahinita, his love, too was with child. Wrestling with his inability to understand how bringing a child into a situation as devastating as this could possibly be viewed as a good thing, a disruption up ahead interrupted Franklin's thoughts.

"Y'all wanted the corn, so let loose of them horses! We made a deal!" Yelled a man sitting on a buckboard loaded with burlap sacks. He had a rifle in one hand and the reigns to the horses drawing his wagon draped over his knee. Two other men were trying to pry a couple of horses away from some Indians who were clearly not happy with what appeared to Franklin to be a deal gone sour.

It had become increasingly common since leaving McMinnville for whites to offer food to the Indians along the trail. Taking advantage of the Indian's emaciated condition, they demanded horses in payment at exorbitant prices for corn, beans, or dried meat.

Several more voices joined in the disturbance, and a soldier of rank from somewhere back in the line rode up to apparently help sort things out in what was quickly becoming a heated argument. He arrived on the scene where three Cherokee Indians on horseback—recruited to assist the military's efforts to keep order on the trail—were speaking with a townsman in the wagon.

"Just who the hell are you injuns, to be tellin' me what ta do with my goods?" the man argued with the Indians on horseback. "Them horses is mine, fair n' square!"

"I am Moses Daniels, Conductor of this detachment. And these men are, Martin Davis, and Jacob Grey Bear, my Commissary agents," the Indian said, referring to his companions. "We have authority to handle any dispute between you and those walking this trail."

"I'll be damned if I'm gonna listen to some savage tellin' me what I can and cannot do!" the man on the buckboard hollered. He cocked his rifle and leveled it at Moses.

"Everybody simmer down!" the soldier ordered. He put his hand up in the air signaling a halt. "What's the problem here?" he demanded of the man on the wagon.

"These here injuns just got handed a bag o' my finest corn me and my boys hauled all the ways outchere. Now they don't wanna pay the fair price I asked 'em for! That was the deal!" huffed the wagon driver.

The Indians on the ground erupted in a cacophony of vehement disagreement, and pulled again at the horses, trying to free them.

"Now these injuns," the man continued, pointing at Moses, Martin, and Jacob, "think they can tell me what I gotta do with my business! Well, I don't listen to no savages, never did, never will!"

"All right, all right!" the soldier raised his voice over the melee. "If you got that bag of corn at your feet from this man, you'll have to pay up," he informed the Indians. "Now pay the man so's we can move along."

One of the Indians picked up the sack of corn. He and some others resumed their complaint in their native tongue.

Franklin turned to Degataga. "What are they saying?"

"They say the corn not good enough for two horses. Not good enough for one. They say the white man is cheating them with corn that is mixed with stones. They say, why don't you feed this shit to your Indian guards like the dogs they are. They think because they ride with the soldiers, they are better than their own people!"

Franklin turned back to the argument and watched as the Indian holding the sack suddenly dropped it. Upon hitting the ground, the bag burst open and a flow of yellow spilled out along with a cloud of dust. The Indian who dropped the bag kicked at the corn and spit at the feet of Moses' horse.

Another eruption of angry voices ensued.

Franklin looked questioningly at Degataga who said, "They are saying that the corn is bad. It is old and mixed full of stones and dirt." The old Indian took Franklin by his arm and pulled him near. "It is true. Those braves riding with the soldiers, they betray us. They have become hated even more than the white man."

"You can't just break open a bag o' corn and then 'spect to walk away for nothin'!" roared the outraged wagon driver. He turned to the soldier and hollered, "I 'spect y'all ta hold them redskins accountable!"

The argument continued, and Franklin looked over at Degataga again for another translation when a movement and a flash of color in the trees off to his left caught his eye. He had gotten so distracted by the altercation going on in front of him, he didn't notice the commotion that was happening about forty yards behind. The women were holding onto each other and crying, their eyes were wide with fear. The reason was abundantly clear. Along side of them sat a single horseman—one of the town militia men—and he was holding a rifle leveled into the midst of them.

The flash of color caught Franklin's eye again, and he saw two militia men struggling with a couple of Indian women just beyond the tree line. They were too far off for Franklin to be able to tell who they were. He tugged Degataga around by the arm, and pointed toward the women in the woods.

"Hiyohisda! Stop!" Degataga yelled. He turned and waved his arms wildly in the air at the soldier who was still arguing up front. "Alisdelvdi itsulaayv! Help us!"

Waya and the three young braves all turned to look, and they immediately recognized Tsula and Ahinita, fighting to break free from the two men. All of them began yelling and waving their arms to get the soldier's attention. With brut strength fueled by fear and anger, they pulled all of the men connected to them with chains toward the side of the road in an effort to get to the women.

The soldier in charge looked up at the new commotion and fired his rifle in the air. "Stop right there or I'll shoot you dead, ... all of you!" he hollered. Then he directed his horse into the opening created by the four Indians. Looking over his shoulder he shouted back at the Indians he had just left. "You broke the damned bag open, so you bought it! Pay up with one horse, not two, and the rest of you," he hollered, directing his gaze at the man in the wagon, "get on outta here! I don't wanna see your sorry ass again! Understood?" He then turned his attention back to the new problem at hand. "What the hell has got into you?"

Moses, Martin, and Jacob rode up along side the soldier. Fingering the triggers of their rifles, they warily eyed their comrades on the ground.

But the Indians weren't paying attention to them, instead they pointed to the woods and cried out in desperation for the women. They strained at their chains, their veins popping out on their necks and arms. The only thing that held them back was the combined weight and strength of all the others who for their own good, pulled against them.

Franklin shouted to the soldier, "Your men took some women into the woods!" As he pointed in the women's direction he saw that one of the men had begun to tear the clothes from one of them. At the same time, the other woman broke away from another man who had been trying to wrestle her to the ground. She clawed at him, and he grabbed at his face in obvious pain. Freed for the moment, she pounded the head and back of the first man in an attempt to free her friend. The militia man rolled off of his victim, swearing vengeance. The two women ran frantically in opposite directions, one deeper into the woods, the other, back toward the line of Indians. By this time, all of the Indians in the area, aware of what was happening, were in an uproar.

Moses said something to the soldier in charge who immediately yelled, "Stop right there! Let them women be!"

But one of the militia men had already drawn his pistol. He fired at the woman running into the woods at close to point blank range. The first shot apparently missed, and the woman darted between two trees where her assailant's horses were tethered. The man fired a second shot and the woman stopped. She turned slowly and stood still, panting, her right hand clutching at her side, where a bloom of bright red was unfolding like a rose.

The man pointed the gun and pulled the hammer back preparing to fire another round.

Suddenly, a loud blast cracked the air just above Franklin's head and he ducked reflexively with the other Indians. His nostrils filled with the pungent aroma of sulfur and black smoke wafting over him from the soldier's rifle. The soldier's horse jumped skittishly at the percussive sound and bumped into several of the braves knocking them into one another. He had either missed, or shot over the militia man's head, because the man was still standing and appeared to be taking another bead on the woman.

The soldier re-cocked his still smoking rifle, and commanded the militia man to put his gun down, but no sooner had he spoke that there was another loud rifle report from the other side of Franklin. The militia man crumpled to the ground like a bag of rocks before he could pull his own trigger.

Two more soldiers, one from behind and the other from up ahead galloped out after the other assailant who, in the confusion, had jumped on his horse and was beating a path into the woods. They gave up the chase, and instead rode back to the two women, then signaled for medical attention.

Jacob's smoking rifle hung at his side, the heat of the barrel sizzling against his snow wet buckskin chaps.

"What you just did, son," the soldier in charge said looking Jacob up and down, "painted a big ol' sign on yourself that says shoot me! The townsfolk around here don't like Injuns to begin with, and they especially don't like Injuns that kill white folk. Now they got them a legitimate excuse to kill you. And they won't stop there." He turned around and hollered to the others. "That means y'all are fair game!" He shook his head. "Hand me your rifle Jacob." Then he turned back to the rest of the Indians. "Get back in line all of you, and move out! Martin, see that woman gets put into a wagon. With any luck she might survive, for all the good that'll do after this.

# CHAPTER 29

The treatment the Indians received in McMinnville was repeated in Murfreesboro. They were met by armed militia on the outskirts of town and directed far around the perimeter rather than being allowed to pass through. By this time, Franklin had undergone—what was for him—a staggering transformation of awareness. What he once believed to be the unquestionably correct handling of the Indians, he now perceived as not only cruel, but patently absurd, and displayed gross ignorance regarding any semblance of understanding regarding the nobility of the Cherokee.

In spite of the bitter cold, many Indians were burning with fever. The dead bodies of those who died from starvation, or succumbed to whooping cough, cholera, dysentery, measles, or small pox, had become a common sight along the sides of the road. Among the living, their raspy coughing was punctuated by an almost constant mournful wail from those who had lost loved ones. The curse of sleet and snow became a blessing in that it often covered the frozen and contorted bodies, softening the lines of their frightened and pain-filled expressions. Those corpses that remained visible reminded Franklin of images he had seen in a National Geographic magazine about Pompeii, where the citizens were frozen in time, their bodies entombed, but with volcanic ash, rather than snow.

As the throng of Indians neared Nashville, more merchants rode out and negotiated with them, offering food for horses. Despite the poor quality of the food, the exhausted and starving Indians had become more willing to trade. More troubling than this, white men had begun to approach both the soldiers and the Indians expressing their desire to purchase women and slaves. The soldiers, who had chased away such scoundrels up to now, although enjoying the comfort and convenience of warm tents and plentiful rations, were tiring, and had become less resistant to the intrusions of these predators. The exception being if the townsmen were interested in a woman already being used by a soldier, in which case, they were summarily chased away like so many ragged dogs looking for scraps.

Nathaniel nudged Franklin. "We comin' ta another town."

Franklin, having trudged for hours through ankle deep snow, he had fallen into a road-weary stupor, and ignored his friend. The group was once again being diverted away from the main road of entry to the north-east, and Franklin felt relief knowing they would soon make camp.

Nathaniel persisted with his attempt to get Franklin's attention, elbowing him with as much force as he could muster, and Franklin, realizing his friend was not going to stop, finally looked up. He immediately spotted a light, and the three men seated on horses alongside the road, just inside the tree line. One of them held a lantern. All three carried rifles. As Franklin and Nathaniel shuffled by with the others, the men nudged their mounts and plodded alongside of them, pacing their slow progress.

"What do we have here?" one of the men said leaning down from his mount for a closer look. He straightened back up, clucked at his horse, and sidled up next to Nathaniel. "Oh Lordy! They's two of 'em! And just when we was about ta give up for the night. What's yer name boy?" the man drawled.

Franklin kept his head down and continued walking. There were no soldiers near by, but despite his vulnerability, he felt his blood beginning to boil.

"I'm talkin' ta ya, boy. Don't get me riled."

"Nathaniel,... suh."

Lazarus emitted a low guttural growl, and both Nathaniel and Franklin shushed him at the same time.

"And this un?" the man said nodding his head at Franklin. "I guess he just don't know how ta talk, or maybe he's forgettin' his manners."

Side-eyed, Nathaniel glanced nervously at his friend.

"Franklin."

After a short silence, the man prodded Franklin's side with his boot and said dryly, "That can't be yer name boy, Franklin weren't no nigger. He was white." The three men laughed at this, and slapped each other on the shoulder.

"This man is Unaduti, and this other is Chuquilatague," inserted Degataga.

"Now, I have heard some funny soundin' colored names before, but these here are somethin' else," the man responded in a sing song voice. "These boys belong to y'all, chief?"

"We don't belong to anybody," growled Franklin.

Degataga gently grabbed his arm to silence him, before he could say more. "They are family," answered Degataga.

"Now let me see if I got this right," the man said with a chuckle. "These two boys are colored, and y'all are injun, but yer tellin' me they's family?"

"That's right," said Degataga.

"Well, now, I can't say as I understand it, but I do respect it, chief. I really do. Now, since there don't seem ta be any soldiers near by, me and my boys could have just rode up here and drug these two niggers right off. But in these tryin' times, what with y'all starvin', and it just gettin' colder and all... . And now, seein' as how y'all are family, well, our hearts just wouldn't feel right doin' that. Instead, I'm thinkin' maybe we could help y'all out some. How 'bout we give y'all a good amount of food and some clothes ta keep ya warm, in exchange for these two coloreds here, who, family or not, technically ain't even yer own people. Stands ta reason there's times when a man needs ta think about his own kind, and protect them over the rest, ain't there? I mean, it just makes sense, don't it? Seems to me that's a mighty fair trade. 'Specially considerin' the alternative I mentioned a while back." The man adjusted himself on his mount, the saddle creaking with his movement, and a look of satisfaction on his face.

Lazarus's growl rose to a rumble, and the man snapped sharply. "Best keep control of that mutt, chief, if you aim ta keep 'im around."

Franklin stroked the dog's ears. "Quiet boy, everything's alright."

"That's where you are wrong," said Degataga, in a firm voice.

The other townsman brought his rifle up, aimed it at the dogs chest, and thumbed the hammer back.

"Put it down. Let's hear the chief out," said the first.

Looking the man in the eye, Degataga continued with his voice steady, "Among my people, family has nothing to do with the color of skin." He bared his forearm and stroked it with a finger. "This is not where the soul of a person is," he said with a tone of incredulity. Shifting his gaze to Franklin and then back again, he continued. "It also has nothing to do with where a person comes from. The soul of a person resides in the heart. So your proposition makes no sense to me or to my people."

"Whoa, chief, what the hell does that have ta do with family or selling slaves?" the man challenged.

Degataga replied with seasoned patience. "What you do not understand, what it seems most white men do not understand, is that family is not restricted to one's race or blood. Because you don't understand this, you feel justified in using anyone who you do not consider family for your gain, or if they cannot be used for your profit, removing them from out of your way. Family has everything to do with the heart and with the soul that lives there. That is what makes a man or a woman what they are. That is what makes them family. Therefore, I do not merely love these men as my brothers, they *are* my brothers. They are not for sale... at any price."

A rifle barrel smacked the back of Degataga's head.

"What y'all savages don't understand," the man countered with a snarl, "is that I came here with my boys ta make y'all a deal. A good deal. Not ta be talked back at by a nigger, or ta listen ta an old heathen flappin' his lips. What y'all don't understand, chief, is that I ain't giving y'all a choice no more." One of the man's companions produced a sledge hammer and a crowbar, and the other readied a rifle. "We aim ta cut these two coloreds loose and be on our way. If y'all don't care ta profit by it, that is okay by me. I'm takin' 'em either way." Turning to Franklin and Nathaniel the man said, "Step on over ta this boulder and we'll just cut them chains right off."

As neither Franklin or Nathaniel budged, the man reached out to grab the chain that connected the two of them. But a sudden rush of yellow fir, and a sound that was half growl and half bark stunned them all as Lazarus lunged forward and sunk his teeth into the man's wrist, then ferociously whipped his head from side to side.

"Yeow! Son of a...! Shoot the damn animal! Shoot it!" the man screamed.

Lazarus, still firmly gripping the man's arm, pulled him off his horse. Straddling him with his full weight, he pinned the man to the ground.

The horse spooked and bolted into the woods, and the other two men dropped their tools, and fumbled with their rifles.

"Haliwista! Ha!" shouted Jacob Grey Bear, who had ridden up to investigate the disturbance. He sat on his mount directly behind the townsmen.

Nathaniel called Lazarus off, and the dog reluctantly released his enemy who rolled from side to side, cradling his bloodied arm in agony. The other townsmen froze where they stood not needing a translation for Grey Bear's command.

"He ain't armed!" hollered the man on the ground. "Shoot the bastard!"

If the man's partners had any thought of complying with their partner's demand, the loud click of a rifle being cocked, immediately followed by a second, they apparently reconsidered, and stood still.

The injured man, his face beet red with anger, screamed. "He ain't gonna pull the trigger, damn it, shoot him!"

"It is time for you to leave," a voice commanded from the shadows behind them. Moses Daniels, flanked by Martin Davis rode up and stood their horses to either side of Jacob Grey Bear, who had situated himself between the Indians and the townsmen. "Jacob may not have permission to shoot you at this time," continued Moses, "but we do."

"I swear on my life I'll never understand savages!" the injured man fumed as he struggled to his feet.

*How sad,* Francis thought, *If I had lived at this time, that could have been me.*

One of the would be slave traders kicked his steed and galloped off into the woods. "Don't just stand there gawkin!" the injured man muttered to the remaining partner. "Get my horse!"

\*\*\*

The flurry of snowflakes quickly grew into an early winter storm, and the Cherokee hurried to make their camp. In the frenzy of activity, Mohe asked Waya to watch over Ahinita who was not doing well from an infection that had set in as a result of her gunshot wound. He then turned and began to wriggle his wrists against his shackles. Mohe, like the rest of the Indians, had lost a significant amount of weight, and with a just a bit of effort, managed to slip free.

"What are you doing son?" Waya asked.

"I cannot allow the man who did this go without punishment." Mohe turned and disappeared into the blinding snow.

# CHAPTER 30

The snow storm abated during the night, and by the following morning the weather had taken a warming trend. As a result the Indians were driven relentlessly through muddy slush, and reached Nashville, a distance of thirty miles inside of two days. The Indians were diverted as usual around the outskirts of the city, but as had happened in the first two towns, Franklin and Nathaniel were held back to be led in chains down the main street. Unlike before, there arose an uproar amongst the soldiers assigned to Indian duty.

Even from the outskirts of Nashville, Franklin understood their complaint. Compared to the other smaller towns he'd traveled through on this journey, this was a bourgeoning city. Franklin estimated that roughly five to six thousand people must live there, not to mention the number of people who came to Nashville to conduct business of one kind or another. The place was bustling, a veritable beehive of sights and sounds. Horses and buggies clip-clopped one way or another down the cobble stoned streets. Men sat outside barbershops smoking pipes or cigars, reading the paper, or engaging in animated conversation. The people Franklin observed appeared to be more sophisticated as well, and dressed more stylishly, than those of the mostly one road towns he'd seen up until now.

Franklin also noticed that while a fair number of the men in town seemed to be busy with the conduction of various forms of business, the few women he saw seemed to fall into one of three categories; those who were engaged in some kind of menial labor, such as carrying bushels of apples, or scrubbing a storefront walkway. While others were managing children. Then there were the prostitutes and the whores who worked an assortment of taverns, and ceaselessly called out to passersby with the promise of a good time. His assessment in the last instance seemed verified by the cat-calls, whistles, and lewd comments made by the soldiers as they passed near these establishments, and the purring and lascivious retorts made in return by the garishly made up women, along with the occasional flashing of an ankle, or less often, a thigh. To Franklin, Nashville was the epitome of a man's world.

"Halt!" the captain of the group ordered as they arrived in front of a lively looking saloon. The sounds of laughter, clinking glass, and a honky-tonk piano, punctuated by an occasional bawdy female shriek floated out from the establishment into the street. Two women walking by the doorway, one with a man by her side, another with a child in tow, turned their noses up and swiftly huffed away.

"Tether these boys to the posts and rails up here," the captain instruct-ed a couple of his men. The two soldiers led Franklin and Nathaniel over to a hitching post, and fastened them by their chains along side of the horses. The captain tested the shackles, and satisfied the two men were properly secured, turned his attention back to his men. "I recommend you boys make good use of your time inside. And make it right quick, so's you can relieve the others still out in the woods, and give those boys a chance at them gals."

"Won't be nothin' left for 'em once we get through in there," boasted the soldier who'd chained Franklin to a wooden rail.

The rest of the soldiers slapped one another on the back and clomped up the wooden steps.

"I've heard tell that for some of you boys, gettin' finished with your business quick won't be a problem," quipped the captain after them.

The men roared with laughter and jostled good naturedly with one an-other as they elbowed their way past swinging doors.

A flyer that had been tacked to the wall of the saloon caught Franklin's eye. It stated in bold, flamboyant lettering that *The Progressive State of Tennessee, Proud to be known throughout these United States as The Volunteer State, has declared the death sentence for murder, no longer mandatory.* The notice further lauded the "enlightened" governing body of Tennessee, for being the first in the nation to make such a change.

"Sweet Jesus in heaven!"

The cry from a woman somewhere behind him disrupted Franklin's attention from the flyer. He turned in the direction it came from and saw her pointing a finger at a cart that was just about to pass by him in the middle of the street. The woman grabbed the two children she had with her and smothered their faces against her billowing, ankle-length dress. Her cry was echoed by others as the horse drawn cart clattered on its steel banded, wooden wheels over cobblestones.

Franklin recognized the man driving the cart as the one who had gotten away in the woods after the attempted rape of the two Indian women. This was the man that Mohe had gone after to avenge his love, Ahinita. "Get back behind that post!" Franklin hissed at Nathaniel, then squeezed himself in between the horses, and out of sight of the rattling cart. Once the cart had passed by, Franklin peeked underneath the belly of one of the horses. Lying upon the bed of the cart, was a man on his back, his face bruised and bloodied. Franklin drew a sharp breath realizing that it was Mohe, the color drained from his body, but still alive. His eyes widened momentarily with recognition when he saw Franklin, but the young brave didn't make a sound.

Franklin glanced over his shoulder at the swinging doors of the saloon. He wanted the captain to finish his time inside so he could tell him about Mohe. But the only thing exiting the saloon was the sound of debauchery. Franklin turned back to the street and watched as a growing throng of townspeople fell in behind the wagon.

The captain finally stumbled out onto the boardwalk with the last group of soldiers, and either failed to notice, or flat out ignored Franklin's attempts to engage him. "Line up!" he hollered at the motley group. "Soldier!" he said to one of the men who had a rather hefty woman still latched to his arm. "Leave her here. You can't be taking the merchandise with you."

Soldiers laughed as they tripped off the boardwalk down to the street.

"What if I ssharzz 'er? They'sh plenty of 'er ta go around," the soldier slurred, then hiccuped.

His comment caused a fresh round of laughter and back slapping amongst the rest of the men.

"I'm afraid you're gonna have to throw 'er back. With any luck she'll still be here when we come back this way."

"What's the missus gonna say about this, Luke?" One of the soldiers teased.

"What she don't know won't hurt 'er," Luke replied.

"Yeah, but if'n she does find out, y'all could wind up dead!"

Luke, wobbling on his feet, rounded off on the man, with his fists in the air, and the rest of the men quickly formed a circle around them and urged their comrades on.

"Enough!" blared the captain. "We've got no time for fisticuffs. You can take care of matters when we get to camp if you still have a mind for it. Now, move out, or I'll have you both chained up with the niggers."

"Speakin' of niggers," Luke said. "Why don't we unload them two we got with us at that auction up the street? Make us a little cash fer when we come back here."

In response to the soldier's comment, Franklin craned his neck to see around a couple of horses. Franklin spotted a gathering of people across the street, and about a block and a half away. They were all facing a platform upon which stood a black woman on one end and a black man on the other. Strutting back and forth in front of them, engaging the crowd, was a tall, thin, mustached man in a black and white striped coat and top hat.

The captain ordered Franklin and Nathaniel released from the hitching post and the group resumed their way through town in the direction of the growing crowd. When they had come to within ten yards of the spectacle, the slave seller directed the crowd's attention to Franklin and Nathaniel in their shredded rags and clanging chains. A collective gasp arose in response from the spectators, and a couple of young boys, about the age of ten or eleven had slingshots, and were aiming right at them.

The stones zinged through the air. One, passed overhead, but the other hit Franklin just to the side of his nose, drawing blood, and making his eyes water. The trader sang out, "Now, gentlemen, … *and* ladies, please do not invest too much of your time with such rubble as you see coming down the road. These niggers are merely like so many pigs being led to slaughter. From the look and smell of them, I have no doubt they are being led to their imminent deaths. They are the refuse,… the dross,… the scum,… which is scraped off the earth and cast away. Only the best meat is sent to market," he said, sweeping his hand, and the attention of the crowd back to the makeshift stage. "Once again, behold the fine specimens I have brought to show you today, and today only, and you will immediately see the difference in quality." He signaled the black man on the platform to remove his shirt and flex. "Don't be shy ladies and gents. Come on up here for a closer look at these work-ready muscles! And remember that after today, any of these I have not sold, will be shipped down the mighty Mississippi to New Orleans, where I have no doubt the people of that great municipality will snatch them up in a frenzy of recognition for the fine servile specimens they are." The Hawker then signaled the black woman, who was wearing a white robe. She untied the belt around her waist and allowed the garment to fall open to her waist.

The crowd in front of her gasped, and pleased with the response, the trader twirled his finger in the air, prompting the woman to turn herself slowly around in a full circle; the gasps following her movement like a wave. "Now, who'll start the bidding?"

Franklin thought that on the one hand, he had never been so happy to be in such a horrid condition in comparison to the clean, oiled, and well fed men and women being displayed on the trader's stage. But in a deeper place, a place where his personal view of the world had seemed over the years to have solidified into a permanent, rock-hard sediment that held any other possibility back, something stirred. More accurately, it roiled. The concrete cover had already begun to crack, the battlements crumbled, and suddenly, the fissure busted wide open. He felt like he was going to throw up. But instead, tears flowed down his grizzled face.

He knew there was nothing he could do to help those people that were being displayed as animals. Franklin realized now that they were objects for others to inflict pain upon, fueled by hatred, or ignorance, or both, together with their own lack of awareness that they, themselves—as he himself had mindlessly been—were the defective ones. Their own hearts, like his, had been turned to stone. In an unconscious, misguided effort to assuage their own pain, and prevent themselves from one day cracking open, they beat upon, and defiled others.

Franklin wondered if he was in hell. That maybe this wasn't just a strange alcohol induced dream after all. He hoped to God that if he was dead, he was instead in purgatory, a condition under which the dregs that fouled his soul would however painfully, be burned away. At least purgatory as he understood it, was a temporary state. *How long Lord?* He cried inside. *How much more do I have to see? How much more do I have to feel?*

As God sometimes does, He answered Franklin, but not with words. And neither did God relieve Franklin of his misery, He added to it. As Franklin and the others continued past the slave auction, he felt a tug on his arm. It was Nathaniel. And in his friends eyes, where before Franklin had seen warmth, and the reflection of his own face, he now saw horror.

Nathaniel's eyes were open wide, his pupils dilated to two big black discs. His nostrils were flared, and he wasn't breathing. Following his friend's gaze, Franklin caught his own breath.

"My God!" he gasped. "What the hell ... ?" The rest of the words caught in his throat as he took in and then tried to make sense of another gathering he saw up the road.

"That be exactly what y'all think it be. They's hangin' that poor man." Nathaniel confirmed.

The man Nathaniel was referring to stood on a box located at the back end of a wagon, hands secured behind his back and a noose around his neck. Even from a distance, it was clear that he was terrified.

At that moment, another man, wearing a heavy, ankle-length, dark coat, and standing beside the one being hung cried out, "Get up!" and clucked his tongue. The wheels of the wagon creaked as the team of horses it was harnessed to slowly moved forward. The man strained to keep his footing to no avail, as his toes scraped along the surface of the box. Once he cleared the edge, the horses stopped, and his body fell about three feet.

Franklin heard the crack of the man's neck as the noose stopped his fall in mid-air. As much as he wanted to look away, he couldn't. The man's legs twitched as though he was trying to kick at the pack of pesky little dogs that were nipping at his ankles. His eyes bulged, and the veins in his neck turned purple as he thrashed around like a caught fish on the end of a stringer. His tongue protruded and swelled to a freakish size. His feet kicked weakly several more times, then became still.

The crowd, who moments before had been cursing at the victim, and cheering his fate, were now silent. The only sound that could be heard was the creaking of the rope as it gently swayed and stretched under the weight of the body. His clothing was ragged. He was clearly not a refined townsman. Blood that covered the man's head obscuring the features of his face, dripped to his shoulders and down his chest.

Franklin stilled himself as the group shuffled passed the corpse, and tried to discern any semblance of humanity that might remain of his face. "Oh, hell," he groaned and seized Nathaniel's forearm, and whispered, "It's Mohe," then froze in place. But as the rest of the group continued plodding along, he was pushed by the butt of a rifle from behind. Stumbling clumsily forward several steps, Franklin caught himself and fell mechanically back in line with the soldiers as they made their way to the north end of Nashville. He and Nathaniel walked in mute silence for what seemed like hours, even though by the time they rejoined the Cherokee, they had only gotten to a mere mile outside of town.

Franklin actually prayed that he would not run into Waya. He didn't want to be the bearer of such terrible news, and hoped he could speak with Degataga, who would then carry the message to his friend. But when he and Nathaniel were situated back into the group of Indians, he found himself walking alongside, not only Waya, but Ahinita as well. Neither of them said a word, but both wore looks of expectancy on their faces. In spite of the otherwise worsening conditions, they and the rest of the Indians also looked upbeat in comparison to earlier in the day when they had been detoured from entering Nashville. The reason seemed obvious enough to Franklin. Unlike it had been on the trail up to now, the soldiers had not separated the Indians by gender.

Franklin looked first at the older Indian, then at the girl, and Waya nodded his encouragement for Franklin to speak.

"For the love of God!" Franklin blubbered helplessly.

Waya closed his eyes and dropped his head to his chest, and Ahinita clutched at her heart. From somewhere deep inside each of them, a sound like that of a cat in heat began to arise. The wailing intensified with each step and spread from one Indian to another, lasting long into the night.

Franklin felt like he was going to throw-up. He kicked the ground with each step until his toes went numb, then kicked some more. The agony of the people he walked with was unbearable. *Wake up, Franklin! You gotta wake up from this fucking nightmare!* he screamed inside his head.

But when he opened his eyes the following morning, Franklin shivered in the cold, then lined up with the others for another days journey. He hadn't taken a dozen steps before he noticed another corpse laying along the side of the road just ahead. Through a thick layer of pine boughs that had been laid over the body and weighted down by several large rocks, he thought he could make out the outline of a face seemingly peering back at him. As Franklin passed by, he noticed that the face belonged to Ahinita. He found out later from Degataga, that grieving over her loss of Mohe, she had gouged her throat open with the splintered, sharp edge of a rock.

Waya refused to eat again after that, and four days later, he collapsed dead in line. The captain allowed the group to stop just long enough to roll his body to the side.

# CHAPTER 31

O ver a period of roughly two weeks, the group of more than one-thousand Indians was driven between ten to fifteen miles a day. The temperature steadily declined until it became bitterly cold, and showed no signs of letting up. They passed Hopkinsville, Kentucky, and several smaller communities before arriving at the Ohio River and Berry's Ferry late in the month of November, 1838.

Unlike the Tennessee River—hundreds of miles to the south—which was too low for crossing at Blythe Ferry until the rains caused its level to rise, the Ohio River had plenty of water. However, the Cherokee were forced to wait for crossing here because of the over-abundance of dangerous, floating ice that jeopardized the likelihood of safe passage across its turbulent expanse. Like the situation at Blythe Ferry, there were already a large group of Cherokee waiting here to cross. There was little shelter in the immediate area, so the Indians huddled together in various sized groups for nearly a mile along both sides of the road. Franklin figured that together with the group of Indians he'd arrived with, they numbered somewhere around two thousand. Soldiers, horses, wagons, scattered slaves, and Indians were forced into such close proximity, they were nearly on top of one another.

Sickness had already become rampant along the banks of the Ohio River, and deaths from illness routine.

Kanuna, along with a couple of other braves had been given permission to hunt, and he returned to his family with a dead muskrat slung over his shoulder. He handed it to his mother, Ayita who took the kill and immediately set about disemboweling, and otherwise preparing it for cooking.

"Edoda," he said to his father through chattering teeth. "I have found a place near here where we might have shelter from the cold. It is there, beside a creek, I found the selagisqua. The surface of the creek is frozen, but the ice is thin, so we can easily break it to get water. I think we should go there to wait for crossing."

"We must be given permission. I will send for Moses Daniels," said Degataga. He summoned Chea Sequa and instructed him to find the Indian conductor of their group.

An hour later, Chea Sequa returned. Walking several feet behind him was Moses Daniels, along with Jacob Grey Bear, one of the two commissary agents. They trudged slowly over to Degataga.

"I am happy to see you will eat today oginalii," Moses said in greeting, then quickly added, "I hope you can accept my calling you friend."

Degataga grunted. "You ride with the white man and watch your own people die. I knew you once, but you must understand that I am not sure I still do."

The look in Moses' eyes was one of deep sorrow. "We knew our brothers and sisters would doubt us and even hate us if we accepted this work. But we understood that it was for the good of our people to do so," Daniels replied evenly.

Degataga scowled back with contempt. "Must you hunt and make such a small meal feed your families?" he challenged.

"Because we do this work of dogs for the soldiers, we eat. But we do this not for the little food they give us. We do this because in return for working for them, we are allowed to watch over you." Moses waited for his words to sink in. "You are only aware of what Jacob Grey-bear did. But there have been many other times we have protected you that you do not know about."

Degataga's face registered understanding at the reminder of Greybear's shooting of the militia man.

"There have been many other times that we have acted and spoken to keep you and your family, and the others safe," Moses said, sweeping his arm along the line of Indians. "And this is another of those times. You may go to the place your son has spoken to you of to wait until the crossing. But to satisfy the soldiers, Grey Bear must go with you. I pray you will treat him well, and one day understand why we have done this work."

The look Franklin saw in Degataga's eyes was one of unfathomable sadness. Moses Daniels reached out his hand to the old Indian, who glanced at his wife. Anita nodded her head, so he slowly stretched out his own hand. The two men clasped forearms and shared the faintest of smiles, then Moses turned and walked away.

"Stiyu," Degataga whispered.

Without turning around, Moses, his shoulders hunched, and back bent with an invisible burden, raised and waved his hand, "Stiyu."

"Uyehi, agasti," Ayita said quietly, and offered a thin strip of blackened meat to her husband. She passed small bits of meat to the rest of the family, then held out the last strip to Grey Bear, who had been standing silent and several steps away.

Grey Bear hesitated and glanced at Degataga, who nodded his assent.

Just then, Franklin heard a low whimper coming from behind some brush about fifteen feet from where they were gathered. He figured Lazarus was looking for a handout. He'd seen the hound following along the entire route of several hundred miles, keeping out of sight so as not to get shot by the soldiers. Whenever the group came to a town, Lazarus had skirted around it, or somehow managed to navigate his way safely through it, and rejoined them on the other side. Each night when the group stopped to camp, Lazarus had waited for the soldiers to retreat into their tents, before he'd sneak in for food and the companionship of his two friends.

Franklin elbowed Nathaniel. "You hear him?"

"Yessuh, I do. But it don't make no sense he be moanin' out there, 'sted of comin' ta us."

It did strike Franklin as odd that Lazarus would be making his presence known so early in the day. "I'll check on him," he said, and made his way out to the brush. As he drew closer, he heard the tell-tale sound of the dog smacking its tail on the ground in welcome. Franklin expected to be pounced on by a mass of yellow fur, albeit, a thin one. But the dog didn't move from the ground he was lying on. Although his tail continued thumping, his head didn't rise. He was panting, and whimpered again softly when he saw Franklin.

Franklin knelt down and passed the palm of his hand carefully along the dog's protruding ribcage, spine, and boney hips, but felt nothing more than the proverbial bag of bones. "It's okay boy. We'll fix you right up," he said soothingly to the dog. Then he scooped him up in his arms and carried him back to the group.

There, Franklin, Nathaniel, and several of the others took bits of their meat and dropped them into a bowl of mush for the dog. Lazarus lapped it up greedily, and Franklin thought he could see the spark of life light up a bit in his eyes. The group finished their bits of meat and small bowls of corn mush with a chunk of hard bread, then followed Kanuna back down the road before they veered into the woods.

At first, other than the fact that they were separated from the crowd and sickness along the road, things didn't look any better to Franklin. They turned a corner around a stand of trees and stretching out before them was an immense bridge of sandstone that jutted out close to two hundred feet alongside a cliff wall, forming an arch about twenty yards long, and thirty feet above the ground. The cliff face was riddled with crevices and caves, some of which could accommodate two or more people each, and together with the arch would offer welcome shelter from the harsh elements. In addition, the creek Kanuna told his father about ran right near this place, and although the sheen of ice could be seen upon its surface, it was indeed thin enough in places that accessing fresh water would be simple.

Several of the Indians went about gathering pine boughs for bedding, while others got to work by the water. A contraption to catch fish was fabricated from branches similar to the one Nathaniel made after the escape from Fort Cass. The ice was easily broken through, and the trap lowered into the stream. Water was collected in animal-skin bags, and Degataga put Franklin and Nathaniel to work gathering wood which was used to build a central fire.

As the gray day gave way to the dark of night, a brave returned from the creek with a string of three brown trout, and another returned with a couple more. The fire was going strong, and Degataga didn't need to call everyone together. The promise of warmth did that for him.

From Franklin's position beside Kanuna, he noticed Grey Bear off in the trees by himself. As far as he knew, the man had not yet even situated himself in a cave for shelter. Franklin thought he could understand how the man must have felt. He had separated himself from his people and associated with soldiers—the oppressors of his own kind. In doing this, he was able to ride, while they walked, and was fed substantially better, while they struggled with what barely qualified as scraps.

The group huddled shoulder to shoulder around the blazing fire. Wood crackled, and embers rose into the air with spiraling white smoke. Franklin leaned into Kanuna to draw his attention, then shifted his eyes in Grey Bear's direction. "Isn't anyone going to get him over here before he freezes to death?" he asked.

"Joining us cannot be forced. He has chosen to separate himself from his people, and he must decide if he wishes to return."

Degataga pulled a pipe from inside his cloak, then tamped some tobacco into its bowl and lit it with a stick from the fire. Franklin hadn't seen him smoke since they first met. Degataga took a puff, then signaled to two of his braves who held small drums in their laps. They started to tap on the stretched leather skins lightly with the heel of their hands, producing a gentle, rhythmic, deep tone. Degataga began to sing in a voice barely more than a whisper, "Weya hay hay haya, weya haaaay ya, Weya hay hay haya, weya haaay." He then repeated these words, each time singing a little louder, while at the same time speeding up the tempo. After repeating the lines the third time, the rest of the group joined in.

"What are you singing?" Franklin asked Kanuna.

"This is a song of welcome. In this way Grey Bear can understand that he is welcome to be one with us again. But, *he* must choose this. I have heard that in your world, your people would kick one like him out forever. Is this true?"

Franklin looked down into the fire and nodded his head. "Lock him up, if we could."

"It is good then, is it not, that you are here."

The group had raised their voices enough now that Franklin was worried the Indians back along side of the road would hear, and mistake it as a welcome for them to barge into their little sanctuary. As the singing reached a feverish pitch, Ayita—which means first to dance—broke from her husband's side, and began to move rhythmically around the inside of the circle, alternating shuffling then softly stomping her feet. She was soon joined by several other women as well as several of the men.

"Do not worry. The others will not join us here," Kanuna said to Franklin, as if he knew what he was thinking. "They know the song is not for them. We are already one."

Franklin stole another glance towards the woods. Grey Bear stood and looked in their direction for a long while, then slowly made his way over to them. As he approached the ring of dancers, the fire reflected on his face, and revealed the tears that were flowing down his cheeks. The group opened up a space, and he joined in the dance, he and many of the others weeping freely.

* * *

The trout was the last substantial food they ate for the next three weeks. But on the positive side, the weather grew steadily warmer. Unfortunately, many of those who had become ill, were not able to recover. Jacob Grey Bear moved freely between Degataga's group and those along the road. He brought word daily of the condition of the other Indians, and that of the river. Each day he told them of new deaths, but this was hardly necessary, as they could all hear the wailing. The lamentations were followed by a new song to Franklin's ears, that quickly became almost as constant as the sound of the wind in the trees. He tried, but was unable to puzzle out the words. Finally, he turned to Kanuna again. "What is this song? Even though it follows all the crying, it sounds happy. Like something good has happened."

"This song reminds us that we are of the Great Spirit. Of course, we talk of this often. We know we are connected with all things. But it is natural when things become hard to question this. We sing this song to remind us, and that our loved one who has left the world of physical things, is finally witnessing the full truth of this great mystery. Before, we could only see our loved one as he or she is. But after we suffer the sorrow of losing them, we can experience the joy of knowing them in each and every thing that exists."

# CHAPTER 32

Clambering suddenly to his feet with the hair on his back standing on end, Lazarus emitted a low growl and glared into the darkened woods. Franklin and the others turned and peered in the direction the dog was facing. Someone, or something, was coming toward them, but not making a sound. Degataga and several others drew their knives, and the Indians stood in unison to face the unseen threat, but it was Moses Daniels, the Cherokee conductor, who emerged from the darkness, his hand raised in greeting.

"I come to tell you we will be leaving this place tomorrow."

"How is this possible?" Degataga asked. "Has the river become safe to cross?"

"I have received word from my Commissary Agent, Martin Davis. He risked his life, leaving here to explore passage on the other side of the river. The ice in the water has been breaking up for the last week, and many of the others have already begun crossing on the boats. I am not happy to be telling you this now that I see that you have found a comfortable place here. Conditions are much worse to the north."

Degataga only nodded his head.

"The message I have received from Davis was that the weather on the other side of the river is the coldest he has experienced anywhere before," Moses continued. "The streams are all frozen, the ice upon them is thick, and the snow almost always falls. He and the first party are still camped in swamplands on the east side of the S-dun."

Franklin looked questioningly at Kanuna, who explained that the S-dun was the Cherokee word for what the white man calls the Mississippi.

"They have been unable to cross the water there because of the floating ice," Moses told them. "Davis said travel to that place was harder than any we have faced. He fears many more of our people will die along the way."

"How much must we pay to cross this time?" Degataga asked. "We have little money left among us."

"The price they demand is one dollar a head; man, woman, or child."

"That cannot be," Kanuna growled. "I have seen the sign posted at the boats. It says the cost is twelve pennies."

"That is true," Moses replied. "But that is the price if you are a white man." Turning to Degataga he continued, "I cannot make them change their price. But if you are willing to sell your horses,..." Seeing the alarm in Degataga'a eyes, he quickly added, "I do not believe they will make it beyond the river. Selling them now would spare their lives, and give you money for this crossing and the ones still to come."

While Franklin watched Degataga contemplate the suggestion as he was stirring the ashes in his pipe with his deer-antler knife, he felt a familiar tug on his arm.

"I don' believe I'll be goin' with ya once we get past this river," Nathaniel said. "Think it's time I be gettin' myself back home and find my family."

"You'll die out there by yourself," Franklin responded. "As long as you stay in the group, you'll have food and protection."

"If'n the cold don't kill me goin' the ways these Indians is, my massah sho nuff will when he catches up with me. No suh, I think it's time I take my chances and go my own way. Your massah probly be comin' for y'all too. Me and Lazarus would be pleased ta have your company."

"I am tempted my friend, and I'll miss you and Lazarus, but I came into this business with the Cherokee, and I think I'll stay with them until I get out of it. How are you planning on getting away?"

"I figure if things are anywheres near as confusin' when we get ta the other side of this river as they was after we crossed the Tennessee, me an' Lazarus oughtta be able ta sneak off easy. And somethin' tells me the other side of this river's gonna be a mess."

"Why not leave now?" Franklin asked his friend. "No one seems to be paying any attention."

Nathaniel cupped his hands and blew into them, then rubbed them briskly together before he shoved them deep into his pockets again. "I wanna have me a river between the massah and me. Besides, the land south of this here river is still pretty much slave holdin' country. The other side is mostly free, makin' my chances of gettin' ta Pennsylvania better. That is if I don't freeze ta death first."

The Indians began to move off to their various sleeping areas, but Franklin and Nathaniel sat for a bit longer by the fire, Lazarus curled up at their feet. "I feels like I knowd ya for a long time," Nathaniel said as he poked a stick at the fire.

Embers twirled upwards into the darkening night. "It does feel like that," Franklin agreed. Then he laughed softly. "But you only know what you see. Funny, I used to tell people that what you see is what you get, like what you see is true. But I'm telling you,... you don't really know me."

"Here ya go again, puttin' y'all's self down, when all I seen of ya has been good. Why, when I..."

"You weren't there when I ate more than my share of his family's food," Franklin interrupted with a snap and pointing in the direction of Degataga. "Even when I knew they were as hungry as I was." He quickly looked around to be sure they were alone. "And you didn't see me when I was lusting over his wife!" Franklin stared silently into the fire, shaking his head. "You have no idea how many times I disrespected him, his sons, his God, his people. And all the while, they were taking care of me. They took me in, and protected me. Cared for me like I was family. They never asked anything of me. And I know... I know they knew all of these things, and still they cared for me."

Nathaniel was about to speak, but Franklin grasped his friend's arm to stop him. "I did nothing to deserve what they did for me. All I did for *them* was give them something else to have to deal with. But, you see? They didn't *have* to do anything for me. They *chose* to take care of me. Even though when they found me I was drunk and belligerent. And that's only a part of me they saw. They don't know the man I was before I came here. I took advantage of everyone I ever knew. I disrespected them, even people I never met." He looked directly at Nathaniel. "I treated anybody who was not like I thought they should be like shit, like they were mindless idiots,... even subhuman." He kept his gaze on Nathaniel, locking eyes with him. "Some people didn't have to do anything for me to hate, disregard, or mistreat them. All some people had to do was be a different color." Franklin broke his eye contact with Nathaniel and stared into the fire, his chest heaving with emotion.

"But I seen ya care for them Indians," Nathaniel began. "I seen how ya cared for that little girl we buried too. Lazarus and I *both* knows how ya been takin' care of him. Why, y'all saved his life. An' I know ya care 'bout me." Lazarus looked up at the sound of his name, then laid his head back down and rested his chin on the toes of Franklin's boots. Nathaniel chuckled. "See what I mean? He'd be dead by now if ya hadn't been lookin' out for him', and feedin' him from y'all's own scraps like ya still be doin' right ta this day."

"Something's happening to me," Franklin mumbled. "I can't pretend I understand it, but maybe that's why I'm here."

Nathaniel shrugged, and Lazarus gnawed on his hind quarters, yawned, then stretched his head up to press into Franklin's hand as he reached down to ruffle the dog's ears.

"I feel like I'm changing," Franklin continued, "from what I was, to something else." Franklin stretched out his hand and held it up to the fire light, taking in the color of his skin. "I gotta admit," he said, "even I kind of like the me that I'm becoming here. But I'm afraid it won't stick. I'm afraid that whenever I do get back to where I came from, I'll forget all this and go right back to pushing my wife around, and all the rest of my crap again. And I have a feeling if that happens, she won't stay around for long." Suddenly, Franklin sat up straight, then reached into his shirt and pulled out the feathers that still dangled from the string of sinew. He played the feathers gently through his fingers, then put them back into place inside his shirt. "What proves—*even to me*—that I'm not my old self anymore, is that I don't think she *should* stay with the asshole that I was. If I can't fix this, I think she *should* leave so that she has a chance to be happy. She's too good for the likes of me. I think I always knew that, but until now, I've been too afraid to say it. When I wake up from this I... "

Nathaniel had sat quietly by, listening to his friend's lament, but spoke up, interrupting the downward spiral. "But that's where y'all is wrong. This woman y'all be talkin' 'bout, it might be she was miserable with ya the way ya say, but she stay miserable, even if she leaves ya."

Franklin was dumbfounded, and wanted to argue, but Nathaniel held a gnarled finger up to his face, stopping him before he could get a word out.

"Listen here. If she loves ya like I 'spect she does, she will only be happy if she has the man she believes ya are, the man I come ta know here, beside her. If y'all love her, and if y'all ever do get back ta her, don't go back beatin' y'all's self up for what ya been. That ain't gonna do anybody no good, and she don't need carry ta that weight." Nathaniel reached over, clasped Franklin's shoulder, and looked him in the eye. "Ya gotta give her that man ya become here. Then she be happy," he said, nodding his head. "That is when everythin' gonna be alright again."

Franklin shook his head. His eyes burned from his tears. He feigned a yawn and wiped them with his sleeve. "I think I'm gonna try to get some sleep. To-morrow's gonna be a big day for all of us. He ruffled Lazarus' ears and stood up. Leaning over, he took a burning branch from the fire, and cupping the flame to keep it from going out, headed for the small cave he, Nathaniel, and the dog had been sleeping in. After several steps, Franklin stopped, his tears freely flowing. Without turning around, he said over his shoulder, "You've been a good friend Nathaniel, you and Lazarus both." Arriving at the cave, he used the flame at the tip of the branch to re-light a small fire at the opening, then laid awake long into the night contemplating what Nathaniel had said to him.

***

The following morning, Franklin rose early with the others. Grateful that the common fire had not gone all the way out as the one at the entrance to his shelter had, he thawed his fingers out over the embers before helping to brake camp. Remnants from last night's fish was doled out, and the group ate as they joined up with the end of a mile long line of Indians waiting to board a ferry that would transport them across the Ohio River.

Heavy, wet, flakes of falling snow obscured his view, but Franklin could still make out the river off to his left through the trees. The line-up of Indians had shifted about ten yards off the road as everyone huddled under the heavy pine boughs for shelter. Other than an occasional branch snapping under the weight of accumulated snowfall, it was as if the volume had been turned all the way down around them. Lazarus, who had wedged himself between the trunk of a tree and behind Franklin's and Nathaniel's legs, suddenly squeezed himself out in front of the men, his teeth bared and the hair standing up at odd angles along the protruding spine of his back. He growled menacingly, looking south in the direction they had come from.

Gradually, a contingent of men on horseback materialized like ghosts out of the grey-white mixture of fog and flakes. They rode slowly, as if with purpose, past the line of Indians and toward the ferry staging area, swinging their heads from one side to the other as if they were looking for something, or someone. Nathaniel had maneuvered himself behind the tree and brought Lazarus with him. He was quieting the dog as the men drew nearer, and he tugged at Franklin to join him.

"I can't say for sure, but if ol' Lazarus' nose is as true as I knows it ta be, those men is slave hunters."

"What do you mean?" asked Franklin, even though he felt he knew full well.

"They's bein' paid ta find runaways and take 'em back ta they's massahs."

Crouching low, Franklin instinctively felt through his heavy fur wrap at the place the feather amulet hung.

"If thas who they is, they come a long ways. When they does that, it usually mean they gets paid a lot, and maybe they don't even gotta bring the slave back alive."

The men on horseback passed by, and before Franklin could register Nathaniel's last comment, the report of a single rifle shot rang out, failing to echo in the thick, cold atmosphere. Franklin felt the coldness in his bones, but now his blood ran cold too. The idea of being dragged off someplace as a slave, or beaten, or perhaps hung terrified him. If he could feel the cold and hunger in his dream, he reasoned he could feel those things as well.

A couple of tense hours dragged slowly by, and as Franklin and his group inched their way along, the dock and the ferry boats came into view less than a hundred yards away. Grey Bear rode up to them and dismounted. "Those men who rode in today are looking for slaves," he informed Degataga. "Right now they're on the boats, checking everybody as they load to cross the river. They already rounded up a few, and showed papers that say they can take them dead or alive. They already shot and killed one poor fool who broke for the trees. Another one jumped off the boat. He tried to swim away, but got hit in the head by a chunk of floating ice and was swept under the water."

Degataga turned to Franklin and Nathaniel. "You must go now. I can no longer protect you." He looked back at Grey Bear. "Will you allow this?"

"They must go," Grey Bear agreed. But not back the way we came. There are more hunters coming. They know that many slaves have hidden themselves among our people and are trying to cross the river into the north."

"So where do we go?" asked Franklin.

"Go back to the rock bridge where you made camp," Grey Bear instructed. "Then move east along the river, but keep away far from shore for as long as you can. The hunters have offered a reward to anyone who brings them a slave, alive or dead. I saw two men already moving east along the river with rifles. You will find other crossings. But you must be careful that slave hunters are not also at those places."

"We'll freeze to death, or starve," Franklin moaned, but before he could say more, he saw Degataga, Kanuna, Chea Sequa, and others breaking off bits of dry fish and putting this with a portion of their corn into a leather pouch.

Degataga handed the pouch to Nathaniel, then draped some leather wraps and two more furs over each of their shoulders. "The feathers we gave to you will help you find your way to where you belong." He motioned to Ayita, and she handed him another pouch. He opened it and fished out a small handful of coins. "When you come to a crossing, this will buy your way to the other side." He then took out his knife and cut a small square of his leather undergarment, and a string of sinew. Degataga placed the coins on the leather square, gathered the ends together, and wrapped the sinew tightly around it forming a smaller pouch, then reached out and took Franklin's wrist, and placed it into his open hand. The old Indian closed his own hand firmly over Franklin's, and with his voice wavering with emotion said, "You must go now."

One by one, the Indians spoke to Franklin and Nathaniel, wishing them well, and safe travel. When it was Kanuna's turn, he grasped Franklin firmly by his forearms and squeezed, then pulled him to himself in a bear hug. "Stiyu, Oginalii," he said evenly in his deep baritone voice, then stepped away.

Franklin looked down and closed his eyes in a failed attempt to hold back the emotionality of the moment. When he looked back up, he saw Chea Sequa before him with his perpetually bright smile. "Oginalii, you and I will forever be connected as one."

Blinking away his tears, Franklin saw the blurry form of Chea Sequa, the Red Bird, move aside. Ayita took his place, and he immediately looked down at his feet.

"You are a good man, Unaduti," she began with a firm tone. Then softening, she continued. "My husband and my sons saw past the shell that had wrapped itself around your true spirit when they found you."

Tears of shame fell from Franklin's eyes, and he stammered, "I looked at you ... in the wrong way."

"Yes, the part of the shell you wore that was alcohol dulled your mind from all that you were meant to be. The pleasure you stole from the bodies of women, another part of that shell, was a way for you to pretend that you were well, when you were broken and lost inside. The feelings you had when you saw me were wrong, Unaduti, but you did not act on them with me. In this way you showed me respect, and I always felt safe around you. This time you have spent with the Cherokee has broken the shell that has held your true spirit captive, and you are becoming whole again. When you find your wife, give this same respect to her. She is longing for it. She will accept you." Then she reached out her hands and brought his face close to hers. She kissed him lightly on each cheek, then stepped back.

Degataga grabbed Franklin in another bear hug that nearly cut off Franklin's breath. "Stiyu, oginalii," he whispered in Franklin's ear.

It looked to Franklin as though Degataga had more he wanted to say, but Grey Bear put his hand on his shoulder. "They must go now, before they are seen. We are too close to the docks already." With that, Grey Bear promptly jumped up on his horse, clucked his tongue, and sped off in the opposite direction that Franklin and Nathaniel were to take. When he had gotten thirty to forty yards away, he reigned the horse and fired his rifle into the air, then charged with a gallup to the west.

Degataga quickly slipped his knife into Franklin's boot. "This is not a blade of steel, but it will do anything you ask of it." He patted Franklin on the back and stepped away. "Stiyu, josdadahnvtli, be strong, my brother."

With Grey Bear's distraction having its intended effect on the slave hunters, Franklin and Nathaniel took their leave from their companions and drifted into the trees and what had become almost white-out snow conditions with Lazarus at their heels.

# CHAPTER 33

Keeping close to the creek, Franklin and Nathaniel followed it to a small waterfall framed with sparkling, crystalline icicles, that stepped its way in silver-blue and green sequences down a steep canyon wall to where they stood. Franklin searched around himself in all directions but saw nothing that gave him a hint of where to turn.

"Would ya look at that," Nathaniel whispered, and nodded midway up the waterfall to a small ledge. Perched on the edge sat a cardinal. The bird chirped, then flapped its wings and hopped up to the rock above it where it stopped and seemed to look down on the two men. It chirped once again, hopped up to another outcropping of rocks, then another, each time stopping, looking down at Franklin and Nathaniel, then climbing higher.

At a loss to explain the birds odd behavior, and with no other direction looking anymore favorable than the one the bird was taking, Franklin stepped onto the bottom boulder, reached above him to a small ledge and pulled himself up. From there, he saw another step he could take, then another. He patted his coat at the place where the feathers hung against his chest, in his mind seeing the small red one, and silently thanked Chea Sequa, then called down to Nathaniel. "It's easy, even "ol Lazarus can do this."

The climb up was simple enough, only requiring them to periodically brush fallen snow off of a rock or ledge for a hand-hold, or better footing. From the canyon rim, they were afforded a view over tree tops, back to the road, the line of Indians, and beyond them, the Ohio River. Franklin was relieved to see that a group of men he figured to be slave hunters, had followed Grey Bear's lead, and were busy scouring along the shore of the river flowing to the south-west.

"They's still men out this ways lookin' for slaves," Nathaniel reminded him. "So I think we oughta stick to the woods for as long as we can. They's bound ta give up some time." He rubbed his hands together, blew into them for warmth, then hugged himself. "I don't think they's wantin' ta freeze they asses off any more'n we do."

The climb down the other side of the cliff was difficult, and occasionally Franklin or Nathaniel would have the duty of passing Lazarus down to the other when the drop was too long for the dog to safely make it on his own. They accomplished this by removing the soft, leather undergarments given them by the Indians, and fashioning them into a harness they fit under the hound's chest and behind his front legs, and twisting the rest into a rope. It was a wonder to Franklin that Lazarus didn't struggle, but put up with the humiliation of looking like some kind of carnival, rag doll as he was lowered— his legs dangling helplessly beneath him—hand over hand from one man to the other. He also couldn't believe that the cold had so many levels to it. Being from Southern California, he simply learned to distinguish between hot and cold. But here, in this time and place, the temperature shifted from cold, to freezing, to bitter, to deathly cold. He imagined that only the Arctic could feel as inhospitable. The wind moaned incessantly, and whipped the wet snow around them, which froze almost instantly to the surface of the boulders it lit upon. This made their descent increasingly treacherous, resulting in numerous slips and falls before they reached the forest floor, and solid footing again.

By afternoon, the men stopped and huddled in the cleft of a lightening scorched tree trunk to escape the biting wind for a while and have a bite of food. But after only a brief moment, Nathaniel encouraged Franklin to move on. "We's warmer if we's movin'," he reasoned. "'Sides, we can chew on this meat while we goin'."

A couple dozen steps later the men froze in their tracks at a crackling sound to their left, the direction of the river, and the slave hunters. It sounded like someone or something, had broken some dry branches not far from their position, but the snowfall had become a blizzard, making it impossible for them to see more than twenty feet in any direction. Franklin had thought of this as a protective advantage, making them all but invisible to the men they were running from. But he now realized the danger the poor visibility also presented. In their mutual blindness, they, and those who sought them, could literally walk straight into one another.

The subtle snap of a fallen branch alerted the men that whatever, or whoever, had stepped clumsily nearby. *Perhaps it was only an icicle that had fallen from an overladen tree branch*, Franklin wondered to himself. But in his mind's eye he envisioned two or three leather and fur clad slave traders with rifles stalking them. Each of them at least six burly feet tall, heavily bearded, probably missing a few teeth, and their hair long, shaggy, and greasy, flowing out from under their fur lined caps. He feared that every one of them was an expert marksman, and could hit their target—even on the run—blinding snow be damned. And each of them has tethered to their waist or boot, a blood-stained knife capable of filleting a two-hundred pound wild boar.

Franklin reached down and felt into his boot with trembling fingers, and despite their numbness, felt the age-smoothed antler handle of the knife given him by Degataga. He pulled it out slowly and turned it over in his hand. It was the knife he'd seen his friend use to strip meat and to stir the ashes in the bowl of his pipe. The knife was beautiful, the handle worn and burnished by years of handling, the black flint blade, still razor-sharp, glistened, even in the dull light. *He was supposed to give this to one of his sons*, Franklin thought incredulous. *But instead, he gave it to me.* He hung his head until the sound of something—very large, and very near—huffing and snorting, alerted him from his wondering.

His heart pounding in his chest, and straining his eyes against the blinding snow, a movement to his left caught Franklin's eye. He held his breath hoping the blizzard would conceal him from whatever it was. Just when he believed he would have to exhale, out from between two trees, the most magnificent creature Franklin thought he had ever seen moved into view. A large Bull Elk, stepped gingerly into a clearing before them, and stopped, seemingly oblivious to the presence of the men a mere twelve feet in front of him. Nathaniel quietly stroked Lazarus to keep him calm.

The Elk stood at least five feet tall at the shoulder, but its head and antlers rose another three to four feet up from there, and spread out from tip to tip a good seven feet. It looked to be as much as eight feet long from nose to tail, and Franklin estimated its weight to be at least seven-hundred pounds. The animal's dark brown belly, neck, and head looked almost black against the cream white highlights along its sides. Franklin counted six points on each side of the huge rack of antlers it carried.

The big bull—it's eyes wide and crazed—raised its snout in the air for a magical moment and huffed, expelling a great plume of mist, and searing its imprint into Franklin's mind, and Franklin slowly slipped the knife back into his boot. The Elk looked frightened. Without warning, the creature turned and catapulted away with a great leap as if propelled by a giant inner spring, sending it gliding effortlessly over the frozen ground. Franklin was stunned at how it navigated its huge form so gracefully between the trees, but his wonder was disturbed by what sounded like panting from one, and then several other unseen animals coming from the direction of the river. He grasped for the knife again, held his breath once more, and waited.

Out from the trees, burst first one, two, then three wolves at a full-tilt run. Their front and back legs stretched out so far in front and behind them, their bellies nearly scraped the carpet of snow. Both men simultaneously jerked backwards towards the cliff they'd just climbed down, and Franklin wondered if they could get up high enough in time to evade the predators. He realized the knife was no match for a pack of wolves, and knew it would be impossible to save Lazarus. But he soon realized his worry was for naught, as the wolves had a bead on the buck. They had either failed to notice the men, or simply paid them and the dog no mind. Their paws hit the ground where the elk had stood just a moment before, and they scrabbled their legs wildly beneath them for a comical moment trying to gain traction, then sprang in the direction the elk had taken.

"If they catch him or not, they's bound ta be busy for a spell," Nathaniel suggested. "So's we best be skeedaddlin'."

The men moved off to the the north-east, gradually edging closer to the river. Continuous, heavy snow and the drifts it created made the going difficult, but Franklin felt relief when he saw how it quickly covered their footsteps, making it less likely they could be tracked. "You know," Franklin mused to his friend, "it's possible in this snow that we could walk right up behind the slave hunters and not even know it until it's too late. They're probably more likely to be along side of the river though, so I think we should keep back away from it for a day or two. What do you think?"

Before Nathaniel could answer, Lazarus, the snow as high as his empty belly, stopped and lifted his nose. Then suddenly, he bolted to the right. A blast of powdered snow exploded up from the ground, and a rabbit took off like a shot with Lazarus in hot pursuit, zig-zagging across a snow field. The chase lasted several minutes with both hare and dog rushing in and out of view. Then, just as suddenly as it had begun, it was over, and Lazarus, panting from his effort, trotted back to the men clutching his prize in his jaws.

"Whooee!" exclaimed Nathaniel, patting Lazarus' head. "This bunny gonna make us a good meal."

Franklin hooted in agreement. "I've never seen a rabbit so big! Look at the size of that head."

"Yessuh, we in luck! That be one of them swamp rabbits. They get real big in this part of Kentucky. Must weigh close ta eight pounds." Nathaniel took the rabbit gently from Lazarus' mouth, tied its hind legs with a piece of leather, then slung it over his back. "Maybe we can find us a place round here ta hunker down and sit out the rest of this storm." He chuckled and said, "Looks like that knife you got is gonna come in handy. We can skin this and have us somethin' real good to eat," he said, ruffling the fur on Lazarus's head.

The men arrived at an outcropping of boulders, and searched its periphery until they found a south facing cave which would conceal a fire from the view of any slave hunters that might look in their direction from the river. The cave itself promised much needed relief from the bone-chilling wind and driving, wet snow. But, despite their eagerness to get themselves inside, they kept a healthy distance away for fear it might already be inhabited by a wolf, bear, or mountain lion. Lazarus pulled free from Nathaniel and padded towards the entrance, his body taut, nose on full alert, warily sniffing the air. Before long the dogs entire body relaxed, and as he had proven his sense of smell with the rabbit, the men breathed a sigh of relief and joined him.

The obsidian-blade knife Degataga gave to Franklin literally sliced through the lean meat and sinew of the hare like warmed butter. Nathaniel fashioned a spit from a nearby sapling, and roasted the rabbit over a fire that soon popped and sizzled with its juices. It was the best meal the two men had eaten since escaping Fort Cass, and after giving Lazarus his share, they licked and sucked the marrow from each and every bone, then settled down for the night, each of them quickly falling into a deep, bone-tired sleep.

They woke while it was still dark to increase their lead on anyone who might be chasing after them, and eager to get closer to the river with the hope of coming upon a ferry that would take them across to free territory. But after only a mile moving in a northeast direction, they stopped. The storm had abated overnight and the atmosphere was crystal clear. Through the trees, and perhaps another half mile or so away, they spotted the glow of a campfire. Not willing to take the chance of running across a group of slave hunters, the men turned reluctantly inland, and after eating a handful each of dry corn, headed directly east.

Just before noon of the second day, they rested beside a frozen creek. Nathaniel picked up a rock and brushed the snow off the solid surface of the water. Then kneeling down, he began to slam the rock into the ice until he broke a hole through it about two feet in circumference.

"What are you doing?" asked Franklin.

Nathaniel raised one hand to silence his friend, as he peered intently into the stream.

"We have snow all around us if you want water," Franklin said, and held out a leather flask to Nathaniel. "But since you already went through all that trouble, use this."

"Watch now,... steady," Nathaniel said seemingly caught up in a world of his own. Then with a sudden, lightening quick movement, he stuck his arm into the water up to his shoulder. He let out a yelp and drew it back just as fast, and held it out from his body, a brownish-grey creature dangling from his fingers by over-sized pincers. Nathaniel looked at Franklin with a gleam in his eye, then dashed the alien looking thing against a tree trunk, freeing himself from its grip.

"Now I know I'm dreaming!" Franklin exclaimed. "What the hell is a lobster doing here?"

"This here's a crawfish." With his back turned to Franklin, Nathaniel plunged his arm back in the frigid water. "Y'all ain't never seen no crawfish?" he asked as he jerked his arm in one direction, and then another. Within seconds, Nathaniel hollered again, pulled out another of the pincered creatures, and knocked it off his hand like the first one. "Ya gotta try it!" he invited, giggling like a kid, and his eyes shining. "They's more of 'em down there, and they's just as sweet as they are ugly!"

Reluctantly, Franklin got on his knees beside Nathaniel and stared into the hole. At first all he saw was the swirl of flowing water, sand, and stones. Then his eye caught rust colored movement about fifteen inches away from the bank. He hesitated, contemplating the wisdom of shoving his arm into ice-cold water in the middle of winter, not to mention the fact that by doing so he was inviting the pain that would surely be inflicted upon him by the fierce looking pincers. Then throwing caution aside, he plunged his arm into the creek.

"Ow! Damn it! Ow!" he howled and yanked his arm back out of the water. One of the creatures had latched its claw onto his hand in the same way it had Nathaniel's. For a moment—in a state of shock—Franklin held his hand out, and looked in disbelief at the crawfish dangling there clacking its free set of pincers in the air. Lazarus jumped excitedly from side to side, barking, which brought Franklin back to his senses, and he bashed the shellfish against a tree, breaking its arm right off, but leaving the severed claw still clinging to his reddened hand.

Nathaniel rolled in the snow, clutching his belly and laughing hysterically, while pointing at the look of bewilderment on his partner's face.

Franklin laughed in spite of himself. Then after regaining a semblance of composure, grumbled, "I don't know if we're catching them, or if it's the other way around! But I expect you're gonna tell me why the hell we're doing this!"

"Cause we can eat 'em. Tonight, I'm gonna fix y'all somethin' that'll make it all worth it."

The two men took turns and pulled out a dozen crawfish, and after tossing one to Lazarus, packed the others in a pouch, then continued their way east.

After a long, frigid, early morning trudge through thick woods, Franklin and Nathaniel found themselves in another snow-blanketed meadow. The sun had managed to break through the thick, heavy mist, providing a much welcomed bit of warmth, but the sudden brightness nearly blinded the men. The sun's rays reflected off the snow field before them, dazzling their eyes with glittering crystals that took their breath away with prismatic beauty.

"There he goes again!" shouted Nathaniel, as Lazarus lunged and took off like a shot. Still somewhat blinded by the glare, the men soon lost sight of him. Although his movements were muffed by the snow, they occasionally heard an echoing rustle—here, then there—as the hound pursued his quarry. Moments later, Lazarus emerged from the woods with a new trophy hanging from his jaws.

"I hate to go back in there," Franklin remarked, gesturing to the edge of the forest before him. The light penetrated less than a dozen feet into the thick woods, promising a cold, dark passage of unknown duration.

Nathaniel took the rabbit from Lazarus, and stroked the dogs head. Then he tied a cord around the rabbits hind legs, and slung it over his shoulder. "Hold on just a second now," he said as he bent forward and stared ahead as though he was trying to see around the trees. "Lookie there," he whispered, pointing into the direction they were heading.

"Damn. I see it. It's a campfire alright."

"Who ever they is, they's eatin' some vittles. Maybe we can scoot ourselves 'round 'em like we did before."

"You think those slave hunters would come way out here looking for us?"

"Probly not, but no sense takin' chances. We come this far alright, and we got food. We can head south a bit, then cut back."

Franklin and Nathaniel moved off even more to the South, taking them further away from their goal of finding a ferry to get them across the river. They kept the light from the camp fire on their left, and circled around by at least two hundred yards. Once beyond the fire, they breathed a sigh of relief, then swung eastward, and veered cautiously back to the north, and the river.

Suddenly, Lazarus began growling again, warning the men of danger. His normally floppy ears were laid back against his neck, and the hair along his spine stood straight up.

"I don't see anything, do you?" Franklin whispered.

"Nothin', but that don't mean nothin's there."

"Let go o' them bags, and put yer hands in the air," a deep baritone voice ordered from somewhere in the forest around them.

Franklin and Nathaniel were in a small clearing, which caused the voice to echo, making it impossible to locate the source. Even Lazarus spun in circles, barking in all directions.

"Take care o' that dog, or we'll take care of it for ya," the disembodied voice rumbled.

Franklin slowly lowered his hands and pulled Lazarus between him and Nathaniel. He stroked its neck quieting the hound, then put his trembling hands back where they were.

The dark-skinned face of a man poked out from around the trunk of a tree before he stepped into full view. He held something against his leg that Franklin imagined to be a rifle. Three other men with various shades of brown skin stepped out from the protection of the forest into the small clearing, each of them holding something in the same manner as the first man.

"Y'all don't look like no slave hunters," Nathaniel blurted out. "We ain't neither," he said turning his hands in the air, which exposed his forearms.

"How we spose ta know you ain't working for 'em?" the first man questioned.

"We don't have guns," Franklin replied.

"Then how you explain that?" the man questioned, pointing at the rabbit still slung over Nathaniel's shoulder.

"Ol' Lazarus here,... *he* caught it. Caught one yesterday too. We got us some crawfish in that pouch over there," Nathaniel pointed. "Nuff ta share with all of y'all."

All four men had moved to within twenty paces from Franklin and Nathaniel. "If you ain't slave hunters, step outta them furs ta prove you ain't got no guns."

"We'll freeze our asses off!" retorted Franklin.

"If we shoot ya dead, you ain't gonna have no ass ta worry about."

Nathaniel started pulling his furs over his head, but Franklin had been looking closely at the men after they stepped out from the trees, and now that they were right in front of him he became suspicious. "I don't think you have anything to shoot us with," he challenged. "I'm not taking my fucking clothes off."

Nathaniel had removed his furs and soft leather undershirt. At his friend's comment he side-stepped quickly a couple of feet away from him. Franklin was stunned at how skinny Nathaniel was. He could count his bones, and he could swear his brown skin was turning blue with the cold. "Do what they say," Nathaniel pleaded. "I don't wanna have ta die out here like this." He was trembling so hard his knees were knocking together.

Franklin put his arms down with exasperation. "We aren't going to die. They don't have guns," he said, looking steadily at the leader. "Put your furs back on. They're not hunters. I think they're slaves by the looks of them. Their clothes look as bad as ours." As he spoke to his friend, Franklin opened wide the fur wrap he wore and turned from side to side, so the men could see he wasn't carrying a weapon. "We were with the Indians being taken west," he said to them. "We were just about to cross the river, when slave hunters showed up, so we ran off, and we're looking for a way to cross." Then he demanded, "What's your excuse for being here?"

The men looked at each other uneasily, and the leader cleared his throat. "We's runaways too," he conceded. We ain't got no guns,... just these sticks. We come up this way cause we been told they's a underground rail-way in Owensboro. If you is willin' ta share yer vittles, we can take ya with us cause that be where we's headin'."

Nathaniel had pulled his furs back on and was vigorously patting and rubbing his arms and stamping his feet for warmth. "We sure is glad ta meet y'all," he said through chattering teeth. He and Franklin fell in with the men, and together they headed in the direction of their fire.

# CHAPTER 34

"Name's Clarence," the leader announced. His was the baritone voice that first confronted Franklin and Nathaniel from the trees. The men clambered excitedly around the new comers as they trudged through drifts of snow toward their camp. "This here's Boney, but you wouldn't know it by looking at him," he said, slapping a rotund man on the back, to the guffaws of the others and Boney himself. "That boy there be Elijah. And Cubbenah, be the old man we dragging along 'cause we got nothin' better ta do," he said with affection, rubbing the shoulders of the man. "He be the only one of us comes directly from the motherland. The rest of us is born and raised in this country. Me and Boney,... we was both born inta slavery. Them others was once what they calls free men. That is till they was dragged south where we was already pickin' cotton."

By the time Franklin and Nathaniel introduced themselves and Lazarus, they were seated and warming themselves around the other men's cooking fire. Cubbenah brought out a pipe that looked as old as he did, and began stuffing it with tobacco. That done, he then plucked a stick from the fire, lit the pipe, and sat contentedly puffing out blue clouds of smoke.

Boney offered a metal, pint-sized flask to Franklin. He reached out tentatively and took the dented and tarnished container, then turned it over in his hand with a look of deep thought on his face. A slight tremor, barely noticeable to him, caused his fingers to dance. After a few moments hesitation, Franklin promised himself he'd limit himself to the bottle once he was back with Gwen. Then he shrugged his shoulders, tilted his head back, and filled his mouth until his cheeks bulged, then promptly spit the contents into the fire. The flames flared up, his eyes bulged and watered, and the other men nodded their heads knowingly.

"Holy mother of,... what the hell is this?" Franklin coughed.

"Why, that be the best shine in Kentucky," Boney crooned with pride. "If a man swallows it, he can feel that burn all the way down ta his toes." He reached over and took the flask Franklin was holding at arms length from himself.

Franklin hadn't had a drink in months, and the heat of the liquor took him by complete surprise. His nose and throat still burning, he watched through watering eyes as the flask made its way to the other men and the whiskey burned its way to his gut. His fingers twitched spasmodically, prompting Franklin to shove his hands inside his furs.

The men, in turn, tilted their heads back and took their swigs, then wiped their mouths and smiled or hooted their appreciation.

The flask eventually made it back around to Franklin, and he reached for it. Once in his trembling hand, he sniffed at the sweet smelling contents, then took a long, slow drink. Before swallowing, he swished it around in his mouth and chewed it thoughtfully, then sat back, and felt the warmth slide down his throat. His eyes no longer watered, but his mouth did as he watched the flask make another round and back into his waiting hand. He noticed that the tremor was gone, and it hit him in that instant. "I'm an alcoholic," he said quietly to himself while staring absently into the fire. He passed the liquor to Boney without taking a drink, then looked from one man to the other and said it out loud. "I'm an alcoholic. I can't drink. I've ruined my marriage. I've lost friends, and any self-respect I had because of drinking. Your shine is wonderful," he said to Boney apologetically. "Sweetest I've ever tasted. But forgive me if I don't drink anymore."

"Thas alright," Boney responded. "No shame in that."

Clarence patted Franklin on the back. "Takes a stronger man to put a bottle down, then to tip one," he said reassuringly. Then he chuckled, as he reached for the flask. "But I ain't that strong."

Boney gave Clarence the eye, then passed the flask to his friend while he scooted next to Franklin.

"Boney told me you're all going to the underground railroad," Franklin said. "The last time I saw any tracks was back at Fort Cass."

"Shucks, Franklin, the railroad ain't only trains," Clarence chuckled. "Oh, they is trains alright. And some of 'em is underground. But they's also wagons, and ferries, and even row boats."

"The railroad is taken us ta freedom," Boney chimed in, a broad smile on his face. "But it's places for us ta hide whiles we waitin' till we can get us some help ta 'cross the river too. Then maybe they's a train over there for us ta ride. But once we gets ta Ohia, it won't matter. They say they ain't no slaves in Ohia."

"Sounds like heaven, if y'all ask me," crooned Cubbenah, his voice still thick with the accent of his homeland.

"Nobody askin' you, old man," teased Clarence.

"Pennsylvania is heaven ta me," Elijah chimed in wistfully. "Got me a wife and children there."

Nathaniel looked up at Elijah's remark. "I'm from Pennsylvania too. Had me a wife, a little girl, and a son. Now, I don't know if they's alive or dead."

The men put their heads down at this comment, and kicked uncomfortably at the ground.

"Where is this hiding place?" asked Franklin, in an attempt to change the mood.

"We gotta find it," answered Clarence.

"I thought you knew where you were... " snapped Franklin, before he caught himself and softened his tone. "What do you mean, you have to find it?"

"We do and we don't," laughed Boney. "They's signs gonna tell us where this place is. Thas what we's looking for."

"You mean someone's put up signs?" Franklin asked incredulous. "No disrespect, but if you can read them, so can everybody else. Doesn't sound planned out. I always say if you fail to plan, you may as well plan to... "

Boney slapped Franklin on the back and laughed again. "They's no need ta worry. They's plenty of plannin' goin' on, thas for *damn* sure. But the signs is secret. Only thems that's makin' 'em, them's that's tryin' ta get ta freedom, and thems that's helpin' 'em knows what these signs is, and what they says."

Franklin's face twisted up with his confusion.

"Look here," Boney said. He took a stick from the fire and began to draw in the snow at his feet. "This here," he continued as he put the finishing touches on a picture that resembled a small, simple, cabin, "is the sign that tells us a place is safe for us ta stay awhile." He scraped over the rough drawing with his boot, then drew a new picture that looked roughly like a bird in flight. "This one tells us we's still headin' north, like the flyin' geese is goin' home." Boney brushed snow over that sketch and put four squiggly lines in its place. His voice took on a serious tone. "This sign warns us slave hunters is near, and we should go another way. They's lots more, and followin' 'em is what got us ta where we is now. But these I just showed ta ya is probly all we gonna need from here."

A rumbling sound came from Clarence's direction drawing Franklin's attention. The man rubbed his belly and cut in, "How 'bout we do somethin' with that rabbit. We should eat and get movin' while the shine is still warmin' our bellies, and we got the sun ta light the way. If we's lucky we can make it ta the safe place by tonight, and not freeze our asses off out here."

Franklin decided to let the reference to luck pass, and not argue semantics, or his philosophical point of view for the first time he could remember.

As Nathaniel untied the rabbit and showed the men the pouch of crawfish—which they admired with hoots and whistles—Elijah produced a couple of well used tin pots, both of them dented, and blackened almost beyond recognition. He dropped the crawfish in one pot and set them over the fire to boil, then cut up the rabbit into the other, and stirred in some corn with his knife. Cubbenah reached into his pocket and pulled out a pouch of his own. He opened it, took out a handful of green plant stuff and reverently dropped some of the matted material into the pot of rabbit meat. "Y'all saved that for a special 'cassian!" Boney protested.

"This here be special enough," Cubbenah said simply. He turned to Franklin and Nathaniel and said with an apologetic tone, "These greens is a little old now, cause I brung 'em all the way from Alabama." Then he sat back and puffed his pipe contentedly while waiting to eat.

As always, Franklin and Nathaniel gave Lazarus a share of their food, and the others tossed the yellow hound some of theirs. After the stew of fresh rabbit and collared greens, they split the pot of steaming crawfish between everyone. Franklin felt like he was going to burst, and the smiles on the other men's faces told him they felt the same.

Their bellies full, and in good spirits, the men cleaned up the camp in the hope that no one who might happen this way would be able to tell that anyone was ever there. They then trudged further northward, and by late afternoon, found themselves on the outskirts of a town.

"This here is Owensboro," announced Elijah. He had returned to the group earlier after doing some scouting up ahead. "This be where we gonna find us a safe place. The river's just on the other side of town. We got us a straight shot ta the shore when we's ready, and I ain't seen no sign they's slave hunters anywhere neither."

The men kept to the periphery of the town to observe things from the relative safety of the forest for a while. They watched the movement of the people they saw, and looked for anything suspicious. Wood smoke was curling up into the air from the chimneys of most of the structures they saw in the town proper, as well as those that were scattered about here and there in the outskirts and deeper into the woods. The sounds of commerce and civilized life; the murmur of voices and dogs barking, the rattle of wagons rolling, wood being chopped, an occasional bell being rung, carried upon the crisp early evening breeze, filtered through the trees to the anxious men. Franklin heard the faint, but distinctive tinkling of a honky-tonk piano and imagined a warm room full of pipe and cigar smoke, and the tang of beer and liquor.

"There," Clarence said in a hushed tone. He pointed to a cabin about sixty yards to their right, and the men responded with broad smiles while clapping one another on the back.

Franklin peered through the pines at the cabin. "All I see is a woman taking some wash down off a line."

A dog's bark echoed through the woods, and Lazarus's tail wagged in response.

"Look there," Nathaniel said. He took Franklin's elbow and turned him slightly to the right, then pointed. "See that square cloth hangin' on the line with the rest of the clothes?"

"I see it, but there's no picture of a cabin, only shapes and colors."

"See how they is blue colors on one side, and red colors on the other," Nathaniel said patiently. "And then they is a black square, smack in the middle of 'em both."

Franklin's expression was incredulous. There were other pieces of fabric mixed in with the clothes. To him, they looked like they could be table cloths, or patchwork bed spreads. He didn't see anything special about the one Nathaniel pointed out.

"The black square in the middle is a cabin," Nathaniel explained. "Thas a symbol it be a safe place for runaways."

"So what are we supposed to do now?" Franklin asked, stunned at the creativity of the desperate.

"We gotta get closer," Clarence answered. "When the lady of the house sees us, we find out fo sho if she can take us in. If somethin' goes wrong, we high-tail it back ta the old camp."

The men moved to approximately thirty yards from the woman, at first keeping to the trees and stopping every few steps to scan the area for any sign of danger. As none was evident they drew to within thirty feet of the woman, and from there, while the rest of the men kept themselves hidden, Clarence stepped out into the open.

"Evenin', ma'am," he said after clearing his throat.

The woman stopped what she was doing and turned toward his voice, her wide eyes betraying her fear. A frail thing to behold, her clothing hung from shoulders so narrow it was a wonder they could hold them up. Franklin, peeking out from around a tree could see that she was caucasian. Her face shone white as the moon from inside her heavy winter wraps, a patchwork of different pieces of fabric—likely rags—all sown together. She brushed thin strands of black hair from her eyes, and looked to be holding her breath.

"The riverbank... be a mighty fine road,... ain't it ma'am?" Clarence asked speaking haltingly.

"I don't know you mister," the woman replied with a backwoods twang, and just above a whisper.

Clarence looked around, as did all the other men. Franklin could see nothing to worry about.

"Thas right ma'am," stammered Clarence. "A friend sent me and some others with me this-a-way. Said y'all could keep us safe awhile while we wait ta cross the river." He pointed at the line of clothes, and zeroed in on the piece of cloth with the symbol in its center. "Said we'd know ya by the sign."

Franklin and the other men came out from behind the trees, and the woman bent down and picked some clothing out of a basket at her feet. "You'll find what you're looking for in the barn." Still bent over, and feigning that she was busily at work, she nodded her head slightly to her left.

Franklin followed her directive to a decrepit looking excuse of a structure that stood thirty yards behind the not much less ramshackle looking cabin. Besides the ruined look of the building, in comparison to the house, it was dark, and there was no smoke wafting up from a chimney somewhere within that would promise the warmth of a fire.

"Be careful when you get inside," the woman warned. She had straightened back up and was hanging a garment on the line that was so threadbare a person could see the trees right through it. "There's a weak spot'er two in the floor. My husband weren't feeling so good for a spell. But now that he's better he'll be tending to it right shortly. You'll find yourselves some vittles and something to drink inside. There's others in there already. Best be moving quick like. There's still enough light people can see you out here. When you're inside, knock three times to let the others know you're not hunters."

Franklin fell in line with the others as they hustled from tree to tree. Each man "thanked the woman *kindly*," as they passed by her to what he imagined at one time must have been a barn, and upon arriving at the door that was hanging half-opened on rusty hinges, slipped into its darkness. The aroma inside was dank and musty, and something ruffled its feathers somewhere above them when they entered. Farm implements hung on wooden beams that supported the rafters, and the stickiness of spiderwebs brushed against their faces as the men shuffled across floorboards loosely covered with hay that muffled their movements. Clarence knocked on the inside of the door as instructed.

The place looked and felt as though it hadn't been used for years, and Franklin wondered if that wasn't on purpose. Narrow shafts of light filtered in through the porous roof and past sagging and broken beams, but barely enough to navigate by. He heard an odd sounding chorus of chirping coming from the rafters, and the floor, sticky with an acidic smelling substance suggested the creatures might be bats. The weathered floorboards creaked as they stepped gingerly around and over dark shapes of barrels, boxes, spools of wire, and piles of hay strewn about haphazardly. Something startled him as it brushed past his ear, and the whispered expression of various expletives by the other men, told Franklin they felt it too.

"Bats!" Nathaniel shrieked under his breath.

"Here it is," Clarence proclaimed. "Help me move these boxes." But before he and Elijah could lean into them, the boxes moved by themselves.

Franklin jumped back, and he didn't have to see them to know that the others had done the same. But even in the darkness, he could see the whites of everyone's terrified eyes. Then a soft, yellow glow of light came up from a two-foot square hole in the floor at their feet.

"Set down and slide yer asses down here," a voice coaxed from below.

Franklin bent down and saw two pairs of eyes reflecting the light peering up at them from a couple of dark faces about twelve feet down. The sizzle of meat cooking, and the smell of something savory also wafted up through the opening, and Clarence wasted no time in sitting himself down, then disappearing as he slid into the hole. The others followed, one after the other, then Nathaniel with Lazarus in his lap. Finally, Franklin took the plunge down a steep, slick wooden ramp. When his feet hit the floor, a strong hand on either side of him grasped him by his arms and kept him from falling on his face. Once he was steady on his feet, those same two strong hands took hold of a rope and pulled. Franklin heard the sound of boxes scraping across the hay strewn floor above, sealing the hole he had just slid down through.

# CHAPTER 35

"Y'all's safe nuff now," a voice as deep as Clarence's but scratchier said. "Is they any more of you comin'?"

"We the only ones we know about," Clarence answered. "How many of you is down here?"

"Just me, and my son Booker. Name's Cleetus. Some others was here before, but they done gone outta this place already. Wasn't 'nuff room for us on the wagon, so we's waitin' on the next time ta go."

"When will that be?" asked Franklin.

"Don't know 'xactly. We finds out when it gets here."

Perturbed by the lack of information, which once again, for him, meant bad planning, Franklin said thinly, "How many of us can go when it does get here."

"The last wagon was big enough for ten men, so we can all fit. You hungry? Got some stew over there." Cleetus pointed to a pot in the corner that was sitting on top of a cast iron, wood burning stove, that as well as permeating the space they were in with the tantalizing smell of boiled meat, emanated a much welcome warmth. "Me and my boy done ate," Cleetus added, "they's plenty for all o' you."

Franklin's eyes had adjusted to the dimly illuminated area enough to take in the relative size of the space which he determined was too small for the eight of them plus Lazarus, let alone twelve fully grown men. He wondered how they all managed to sleep in such a confined area, or take care of their business, but the unmistakeable scent of urine, coming from a corner, found its way to his nose, and he decided not to think about it anymore.

Cleetus sat himself down on a bale of hay and encouraged the others to join him on other bales that had been arranged in a circle. "Booker and me come up here all the ways from Alabama. We was headin' for a place called Paducah, but we got lost somewheres and ended up here. Where you from?"

Booker passed around cups full of aromatic broth with chunks of meat and chopped up carrots and potatoes floating in it, and the grateful men ate as they shared their names and stories. Although the son and his father, and the other four men looked at Franklin in wide-eyed wonder when he shared his, no one questioned him.

Franklin and the rest of the new arrivals were dead tired, and shortly after eating, they moved off and scraped together piles of hay to lie down upon. As he lay on his back contemplating all he'd been through, Franklin heard someone lightly drumming on the bottom of a tin bucket. The drumming reminded him of when this journey for him began—which now seemed like a very long time ago—and when he closed his eyes, he saw again for a moment, the smoky interior of the Cherokee dwelling. Then a deep voice he took to be Cleetus', began singing in a whisper.

"Follow the drinkin' gourd, follow the drinkin' gourd. For the old man's a-waitin' for ta carry you ta freedom. Follow the drinkin' gourd."

Franklin raised himself up on his elbow, as did the others, and they all listened to their host. Cubennah lit his pipe and puffed out plumes of blue smoke. Boney brought out his flask again, and soon all the men were once more sharing the liquor. Franklin allowed the flask to pass him by, and soaked in the warmth of being in the presence of this remarkable camaraderie such as he had never known.

"When the sun come up, and the first quail calls. Follow the drinkin' gourd. For the old man's waitin' for ta carry you ta freedom. Follow the drinkin' gourd." Cleetus sang the first verse and repeated the opening chorus, took a sip of whiskey, then began the second verse. "The riverbank'l make a mighty good road, the dead trees show you the way. Left foot, peg foot, travelin' on. Follow the drinkin' gourd."

Booker and the others joined in to sing the chorus, then before Cleetus could sing the next verse, his son asked, "Do you think Peg leg Joe was a real man?"

"Don't know, son. All I knows is he's in the song, but it don't matter. What I do know is when we get ourselves back home ta your momma, I'm gonna write this song down and hang it on a wall some wheres in our home. Without it, and the Good Lord, I don't knows how we'da found our way."

Booker closed his eyes and leaned against a post as Cleetus finished the song. And one by one, while the last lines were being sung, the men retreated to their piles of hay. Tired as he was, Franklin found he couldn't sleep. So he laid back quietly, his fingers clasped loosely beneath his head, listening to the men breathing and mumbling in their sleep. Soon, images flashed through his mind of all the people he had met during this odd, prolonged, and harrowing experience. There were many cruel people like Hawley to be sure, but him and those like him weren't the ones he focused on. Instead he thought of Degataga and Ayita, and their sons, Kanuna and Chea Sequa. He thought of Nathaniel and his dog, Lazarus, then Moses Daniels and Joseph Grey Bear. He thought about all the men that lay sleeping around him now, Clarence, Boney, Elijah, and Cubennah, Cleetus and his son Booker, and the woman, whose name he'd probably never know, and her husband, whom he'd not yet seen, who were allowing him and the others to sleep in their barn, offering protection to complete strangers; and this at their own risk. Franklin realized that unless he woke up from this prolonged dream, there would be others, and that all of these people were willing to risk their lives so that he and others could be free.

The images of these people faded away like guests leaving after a short, bitter sweet visit, and Franklin's thoughts turned to Gwen. He realized now that there was something she had in common with all of them, something he lacked in himself. It wasn't just that they weren't judgmental like he was. Nor was it that they weren't cruel, crass, unkind, or self-serving as he had been. There was something else, something more. He wrinkled his brow trying to figure it out, but nothing solid materialized in his mind. Instead, a thought seemed to filter down to him softly like the sunlight that had filtered down through the heavy, snow-laden grey clouds in the frozen meadow only a day ago, that instantly warmed him in spite of the blizzard he heard blowing outside in the dark that now surrounded the safe place. Or was it that it welled up inside of him, spreading a nourishing and comforting warmth throughout his body, in the same way the warmth of the stew he'd just eaten spread from his stomach to the rest of his being. Either way, Franklin felt a change was coming over him, working its way from the inside out. How this change was happening, he couldn't say. He only knew it felt good. He only knew that each of these people had given to one another, and to him, in spite of his ugliness, from the very little they possessed. And this, often at the risk of their own peril. "That's what it is," Franklin whispered to himself. "That's what they all have in common." As he drifted to sleep, another thought threaded its way into his consciousness. *If we are to be judged for how we've lived our lives, I no longer believe it will be for our not somehow obtaining more for ourselves. Rather, I think it will be for our failure to do all we could for others from what we've been given, however much, or little.*

Franklin awoke with a start. He couldn't tell how long he'd been asleep, but he knew without a doubt that a rough, and heavy hand had been clamped tightly over his mouth. Opening his eyes wide, he looked up into the face of Boney, who held a finger to his lips, his own eyes wide with fear. Seeing that Franklin was awake, he pointed to the ceiling.

"Y'all are gonna wanna come on up outta there right quick, and I'll tell ya why," a gravely voice growled from the floor above. "We're 'bout ta set fire ta this sorry excuse for a barn. And we aim ta do it whether or not y'all come up. Get paid the same either way. I know y'all ain't too dumb ta understand that. But just in case, I'll even tell ya why it won't be a good idea for y'all not ta come outta that hole. Once this structure starts ta blazin', yer asses are gonna get roasted even blacker'n they already is!"

A chorus of snickers and several weapons being cocked was heard above Franklin and the other men's heads.

"Now just climb on up outta there, and show yer hands, and y'all might not get yerself shot."

Clarence went up the ladder first, and as soon as his head emerged from the cellar, he was grabbed by the collar of his shirt, and dragged the rest of the way up, then thrown to the floor with a thud. His son Booker went next with the same result, then each of the others.

Terrified, Franklin heaved Lazarus up to Nathaniel who had climbed part way up the ladder. Nathaniel grasped the fur covered bag of bones and shoved the dog the rest of the way out the hatch opening. Lazarus yelped, and Franklin assumed he'd gotten the same treatment as the men who'd gone up before him. Frantic, he looked around himself, but saw no other way out, and no place to hide. He prayed once more that he'd wake up before meeting whatever fate awaited him, then he took a deep breath and exhaled slowly, then climbed the last few rungs of the ladder. Before his eyes could adjust, he was grabbed by powerful hands and thrown hard to the floor. He shook the dizziness from his head and saw Clarence and the others sitting together against a wall. Lazarus trembled in Nathaniel's arms, and as strange as Franklin thought it was, the dog seemed to be looking directly at him, as if he was asking him what he should do.

"Go boy!" Franklin croaked, and immediately, a boot caught him beneath his chin, flipping him onto his back. But not before he saw Lazarus scrabble for purchase on the barn floor and take off like a shot. The yellow hound zig-zagged his way in between the men, startling the slave hunters enough to enable him to make it out the door and into the woods before any of them could get a bead on him with a rifle. Franklin chuckled in spite of the throbbing pain. He knew the dog had plenty of practice at get-aways. And he knew he'd be following close by wherever these men intended to take him and the others, waiting for an opportunity to help them escape.

The angry cursing of one of the gunmen brought Franklin's attention back to the moment. The moon provided plenty of light for him to see that there were three men holding him and his friends at gunpoint. And each of them were as large, and just as frightening in appearance as he had imagined.

"Some of ya might be thinkin' of runnin' for it, like the mutt, but I don't recommend it." The man speaking, spread his wrap aside to reveal that in addition to his rifle, he was also carrying a pistol. "Boys," he said to the men with him. And the two men displayed their additional side-arms.

"Lucky for us, while we was havin' ourselves one last drink before call-in' it quits earlier this evenin'," the man continued, "we just happened to overhear a conversation between a couple of boys at the tavern. Sounded like they was discussin' a pick-up for tonight. So, on a hunch, we followed those two boys here ta take a look for ourselves."

Franklin noticed that one of the men was holding the end of a rope, and that the other end was wrapped tightly around the woman that had showed them to the barn, and a man with a swollen face and bleeding nose. He suspected the unfortunate man was her husband.

"Now that we got this here wagon," the slave hunter said with a laugh, "it looks like we ain't the only lucky ones here, 'cause now y'all won't have ta walk back with us. Tie these two nigger lovers up with the coloreds, and get 'em all up inta the wagon," he directed his partners. Turning to the pulverized man, he said, "Looks like y'all ain't too beat up ta drive this rig, but don't try nothin' stupid cause we'll be ridin' right along beside of ya. Boys," he said to his men, "Torch this place, and let's go get us some cash."

After loading Franklin and the other men onto the wagon, one of the slave hunters picked up a kerosene lantern from the porch of the house, and walked over to the barn. He tossed the lantern onto a mound of hay, and the dry, broken structure roared into flames.

The sudden burst of fire spooked the horses that were harnessed to the wagon. They took off with a start, catching the slave hunters by surprise, and ran blindly down the road from the barn in the general direction of town. The erratic behavior of the two draw horses caused a chain reaction with the slave hunter's horses, who stutter-stepped into one another, then reared up on their hind legs, pitching their riders to the ground.

The beaten up man and the woman made clucking sounds and used voice commands that steered the horses toward the main road to town, while the cursing slave hunters staggered to their feet and tried to regain control of their mounts. The wagon hit the turn at the end of the couple's road hard and fast, throwing a mix of mud and snow into the air, and nearly flipping it over, but by that time, the beaten up man had managed to free his hands. Grasping the reigns, he regained control.

"Name's Ben!" the driver hollered. "Y'all already met my wife, Hannah! The docks are this way! There are two boats waitin' for ya there! One on each end of town!" Ben snapped the reigns, and the horses moved even faster. "Try ta get yerselves untied!" he yelled. "We'll have ta move fast when we get there!"

Clarence had already managed to free his hands, and was busy with the ropes that still bound his companions. Nathaniel had also gotten loose. He steadied himself in the jostling wagon, then untied Franklin.

Franklin rubbed his wrists and thought for a second, then asked, "Won't they just grab a boat of their own and come after us?"

Ben pointed at his head, then gave the thumbs up sign, indicating he'd already thought of that. "Which ever ferry we *don't* take'll act as a decoy. So if we get there fast enough, them slave hunters won't know which one ta go after."

One of the wagon wheels caught a rut in the road, and veered erratically to the right, and Ben stopped talking, quickly grasped the reigns with both hands, and guided it back on course. Once the wagon was steady, he continued his explanation, "The few row boats on the shore won't take 'em too far," he laughed, slapping his knee, "cause they's got holes drilled in 'em." He laughed again at the look on Franklin's face. "Been doin' this a while my friend. Most of us in this town is friendly ta yer cause, and the rest don't really pay it any mind."

Franklin's emotions had downshifted from sheer terror to guarded optimism. He figured that now there might be a fifty percent chance of getting away, which was a great improvement on their odds from just a couple of minutes ago.

"When we get ta the river, we're gonna have ta ditch the wagon!" Ben yelled over the clatter of the wagon and the rhythmic huffs of the horses as they galloped toward town. "The road there is too rough going either direction. When we come ta a stop, we all gotta high-tale it and hope the boat pulls out before those bastards get ta us."

Franklin thought it was a good thing that it was not yet daylight. Otherwise the roads through town would be congested with wagons, horses and townspeople, forcing them to slow down. The town and the river were still far off, and he stole a glance behind but didn't see any sign of pursuit.

All the men's hands, now freed, were clutching the sides of the wagon, their knuckles blanched white from their effort to hold on as it careened down the road. Chancing another look behind them, Franklin thought he saw a small cloud of dust rising up into the still dark sky just beyond the hill and tree line blocking from view the barn they'd stayed in. He feared it was a harbinger of the wrath the slave hunters would rain down on him and the others should they manage to catch up.

Finally arriving at the edge of town, Ben guided the barreling wagon down a street that transitioned from dirt to cobblestone, taking them past a blur of establishments. Franklin was surprised to see some of them beginning to show signs of life. To one side of him a merchant was already arranging barrels on the walkway in front of what looked like a market, while on the other side of the street he saw another man toss water from a bucket onto the boardwalk in front of a tavern, then take a broom to it.

The combination of the horses hooves clacking and the wagon wheels grinding on the cobblestone surfaced street, and all of it echoing off of the buildings on either side of them increased the noise level to a thundering roar. The horses were slathered with foam from their exertion, and it flew off of them in globs into the faces of Ben, his wife, and the fleeing men.

They were making great progress, when Franklin saw a cart that was being drawn by a mule moving slowly down the middle of the road, directly in their path. The mule's back was swayed, and the cart was loaded with large, stacked metal containers. The wagon was gaining fast on the cart and flea-bitten animal, and just as Ben veered to miss a pothole, the mule reared up braying obnoxiously. The driver of the cart jumped for the safety of the boardwalk as the cart tipped over spilling its canisters directly in their path.

Ben pulled hard with the reigns and guided the horses to the left in an attempt to avoid hitting the toppled over canisters, several of which had burst open, spilling creamy white liquid into the street. The wagon slid sideways in white froth for a heart-stopping moment, its iron lined wheels creating sparks as they dragged across the cobblestones. It tilted precariously, threatening to dump Franklin and the others, but the men reacted in unison, each of them repositioning their weight to the opposite side of the wagon, which kept it from flipping. Finally, the wagon driver managed to regain control, and they continued their course through the center of town with the horses at a full gallup.

Approaching the other end of town, the river came into view, and Franklin's initial relief at nearing their goal changed to fear that at the speed they were going, they might run straight into it. The other men must have had the same thought because they all braced for the impact. Ben stood up and pulled back on the reigns, the veins bulging in his neck. He called out, "Whoah!", and remarkably, the horses and wagon stuttered to a stop. "Head north!" he shouted, then jumped down from his seat. While helping his wife down he added, "It's the closest boat from here. Let's go, they're waiting for us!"

"What about you?" Franklin asked the couple. "Where will you go?"

"North, my friend, just, like the rest of y'all. There's no place for us here no more. They'll find us, and lynch us, or worse for what we done. But don't worry. We got us some family in Ohio."

Nathaniel and Lazarus were mere steps behind the other men who had already jumped off the wagon, and were ducking out of site behind a thick patch of reeds along the shore of the river. Ben and his wife wasted no time themselves, and were doing their best to catch up. Franklin looked after them, then back up the road they'd all rattled and clattered so wildly down just moments ago. He could see the forms of the men pursuing them in the distance as they had just entered the far side of town. At that distance, they were merely dark silhouettes that merged and then separated from one another as they galloped down the main road, heading straight for him. Franklin's legs were screaming at him to run, but his instincts told him he and the others didn't stand a chance of making it to the boat and taking off in time. The slave hunters were coming on much too fast.

An idea was forming in Franklin's mind, and it was materializing as fast as the slave hunters were approaching. He had a decision to make, and he needed to make it now. Should he high-tail it after the others and the unlikely hope of freedom in this seemingly unending dream, or should he make a run for it in the opposite direction, to the west, which just so happened to be the direction the Cherokee believed was the way of death. Franklin thought how ironic it was that if he didn't wake up now, he'd die either way.

"Franklin! Come on, now! We gotta go!" the faint, yet urgent voice of Nathaniel implored from the reeds. Franklin looked at his friend and the others. They were hunched down trying to hide their presence there, while at the same time waving wildly at him.

For one frantic, blink of an eye moment, Franklin agonized over his choices. Then suddenly, just like when a key unlocks the mechanism that opens a door, the way he should go was opened to him. He patted his chest at the spot the feathers hung underneath his coat and smiled.

The only time Franklin had ever seen a buckboard wagon before was in one of those "Old Town" parks he once visited. He certainly had never operated, let alone sat in one. So he was surprised at how springy the wooden bench seat was after he'd taken three precise steps, then vaulted up and onto it. Without taking any more time to think about it he grabbed the reins, then with one last look back at his friend, Nathaniel, waved him off. Nathaniel turned and followed the other men, leaving Lazarus to bay his goodby to Franklin before leaping into the reeds after them. Franklin wanted to take off immediately, but he waited, his nerves screaming, as he watched the slave hunters close the distance between them. When he believed they could see him he snapped the reigns to engage the horses as he'd seen the wagon driver do, and hollered, "Yah! Get up!" then pulled their heads to the west.

The horses responded like a well-tuned machine, bolting in his chosen direction, and the wagon rumbled along behind them. Franklin looked to his left and was stunned at how much closer the hunters were. He hoped they saw him, only not so clearly that they'd notice that he was alone. But he wouldn't know for sure unless they made the turn west themselves.

The buckboard rattled like a proverbial bucket of bolts. Its steel wrapped wheels grated on every rock, and snagged on every bump and indentation in the road. And, if there wasn't a groove in the road already, they made one. Besides the reins, the horses were connected to the wagon by a leather harness fitted to wooden poles. These kept the wagon from coming up to close behind the animals when they slowed. Leather straps were threaded through metal fittings at the ends of the poles, and Franklin wondered how something like that endured the beating they invariably took, especially at a run, and particularly on such an uneven, rock strewn and rutted surface as the one he was on.

The badly rutted road snaked along the winding river, and varied from twenty yards to as close as five feet along a ridge that undulated up and down in elevation beside its bank. Franklin heard something "zing!" past his ear, followed by a "thunk!", and his blood ran cold with the realization he was being shot at. Stealing a glance behind him, he saw with a strange mixture of terror and relief that all three of the slave hunters were pursuing him. They were closing ground. In spite of the fact that they would be on him in a matter of seconds, Franklin beamed to himself, knowing now that his friends would make it.

"Bam!" The wagon hit a rut and careened away from the edge of the ridge. Franklin corrected course by steering back to the right, narrowly missing the thick trunks of a stand of trees. One of the hunters had managed to draw up along side of the wagon and was leveling a pistol at Franklin. "Pull up!" he hollered, and cocked the hammer back on the gun.

The wagon slammed into a pot hole and lurched sharply to the right, and Franklin heard an ear-splitting, cracking sound. The jolt had broken both of the poles connecting the horses to the wagon, and in what felt to Franklin like several slow motion minutes, the horses turned their heads to their left. Their coats were slick with sweat, their eyes bulged with adrenaline charged fear, and their mouths frothed. The horse on the left bumped into the mount the slave hunter rode sending the man air born. His gun discharged harmlessly into the forest canopy just before he hit the ground with a hard thump. Franklin laughed in triumph, however, his celebration was cut short when both of the broken harness posts jammed into the ground, locking back up against the oncoming wagon, and Franklin was instantaneously catapulted off his seat.

He soared, summersaulting in the air, and while twisting head over heals caught a glimpse of the still blackened sky, tinged with the lightest blue, vibrant pinks and splashes of orange along the eastern horizon. As Franklin's body continued to flip helplessly, his view shifted from the tops of the trees, to the cloud studded sky, to the roiling steel blue-blackness of the Ohio River thirty feet below. The rivers surface was coming up fast, and the glint of early morning light refracting from jagged shards of floating ice found its way into Franklin's eyes.

Just before hitting the water, Franklin's body turned again so that he was looking back at the ridge line above the river. There he saw the silhouetted form of the lead slave hunter sitting on his horse. The man holstered his gun and turned his mount west, then disappeared from sight. *Was that lucky or what?* he thought to himself with a chuckle, *Chea Sequa would have loved this!*

# CHAPTER 36

Franklin's body plunged into the river with a terrific splash. He likened the pain he felt to what he'd expect if he had smashed through a plate glass window, and he was submerged instantly into a wet blackness that was only surpassed by the intense cold. The impact knocked the breath out of him, but he remained conscious, and remembered to hold his breath rather than fight for air. Although he was disoriented, he became aware of the sensation of sinking. Suddenly, his survival instinct took over, and he kicked his legs and flailed his arms wildly. He figured his chances were fifty-fifty that he'd reach the surface, and those odds would have to do for now. His body was so cold his head hurt. His ears had popped, and his lungs were burning from the pressure of holding his breath. He was running out of time, and knew that it would be over for him if he didn't surface soon. Franklin thought to himself, *I'll finally know what happens to a person who dies in a dream.*

When he reached the point he thought his lungs might burst, Franklin broke the surface and gasped, filling his lungs with life giving but frigidly cold, pre-morning air. His water-soaked cloths tugged him downwards, forcing him to kick against the weight with his numbing legs to stay afloat. Franklin became aware of the strong pull of the current and realized he was being swept downstream to the west. He also noticed with disappointment that the current had brought him closer to the center of the river, making a swim to either bank nearly impossible for anyone but an olympic athlete, much less somebody in his current condition. Endurance was in short supply at the moment, so rather than increasing the risk drowning with an attempt to make it to shore, he searched the water around him for something to hold on to and keep him afloat.

All around him were chunks of ice, but they were slippery, and so small they only sank under his weight. A small mass of broken branches floated towards him but just as he reached for it, the debris twisted in a strong eddy. Branches jabbed him in the arm, leg, and gut, with enough force they ripped through his leather wraps, cutting him in several places. Franklin re-coiled in fresh pain, searching frantically for something else to cling to.

Like the branches, the current spun Franklin in maddening circles, then spit him out and picked up speed. Struggling to stay afloat, he spotted a large dark, triangular shape looming in the water up-river from him. He had drifted into some rapids, and knew from experience that he should be floating on his back with his feet down river to enable him to kick off from any rocks he might encounter thus avoid cracking his skull. But the object bobbing in the water toward him looked as though it might be a boat. Franklin reasoned that if it proved to be one, he would call to who ever was on board at the right moment in the hope he would not be missed. He feared however, that he didn't have long before he would sink from the weight of his water soaked clothing and shear exhaustion.

Finally, from out of the darkness still shrouding the river, the object bobbed into view. It was a large chunk of ice as dark as the river itself, and twice the size of a row boat. Franklin reached out as he began to slide by it, and his fingers slipped across the cold surface. Struggling to find a handhold, his body bumped hard against a large rock jutting up to just below the surface, and once more had the wind knocked out of him. Gasping for air, Franklin grabbed the end of a branch that stuck out from the ice. It bent like a bow under his weight, and he feared it would snap, but the branch was flexible, and held up long enough for him to work himself up to a shelf of ice that served as a hand hold.

Every muscle, each and every fiber of his body, all of his nerve endings, and the full and raw desire of his will to live, was strained to the limit as Franklin fought to hold on to the floating ice while it twisted in eddies, and bumped into rocks, nearly toppling over from the force of the impact, then righting itself to point down river again. Finally, he managed to lock his armpits securely over a sturdy looking branch, giving his hands some relief from the cold ice. With nothing more to do but hold on, weariness overtook him. He'd had no more than a couple hours of sleep at best in the last day and a half. Franklin leaned his weight onto the branch to satisfy himself that it wouldn't break. His numb limbs seemed no longer to belong to his body, and his legs now trailed behind him as he no longer had the strength hold them out in front of himself. The combination of the cold, physical and emotional exhaustion, and lack of sleep overtook him, and his eyelids closed to mere slits. "Perhaps I'll just take a nap... ."

Franklin's words trailed off before he could finish, and he awoke perhaps two or three hours from when he nodded off. The sun was low in the east, so he assumed it was mid-morning. He could no longer feel any part of his body, and he assumed he was able to hang on simply because his limbs had frozen in place. It seemed to him he had become one with the ice, and as he resigned himself to the fact that he would surely die, an oddly familiar looking shadow appeared ahead in the mist rising from the river. As the current brought him closer, the shadow became a boat, then the boat, a ferry.

His heart leapt. *What are the odds,* he wondered, *that I've drifted all the way back to Berry's Ferry, and am gaining on one of the boats?*

Through the morning fog, Franklin could barely make out the shapes of people on board. He tried to call out, but he had become too weak. To his alarm, the boat seemed to be picking up speed and was pulling away from him, when it suddenly spun sideways in an eddy. What luck, he thought, as the huge mass of ice he was hanging onto appeared to be on a direct course to collide with the ferry within the next few moments. Someone was leaning over the edge of the ferry, and Franklin's heart leapt in his chest. He couldn't be sure, but it looked as though whoever it was was reaching for him. Franklin again tried to call for help, but his effort was in vain. All he could utter was a hoarse rasp.

The floating ice suddenly came to a jarring stop, then swung around in a lazy circle having bumped up against something below the surface of the river. Franklin heard a cracking sound and the branch he was hanging onto broke. A smaller branch slipped in through his coat to the leather strap that held the eagle and cardinal feather talas. Franklin fought to hold onto the broken branch, only to find that it had become too water-logged to stay afloat. He flailed his hands wildly, grasping at the slick ice to no avail. Finally, and only when he felt he no longer had a shred of energy left in him, he stopped struggling and slid silently below the rivers churning surface. The strap, snagged on the smaller branch, and the precious feathers were pulled from around his neck.

Franklin didn't bother to take another breath. His body sank, and the light dimmed incrementally with the depth until he was in total darkness. And still he felt himself sinking. His ears began to ring with the pressure, then they popped. He bumped up against something unseen as the deep current of the river swept him tumbling like a leaf in a stiff, blustery breeze. His numbed hands felt the heavy, mushy flatness of what he decided must be a water logged plank. Then he felt another, *maybe the remnants of an old pier*, he thought groggily, *or a sunken vessel*. Bright colors and flashes of light began to burst before his eyes, and his instinct to draw breath into his oxygen depleted lungs overtook reason. Thinking once more of all those he had hurt, and all whom he now—but too late—held dear, he gasped deeply, drawing the frigid water deep into his lungs. The ringing in his ears stopped, and he drifted weightless and silent in a cold, blackness he felt could only be death.

\*\*\*

Franklin thought it odd when he felt a distinct thump against his chest, then decided that perhaps it was merely a part of the dying process. But there it was again, another thump, then another, each one increased in intensity. A fourth thump, much harder than the first three, caused him to gasp even more deeply than a moment before. Then the ringing in his ears returned, followed by a rhythmic assortment of odd beeps. The sounds became progressively louder, and he suddenly felt intense, crushing pain in his chest. A light appeared. It was faint, and seemed far away. Franklin couldn't decide if it was drawing closer, or becoming brighter, or both. He thought incredulously, *And I always thought people who talked about going to the light were full of it.*

He tried to stroke upwards through the dark water, but his arms became entangled in something that held him firmly in place, and he thought he heard the voice of a woman breaking through all of the commotion, but it was garbled, and again, sounded like it was coming from far away.

"Franklin. Mr. Carlyle. Can you hear me?" the voice of a woman repeated.

*God's a woman?* he asked himself. A blurred form manifested in the center of the light that had become blinding. It looked remotely like a face that floated just above a white gown, but he couldn't be sure. Two indistinct appendages branched off from the gown, and Franklin realized that they were what kept him from surfacing.

"My God, If I hadn't seen this for myself, I wouldn't believe it," the face announced. "I've never seen anyone in a coma for this long, who codes, and then comes back. But, I'll be damned! I think we've got him. I think he's with us!"

With one last feeble stroke, Franklin thought he had broken the surface of the river. That was when the previously calming, muffled sounds of his underwater sojourn suddenly became blaring and harsh. The ear splitting, repetitive sound of an alarm came from somewhere behind him, accompanied by other equally annoying beeping noises. Light blazed into his eyes, and other lights flashed on and off in his peripheral vision keeping pace with the beeps. Then the amorphous face of God appeared. All of this stimuli seared its way into Franklin's head, resulting in a massive headache.

"Mr. Carlyle, if you can hear me, blink once, or raise a finger," the blurry face instructed.

*Can't a man even die in peace?* he raged silently to himself. *Yeah, sure, I'll give you the finger!* he snapped, still in his head. But he thought better of flipping God off, and lifted his index finger, which felt like a piece of rolled, uncooked dough. The face became clearer, and he saw a woman with some kind of blue wrap around her head. A stethoscope hung from her neck, partly covered by a white gown, or coat of sorts.

*I'm back*, Franklin thought with relief, and foggy memories of an ambulance ride and laying in a hospital bed looking at his crying wife came back to him. Tears formed in his eyes, and he tried to speak. He realized that he had been in a coma, or possibly even died and came back, but he suddenly felt the loss of the people he met during his dream. Although relieved to finally be home again—or almost home anyway—he resolved to do some research as soon as he could on slavery, and the actual Trail of Tears history.

Franklin tried to move his mouth. He wanted to say something, to ask about Gwen, but no words came.

"Don't try to talk yet, Mr. Carlyle," the face said. "You're far too weak. Rest now. You've been through a lot, and there's still a bit more to go."

\*\*\*

The next time Franklin opened his eyes he was certain he was back in the dream. Standing several feet away from him, and looking out the window of his hospital room, was Gwen. The fact that she was standing with her back toward him made him nervous. The last few times this occurred, things went horribly wrong. Finally, when he could stand it not longer, he cleared his throat and winced when it felt like he was swallowing razor blades. "Gwen?" he rasped.

She didn't jump as she had the other times. She turned slowly, and in a manner that seemed both gracious and purposeful. Franklin noticed with surprise that she wasn't fidgeting nervously with her hands. Instead, her arms were at rest along her sides, her fingers relaxed. He saw that her eyes weren't wide with that deer caught in the headlights look either. Instead, her blue-green eyes were soft, and she wore a pleasant smile. He knew she couldn't have gotten any younger, but she looked as though she had.

"Franklin, I'm so glad you're back," she said quietly.

"Where would I go?" he asked in a weak attempt at humor, then coughed several times, the pain of which had him seeing stars. "Excuse me," he continued as his vision cleared once more. "What am I doing here?"

"You've been in a coma."

"How long?"

"It's been over three months."

"Three months?" he mused. Then turning his focus back to Gwen, he asked, "What's wrong with me? What caused the coma?"

"Drinking," she answered flatly, and her eyes flashed a moment before softening again. Gwen stayed where she was, a full arms length away, and Franklin was acutely aware that she hadn't reached out to touch so much as his arm.

"Are you here to take me home?" he asked meekly, then quickly added, "I promise, I'll never drink again."

"I don't know when you'll be able to leave here," she answered, her voice rising as she spoke. "You're very sick. You've nearly destroyed your liver." She paused and looked at him with her softened eyes that somehow still seemed to penetrate his soul. Lowering her voice, she said, "When you leave here isn't up to me. Aside from that, I haven't decided yet what to do about you coming home at all."

"What does that mean?"

Ignoring his question, Gwen continued. "I'm not sure we have what most people would call... a home. You've done so much with your attitude and your behavior to destroy that dream. So, I'm not ready to answer your question."

Franklin was speechless. Gwen had never spoken to him so directly and abruptly, and she had most certainly never spoken to him with such a tone.

"What I can tell you is this," she went on. "I'm here right now because I'm still your wife. I've been your partner for a very long time, even if you haven't been mine, and I'm not going to leave you in your time of need."

"Thank you,... I... "

Gwen raised her hands, palms out towards her husband. "Please," she interrupted, "just listen." She waited until Franklin's opened mouth closed, then continued. "There are a lot of things that will have to change if you and I are to go forward from here as a couple. I've spoken to a counselor, and I've thought and prayed about this during the time you've been here. And I've become clear on several things."

"Anything, Gwen. Just tell me... "

"*Listen - to - me, please*," she insisted with a voice imbued with an inner strength Franklin could not fathom was actually coming from her. "Before I tell you what I need, I think you should understand what *you* need. Just for you to get well. And even *that*, according to the doctor, is not a guarantee at this point."

Franklin kept quiet, looked directly at his wife, and waited. He saw a momentary look of confusion on her face, and shuddered from the realization that his being quiet and actually listening to her was a new experience for Gwen.

Gwen took a pronounced breath, and the words she spoke next seemed to tumble out of her as if she was finally getting rid of something she'd been holding onto for too long. "You need a liver transplant, Franklin. Without it, you'll die."

"I'm ready for... "

Gwen cut him off again, "To get it, the transplant, you will have had to have gone without drinking for at least six months, and *that's* just to get on the donor list." She let that set in, then continued, "Because you've been in a coma this long, you've already completed the first three. *If* you manage not to drink for *three more months,*" she said, strongly emphasizing the 'if', "you'll probably have to wait at least six more months after that for a liver. But you have to understand that a new liver is not guaranteed. *You're* not guaranteed to survive that long even if you no longer drink. This is the best case scenario." Gwen took a breath, crossed her arms tightly against her chest, and her eyes searched Franklin's face for a shred of understanding.

"I am pretty sick, aren't I?" Franklin offered in a weak attempt at humor.

"You nearly died! The doctors say you *did!*" Gwen yelled. Her voice trembled, and tears welled up in her eyes.

A nurse walking by the room stopped abruptly, her heels squealing on the polished floor, and peeked around the privacy curtain. "Everything all right in here?"

"Yes, thank you. We're fine," Gwen answered before Franklin could open his mouth.

The nurse pulled the privacy curtain back in place, and Franklin listened to her footsteps squeak away down the hall. "I'm, I'm sorry, Gwen. I'm kinda groggy. It's no excuse, but I am listening, and I'm taking you seriously," Franklin said carefully. Then with as much compassion as he could convey, he said, "I know it's hard to believe, but think I'm beginning to understand how you're feeling."

"How Franklin?" Gwen snapped. "How could you wake up from a three month long, alcohol induced comma, and *suddenly*," she said, trembling, "*suddenly*, after years of neglect and self-centeredness, understand how I feel? Can you explain that to me? Because, I'm not sure you've ever cared about *anyone* but yourself, or gave *two hoots* about how I ever felt, let alone anybody else!"

"You're right," he quietly agreed. "But let's save my explanation for later, can we?"

Gwen started backing away from him. "That's just what I'd expect! Let's put it off and forget all about it, right?"

"I'm exhausted, Gwen. It's like I'm all out of gas. I just don't think I could talk for as long as I'd need to tell you everything. Besides, I wouldn't expect you or anybody else to believe that I've changed. I'm going to have to show you." He stopped and coughed horsely, then took several raspy breaths. "In the meantime, I think I have enough left in the tank to hear you out. Would you please,... I know you've told me a million times before but,... just once more, please tell me what you need?"

From the look on her face, Franklin worried Gwen had gone into shock. *Hell, I'm in shock,* he thought to himself.

"All right, thank you," she said after the glazed look in her eyes had dissipated. Then she continued with a bit of tension still in her voice. "But before I tell you *my* needs, let me tell you what you need. First, as I already said, you need you to stop drinking. Completely." Gwen studied her husband's face again, but his expression didn't change, and surprised as she was, he seemed to be listening. "Second, you need to survive."

"Done, and done."

"Third," she said, shaking her head slightly at his interruption, "you need to go to therapy. And I don't mean only rehab. You also need to see a psychologist,... on your own, and whether your doctor says so or not, you need to join some form of alcohol abuse treatment group. You might even have to go into a residential program, but we'll see about that as we go."

"Can't I just go to an AA meeting?"

"First of all, it's not going to be *just* a meeting. You have to go for as long as it takes. I've done some research, and I've learned that quitting drinking in and of itself isn't enough. Alcohol is just the symptom of your problem. You need to see a therapist to sort that out and decide if you are willing, and, or able to become the man I need you to be, which brings me to my needs." Gwen took a deep breath at this point as she changed the focus from her husband to herself, something she'd had little experience with in the course of their relationship. "I want you to need me. And I *need* you to want me. And I don't mean like the trophy you once saw me as either. I mean as your wife, your lover, your partner, your friend. I *need* for you to value me. And by saying all of that, I want you to understand this doesn't mean that I can't live without it, or you." Gwen stopped a moment to let her words sink in, then took a step toward her husband. "I've grown while you've been gone, Franklin. I've learned about, and recovered who it is I am, and I'm perfectly capable of going on without you. I need you to do these things I've asked because you truly value me, and for no other reason. If you do these things, and make progress in therapy, then I'll consider joining you for couple's counseling."

For the first time since he'd awoken from the coma, Franklin brightened a little.

"But even then," Gwen continued, holding up a finger to keep him in check, "none of this guarantees that I'll take you back. You're really going to have to work. You'll have to pursue me, and I'm not going to make that easy for you."

The look of confusion returned to Franklin's face.

"Do you know what courting is?" Gwen asked, her eyebrows raised.

"I, I think so."

"Well, you need to be sure. It's not at all like the dating that goes on today, and I'll accept nothing less." She crossed her arms across her chest, and waited for that last bit to sink in a moment. "Talk to a therapist, ask around, read some books, watch some movies to find out. Without understanding this, you won't stand a chance with me. You're going to run the gauntlet Mr. Carlyle." Gwen stepped back from Franklin again. "This may be hard for you to hear Franklin. And even if you're finally listening, it may be hard to understand. I am no longer your servant, or your maid. I'm not your trophy. You showed me over and over again that I've not been your sweetheart for a very long time. I guess I was in what they call denial. I just refused to see it. But I've come to understand it, and that I've been fooling myself all this time pretending that I meant *anything* to you. I may still be your wife, and because of this I'll do what I can to see you through your recovery, but I'm not your lover anymore. You've lost me, and you're going to have to find me again." Gwen took a step back and indicated she was done talking. She wiped tears from her eyes, took a handkerchief from her purse, and blew her nose, then dropped her arms to her sides and waited for Franklin's response. Inside, she was trembling, but she didn't let him see it.

Franklin, trying to digest what Gwen said, stared at her in stunned silence. He felt as though he was seeing her for the first time. *God*, he thought to himself, his thoughts racing. *She's beautiful. How could I have not seen this? How could I have not known?* "Thank you," he choked.

She didn't respond, but waited for him to go on.

"Thank you for standing by me all these years. For putting up with me. I've given you plenty of reasons to leave long before this. Everything you said is true. I've needed to hear it, but I don't think I could have until now." Franklin had been looking at Gwen with a penetrating stare, hoping against hope, while at the same time knowing it was foolish of him to think these few feeble words of his could make up for the years of pain he'd caused her. His eyes softened with the realization. Franklin cleared his throat resulting in fresh razor blades of pain, then said slowly and as clearly as he could, "I have no right to ask anything of you, Gwen. If you leave me now, I wouldn't blame you. But if you do stick around a little longer, I can only hope you'll be able to see the difference I intend to show you."

"I'll be back in the morning," Gwen said without ceremony in order to maintain the boundaries she had set. She wiped her eyes again, then turned and left the room.

"A man can dream," he said, and laughed weakly at himself as the door closed behind Gwen. "Perhaps, I'll get lucky."

# CHAPTER 37

Franklin remained in the hospital for the next three months. On the one hand, Franklin found it a luxury that he was in the hospital during the next three months. It was refreshing to not be constantly on the move, and he slept. A lot. On the other hand, in a cruel twist of irony, although he was offered all the food he could eat, Franklin struggled keeping it down. He lost seventy pounds and became so ill, he was unable to see for three weeks. One morning, after shuffling to the bathroom, he glanced in the mirror and was shocked to see that the pale, yellowed skin of his face was virtually hanging on his bones. He leaned in for a closer look, then after contemplating his reflection, laughed weakly. "At least I'm not drinking."

Franklin channeled the little energy he had into doing research on the tablet Gwen brought him. He read books and articles on relationships, communication, and love, and studied the art of courting. He came to favor the notion of courting over dating, as he believed the later was too casual for what he felt he must do if he stood a chance of winning Gwen back. He learned that among other things, courting involved a fair amount of chasing, and although he couldn't do much of that now, he hoped and prayed his time would come. In the meantime he focused on listening deeply to Gwen when they talked on the phone, and when she visited.

In addition to this course of study, Franklin researched everything he could find on the Cherokee Indians, and the Trail of Tears, as well as the history of Slavery in the United States, and was surprised one day to discover that there also existed something referred to as the Slave's Trail of Tears. According to the information he found, perhaps as many as a million men, women, and children—many of them in chains—were forced to walk in formations called coffles, along dirt roads and wilderness trails that stretched from Richmond, Virginia, to New Orleans, Louisiana, a distance of a thousand grueling miles. One article he read estimated that up to twenty times more slaves were forced to move along this trail than all of the Indians on the Trail of Tears combined, and this they did either walking barefoot through both hot and cold extremes of weather, or packed like sardines in the holds of boats, then shipped down the Mississippi River to the slave markets in Natchez and New Orleans.

Compared to the relatively small amount of information Franklin was able to find on the slave's trail of tears, there was considerably more available regarding that taken by the Indians. He was surprised to read that the Cherokee were not the only Indians on the Trail. Creek, Chikasaw, Choctaw, and Seminole Indians were also forced from their homelands in the Eastern United States to Oklahoma, and each of the respective tribes took their own route during the removal process. He learned further that the name Trail of Tears, or Nunahi-Dun-Dio-Hilu-I, which translates to The Trail Where They Cried, was meant primarily as a reference to the Cherokee Indians forced removal which itself involved numerous trails to Oklahoma. From what he could deduce from his research, Franklin believed that the group he walked with during his coma took the longer of the trails that spanned a thousand miles from start to finish. Although accounts on the matter differed, he read that out of the combination of all the tribes, an estimated 46,000 men, women, and children, or one-third of those who underwent the removal process, died during the forced march. He shared his dream and all that he learned with Gwen during her visits.

"Reading again?" Gwen said as she entered his room.

Franklin sat his tablet on the plastic tray that extended over his bed. "Even if I had more strength, they have me hooked up to so many things I couldn't get out of bed on my own if I wanted to. Besides," he continued with a rare gleam in his eye, "this gown has that built in air conditioning, you know? Wouldn't want to frighten the staff."

"My, you're in silly mood this morning. It's nice."

"It's the new me. Hope you can get used to it."

"I want to think I can, but it's going to take time."

"Well, that's one thing I have a lot of these days, so luck... is on my side."

"*Luck*?" Gwen exclaimed with surprise. "*You* talking about luck? Now, *that's* different," she teased, as she drew nearer to him.

"Yeah, kinda just popped out really, but what the heck. Just more proof that people can change. Even me. I just hope the luck holds and my number comes up soon for a liver. Last time I saw myself in the mirror it looked like I could use one."

"We knew it could take some time. You've only been on the list for two months," Gwen reminded him in a serious tone. Then, brightening her voice, she asked, "So what are you reading so furiously today?"

Franklin realized he was pushing a little too much, causing her to change the subject, so he adjusted, and went along with her. "You really want to know?" he asked, to which she nodded.

"I'm still reading about the Trail of Tears. It breaks my heart knowing how difficult they had it after I left them. So many died."

"Honey, you were in a coma," Gwen gently reminded him. "You only dreamed of them. You were never really there."

"It still feels real to me. I can't help thinking about them."

"The doctor told me it will eventually pass." Gwen turned away from him and looked out the window. "He said that even though you were in a coma, the dreams you had may have felt real and traumatizing enough to cause you mild PTSD. Maybe you should spend more time reading up on that, and recovering from alcohol and living sober."

Gwen's comment felt like a kick in the stomach, and Franklin had to fight inside himself to not over react. He took a deep breath, then smiled. "I'm working on it Gwen. You'll see."

"Would you look at that?" she exclaimed, distracted. "What's a bird like that doing around here?"

Franklin craned his neck to look over Gwen's shoulder, and caught his breath. Sitting on a branch just outside his hospital room window, was a brilliant, fire-red cardinal, complete with pointed crown, red beak, and eyes that seemed to sparkle, outlined in black. It seemed to be looking right at him. "What's it doing here?" he asked. "They're not native to San Diego."

Suddenly, the bird hopped up the branch to the window. It bent forward and tapped the glass with its beak, then ruffled its feathers and flew off.

"Didn't you say one of the Indians in your dream was named for a bird?" Gwen asked, turning to look back at her husband.

Tears brimmed in Franklin's eyes, and he touched at the place on his chest where the feathers of an eagle and a cardinal once hung. "Chea Sequa," he said. "His name means red bird."

"I don't understand how you seem to know these things. You've never cared about birds, or Indians before. How could you possibly know what Chea... whatever means?"

"He told me," Franklin answered, a far away look in his eyes. He suddenly felt exhausted. "You know, I'm pretty wiped. If it's okay with you, I think I'm gonna try to get some sleep."

"Sounds like a good idea. The doctor said you'd probably need a lot of sleep. You'll feel better, you'll see." Gwen stepped over to the bed, where she bent down over her husband. With her finger she wiped the tears that had escaped his closed eyes, then gently kissed his forehead. "I'll come back tomorrow."

"I'm a lucky man," Franklin whispered, as he relished the sweetness of the kiss. It was the first he'd gotten from her since awakening from his coma five months ago.

"You're lucky to be alive," she agreed soberly. Worrying to herself, she wondered if there was more to her husband's condition than liver damage. Perhaps the alcohol had caused some amount of brain damage too. Deciding she would follow up on this with the doctor, she smiled and added, "And you're damn sure lucky you've got me around."

Franklin opened his eyes in mock surprise, and Gwen winked playfully. But as she turned and walked out of the room, Franklin could tell she was wringing her hands.

Over the course of the next three months, Franklin continued working on his relationship skills, and was feeling encouraged that Gwen seemed to be warming up to him. However, his condition worsened. He was getting progressively weaker, had lost his appetite, and now had to be fed intravenously. The day came when he was no longer able to walk to the bathroom without assistance, and he seriously considered the possibility that he may be dying. But in addition to Gwen's renewed show of affection, there was another element that he held on to which gave him hope.

This morning, as it had every day at the same time for the past three months, a cardinal landed upon the branch outside Franklin's window. He could tell it was the same bird because of the slight limp it had. After tilting its head from side to side like it did each time, it stopped and seemed to stare at him. But today was different. This time it hopped over and tapped at the window with its beak, then stared some more. Finally, it ruffled its feathers, and abruptly flew away.

"Like it's trying to tell me something," he mused before drifting back to sleep.

The following morning, Franklin woke groggily to the sound of tapping at the window. "Can't you let an old man sleep?" he muttered, and allowed his head to flop over so he could look at the crimson bird. It flapped its wings and looked back at him, flapped them again, then tilted its head up, pointing its beak to the sky. Curiously, it opened and shut its beak several times, looking as though it was singing. Transfixed, by the bird's antics, he was startled when Gwen entered the room and briskly approached him. Then suddenly, as if changing her mind, she turned to the window and cranked it open. Swinging back around on her heals to face her husband again she said breathlessly, "Franklin,... you have a donor, you're getting a liver!"

Franklin exhaled for a long moment, tears falling freely from his eyes. Fully immersed in the moment, his wife's hand in his, he felt as though time had stopped. Sweet chirps and shrills flooded the room, and Franklin felt as if the red bird was celebrating along with them.

# CHAPTER 38

The following morning Franklin was moved into a shared room where he began to mentally prepare for his upcoming procedure. In stark contrast to his old way of thinking, it had become overwhelming for him to think that *he* of *all people* would get a second chance. Franklin was in the midst of wrestling with his emotions over his good fortune when he overheard the conversation of a couple regarding the patient who was staying in the bed next to his. From the other side of the privacy curtain, he heard a mother and father talking tearfully about their son's chances of survival from his liver disease.

Gwen was unable to visit Franklin that day, but was there first thing the next morning.

The boy on the other side of the curtain was apparently asleep, and his parents were engaged in another tearful exchange. Besides the daunting prospect of undergoing such an operation and surviving, they worried their son was too far down on the list of candidates and might not live long enough to even receive a transplant.

Gwen held Franklin's hand and looked at her husband, her eyes open wide. She whispered sadly, "Those poor people."

Franklin new in his heart that Gwen had not come to the point that she was able to fully commit to him again, and he didn't blame her. He'd put her through too much. Too little too late, he thought. But he had also come to the conclusion that the change he was working on had to continue whether she would take him back or not. He squeezed her hand and cleared his throat. "Excuse me,... folks. Would you mind if I said something?"

Gwen looked at him with alarm, squeezed his arm, and shushed him.

A hand pulled at a section of the curtain, and a man Franklin figured to be somewhere in his mid-forties poked his head around its edge.

Franklin winked at his wife. "It's okay, Gwen. Please give me a moment."

"I'm so sorry, I hope I'm not interrupting," the man said.

Franklin crossed his arms carefully to avoid tangling his IV line. "Actually, I'm the one who interrupted you. I overheard you and your family... "

"I'm so sorry," the man said hastily before Franklin could finish. "We didn't mean to disturb you."

Franklin saw—out of the corner of his eye—that Gwen was vigorously wringing her hands. He chuckled to himself suspecting that she feared he was going to be characteristically rude.

"Like your son," he went on, "I need a liver transplant."

The man's face drained of color, apparently convinced he had offended Franklin. His voice shaking, he blurted out, "Liver disease runs in my family. My father and my older brother died because of it."

"Sorry to hear that," Franklin offered with a tone of compassion that surprised even him. "I pretty near destroyed mine because of drinking. How old is your boy?"

Still attempting to regain a semblance of composure, the man stammered, "His birthday is in two weeks. He'll be thirty-four..." The man's lips continued moving, but no sound came out, and tears welled up in his eyes.

"If he makes it, right?" Franklin said matter of fact. He glanced from the man to Gwen and understood by the looks on their faces that he'd touched a nerve in both of them. Franklin grinned inwardly, figuring his wife was thinking nothing had changed with him. "Tell me," he continued, "how much does your boy weigh,... I mean when he was healthy, how big was he?"

The tension in the room had become palpable, and Franklin could see the man was struggling to suppress his feelings.

"He was one-hundred and eighty-three pounds before his liver started failing," the man said, his voice trembling. "Solid. He was always athletic. Played sports in high school and college. Health was a priority to him, so alcohol was never an issue," he said, his voice rising slightly. "My son was coaching *his son's* soccer team when it hit him. He lost his job, and his wife left him... . I don't know why I'm telling you all this," he said, clearly flustered. The man turned to Gwen. "I'm sorry, you've got enough of your own worries. I hope you'll both be okay. I've got to get back to my family now. Perhaps we can talk another time. Sorry if we disturbed you." The man let the curtain fall closed and rejoined his family.

Franklin saw the bewildered expression on Gwen's face. It wouldn't have surprised him if she gave him a slap, and left him for good. But she stayed put, seemingly stunned by her husband's comments. He winked at her again, took a breath, then with a firm, loud voice said, "I weighed between one-eighty and two hundred pounds when I was healthy."

Gwen positioned herself between Franklin and the curtain separating the two families. "That's enough!" she whispered, her tone firm.

The conversation on the other side of the room ceased.

Franklin gently took his wife's hand. "I know what you're thinking," he whispered, "but, give me one more chance to show you I've changed. This is not what you think it is."

Gwen closed her eyes in an attempt to still herself.

"If I'm not mistaken," Franklin continued, "I thought I heard your boy's blood type is AB. As luck would have it, that's the same as mine, and the same as my donor. It's gotta be the same to work you know." Franklin relished the sense of anticipation he felt was building on the other side of the curtain, but even more, he rejoiced in a deep feeling of liberation that was growing inside of him. Holding Gwen's hand firmly he said, "I would like your son to have that liver. And, knowing my wife as I do, I'm certain she feels the same."

In the stunned silence that followed, Gwen looked at Franklin with tears in her eyes. "You know there isn't another liver available, and we don't know when another will be," she whispered, a tone of desperation in her voice. "Am I to lose you, at the very moment you finally come back to me?"

"Gwen,... you said it. I'm a lucky man. I've lived long enough to give to the world something of worth after all of my selfishness. If you'll tell me you'll take me back, I promise I'll do everything I can to hold on for another donor. I believe I can do it. I read that the number one criteria for donating a liver after blood type and body weight, is doing it for altruistic reasons. Please let me do this one thing right, and I promise to show you so much more."

"But honey, didn't you tell me you gave your life for your friends?" Gwen cried.

"That was just a dream, Gwen. You know that."

"What about me? What about us? Franklin, I love that you're willing to do something so wonderful for others, I really do. But part of me feels like this is just another way of you making a decision without considering my feelings. It may be for a good reason, but it's what you've always done."

Franklin swallowed hard, realizing the truth of what Gwen said, and he was shocked at how viscerally powerful the initial reaction of asserting himself against her challenge was. It was almost as if nothing had changed at all.

A tapping sound coming from the window interrupted his thoughts, and turning towards it, Franklin saw that the cardinal had returned. He felt again that it was looking at him, that something about its gaze was penetrating right through him, shining a blindingly bright light on who he had been, and the remnants of who he still was. And now, he saw it too. The solid, dark mass that had strangled his being over the years, was melting. Far from gone, however, it was now a thick, viscous muck that filled all of the empty spaces within him, and still oozed through his heart. He saw that it could easily solidify again and destroy the hope of his relationship healing forever. After that, he would have no hope at all.

"You're right Gwen. Even this has been about me. I didn't see it until now. Please forgive me." Franklin looked directly at his wife, and said slowly and deliberately, "If I am to do this, it has to be because we agree together that it should be done, as will everything else we do from this day on." Watching his wife for even the slightest sign of understanding, he added,

"That is, if you'll still have me. I love you Gwen. Please, just tell me what you want."

Tears streamed down her face as she leaned over and embraced him. "Thank you, she sobbed. "You've told me everything I've ever needed to hear from you. Of course this is right. I don't want to lose you, but this is right. It's what you've got to do."

In spite of her trembling lips, the smile that appeared on Gwen's face was the most beautiful he could remember seeing. Gwen sobbed, and tears filled Franklin's tired, jaundiced eyes. The cardinal ruffled its feathers, lifted its beak to the sky, and once more, its music filled the room. The father and mother opened the curtain that separated the two families, and for the first time Franklin could see the boy. His face was pointed at the ceiling, looking every bit as emaciated as his own.

Franklin could not keep himself from studying the young man's features, from the tips of his boney toes that stuck out from under the sheets, to his thick, black eyelashes, that seemed disproportionately healthy in comparison to the rest of him. Suddenly, the kid's head flopped over toward him, and Franklin caught his breath. The young man's cheek bones and nose were so dramatically pronounced that he could see the contours of the bones and the cartilage beneath the taut, jaundiced flesh. His eyes were so dark and deeply drawn into his face that Franklin felt he was looking directly into the eyes of death itself. Gathering up all the courage he could, Franklin smiled. The young man smiled weakly back and gave Franklin a boney thumbs up.

"I'm sorry to have to interrupt," a voice broke in. "May I have a moment with these two?" one of the nurses who had been caring for Franklin asked the young man. She drew the curtain closed again, then turned toward Franklin. "I was standing by the door, and couldn't help overhearing some of your conversation. Did I hear you right? Did you say you wanted to postpone your operation?"

"Yes, if it's alright," Franklin answered, still holding Gwen's hand. "We'd like it if the boy could take my place."

"Mr. and Mrs. Carlyle," the nurse said, squinting her eyes and looking from one to the other of them. "If the boy is a match, you *do* understand we have no way of knowing if another donor will come available in time for you?"

Gwen spoke up before Franklin could answer. "We've talked it over, and we're sure."

"I'll make it happen," the nurse answered while jotting some notes on a pad she pulled from an inside jacket pocket. As the nurse left the room, Franklin and Gwen held one another. The only sounds they heard were from the medical equipment and the squeaks coming from the nurse's shoes as she walked away down a corridor. They looked at one another, then at the same time, burst out laughing, while tears of joy streamed down their faces.

Both were crying freely, when suddenly Franklin felt Gwen lean in and wrap her arms around his neck. In the midst of her embrace—one he hadn't felt for years, and wasn't certain he'd ever feel again—he heard the father's voice call tentatively from the other side of the room. "We don't know how to thank you."

"Accept it, and take care of your boy. That'll be thanks enough."

"Dad," the dry, weak voice of the young man spoke up. "The pups,... tell him about the pups."

"Son, I don't think they'd be... ."

"What about a pup?" Franklin croaked.

"Well, it's just that our dog is due to have pups in a few weeks," the father said. "I think my son would like you to have one as his way of thanking you. But I'm sure that bringing a dog into your life right now, would have to be about the last thing on your minds, let alone a puppy. We understand if you're not interested."

Franklin noticed Gwen's eyes had brightened over the last couple of moments, and he saw a familiar sparkle at the mention of a dog. "What kind of dog is it? I've heard that dogs can be good support animals," Franklin said, giving Gwen a wink. "My wife has a lot on her plate in caring for me. She might be able to use a little help."

"Show them her picture." The young man's voice urged with a ragged voice.

"Yeah, bring it over. Let me take a look at her," Franklin encouraged.

The man stepped over to him looking sheepish, and held out a cell phone. Franklin reached out, and with hands that were shaking with weakness, took the phone. Turning it to himself, he saw a beautiful, smiling, and obviously pregnant yellow lab. Although she was not a hound, Franklin uttered impulsively under his breath, "Lazarus!"

"What is it, Honey?" Gwen asked.

Franklin handed her the phone. "Just reminds me of an old friend. You okay with this?"

Gwen only smiled and nodded her head.

Less than two hours after Franklin's decision to give up the liver he had been slated to receive, the nurse returned to his room, with a look on her face that betrayed her excitement. The young man in the next bed had been wheeled out several minutes earlier for his procedure, and Gwen had gone along with the parents to offer her support. Franklin looked at the nurse and laughed. "You look like the cat who ate the canary," then coughed so hard his head hurt.

"Mr. Carlyle, we have another donor!" she blurted out. "We just got the patient's final approval, and it's a perfect match." Then the nurse's face took on a more serious expression. "Unfortunately, this is one of those cases where there is good news and bad news."

"Give me the bad news first, I don't want to get my hopes up just to crash."

"Well," the nurse began, "in all seriousness, the bad news is there's no one else on the list anywhere near as critical as you." She stopped and let Franklin contemplate the information for a moment before continuing. "But the good news," she said with her voice bordering on hysterical, "is there's no one else on the list anywhere near as critical as you! I double checked!"

Gwen had returned to the room and overheard everything. She looked as though she was about to faint.

"Forgive me," Franklin said, "but I've been in a coma for a very long time. I'm a little confused. Sooo... could you please just tell me what you're getting at?"

"So... ," the nurse replied, stretching out the word as Franklin just had. "It's yours if you want it!"

Franklin looked at his wife who returned his gaze with pleading eyes.

"Incredible," Franklin mused. "Why wouldn't I want it?"

The nurse became serious once more. "There's something you need to know before you decide."

"I can't imagine what could change my mind at this point," Franklin said, and took a sip of water.

"The donor is from a different ethnic group than you. There is no evidence to suggest this would pose any problems, but we understand that some people object to receiving an organ from someone who is other than their own race, so we have to ask if you would be okay with this."

Franklin laughed out loud, spitting his water in the process, then winced from the pain. "It's not an issue for me. In fact, I couldn't be happier about it."

"Excellent. There's one more thing. The donor is being prepped as we speak, and his family is with him for support, so the usual meet and great isn't possible. I hope that's okay."

"Honey," Franklin looked at his wife. "Are you okay with this?"

"I can't lose you," was all she said.

Franklin patted Gwen's hand. "What are we waiting for? Let's do this thing."

# CHAPTER 39

Franklin handed the aluminum foil covered plate of freshly baked cookies to the men who were taking a break from maintaining the landscape around his home. "Gwen's specialty," he said, then sat the pitcher of iced tea down on the garden table along with a stack of plastic cups.

The men took turns petting Laz, the robust ball of gold-colored energy that had become a fixture at Franklin's side. In response, the dog wagged his tail and entire hind end so ferociously, someone had to grab the table to keep it and the refreshments from being knocked over.

"Come-on Laz, let's leave these guys alone and see what momma's doin'," Franklin said to the dog, and he padded along beside him as Franklin returned to the house.

Seven months had passed since Franklin's operation, and it had indeed been, as he had been forewarned, the battle of his life. The two days he spent in intensive care remained a complete blur to him, and the longer than usual fifteen day post-op stay in the hospital was a time of immense, and unbelievable physical pain. Up until a couple of weeks ago, Franklin honestly didn't know if he'd be around for another three months. But now, he had hope. His one regret, post surgery, was that he never got the opportunity to meet his donor. He'd thought about it every day, and he felt the time had finally come to do something about that.

"I still can't believe it, my love."

Gwen looked up from a book she was reading, her eyebrows comfortably arched in question.

"I mean, what are the odds my donor would be Cherokee, let alone an Indian?" he said, shaking his head. He picked up a photograph that was laying on the counter, and gazed at it. "I really wish I could have met him."

"You're doing well. What's stopping you?"

"I don't know, it's probably nothing," Franklin mused as he patted Laz's broad, yellow head. "Just a crazy idea, really. It's not even a good photo, kind of grainy. But the guy looks familiar." He tapped the photo with his finger, traced it along the printed name at the bottom, then wistfully closed his eyes. "Bird, Luke Bird... . What are the odds?"

"They don't live so far away. We can just drive out there," he heard Gwen say from somewhere beyond his thoughts. "Besides, it would be good for you to get out a little. I'll call them to make sure it's alright with them, then I'll look for a hotel that allows pets. It should be pretty out there this time of year." Before Franklin could respond, Gwen had her phone in hand and was punching in some numbers.

Franklin laughed to himself at his wife's exuberance, and remembered with a chill when he would have silenced her for just such behavior. Then, he felt again what had become an almost constant nagging feeling that something was missing. It was as if in spite of the fact that he had survived the transplant and things had been going so well with Gwen—despite the fact that his behavior had radically improved, and he felt almost literally like a new man—there was something missing. Something, that without it, he would remain inexplicably not quite whole.

\*\*\*

It had been a while since Franklin and Gwen had been out on highway I-395. In fact, they hadn't been on the open road, away from the typical glut of traffic back home—since Franklin fell into the coma. After four hours of travel, they left the last of the urban sprawl behind them, passed through desert, and entered the southern most edge of the Sierra Nevada Mountains. Due west and directly in front of them, was Lake Isabella, sparkling in the sunlight yet several miles away. Soon they would veer northward again with the Kern River on their left. Driving through a valley, dotted here and there with gigantic oaks and an occasional pine tree, they were surrounded by mountain peaks lightly dusted with snow. The fresh, crisp air felt good, yet Franklin shivered deep in his bones.

"Gwen, could you drive for a while? I'm gonna rest up before we get there."

After trading places, Franklin tilted his head back and closed his eyes, and immediately the image of deep snow, mixed with mud, and a line of people dressed in rags and furs materialized in his mind. The Indians were bent with sickness and starvation. Men, women, and children trudged along a winding trail, illuminated only by the moon, its soft light shimmering weakly through the falling snow. The intensity of the storm was such that any color had faded to blacks, whites, and shades of grey, and the faces Franklin saw were etched both in agony brought on by their circumstances, and their determination to survive. Franklin strained within himself to recognize any of them, when a flash of color startled him, and he gasped at the beauty of a singular cardinal emblazoned in crimson that streaked by overhead.

"Honey, wake up. We're almost there."

Gwen's voice startled him, and Franklin woke, wondering if he'd had a vision, or had only been dreaming. He opened his eyes in time to see a welcome to Kernville sign and a few scattered rustic looking homes and other small out-buildings. The place was beautiful and reminded him a little of the mountain area in his dream where he first encountered the Cherokee. He even noticed behind several of the homes they passed, structures resembling the dwelling he was cared for in by Ayita and Degataga.

A rust colored hound that had large floppy ears that almost dragged the ground scampered awkwardly down the drive to meet them as Franklin and Gwen pulled into a gravel driveway. Then it turned and loped along side of the car, tongue lolling from its mouth, as they made their way—tires crunching in the gravel—toward a clean, but simple looking home. On the way up they drove past a mail box with three cutouts of birds—all painted in bright red—and a dog that roughly matched the color of the one now scrambling to keep up with them sitting on top of it.

A man standing on the porch up ahead cupped his hands to his mouth and shouted, "Come on up!" Next to him, stood a woman and a young girl, both smiling and waving.

Franklin put his surprise at seeing the birds aside for later and pulled up in front of the porch. And when he opened his door, Laz, uncharacteristically bounded over the seat back and plowed into the hound. Before anyone could react, both dogs, tails wagging wildly, jumped and rolled as they sparred in play, then together bolted into the surrounding woods. The young girl hopped off the porch, laughing, and by doing so, revealing a missing tooth, shouted, "Hi, I'm Addie", then took off after the dogs, hot on their heels.

Franklin took Gwen's hand, and as they walked the remaining distance from the car to the house, he caught periodic flashes of rust, yellow, and brown in between the trees. He thought wistfully of Lazarus, and wondered if he'd have made it through his ordeal without the hound.

The couple welcomed Franklin and Gwen, and introduced themselves as Luke and Joy, and after Franklin introduced Gwen and himself, Luke led them into their home, which opened up immediately into a large rectangular living room space. The room—not primitive in any sense—was warmly paneled and hung with paintings and framed photos. The floor was deeply grained wood overlaid here and there with thick, colorful rugs. To the left, he could see into a modest kitchen, and next to that was a hallway leading to the back half of the home. Against the wall beside the kitchen stood a black wood stove that had a kettle steaming on its iron surface, and beside it were two comfortable looking chairs and a lamp with a low table between them, all of which was situated in front of a large square window. It had gotten a bit chilly outside, and Franklin was grateful for the pleasant warmth that engulfed him and Gwen immediately upon entering the home.

Joy offered everyone coffee or tea, and Luke led Franklin and Gwen to the right side of the room where there was a larger seating area complete with two overstuffed leather sofas. These were overlaid with colorful blankets and arranged across from each other, with a large wooden coffee table between them. Two equally overstuffed leather chairs sat at either end of the table. The floor in this seating arrangement was covered by two luxuriously thick, dark brown bear furs, laid side by side. A large bay window through which the woods were visible, was the centerpiece for the front wall, and the opposite wall was dominated by a large stone fireplace with a beautifully lacquered pine mantle that matched the coffee table. After Franklin and Gwen were seated on the sofa, Luke excused himself and went to the kitchen to help his wife. Thinking better of the impulse to remove his shoes and socks in order to feel the fur on his bare feet, Franklin kept them on. But he leaned over and ran his fingers over it, remembering the scent inside the Cherokee dwelling of his dream.

While Joy and Luke were in the kitchen, Franklin got up and stepped closer to the mantle to get a better look at a colorful framed picture that was hanging above its center. It featured a geometric design that he recognized as a Medicine Wheel. He remembered from his dream that the wheel was a symbol of the journey each person must take to find their own path in this world. The circle of the wheel was representative of the circle of life, and within the circle were the Four Cardinal Directions, each tinted with the Four Sacred Colors, of Blue/North, White/South, Red/East, and Black/West, the last of which Franklin remembered with a chill, was considered by the Cherokee to be the direction of death.

On the mantle to the right of the framed Medicine Wheel was a bowl made from a gourd. It looked like it had seen a lot of use. In the bowl there appeared to be bone fragments and seeds. Franklin leaned in and sniffed, and a surprisingly familiar, pungent aroma filled his nose, stirring up memories and emotions. He shook this off and laughed at himself for being so sentimental about a mere dream, however prolonged and intensely realistic it had been.

Franklin's eyes trailed away from the bowl over to the left of the MedicineWheel. They landed on a worn, time-rubbed chunk of antler that had a finely chiseled, six inch obsidian blade fastened to one end. He thumbed the edge of the blade and goose bumps rose on his arms. *I'll be damned*, he thought, *I bet this thing could split a hair.*

Alongside the knife was a rough hewn obsidian pipe with a reed-like stem adorned with three badly tattered eagle feathers fastened to it with age-yellowed sinew. On closer inspection, Franklin saw that one of the large eagle feathers had fragments of a much smaller feather threaded to it with a very thin and equally aged tendon. This feather was crimson.

Franklin's hands began to tremble, and tears welled up in his eyes. "Gwen, I can't explain it, but these things are familiar to me. It's like I know them. When I touch them, I feel a kind of energy coming from them." He ran his finger along the rim of the bowl. "I know I must sound crazy to you, but I remember drinking from this."

Before Gwen could answer, Joy returned with refreshments followed by Luke.

"Thank you," Gwen said as she accepted a cup of tea. She glanced at her husband with a worried look, and Franklin broke from his musing. "Did you say your daughter's name is Addie? She is so sweet."

Joy beamed. "Addie's name comes from Adsila, which means blossom."

"How beautiful, children really are so much like flowers."

"My Cherokee name is Ahyoka," Joy continued, then looking over at her husband, she said smiling, "It means, she brought happiness."

"Although true, the name seemed a little long," Luke laughed. "So we shortened it to Joy."

"Your names are perfect," Gwen said.

"How about you Luke?" Franklin asked.

"My given name is Adahsnuh tsisqua. It means Lucky Bird, but after a while people took to calling me Luke, and it eventually stuck."

Franklin and Gwen exchanged glances.

"Is everything alright?" Luke asked.

The two of them only stared at one another.

"I apologize," Luke offered. "You must be tired after such a long drive. Joy has prepared some food for us. Perhaps this would be a good time to eat, and if you'd like to get some rest after, we have a room ready."

"No, we're fine," Franklin answered, but inside he was feeling off balance again. His odd sense of familiarity with the artifacts on the mantle were one thing. But the coincidence of the meaning of Luke's Cherokee name, coupled with the red feather, took him by complete surprise, and he was momentarily flooded with memories of Chea Sequa and the others from his dream.

Seeing her husband's discomfort, Gwen chirped, "That sounds lovely. We could smell something wonderful cooking when we first pulled up."

Feeling as though he was losing his mind, Franklin welcomed the break. "Now that you mention it, that drive did work up an appetite."

Luke and Joy's daughter, Addie, suddenly burst in through the front door, back from her romp with the dogs. Flashing a smile at the adults, she rushed in and grabbed two bowls and a bag of dog food, then bolted back out the door, talking over her shoulder, "Those two sure are thirsty and hungry!"

"I'm a little surprised, Luke," Franklin remarked while shaking his head along with the others, "that you're living way out here in Central California. I've read that most Cherokee still live in or somewhere near Oklahoma."

"Many still do. In fact, over three hundred thousand of our people still live in and around Northeastern Oklahoma, which is the area our ancestors were assigned to in the 1800's. But, over time, the government began to decrease the size of what they called Indian territory, and eventually eliminated it completely in order to recoup the land they had given us."

"I've always enjoyed reading history," Franklin said. "While I was in the hospital, I read up a little bit on your people."

"*A little bit?*" Gwen teased. "Be honest honey. That's almost all you've done since coming out of the coma."

Franklin laughed. "Seriously though, I think I read somewhere that Cherokee Indians fought on the Confederate side during the Civil War. I found that remarkable. Is that true?"

"Actually, a large number of our people allied with the Confederates because they felt betrayed by the US government forcing them out of their homelands. On top of that, the South promised our ancestors a state which they could control on their own if the Confederacy won the war." Luke sipped his coffee, then continued. "After the war, the government offered new treaties to us, but these turned out to be no better than the paper they were written on. Even though we signed them in good faith, the land we had been moved to was continually encroached upon and settled by whites, until as I said, there was no more Indian territory. As a result, the Cherokee people began to go wherever they felt their path was leading them, and my parents eventually came here."

Addie burst back into the house, and after washing her hands at the kitchen sink, she skipped to the table bubbling over with stories of her play in the woods with the two dogs. Her antics brought laughter to the adults, and dominated the remainder of the talk during the meal.

It had been a long day for Franklin. The drive alone was a bit much for someone who'd barely left the house for months, let alone undergone a liver transplant. But fortified by good food, relaxing conversation, and another cup of coffee, Franklin felt he had another couple of hours in him. He looked at his wife and was happy to see that Gwen and Joy seemed to be enjoying their time together, but he hoped an opportunity would arise to continue the conversation from before dinner. He was intrigued by his feelings of familiarity with the artifacts on the mantel, the red birds on the mail box, and by the coincidence of the meaning of Luke's Cherokee name.

"Excuse me for just a moment," Joy said. "I'm going to help Addie get comfortable in her room. If you're feeling up to it, the four of us can enjoy some more time together in the living room." No one objected, so she guided Addie down the hall, and returned a moment later. Joy asked Luke to light the fireplace, while she lit a couple of oil lamps. After adjusting them to a soft, warm glow, she joined her husband who was seated across from Franklin and Gwen who had retaken their original positions on the oversized sofa.

# CHAPTER 40

"It's kind of silly," Franklin began as the fireplace crackled and popped to life, "but... well, every day while I was in the hospital waiting for a donor, a bird would come to my window." Franklin sat forward, and as he continued, he used his hands to illustrate his words. "I mean, it would swoop in, hop right up close, peck at the window, and look straight at me. It looked as though it was staring into my soul. Then the darned thing would sing. I felt like it was encouraging me, telling me that my luck had finally changed. Funny thing though, on top of this, it was a red bird. You know,... a cardinal." Franklin sunk back into the couch and laced his fingers together in his lap. "I don't know if you're aware of this, but they aren't native to California. But that's not the only thing about it that struck me as odd." Franklin stared out the window, and with his fingers still entwined, tapped his thumbs together nervously. "While I was in my coma, I had a, uh ... let's just call it a pretty peculiar dream." Franklin glanced at Gwen, who smiled slightly, then nodded her head encouraging her husband to continue.

"I promise you, I'm not crazy," Franklin continued as he looked from his wife, to Joy, then to Luke. "Or at least I don't think I am." Luke and Joy smiled back reassuringly, so he went on. "There was a person in my dream,... correct that, a lot of people in my dream, who I grew close to. Most of them were Indians,... Cherokee." He stopped and waited for a reaction from his hosts, but none was given other than their attention. "One of these individuals," Franklin continued, nodding at Luke, "told me he was named for a cardinal. And it was because of him that I eventually became open to the idea of luck." He looked at Gwen again. Although he was certain she was struggling to understand, he believed he saw such a deep compassion in her eyes, it brought tears to his. "I guess I'm being foolish, but that dream feels like it was almost as real as life itself, so when that cardinal showed up at my window, I felt something that I just can't explain." Franklin's hands began to tremble, then the trembling crept through his whole body. "It was like some kind of connection to,... to something beyond me, beyond my circumstances. It gave me hope. I'm not sure I'd have lived without it. And now, coming here and seeing the red birds on your mail box. Then meeting you, and finding out that your name literally translates to Lucky Bird, well... there's got to be a reason for it all." After he'd gotten it all out, Franklin shoved his hands between his quaking knees and put his head down, certain he'd be taken for a fool.

The room was quiet, save the soothing crackle of the fire. Aside from that, one could hear a pin drop in the silence that followed Franklin's comments. After a few moments, he looked up into the wide-eyed expressions of Luke and Joy. They appeared confused, as if they were stunned speechless. Franklin fidgeted, nervously wondering if he'd gone too far.

Finally, Luke spoke, breaking the awkward silence. "Do you remember exactly when you first saw the bird?"

Between the four of them, they determined that the day Franklin had first seen the cardinal at his hospital window, was the same day that Luke and Joy began the process towards Luke becoming a liver donor. They further realized that the date of Luke's surgery was exactly one week after the day Franklin and Gwen decided to give the first liver he was offered to the boy in the next bed, and the day the Cardinal sang so gloriously at his hospital room window.

What to others might have seemed no more than mildly interesting curiosities, were for Franklin, mind-boggling coincidences, or what some consider moments of profound serendipity. His nerves strained to their limit, Franklin once more began to question his sanity when another crackle and pop from the direction of the fireplace reminded him that he was in a safe place, and among good people. Even then, it was all he could do to sit there and try to maintain a semblance of composure.

"Would you do me a favor, Franklin?" Luke asked. "There's a box under the coffee table. Would you please reach under there and pull it out?"

Franklin bent over and felt around until his hand touched the smooth surface of a wooden container. Feeling along its side his hand caught on something that felt like a rough rope handle, and he pulled the box out.

"Please, put it on the table in front of you," Luke asked. "There are some things inside I want to show you."

As Franklin raised the box up onto the table, Joy came over and sat next to Gwen. The box was old and worn, with handles on each end that looked like pieces of an old leather belt. When he lifted off the top and set it on the table, his senses were immediately filled with a mixture of aromas reminiscent of grease, smoke, wood, and herbs. Inside the box was a tanned leather pouch that like its container, was also aged and stained by the passing of time. The pouch was thick, a little larger than legal letter sized, and it had a flap that was tied shut with braided horsehair.

"Go ahead, take out the pouch and open it," Luke prompted. "Just watch out for the dust."

Franklin laughed a little nervously as he unwound the tie, then pulled the flap back. This time, mixed with the smell of leather, was the scent of old parchment. Grasping the ends of the material lightly between his finger and thumb, Franklin slid the contents of the pouch out onto the table. Before him now were several plastic sleeves, inside of which were folded rectangular pieces of yellowed paper, each protecting what appeared to be photographs from a time long passed. Under these were two large mailing envelopes.

With trembling fingers, Franklin opened the first of the plastic sleeves and allowed its contents–a very old looking lithographic picture–to slide out onto the table. The lithograph had been smoothed, but still bore the marks of having once been badly crumpled. The corner was torn, and it bore a faint, yet distinct boot imprint, the sight of which caused the hair to rise up on the back of his neck, and his heart to pound.

"Franklin, are you alright?" Gwen asked. "Do you need to lie down?"

"I've seen this before... in my dream. It's a picture of John Ross, the Chief of the Cherokee." His voice began to trail off as if he was talking to himself. "I picked it up off the ground out of a broken frame. It had been crumpled up and torn by looters, and someone had stepped on it... just like this." Franklin lifted his eyes to look at Luke. "I also drank from a bowl just like the one you have on your mantle. I... I... I don't understand."

Luke got up and stepped around the table, then knelt beside Franklin. He opened the next sleeve, slid the contents onto the table and spread them out like playing cards. Then he placed a hand on Franklin's shoulder. "Take a look at these."

Barely breathing, Franklin laid the image of the old Indian leader aside. He felt as though his heart had stopped. Facing up from the table were four grainy, black and white images. He touched the edge of the first of them lightly and breathed, "Degataga," and a tear trailed down his cheek. He stared at the man for a full minute. Ignoring the tear and the several that followed, Franklin's hand shifted to the next photo, "Ayita," he said, feeling a familiar twinge of guilt. Franklin shifted his eyes to the next image, and although what he saw was a man in his forties, he immediately recognized Kanuna. Finally, Franklin turned his attention to the fourth photo. He picked it up and held it out before him, like the priest held up a communion wafer to those seeking to receive it back when he used to go to church. In a voice barely audible to the others he whispered, "Chea Sequa," then he sat back as if in a daze.

Gwen watched her husband silently as he looked at the pictures. With each comment he made, her eyes grew larger with confusion. She waited until he was finished, then tugged at his arm. "What are you saying? Who are these people, and how could you possibly know them?"

"How is it you know their names?" Luke added, his voice mirroring Gwen's astonishment. "Chea Sequa is my great-great-great grandfather, and Kanuna, was his brother. Their parents were Degataga and Ayita. They lived over two-hundred years ago. How can it be that you know them?"

Franklin looked at Gwen. "I've told you some of it. But, I think it's time I told the rest. I don't understand it, but I think this is why we're here." He turned to his hosts. "This could take a little time."

"How about I get us some tea," said Joy, breaking the tension that had filled the room. "I know I could use some."

"Would you mind bringing both the coffee and the tea pots back?" Franklin asked.

Over the next hour, Franklin unfolded his story to them in vivid detail, from the moment he first found himself in Degataga's and Ayita's primitive dwelling, and discovered he was a run away slave, to when he felt himself drowning in the Ohio River, only to wake up in the hospital.

"I know it's hard to believe," he said upon finishing. "I'm having a hell of a time believing it myself. And I wouldn't blame anyone for thinking that I'm crazy. But can any of you explain how else I could possibly know the names of your ancestors?" Suddenly, he stopped short. "Unless... I read about them in some book, or article. That must be it!" he said, smacking his fist into his hand. "Their names must be recorded somewhere." He didn't believe this explanation. And something inside of him didn't want it to be true even if it was. To him there was something incredibly rich about his experience. He felt it had to mean something more than a nearly lethal, alcohol induced coma.

"I'm sure that's all it is honey. It really is an incredible story, but you've done almost nothing but research since you woke from the coma. That's the logical explanation," Gwen reasoned.

"I'd agree with you, but the truth is, I knew these names and all the rest of it before I started to read. I'm telling you, it's like I actually lived all of it."

"Franklin," Luke interjected. "There's something else you should see." He picked up the two envelopes, one in each hand, and held them out in front of himself. "This one," he said, holding one of them out to Franklin, "is full of newspaper clippings about my ancestors, before, during, and after the Trail of Tears. But this one," he held the second envelope out and gave it a shake, "I think you'll find especially interesting." He handed the envelope over to Franklin. "Apparently, Degataga, liked to write things down. That envelope holds his journal. At least as much of it as we could find. I'm afraid some of it has been lost over the years."

Franklin gently slid the contents of the envelope out, and began to flip the dry, yellowed pages delicately between his thumb and forefinger, and noticed right away that it was written in a text unknown to him. He assumed it was the Cherokee language, and shrugged his shoulders. "I may believe I spent some time with him, but I apparently never learned to read the language," he said, and offered the pages back to Luke.

Luke pushed the papers back to Franklin. "Keep going."

Franklin continued thumbing through the aged and cracked pages, scanning the unrecognizable script. Eventually his eyes settled on some sections that were written in English. He squinted his eyes and scanned over the words, and saw that each of the entries was signed Degataga. One of them spoke of the time during which the Cherokee were in Illinois, where so many lives were lost because of the extreme cold. Degataga wrote that it took them almost three months to travel as little as sixty miles through the worst winter he could remember in his lifetime.

In another segment, Franklin recognized the name Waya, and read about the death of Waya's wife Ahyoka, and later on, the hanging of his son, Mohe. Franklin knew that Degataga couldn't have possibly known how Mohe died, except that he himself had told him.

Franklin found several entries referring to the captivity of the Indians at Fort Cass, and another about the time the group encountered Nathaniel, the runaway slave, and his yellow dog, Lazarus. Tears formed in his eyes, and trailed freely down his cheeks as he continued flipping through the sheets of paper, while Gwen and the others looked quietly on. Midway down one of the pages, Franklin recognized another name and read it in a whisper. "Unaduti," he choked. "That's me, Unaduti." He reached up with both hands, and ran his fingers through his straight and thinning hair. "They gave me that name because they said my hair was like wool." He put his hands out and turned them over looking at age spots that had formed over the years on his pale skin. "How could that be?" he asked absently.

Gwen, Luke, and Joy, sat quietly, waiting for him to continue. So Franklin decided to thumb through the remaining pages. "Here I am again," he blurted out. About a quarter of the way through a section subtitled Berry's Ferry, he touched a spot just below the name Unaduti.

"Please read it to us," encouraged Luke. He and Joy were both sitting forward with anticipation. "There is something in this section we've wondered about for a very long time."

Franklin choked back some tears and cleared his throat, then read, "After leaving the area of Nashville, Tennessee, we walked in an almost constant blizzard for close to one hundred and fifty miles. The storm was so heavy, those of us who fell along the way were covered immediately by a blanket of snow, and became almost unrecognizable to the rest of us as we passed by them. We finally stopped at a place near the southern bank of the Ohio River, named Berry's Ferry, where nearly a thousand more of our people had already gathered along the side of the road. It was very lucky for us that my son, Kanuna found us a place to shelter, a place where we were able to keep warm, and even to find food while we waited for the river ice to thaw so that we could continue the trail. It was there also that we made peace with Grey Bear. Soon, the day came for us to move again, but after we had joined all the others, we were warned by Grey Bear that slave hunters were searching among us for runaway slaves. It was time for those we were hiding to leave our protection, or they would be captured and most likely killed. We do not know where Unaduti and Nathaniel came from. This does not matter to us. When we found them, we took them in and protected them as we would any other human being. Over the many miles we walked together, one of them grew to be as a brother to me." Franklin choked up as he read those words, and had to stop to regain some composure before he could continue.

Franklin sniffed and wiped his nose unashamedly on his sleeve, then went on. "Sending Unaduti away has been one of the most difficult things I have ever had to do. I think a part of me died that day. He often told us that he came from another time, and that his name there was Franklin. He told us many times how he believed he had failed in his other life, and especially how he failed the woman he loved there. He said during the time he walked with us, that he began to learn how to live right, and to not judge others who were different from him. And he longed to return to his own time, and to his wife, so he could love her as he should."

"The ways of the Great Spirit are a mystery to man, and many times we curse what we do not understand. But these ways, often beautiful, while at other times cruel, are always in the service of the earth and all of its life forms, including man."

"I sent Unaduti away, because I knew that for him to go any further with us, was not only dangerous for him, but it also no longer served his purpose. He had learned all that his coming to us had meant for him to. I sent him away so that he could follow his path. Even though he was only a little younger than me, I sent him away, loving him in my heart both as a friend, and as a father loves a son."

Franklin could read no longer. His tears had made it impossible for him to see.

Gwen gently pulled the journal from his hands, and continued reading for him. "I pray to the Great Spirit every day, that when we have each completed the path the wheel of life has given to us, we will be together once again."

Luke stood up slowly, and stepped over to the fireplace. After a moment, he picked up the pipe and returned to his seat. "This pipe belonged to Degataga. He passed it on to Chea Sequa, and he in his time passed it on to his son. In this way it has come to me."

Franklin wiped his eyes and looked at the pipe.

"There is another story written in the papers about the three eagle feathers you see fastened to this pipe," Luke said. "According to Degataga's journal, it was two days after sending you off, before he and the others boarded a boat that took them across the Ohio River. He wrote that the river was rough and still full of floating ice that made the crossing difficult, and it took them a long time before they reached the opposite shore. As the story he tells goes, a large submerged branch caught the front end of their boat, turning it sideways in some very dangerous rapids. And he feared that if the boat capsized, many of them could drown."

"When the boat hit the branch, it slowed down, and a large piece of ice that had been floating toward them, caught up with the boat and bumped into it, causing it to correct its course, and freeing it from danger. Degataga wrote that while this was happening, he spotted something hanging from a broken branch that stuck out from the ice. He reached down and pulled a string of feathers from the branch, and realized they were the ones he and his sons had given to you. He took this as a sign that you had finally gone home that day. And he believed that the luck of those feathers coming back to him as they did were what helped them to make it across the river, and enabled him and the others to survive the rest of their journey."

Luke unwound the sinew that fastened the frayed eagle and cardinal feathers to the pipe. He gently tied the ends of cord together, then got up and walked around the table to Franklin. "These are those feathers he wrote of. I believe Degataga would want you to have them again." Luke placed the necklace he'd fashioned over Franklin's head so that the feathers hung down against his chest. He then returned to the mantle, and came back to Franklin holding out the knife. "I know he will not mind if I give this to you as well."

Franklin took the knife with his free hand as he stroked the feathers with the other. The fire light reflected off the chiseled stone blade like it did that first night he sat with Degataga at the cooking fire in the mountains. Words he had read or heard somewhere before echoed in the recesses of his mind, *If we are to be judged for how we've lived our lives, I do not believe it will be for our not somehow obtaining more for ourselves. Rather, I think it will be for our failure to do all we could for others from what we've been given, however much or little.* He closed his eyes, sobered by these words and all he'd experienced while in his coma, and realized that although there were many steps still remaining for him to take along his path, his time on the Trail of Tears had given him all he needed for the remainder of the journey.

# Acknowledgements

Writing a novel is both a pleasure and a difficulty not to be taken lightly. But the process of researching the history of a people who have suffered much more than any author, and integrating their experience into a story of one man's transformation, was made easier by the support and encouragement I received from my family. For that, I especially thank my wife, and my daughters.

I am also grateful, and indebted to Veronica Golovan, who graciously took on the painstaking, and exceedingly tedious task of editing this work of fiction. Without her help, readers of my novel, would not be able to do so without tripping over the numerous grammatical errors that, despite the fact that I see what I want to say inside my own head, these ideas far too often do not make it to paper.

# About the Author

Mark W. Stevens is a Clinical Psychologist, Artist, and Author, living and practicing in Southern California. His interest in writing began after being prompted by his youngest daughter, who asked that he write down the stories he had told her and her five sisters while they were growing up so that they would still have them after he was gone. Paragraphs grew into short stories, poems, essays, novels, and children's books.

Now that his daughters have left the roost, Mark and his wife live in a home filled with dogs and cats. When not at his office seeing patients, or simply spending time with his family, he enjoys drawing, painting, music, travel, nature, and of course, writing.

Drawing from his work of more than twenty years as a psychologist, his writing is an investigation of human nature in the context of environmental and psycho-emotional challenges. As an author, he writes about human and animal nature and transformation that occurs in the midst of life's difficulties.

# Other Books by Mark W. Stevens

## — ADULT FICTION —

**ABDUCTION**

Fireworks, in almost dreamlike fashion, grace the evening sky with their thunderous booms and veritable explosions of color that bloom like bright and glittering flowers, then shower shimmering tendrils that drift grace-fully back to the ground. While those celebrating with "oohs" and "aahs", the gift of their freedom—the significance of which the pyrotechnics rep-resent—there are millions of people in this world who in a variety of ways have lost theirs. Whether an individual's freedom is taken by the actions of another, or lost because of a bad or poorly timed decision of their own, or by simply being in the wrong place at the wrong time as sometimes happens, once lost, that person must often be willing to go to extraordinary lengths if they hope to regain what has been taken from them. ABDUCTION explores the journeys of several such individuals, whom, having lost their freedom, decide to take the risks necessary in an attempt to recover it, and this, in the context of immense and brutal environmental and psycho-emotional challenges.

**PREY** – *Coming soon!*

Jake, a clinical psychologist, and his wife, Marisa, in celebration of Jake's retirement, embark on a trip of a lifetime, exploring the Sea of Cortez in a rented sail boat. The couple sailed azure waters, home to the majestic Blue Whale by day, immersed themselves in the regional foods, tequila, and mezcal, and danced with the locals in the streets during the evening, before retiring to their boat where they floated in a sea of stars until morning. Idyllic, would describe their time in Mexico, until their boat was boarded by drug runners, who planned to use the couple as mules to transport meth across the border into the United States. What follows is a life or death struggle with the sea itself, the relentless drug runners, and Mexico's vast, inhospitable, and punishing Sonoran desert, as the couple, straining under their unforeseen circumstances, struggles as much for the vitality of their relationship, as for their very lives.

**THE GRAPEVINE** – *Coming soon!*

Hoping to salvage whatever might be left of the faltering relationship he shares with his wife and sixteen year old daughter, Stanley takes the two of them on a family vacation up north of Los Angeles. But an incident on a stretch of California's Interstate 5, known as the Grapevine, only makes matters worse. The family slowly comes to the realization that they, "aren't in Kansas anymore," when they find themselves seemingly stuck in the central valley, with dust storms so fierce, they sand the paint off of cars and trucks down to bare metal, the eighteen-wheeler, big rigs bear down on them like predators to prey, and the line between the living and the dead becomes much too thin.

# — CHILDREN'S BOOKS —

## THE DAISY STARSHINE ADVENTURE SERIES

*Book 1.Daisy Goes to the Races*

In the first book of this author-illustrated children's series, Daisy, a young orphaned, and disabled donkey, dreams of becoming a unicorn as her way of coping with her self-perceived inadequacies. When she starts working at a local race track, she is crushed that the other animals and employees there tease her for her small stature, and the brace she wears on her short, front leg. When an angry groundskeeper sets fire to the stables that house her and the other animals, Daisy discovers a strength she didn't know she had, and finally discovers the happiness that comes from accepting herself just as she is.

*Book 2.Daisy: Lost in the Rainforest*

This second author-illustrated book in the Daisy Starshine series tells the reader how Daisy had become tragically separated from her family. Lost, and on her own in a dark and mysterious rainforest, Daisy faces obstacles that would challenge the best of us, from a crocodile infested river to a pack of large, ravenous, Spiney-tailed Iguanas. She also discovers Mayan ruins, and makes wonderful friendships, one of which will last a lifetime.

*Book 3.Daisy's Grand Canyon Adventure*

In the third author-illustrated book of the Daisy Starshine series, Daisy goes along with her adoptive family and best friend, Clarissa, on vacation to the majestic Grand Canyon. But it isn't long before she finds herself caught in another wild adventure that tests her ability to cope with fear and uncertainty. There, she braves the rapids of the mighty Colorado River, tangles with a trio of bumbling bank robbers, is guided by mysterious, riddle-singing Condors, and stumbles upon a surprise beyond her wildest imagination.

Made in the USA
Monee, IL
06 June 2023

35110239R00187